UNSPEAKABLE HORROR 3:

DARK RAINBOW RISING

EDITED BY
VINCE A. LIAGUNO

Let the world know:
#IGotMyCLPBook!

Crystal Lake Publishing
www.CrystalLakePub.com

WELCOME
TO ANOTHER

CRYSTAL LAKE PUBLISHING
CREATION

Join today at www.crystallakepub.com & www.patreon.com/CLP

ALSO BY VINCE A. LIAGUNO

NOVELS

The Literary Six

COLLECTIONS

Unspeakable Horror: From the Shadows of the Closet (editor, with Chad Helder)
Butcher Knives & Body Counts: Essays on the Formula, Frights and Fun of the Slasher Film (editor)
Unspeakable Horror 2: Abominations of Desire (editor)
Other Terrors: An Inclusive Anthology (editor, with Rena Mason)

For all our trans brothers and sisters, murdered in the darkness of cowardice and hatred, may your memories shine in the perpetual light of your truth and beauty.

UNSPEAKABLE CONTENTS

INTRODUCTION:
IT FOLLOWS

VINCE A. LIAGUNO

AS I SIT and pen this introduction to the third volume in the Unspeakable Horror anthology series on a sunny, post-snowfall day here in the mitten-shaped state of Michigan, I marvel at how my procrastination in writing this has been good providence. Not *good* in the conventional meaning of the word, but good in a manner that's advantageous to the larger point I hope to make—both in this preface and with the anthology as a whole.

When I decided to embark upon the third Unspeakable Horror, the concept was decidedly more thematically dense than its two predecessors—the effects of the proverbial closet in *From the Shadows of the Closet* and the dangers of desire run riot in *Abominations of Desire*. I saw *Dark Rainbow Rising*, in its infancy as an idea, as being about political and cultural pendulums and how they swing back when pushed to an extreme—or perceived extreme—with even greater force. I saw the collection exploring this idea of how the LGBTQIA community, in light of its political and cultural gains, had to brace itself for the inevitable backlash.

That idea—of being in a suspended state of anticipatory apprehension, of always having to look over one's shoulder for what's next—reminded me of an indie horror film called *It Follows* that was shot in and around Detroit in late 2013 and conceived by a native Michigander named David Robert Mitchell. The premise of the film, which is essentially a fever dream committed to celluloid, is that a supernatural curse is passed on through sex. The recipient is subsequently and forever stalked by grotesque personifications of said curse until they either pass it along themselves to someone else through sexual intercourse or it catches and kills them. I remember seeing the film in early spring of 2015 and its vivid images of Maika Monroe constantly looking over her shoulder, knowing with certainty that something was following her. Something malevolent that needed to be dodged at all costs lest it destroy her.

This idea of sidestepping a continuous and looming threat stuck with me, and as I crafted the submission guidelines for *Dark Rainbow Rising*, the cause-and-effect relationship between gains and backlash within the LGBTQIA community came into sharper focus. In the wake of the Supreme Court's landmark 5-4 decision handed down in Obergefell v. Hodges, which ruled that the fundamental right to marry is guaranteed to same-sex couples by both the Due Process Clause and the Equal Protection Clause of the Fourteenth Amendment of the Constitution, the LGBTQIA community has been enjoying unprecedented political and cultural visibility and societal parity. But for many—especially those among us old enough to remember the ebbs and flows of other civil rights movements in this country—there was always a darkening on the horizon just beyond the expanding colors of those bright rainbows.

The *it* that's been following the LGBTQIA community like the supernatural entity that pursued Ms. Monroe in *It Follows* is, of course, the personifications of homophobia and transphobia in our political, religious, and cultural arenas. Bigots with titles and public platforms to poison minds and stoke baseless fears in the hearts of everyday people. Everyday people who then mobilize and vote in larger and larger blocks for even more fringe politicos who go to Washington with their own brand of hate seeds to sow. Everyday people who then take to the Internet with podcasts and YouTube videos that attract growing audiences with their conspiracy theories and incendiary thinking. Everyday people who then demand that certain books be banned from public libraries under the threat of withdrawn funding.

As a community, we're forced to play a constant game of one-upmanship. When SCOTUS Justice Clarence Thomas sounded a clear dog whistle about the questionable ground the Obergefell v. Hodges decision was left standing on in the wake of the successful overturning of Roe v. Wade in June of 2022, LGBTQIA supporters in Congress mobilized and successfully enshrined same-sex

INTRODUCTION

marriage into law with President Joe Biden's signing of The Respect for Marriage Act in December of that same year.

But for every swing of the pendulum to the left, comes an equal—if not stronger—swing of the pendulum to the right.

We're now watching—horrified and momentarily paralyzed as I write this—as anti-LGBTQ+ legislation is springing up all across the country. In the focused crosshairs of our enemies this time around are our trans and non-binary brethren, who are being systematically targeted with politically enshrined hatred aimed at banning everything from drag entertainment to gender-affirming medical care. According to a tally by the American Civil Liberties Union, there are more than 300 bills introduced by state legislators across the country that target LGBTQ+ rights.

Here we are—the Maika Monroes of our own horror movie—looking over our shoulders once again and likely in perpetuity across the spans of our lifetimes, being followed by an enemy of insidious evil no longer even bothering to masquerade through the mainstream.

Therein lies the theme of the anthology you now hold in your hands—this idea of a rainbow darkening at its edges even as it continues to rise from the horizon. The authors who have contributed their magnificent and thought-provoking stories to this latest volume have each tackled this cerebral premise through interpretations that range from narrow to broad, from literal to symbolic. The international group of voices who have gathered for this compendium are diverse and distinct—those who identify as gay, lesbian, bisexual, transgender, and non-binary, as well as male, female, and gender non-conforming, offer tales as only those on the inside looking out can. A few straight allies join them with their own thematic interpretations from the outside, looking in.

Together, these contributors use their blood-tipped pens to show you—in sometimes uncomfortable and unflinching ways—the horror of the dark rainbow rising on the horizon.

March 5, 2023

THE TATTOO ARTIST

CHAD HELDER

The tattoo artist writes their queer horror
on the body,
blood an essential component
of the genre.
A fresh tattoo is always a wound,
every queer horror tale the same.

The nonbinary tattoo artist wipes away
the weeping dribbles
as their buzzing needle penetrates,
injecting stories into dermis:
inhuman figures like cave paintings,
iconoclastic imagery,
and bits of incantation
to summon archangel protections
or exorcise the litany of symptoms
from the latest DSM.

So much stabbing and chopping in the horror genre,
but their tattoo needle moves
with a graceful determination
like a dorsal fin across the skin.

THE TATTOO ARTIST

They tattoo the classics:
the bright pink triangle,
the holocaust armband transformed
into a dream of solidarity;
a patchwork of quilt squares across the chest,
one for every deathbed lover,
the tattoos that bleed the most.

They tattoo a track of zipper teeth
right through the nipple,
later to be unzipped
for hopeless broken heart repairs
in a succession of black bedrooms.
A repeat customer:
the straight razor clears a bare patch
for the stained-glass face of Saint Matthew
to hover above that broken heart.

As the tattoo artist moves in
like a date with Bela Lugosi,
you smell the ancient coffee breath
and discover they are
just a nonbinary Anubis
armed with a penetrating instrument.

What started out
as a cubist orgy back piece,
inspired by unspeakable frat fantasies,
has evolved into
dense geometric designs of the damned,
a black magic collage
with a dark rainbow tramp stamp,
a symbol of the covenant
with the God of Monkeypox
who casts projectiles of shame
like baboons throw turds at zoo patrons.

CHAD HELDER

In the end, you didn't choose these tattoos,
and the tattoo artist never gives a refund.
Once upon a time,
we gathered together at the community bar,
pushing up sleeves, unbuttoning shirts
to compare our tattoos, our
queer horror stories,
the battle scars all of us have,
but now everyone turns away,
scrolling alone on their smartphones.

BAD WITH SECRETS

HAILEY PIPER

MAY HABERMAN HAS the Important Thing, and also her tongue, but that is an unimportant piece of her. No one will believe her tongue alone. If those who give chase pry her mouth open and saw out her tongue but leave her with the Important Thing, that's enough to damn them.

Better the day not come to that. She's walked a long way down a dusty road, the world full of sand, stones, and parched trees. Her sweat is a second skin, but she keeps her thick coat on, a third skin, for secrets. A dusty two-floor house looms over her, its fence a layer of ramshackle decaying teeth. She doesn't want to bother the people inside, but at least they're not her pursuers.

The dust forms a second skin for the house as she climbs the wooden porch steps and crosses the dark front doorway. Lights glow inside, but after walking in the sunshine, May needs a moment for her eyes to adjust to the round tables, glass-dotted bar, myriad stools, shelves full of bottles, radio gone silent, a single-sheet 1953 calendar with X's running down the past several months.

And the men.

"Afternoon," says the one behind the bar. He carries softness in his stance, shape, and the smile on his pale face. "Welcome to Rickie's—that's me."

The other man mops at the floor, a rag thrown over his sun-kissed shoulder. He's tall, with a rogue's grace and a rakish gleam in his eyes.

"And that's Bruno," Rickie says. "Get you anything—"

"Gasoline," May says, before she can hear the rest of the question.

"—to drink?"

Bruno pauses mopping to chuckle, and May feels the air squeeze her coat-skin, sweat-skin, skin-skin. She is not a small woman, and she's certainly not as frail as she thought before three days ago when she fled Washington, D.C. with the Important Thing, along with her precious tongue and broken heart, but could she fight these men if she had to? Better the day not come to that.

"For my car," May says, pointing out the door. "Ran dry a couple miles up-road. If you have a jerrycan, or anything, I'll buy it off you."

"You walked in that heat?" Bruno asks, gentler than May expects. "With that coat?"

May stiffens, every skin going cold. Could Bruno know she hides the Important Thing, or is he only concerned?

"You can take the gas for free," Rickie says. "On the house."

"I'll drive you back." Bruno sets his mop against one wall and maneuvers between tables. "Let me fill a can, and we'll hit the road."

May thanks them and accepts a glass of water at the bar while she waits. She vaguely remembers a practice she heard of in college wherein ancient Greeks were said to aid any mysterious guest lest they accidently spurn a god in disguise. These men might think her as one so disguised.

With the Important Thing in her coat, she might be that significant for once.

Bruno is careful with his rusty car, as if he drives for a princess. Nothing like the storm May has torn across the country in her mad rush for California, where Anton Headley at the *Los Angeles Examiner* promises publication of the Important Thing. Once her car's gassed up, she can plow through this desert, unfold her map as she approaches some semblance of civilization, and maybe reach L.A. by tomorrow morning. Earlier, if she's lucky.

She shouldn't have had to come this far alone, except Gertrude Sheldon's heart went rotten back in D.C. Last time she and May spoke, Gertrude wanted nothing to do with their past, their present, any relationship between the two women. Even to remain friends was too big a risk to her job. Dating men by the next night wasn't anything May could fault Gertrude over, but her passing jab was another story.

BAD WITH SECRETS

I've chosen the way of God and country, she said. *You should do the same.*

As if the State Department hasn't been hunting their kind within the government for years before Joseph McCarthy really got his hackles up. Does he know about May beyond what she carries? You don't need to be a homosexual for McCarthy to accuse you, but it certainly helps. May imagines it's the same for his alleged communists. Didn't he tell the press what kinds of people are his enemies? And if his enemies fall outside those categories, he only has to accuse them, and in they'll shift.

No shifting necessary for May, but Gertrude has made a habit of lying to herself. She loves men and women alike, but she's drowned the latter part of herself under expectation.

May supposes anyone could call what followed a vendetta. Was her purpose against McCarthy righteous, or was it vengeful? Why should the latter taint the purity of the first? She should be entitled to some vengeance. At least for her heart.

Those who hunt her might disagree. They didn't know of her hiring private investigator Thorn Bannerman until after he passed the Important Thing to May. They must have questioned who he worked for, and either he told or they found receipts. Something to point them in May's direction before McCarthy sent his men hunting. They pulled everything they needed out of Bannerman.

And then they murdered him. May watched it happen.

She's still watching it happen, replaying the scene behind her eyes like two film reels stuck in an infinite loop. She sees thin, mannish shapes crawl from Bannerman's glovebox, unfold to her height, his height, greater, a wolfish pack of arcane thin men filling his car, grasping for him, and then—

"Christ almighty," Bruno mutters from behind the wheel.

His voice shakes May from the past. Leather seating burns hot beneath her, and beyond the sun-glaring windshield, twining pillars of smoke rise like black heaven-bound snakes.

From the place where she left her car.

It isn't her car anymore, not really. It's not Bannerman's car either, though the resemblance is uncanny. After the thin men finished with his flesh, the men in coats came to torch the remains. Had the thin men come while May walked to Rickie's? Or only the men in coats? Either way, her car is a similar burnt-out husk to Bannerman's.

"Keep driving," May says, sinking low in her seat. Inside her coat, the Important Thing crunches against her chest.

Bruno slows along the wreck but doesn't stop. The fire chews at May's car. He drives on after a moment, as if heading to some nowhere town for supplies.

"You can stay at our place," Bruno says. He clears his throat. "The night. If you like."

The words are shaky, as if he lives in constant fear that his generosity will be mistaken for desire. Maybe someone in his life tried forcing him to see the world that way, only tit for tat, unbelieving in genuine kindness.

Bruno tries anyway. "Or I can take you to town, see if there's a hotel." He glances May's way for confirmation.

She starts to nod, but her chin presses against papery corners. The Important Thing has risen from inside her coat and now sticks out tongues of large black-and-white photographs. She sits up and stuffs everything back beneath her collar.

Bruno is confused. And curious. Were May to let him drop her off in some no-name town, and then the men in coats came to Rickie's to question, and neither man knew to lie—May saw the thin men unfolding from Bannerman's glovebox. They would come first. And then the men in coats. Maybe Joseph McCarthy himself would clamber from the shadows, those soulless, almost disinterested eyes always watching. She has seen him in person once, a phantom lit by the dancing fire of Bannerman's car, his fist closed around a violet jewel, his stare thoughtless, as if he watched through the flames and the night to some terrible future May might never know.

She hopes to burn that future. Her arms hug her chest, clutching the Important Thing and its photographs close.

"Your place," she tells Bruno.

May telephones the number she has for the *Los Angeles Examiner*, kept on a scrap of paper in her coat pocket, but there's no answer. For all she knows, death has intercepted journey's end, with thin shapes having crawled from beneath Anton Headley's desk, meaning he won't be there anymore to publish her photos. So close, only for McCarthy's men to take this matchhead-flammable plan and strike it down the side of their master's shoe.

BAD WITH SECRETS

Drinking eases May's anxiety, and Rickie offers plenty to drink. She watches the casual way he and Bruno navigate each other, a light touch here, a smile there, and she remembers Bruno's tone when he said, *Our place.* Doubtful she could have found a better refuge.

As night falls, the desert begins to rage. Wind batters the outside of the house like an unwelcome guest banging to be let in. If wind is tonight's only intrusive presence, then May's pursuers might have taken their hunt farther afield. They couldn't even catch her in D.C., after all. Did they come for Gertrude? If so, she would have used her man of the week as a heterosexual-looking shield. Would McCarthy push that point? May doesn't know, but she'll keep Gertrude's secret hidden under the same tongue that once explored Gertrude's body.

May imagines she can still taste Gertrude here and now. Is it a crime to have a tongue? To have a heart? In McCarthy's world, it seems so.

The clink of glasses pulls May to the bar. There have been no other customers at Rickie's. Have there ever been? Maybe this establishment is another shield should anyone come poking. Through the evening, the men only ask one question each.

"Who?" Bruno mutters. He's sitting at the barstool beside May, nursing a brown bottle.

"Government," May says. "I have pictures they don't want anyone to see."

Bruno nods. "Eisenhower."

Funny he should bring up the president. The roots of hatred dwell deep, but the flowers have budded in modern ways throughout and since the war, and many names have grown on their petals. Truman, Peurifoy, and sure, Eisenhower have all handed out matches and gasoline, but it is Joseph McCarthy who dreams of hellfire. May says as much.

"Why not mail these pictures of yours?" Rickie asks.

"If I let them go, he'll know," May says.

The defense sounds frail. How to explain McCarthy's methods? Power lurks in his words, but there are other forces at work far older and stronger than the government of the United States. In the same way the thin men sniff out McCarthy's enemies, they sniff out what threatens him. To let these pictures fall into a manilla envelope, a mailbox—they would never see California.

They might never see California anyway. The wind thrashes the house, the lights shift, and May wonders if there are thin men waiting in the shadows.

"I'd like to see these pictures," Bruno says. Rickie shoots him a concerned look, but Bruno doesn't notice. His kind eyes gaze into May.

She hugs her chest where the Important Thing hides in her coat, as if the wind outside is cold and filled with all teeth. She thinks of her tongue again, and now Bruno's tongue, Rickie's, their muscly messengers. Who could they tell? Would it really hurt to show them?

The clock ticks a late hour when the lights stutter out. Without their radiance, there will be no showing of any pictures. Maybe this is how McCarthy will stop May, by dousing all the light. The sun might not shine tomorrow because McCarthy has willed the Earth to stand still. He regularly preens to journalists as if he holds such power.

A subtle glow rises from the far side of the bar as Rickie lifts an oil lantern. "That'll be the fuse box again."

May's hand twitches to reach out, stop him from leaving, but in a blink he's heading into the wind. The front door bangs behind him. Open, shut, open, a wooden heart valve between outside and in. The uncertain doorway offers a dwindling view of his lantern as it sinks to a pinprick in the far darkness.

Bruno's barstool creaks, jerking May's attention to the black bar again. A flashlight cuts across the room.

"You can show me," Bruno says.

"If I show you, he might kill you," May says. "He's done it before. A private investigator, named Bannerman."

From the corner of her eye, she notices the lantern light through the front doorway. Rickie must be coming back—was the fuse box out past the fence somewhere? May isn't sure, and the wind keeps its open-shut-open pattern with the door, but the light is growing again. A pinprick becomes a pebble.

Bruno retakes his seat. "And what's he done to Bannerman?"

May isn't sure where to start. From this desert, Washington, D.C. must seem no more real than the Emerald City of Oz, or Neverland in *Peter Pan*. Neither Bruno nor Rickie have likely thought of so distant a place as Berlin in some time, or dead Hitler, or his desperate search for arcane powers to win his vicious war.

BAD WITH SECRETS

Little thought would cross their minds that Senator Joseph McCarthy might have found such a power or that it might aid his hunt through the government for communists and homosexuals. In his eyes, they were two breeds of security risk, prone to loose morals, easy to blackmail, and bad with secrets. Hasn't May proven the last with her eager tongue and cross-country escape?

Through the doorway, the pebble of lantern light grows to a fist. Rickie again. Except if he's coming back, the house's lights should have returned.

Bruno cleared his throat, waiting for an explanation.

"The thin men come from small places," May says, voice tremulous, trying her best. "Dark places. And when he commands them, they start to cut you. They make it slow, like an interrogation in flesh."

She can't make out Bruno's face. He's probably confused, and can she blame him? She hasn't been clear, doesn't want to be. How to explain that a violet stone commands the thin men to uncurl from shadows? Even Bruno's kindness would go as dry as her gas tank before the car fire should she speak of devils in a senator's hand.

The lantern is the size of a head now, almost reaching the door. It clacks shut against the light, startling a gasp out of the lantern's carrier.

The voice is not Rickie's.

May scuttles off her barstool and ducks among the tables. Bruno turns, clearing his throat again, ready to ask a question as the door slams open. This time, the wind can't find it. A hand holds it still, lit by the lantern as it rises, revealing a white coat, curly hair, and a familiar pale face.

"May?" Gertrude calls.

The need in her voice is a punch to May's heart. She rattles up from behind the table, her body a suggestion at the edge of lantern's light.

"Gertie," May says.

She's supposed to ask what Gertrude's doing here. She should be relieved, joyous, needful. Wasn't she thinking of touching Gertrude earlier tonight? In a way, she's always thinking of Gertrude. Or Bannerman's death. Those two moments cleave her mind and fight for territory.

"Why did you leave?" Gertrude asks, stepping deeper into the house. "I meant to come back to you. Needed time, that's all."

Bruno says what May won't, or can't: "Ma'am, where's the man who was holding that lantern?"

Gertrude keeps her eyes locked on May, each reflecting the lantern light. "Come home."

"What happened to Rickie?" Bruno asks. There's a creak in his throat. "Where is he?"

"Look," Gertrude snaps, same tone as when she ended her relationship with May.

There's more inside Gertrude's mouth than voice, teeth, and tongue. A black gap stretches between her lips, dark as an open glovebox. Narrow fingers crawl from inside like frantic spider legs. They draw out a hand, and then a forearm. Gertrude leaks the beginnings of a thin man into the house, uncurling at his master's command, wherever he is.

May charges from behind the table and slams the heel of her hand beneath Gertrude's jaw, desperate to shut her mouth. Her once-soft skin now bears a papery texture. Maybe it's the dry desert air. Maybe it's what McCarthy has planted inside her.

The thin emerging arm whips left and right from Gertrude's lips, fighting May away, and Gertrude fights as well. It's too much for May alone.

Bruno rushes beside her. The kindness she's seen in him gives way to powerful muscles as he grasps a mop and slams it under Gertrude's jaw.

She falls beneath May's and Bruno's combined strength, and the lantern shatters. Oil paints the floor in shimmering flame, but Rickie isn't here to help put it out, and it takes every hand working with the mop to keep the horror from popping out of Gertrude's mouth.

Her teeth pinch the thin man's arm, and he jerks back into her inner darkness. The withdrawing force cracks her skull against the floor. Jamming her mouth shut against the thin man is physically doable, but emotionally it is a hammer in May's chest, and her heart is already broken. They could have been happy in D.C., ignored by others who thought them two untouched spinsters, the way women in love have hidden in plain sight for generations. None of this should have happened.

And none of it would have if not for the shape now filling the house's doorway in Gertrude's place. He is a man May recognizes by dancing firelight better than she recognizes him from broadcasts or newspapers.

BAD WITH SECRETS

Senator Joseph McCarthy wipes his damp brow with a sigh. "That was an olive branch, Miss Haberman." In his left hand, he clutches a violet gem. "But I see you've chosen burning."

Men in coats haunt the doorway behind him, but none will set foot inside unless McCarthy gives the go-ahead. He has complete control here, as in D.C. Had he always lived that way, or does he have the gem to thank?

Bruno begins to rise, but fighting the thin man in Gertrude's mouth has taken his strength. Dark fluid paints his arms as he glares up at the senator.

"Like I told the press, if you want to be against McCarthy, you've got to be either a communist or a cocksucker," McCarthy says. "And I take you for a cocksucker." He points across the room with a damning Uncle Sam-like finger. "But we're not in Wisconsin or Washington, so I can look the other way if you don't make a fuss. From you. From your fella out there, bumped on the head but no worse for wear. Give Miss Haberman to me, get off scot-free, and do some good by your country."

May scuttles backward, but the crabwalk betrays her no different from Gertrude. Her coat jerks around her torso with each shuffling step until a manilla folder slips down the hem, the word Important scrawled across the front in black pen. The Important Thing vomits every precious picture across the floor. Some of them spill into the lantern flames.

In the firelight alone, each could remain an innocuous black smudge, but Bruno leans closer. He's the one who wanted to see the pictures. Now he has the chance.

May has seen enough since she first accepted the photographs from Bannerman. They paint an evening in still shots—McCarthy at a poorly lit curb. McCarthy meeting a younger man at a doorway. McCarthy and the man standing behind window glass, sitting behind window glass. They are with clothes. They are without clothes. They are touching, and there is more to them, too much of them, too much like everyone McCarthy has hunted without mercy.

Bruno lifts one of the photographs and glances to May. "Blackmail?"

"Exposure," May says, her voice faint. "People need to see the truth."

"This isn't right," Bruno says.

"Right?" May points at McCarthy, who wears the expression of a man inspecting drywall. "He's a hypocrite. He's one of us, and he hunts us."

Genuine anguish presses Bruno's features. "No one will take that to mean they should accept us, or that they shouldn't have listened to him. It'll prove to them we're what he says. Lurking everywhere. Monsters. We even got to him, is what they'll say."

"That isn't—" May falters, uncertain. She's been fixed on Gertrude's wrongness, and the evil in McCarthy's grasp. Could Bruno be right? She doesn't know; she's only certain McCarthy needs exposure, from the *Los Angeles Examiner* or somewhere else. Let him hunt himself. Or be hunted.

"You've got a good head on your shoulders," McCarthy says, clapping Bruno on the back. If his hand lingers too long, Bruno doesn't notice. "Use it, by God and country."

"I want to live in peace." Bruno says. He looks from the burning celluloid to the secure photo clutched in his hands. The kindness in his eyes has faded beneath firelight's reflection.

"You will, my boy." McCarthy squeezes his violet gem tighter as his free hand trails Bruno's shoulder, then his neck, and then cups beneath his jaw. "All I need from you is an open mouth. A small, dark place. Can you do that for your country? For me?"

He squeezes Bruno's cheeks and chin until his mouth pops open, one more black hole for the house tonight. Violent light shimmers between McCarthy's fingers, and spidery fingers uncurl from the dark space of Bruno's mouth.

The thin men are here, and there's no stopping them this time.

May jolts up and back to make for some exit, but she's caught between fire and evil and a dark, dark house. She darts right, only to bang into something bony and firm—a thin man. She's never touched one before, and his skin feels oddly papery like Gertrude while also sharp as a knife.

Another thin man crushes against her back. They're spilling from Bruno's mouth like baby spiders from a burst pod, no end in sight. As many thin men as McCarthy needs. If the violet stone has a limit, it doesn't show. Although it would be much like him to push and push until his power shatters someday, May doubts that will happen tonight. Only the future can tell if McCarthy and his power will crack.

May thrashes, kicks, but here comes another thin man, and

another, until hands wind snakelike around her limbs, and arms tangle around her torso, and sharp-glassed fingers clutch her head.

Two fingers pinch the corner of May's final unburned photograph and slide it across the wood floor toward McCarthy. He bends. Lifts it. Stares with a fond twinkle in his placid eyes.

He then he dips the photograph into the fire with the others. The flames lap at Gertrude's coat. Bruno kneels, a trembling wreck but alive. He won't stop this. Maybe Rickie would have, but if McCarthy's telling the truth, Rickie lies unconscious outside. Bruno can tell whatever version of events he chooses later. Same as McCarthy.

May spits on the floor. "You're full of shit, you know that?"

"Could be," McCarthy says. "What good's it to you? Ashes are the truth now, alongside whatever I say. And what I say, goes."

"You're so hellbent on lying to yourself, there's nothing true inside you," May snaps. "You have no place. No self. Nothing. There'll be a day when everyone else turns on you, and you'll have no one but your kind, the ones you spit on. And maybe we won't be there, and you'll die alone like you deserve. Or maybe we will, but you'll know same as us that you don't deserve us, and the knowing will crush you."

A pall coats McCarthy's face. Some concerned darkness haunts his eyes, a memory locked away. He might have known someone before who counted on him, or he might have counted on someone else, but since then all bonds to his fellow humans have shriveled in a mad grab for the power to save his skin.

"I don't—" McCarthy wipes his sweaty brow and then flicks a commanding hand toward May. "I don't want to hear her talk anymore."

The thin man who holds May's face slides one sharp set of fingers beneath her jaw, where fingers squeeze until her mouth pops open. Same as McCarthy to Bruno. Same as Gertrude.

May thrashes again, desperate to clench her teeth, close her mouth, anything. She doesn't want to be another vessel for thin men, sent to some other lesbian's hideaway to deliver wrath, or to some communist, or even a helpful working man like Bannerman. McCarthy has fed every piece of the Important Thing to the fire. He has all the unimportant things too—May's comfort, her dignity, Gertrude's life. He has it all, but he needs more, a gluttonous fish eating and eating until he bursts at the seams with secrets and hatred.

But no thin man's fingers climb from within May's throat. Instead, they dig between her lips and teeth from the outside.

May can only grunt with another revelation. She isn't about to be made useful for McCarthy like Bruno; she's caused too much trouble for that. McCarthy has taken so much from her that there shouldn't be anything left, but he's looking to collect another piece of her. It's a piece no one will believe without the photographs anyway, useless, yet his desire is enough reason.

The thin men don't ask why; they only take. May feels glass-sharp fingers cut at thick muscle inside her mouth. In this moment, her tongue has become the new Important Thing. The piece that's bad with secrets.

And McCarthy wants it.

SUCH A LOVELY PLACE

MATHEW L. REYES

MINE ISN'T THE sort of family that commits murder. We tend our own garden, mind our business. My husband, Andrew, teaches high school English and was voted most popular among the students. I work from home as an editor. And our adopted son—my nephew, Nathan—is a great kid. Does his chores with no complaints. On Friday nights we watch movies, and on the weekends we hike and putz around the house. So, yes. As a general rule, we don't kill, but needs must when the devil knocks.

There's always a period of adjustment when moving to a new home, anyway.

The house was perfect. White clapboard siding, an ample garden, space in the backyard to grow a family's worth of memories. It rested at the end of a cul-de-sac in Good Earth, one of those subdivisions where the sun is kinder and the wind gentler as it kisses the faces of laughing children and parents. That is, so far as one is the *right* sort of child and the *right* sort of parent.

We found that out on our first day in the house.

I was in the front garden, turning cake-like soil in my hands and scooping piles around newly planted poppies. They were my own variety and now formed a colorful wall around the front siding. I was elbow deep in a sea of lilac and pink and red and white when someone cleared their throat behind me.

"Hello!" I turned. A woman in a white dress stood on the grass.

I stood, smiled, and said, "Morning! I'd shake your hand, but." I held up my dirty hands. "It's great to meet you, though. I'm Danny Meyer."

She nodded. Blond curls fell around her cheeks, and the sun played against her pink, glossy lips. "Annalee Ransom-Jones. My husband, John." She gestured behind her. How I had missed the man and two little girls standing behind her, I don't know. He wore gray shorts and a white polo shirt. The two girls, porcelain miniatures of their mother, smiled at me.

I waved to John. "Good to meet you."

"And our daughters," Annalee said. "Pearlie and Mary-Beth."

John walked up the driveway, guiding his daughters. "We saw you moving in, but didn't want to bother you."

"No worries." I smiled. "My husband and I and our son just moved from the city. It's nice. Quieter. Cheaper." There it was: the confession of my family's dynamic that by now ought to have been a matter of course but still felt like a confession. I braced myself, hoped for the best.

Annalee's smiled widened. "I thought I saw the two of you yesterday, and with a boy much too old to be, well, your son unless—he's adopted?"

I swallowed, smiled. "My husband, Andrew, and I are both twenty-nine. Nathan is fourteen, but he's my nephew. His mother was my older sister. She and her husband died last year, bus crash in the city. Andrew and I took him in. We're here for a new start, away from the city and its memories. Nathan needs stability, too."

"So true," John said, "children need stability."

"And what a home you've made," Annalee said. She gestured to the flowers. "Those are poppies? I've never seen any so brilliant."

I grinned. "My own cultivation. Eleusinian Poppy, I call them. I can give you some seeds?" It was perfect: a potentially shared hobby, a way to make friends. I thought I could bake lemon cake to bring over, too.

Annalee smiled. "I would love that."

One of the children spoke up. "What's *that*? That rock looks weird." She pointed.

"Pearlie!"

"It's okay," I said. I nudged one of the flat, gray rocks with my bare foot. It was a gray disc with one red symbol and one black etched into it. "I like decorating my garden. The red stick with leaves is a chaff of wheat, and the black spiral behind it is, well, a spiral."

"What does it mean?"

SUCH A LOVELY PLACE

I tried to answer, to convey with simplicity the idea of abundant harvests, when Annalee said, "No more questions, Pearlie." She turned to me. "I hope you love it here. Please let us know if you have any questions about the fees, too."

"Fees?"

"Didn't the realtor tell you? I'm the HOA president. We're excited to have you. In fact, next weekend we'd like to have you for a cookout at our place, just across the way." She pointed to the immaculate white house with the well-trimmed lawn and sparse garden on the opposite end of the cul-de-sac. On the edge of the lawn, a small sign read 'All Are Welcome Here.'

I nodded. "Gotcha. Yeah, the realtor mentioned an HOA. We'd love to attend, of course."

Her business seemingly done, Annalee wished me a good morning and herded her family home. I'd hoped to have chatted more. We wanted friends here, along with a reassurance that we wouldn't get any trouble for being ourselves. But things had changed in society; acceptance was widespread.

And yet I felt an unease, a sense of underlying coldness under Annalee's sunny smile.

Several days after moving in, we had a small affair for the friends we'd left in the city. Our living room had one of those mid-century conversation pits, with beige leather sofas arranged around a white table. I sat against Andrew, who ran his hands through my black hair. Across from us sat Bryce, one of our oldest friends, and in the middle section sat Jace and his partner, Chase. It was early spring, so we had a small fire in the hearth. Music played from a new turntable.

As the record ended, Nathan, carrying a pewter tray of smoked salmon canapes, entered the living room from the kitchen. He set the tray upon the table.

"Nathan, could you put Four Seasons on?" Andrew asked.

Nathan smiled. "Sure." He favored me; we shared black hair and narrow faces with high cheekbones. His hair was longer, though. He wore a lilac blouse with bell bottom jeans. Playing with gender was the only thing he was unsure of now that we lived in suburbia, but we encouraged him. With fingers tipped with purple-lacquered nails, Nathan set a new record on the turntable.

Vivaldi's Spring Allegro flowed like clear waters from hidden speakers.

"Ooh, show us the dance," Nathan said.

Andrew nodded and stood as Jace and Chase nibbled on smoked salmon and deviled eggs. Bryce sat, one leg crossed over the other, staring. With fingers clad in gold bands, he brushed long yellow hair from his eyes.

"Crown," Andrew said. He hunched as Nathan set upon his head a crown of blood-red poppies I'd woven earlier in the day. They clashed with Andrew's orange curls. Andrew began to dance to the music, holding his arms out and up at the elbow, forming right angles with palms facing outward. He spun in front of the fire.

His feet bare, his palms facing outward, his hair glowing in the firelight, Andrew looked to me a God, ascending amidst flames. He stopped eventually, and I felt as though I'd lost something precious. He rejoined me on the couch, setting the crown upon my hair.

I kissed him on the cheek.

Nathan dribbled a splash of white wine into the fire. He whispered indiscernible words before joining Andrew and me on our side of the couch.

Our party enjoyed several minutes of amicable chatter.

"You know," Bryce said as Vivaldi's spring turned to summer, "keeping up the hippy act doesn't change the fact that you've left us for the 'burbs."

I tilted my head. "What do you mean?"

He gestured vaguely. "You can move to the burbs, honey, act like one of *them*. But you're still a family of fags in a straight world. You really think these people are going to *actually* accept everything? I mean, for Chrissakes, Andrew, your *hair*."

Andrew sat up. "What's wrong with my hair?"

"It used to be down to your waist. Now it's—like a Republican cut. Pure fucking assimilationist."

"I donated it," he said. "To cancer patients."

Bryce crossed his arms and sat back, holding his wine glass at shoulder height. "Whatever you say, dear."

"And maybe don't call us *fags*," I suggested. "Not in front of Nathan."

"It's okay, Uncle Danny," Nathan said. He nudged me with his elbow. "I've heard worse at school."

"And you'll hear *worse* at your new school," Chase said, prying himself from Jace and reaching for a deviled egg. "Maybe fag's a strong word, but you can't be properly and radically queer in a radically *straight* world."

I chewed my lip. "You know guys, there's no *right* way to be—us, you know? Starting a family doesn't—"

"Family," Bryce said, snorting. "You tell me, then, what were *we* all the years you lived in the city, if not a family?"

"I can have more than one family." My blood began to pump hotter. "If you don't like how we live now, fine. But don't say we're *assimilating*. What's gotten into you, Bryce? Is this what you all think?"

Silence.

I sat back. And then I stood. "Well, you don't have to like what we're doing. You don't have to agree with it. But if you're our *family*, you'll respect it, as we respect you."

"These people out here," Bryce said, standing as well, "they don't get you like we do. They're not like us. Just because you *can* get married and move out here doesn't mean you *should*. They'll never accept you."

"And what's this you're doing? I feel so accepted." My voice was iron.

Bryce's eyes hardened. Chase and Jace looked at each other, and then to the parquet floor. Andrew stood between me and Bryce, and smiled.

"I think Bryce misses us, and this is how he's expressing it." I leaned into Andrew. Bryce looked ashamed of himself, so we six decided to let the thing go; we sat at the dinner table as the Winter Allegro Non Molto played. I served spring risotto and a strawberry pie. The food was good, but conversation was stilted.

Toward the end of the night, I said, "You know, we *are* still family. Distance doesn't change that. Besides, it's only a twenty-minute drive here." Bryce had the good manners to not scoff. Andrew reminded them of their promises, and urged them to keep faith with us. In the end, there were hugs all around, albeit stiff, and our friends left.

The doll's eyes stared at me when I opened the front door and stepped out onto the porch that Saturday. I recoiled. It was one of those Victorian-style dolls with glossy, dead-baby eyes. Silky blond hair fanned around it. The head, decapitated from the doll, was coated in red substance. I ran a finger through it, and then sniffed. Blood.

I gagged and started to run my finger against my pants, thought better, and went back into the kitchen to wash my hands. Andrew, casserole in hand, and Nathan, today in a pink chiffon top and denim shorts, stared at me.

"I—the porch. Someone left a doll head."

"A *what?*"

"Covered in blood," I said, putting my hand over my nose, though the iron stench clung to my nostrils.

Nathan's eyes widened. "Cool!"

"No," I said. "Not cool. It's just there, like . . . like it was positioned so I'd see its eyes first."

Andrew went out. He returned seconds later, his face red. He went to the kitchen, came back with an empty garbage bag, and disappeared out the front door again.

"Do you think someone is playing a prank?" Nathan now seemed unsettled.

"I don't know," I said, pulling him into a one-armed hug. "Seems targeted. They probably knew we'd find it since we're going to the Ransom-Joneses for the welcoming party.

Andrew returned, slamming the front door behind him. He washed his hands in the kitchen, then rejoined us.

"I threw it away," he said. "The hair soaked up most of the blood. We can clean the rest later."

"Who would do something like that?"

Andrew picked up the casserole he'd baked that morning. "One of our lovely neighbors. Surely not because we're . . . . I guess we can ask Annalee if she has any idea who did this."

Anger bubbled in my throat, but I suppressed it and nodded. It was best to make as few waves as we could, since they could not *all* be behind this. Surely they liked us. One bad actor, I told myself. It was just one bad actor.

The sun shone in perfect temperament on Good Earth's green lawns and white houses as Andrew, Nathan, and I joined the cookout at the Ransom-Joneses. Their lawn was evenly clipped.

SUCH A LOVELY PLACE

Rows of cream-white snapdragons lined the brick path to the backyard. Mingling chatter and laughter floated over the white fence separating the front from back.

Andrew opened the gate. When we three stepped into the backyard, the voices hushed. A cluster of a few dozen people, all clad in white and khaki, turned in unison to look at us. All around us were smiling faces framed by neatly styled hair that remained perfect in the warm suburban wind. They'd been forming a semicircle around Annalee, who wore a lacey white sundress. Her blond hair fell like goldenrod around her lovely face, and she smiled and waved.

"The Meyers!"

Swallowing the feeling that we were on display, I waved back and said, "Got lost on our way, but we made it!" It was a silly joke, and I expected half-hearted chuckles. The robust laughter threw me off.

Annalee and John welcomed us and introduced the neighbors. There was the Desmond family: Patrick and Polly, husband and wife whose smiles outdid the Ransom-Joneses, and their son, Parker, who glared at Nathan. We were introduced to the Sheehan family, an older couple, and the Dodson family, another young couple with two children that were running around with Pearlie and Mary-Beth.

As the group split into several conversations, Polly Desmond pulled me aside and said, "So, you're our new *gay* family! Isn't that just wonderful?"

I smiled. "I . . . guess?"

"I hope you love it. Your son is fascinating—is he uh, your son, daughter?"

"My nephew," I said. Polly nodded, saying 'ah' as though she'd always known this. I said, "He's genderfluid. We're worried he might face some hardships out here, but best to be himself, right?"

"Of course!"

She was not the last to ask. Andrew later told me that Mr. Sheehan had similar questions, and that Paul Desmond had asked whether it was appropriate for a kid to wear shorts that short. 'Someone,' he'd apparently said, 'might judge him, and it's a harsh world.'

Never had kindness unsettled me so. Surrounded by these smiling strangers that I wanted to befriend, I questioned whether

Bryce had been right. Was the neighborhood truly going to accept us as a family on our own terms? I put a smile on my face, opened myself to them. Once they got to know us, it'd be better.

Annalee approached me an hour into the cookout. I said, "Oh good, I'd wanted to talk to you, Annalee."

Her red lips smiled. "Oh? Well, so did I!"

"Look," I said, "do you happen to know if anyone has a problem with me and Andrew being here? This morning someone left a doll head covered in *blood* on our doorstep."

She put a hand over her mouth. "No, that sounds horrible. I can look into it. I can't imagine anyone here doing that. How ghastly!"

"I'm a little creeped out," I confessed.

"Well," she said. "I'll get to the bottom of it. Speaking of, I wanted to talk to you about your flag." We'd hung a rainbow flag from the side of the house where most families had the American flag.

"Oh? Yeah, I've had it since college."

Annalee smiled and knotted her brows. "Well, the thing is, your flag is . . . it's not compliant with the HOA. No need to look worried! It isn't a *gay* thing, it's just, political flags aren't permitted, you know. We find it best to avoid displays of a divisive nature."

"I see."

She put a cold hand on my forearm. "Please don't think we're anti-gay here. You're welcome to have one of our 'All Are Welcome Here' signs." But the signs weren't rainbow; they were grey with black wording.

"I'll think about the sign," I said. "But . . . can't the HOA amend its rules?"

She tilted her head and shrugged. "I wish I could, really. But it's difficult to change things every time a new neighbor comes, you know? But we are so *glad* you are here."

My chest tightened. We'd heard it before, that particular excuse. I grasped at something to say, but how to be noncombative? All they needed was to get to know us more, and they'd be fine with the flag, with us, with Nathan's gender. Surely.

"Truly," Annalee said, "We are glad. In fact—" she clinked a fork against her glass of wine. Raising her voice, she said, "everyone! If you'll give me your attention."

The chattering fell silent. Even the children quieted. Everyone gathered in a semi-circle around Annalee, who rested her lacquered nails on my shoulder. Andrew and Nathan crowded next to me.

"A toast," she said, "to the Meyer family, our first gay family. I'm so happy for them and the diversity they'll bring to Good Earth. Now that we've gotten to know them, I can say with certainty they truly will be one of us. Cheers!"

"One of us!" echoed the neighbors. They clapped. Nathan edged closer to me and burrowed into my shoulder. I pulled him in. A semicircle of white-clad neighbors clapped and smiled, clapped some more, and smiled brilliant, white-toothed smiles. Their stares became wider, their smiles whiter, and the claps louder, until my family drowned in this grotesque hospitality.

Nathan woke me and Andrew with his screaming on the morning after the cookout. He'd found a second doll head. This one came with the rest of the body and was strung from a ribbon on our front porch. It was soaked in blood.

As Andrew put his arms around Nathan and pulled him inside, I stared at the abomination. This one was a Raggedy Andy doll. His midsection was split down the middle; stuffing leaked out in bloody tufts.

Worse, the blood formed a trail of droplets that led to the rainbow flag. We had decided to leave it up, refusing to prove Bryce right by *assimilating* to the tastes of this neighborhood. But somebody had taken offense. The flag was soaked in blood.

Luckily, we had a spare.

On Monday we received a missive from Annalee, handwritten, ensconced in a perfumed envelope.

Hello, Meyer family!

Deeply regret that someone defaced your lovely flag on Sunday and left those ghastly dolls. Haven't identified the culprit. HOA is on it. We have some authority in Good Earth, and we protect our own.

Please consider replacing your rainbow flag with a U.S.A. one as discussed Saturday. Your poppies are beautiful—but might cause issue with garden color regulations. In addition, some members believe the stone symbols in your yard have a (not my word) 'pagan' feel to them. HOA to meet and decide on both issues soon. Once your garden/yard are HOA-compliant, we will take your HOA fees and admit you into membership.

Merrily yours, Annalee Ransom-Jones.

I wrote her back immediately:

Dear Annalee,

We got your note—thank you for the reassurance that somebody is looking into the attack on my family. We would like to query the HOA on changing its flag and garden regulations, and should like to keep our flag up pending that. As a show of goodwill, perhaps the meeting can be held at our home? We'd love to return your generosity so, if not the meeting itself, perhaps a late-spring cookout. Saturday? It'll be the spring equinox, perfect day for outdoor activities.

Best, Danny Meyer.

And on Wednesday:

Hello Myer family!

Meant to return this note sooner, but of course I heard about the brick thrown through your window and had to re-write this. As I said to you this morning, we deeply regret that someone is doing this to you. HOA investigating.

One note—some of our older members are not comfortable with Nathan's choice of dress. Of course we fully accept and celebrate his differences, but the skirt he wore yesterday while gardening was, Mr. Sheehan suggested, inappropriate for any age. Beg to remind you this is a neighborhood for all families, and age-appropriate dress is important.

The HOA has a long reach, and when you pay your fees and have a compliant yard, I am sure these issues will resolve themselves. Your family brings much desired diversity to Good Earth, and to grow a prosperous community is my sincerest desire. Unfortunately, we cannot hold the HOA meeting at your home, and prefer the flag to come down now. Cookout on Saturday is a lovely idea. I will spread the word.

P.S. I hope you enjoy the gift of pomegranates. A little bird

told me that you and your husband favor pomegranates in addition to poppies. Little birds tell quite a lot.
Merrily Yours, Annalee Ransom-Jones.

Her allusion to pomegranates frosted my blood. When Annalee brought them Tuesday, the day after a brick was thrown through our side window, I thought it an odd choice. Annalee claimed she had spares from a recipe. But her Wednesday letter, indicating that a *little bird* had told her, chilled me.

"How does she know about our 'favoring' pomegranates," I said to Andrew Thursday afternoon. "How could she know?" I'd been making a lunch salad for us, but in my fear and anger, I couldn't focus. The doll heads, the brick through the window, the subtle commands to conform to the HOA's demands. Acceptance was, I knew now, conditioned on conformity.

Andrew's face, normally serene, was red. "Do you think it was . . . "

"Bryce? Or Jace or Chase?"

Andrew nodded.

My heart pounded. "No. I refuse to believe that. Bitterness over us moving here is one thing, betraying everything about us is another entirely, and they know the consequences."

"Do they? Maybe they thought everything—the rituals, the dancing, was a joke?"

"The vows they took to keep the faith and our secrets were serious," I said. "I made that clear to them. But if they betrayed our secrets to someone here, we're screwed."

Nathan appeared in the archway between the living room and kitchen. "So what do we do? Are we going to have to move back to the city? Or just erase everything about who we are?" He swallowed. The brick had come within feet of hitting him as he read in our dining room.

"No," I said. I set the knife on the cutting board. "We can't afford it. We stay. Live on *our* terms." I pulled Nathan in for a hug, ruffled his hair. A natural hugger, he didn't let go. I swallowed and said, "If they want to push us, we can push back. I'd rather we have friends, a community like what we had in the city. If not, so be it. But I won't change a thing about this family. Now. Lunch time."

The salad was filling. Composed of gifts harvested from our back garden, from the mother herself, it nurtured us, but only for so long. Another note came, this from Polly Desmond, begging us to reconsider the 'distractingly colorful' poppy garden, as it was seeming 'to grow a bit wild.' Nevertheless, she said, she was looking forward to our cookout on Saturday.

That afternoon, I called Bryce, to see if we could get answers. He didn't pick up.

Friday morning, the doorbell rang.

I'd been washing dishes. Andrew was putting together a menu for the next day's garden party. He answered the door. I assumed it was a neighbor, stopping by to again harass us.

"Danny?" There was a hitch in Andrew's voice. I turned the water off, dried my hands, and turned. A man stood beside Andrew. He wore an ill-fitting suit and smelled of the dust and mildew of bureaucracy. This he confirmed by showing his ID, identifying him as Arthur Flannigan from Child Protective Services. Behind Andrew and Flannigan stood a police officer, a burly man tightly squeezed into his dark blue uniform.

Flannigan said, "I'd like to discuss your uh, nephew. Nathan Meyer. Is he here?"

"Yes." My voice was cold.

"I've received several reports," Flannigan said, "from this neighborhood, alleging mental abuse of a minor male child, as well as potential sexual abuse by one or more adults in the household. We have claims that you conduct . . . rituals of a dubious sexual nature with the minor child." *Rituals.* Someone had betrayed us—only they'd lied, for *She* never required that sort of filth to succor her; the Mysteries were nothing like that.

"Excuse me?" I picked up the knife, but the cop put his hand on his holster.

"Easy, sir."

Flannigan said, "Can you call him down?"

I did so. Nathan must have sensed something in my voice, for he poked his head around the corner of the stairwell before coming into the kitchen. He wore a green dress. Flannigan twitched his mustache and turned to me. The cop looked at Nathan with unbridled disgust. I suppressed the urge to lunge at him with the knife.

"I find the reports credible," Flannigan said to the officer. "The minor child is in clear, imminent danger of mental abuse and likely sexual abuse." He turned to us. "Mr. and uh . . . whatever Meyer, we're going to have the minor come with us."

SUCH A LOVELY PLACE

What happened after that was a blur. I got tunnel vision and felt the earth rushing to meet me, but someone caught me. Nathan's screams, and in the distance, a door slamming, flashing blue and red lights, a whirl of horror. I screamed, someone held me, and I screamed again.

An hour later, with a shot of whiskey in my system, I waited for the other end of the line to pick up. It clicked after several rings.

"Danny?" It was Chase.

"They took Nathan," I said. I explained everything to him, including how Andrew and I had been betrayed by someone who knew only the Lesser Mysteries and had reported us to the neighbors, had concocted a story of abuse that played into their assumptions about Nathan's way of dressing.

Silence on the other line.

"Are you there," I said.

"It was Bryce," Chase said. I closed my eyes. He continued, "He told us a few days ago that he'd done something to prove to you that you'd never be welcome in Good Earth. We asked him what, but he won't talk to Jace or me about it. Since he doesn't know the Greater Mysteries, he probably told them what he knew, and they went from there."

"Bring him," I said.

"Are you—"

"Bring. Him." My blood had frozen with grief and rage. "They *took Nathan.*"

"I understand," Chase said. His voice hardened. "He didn't expect anything to come of it. But that doesn't matter, does it?"

"No."

"I'll have Bryce there in an hour."

That evening, Andrew and I huddled in the kitchen. I scrubbed at my hands, trying to remove the dark stains on the webbing between my fingers and under my nails. Andrew was on mood stabilizers, but I was sober. Chase and Jace had just left with a promise to return tomorrow for the garden party. They, at least, had kept the faith. They had not betrayed my family, taken my nephew.

The doorbell rang.

It was Annalee. She wore a white cardigan and an indulgent grin.

"May I come in?"

I gestured inside.

We settled in the living room, Annalee with a glass of water and I and Andrew with nothing but our sorrow. Every moment Nathan was away from us was agony; yet she sat there, smiling.

"I saw what happened this morning," she said. "With Nathan. I'm sorry."

Andrew said, "How many of you reported us to CPS?"

She set her glass on the table. "Myself, Polly Desmond, Mr. Sheehan, Mrs. Dodson. I told you that the HOA has a wide reach. Danny, Andrew, I think we can all sort this out easily. I can have all of this settled within an hour and have Nathan back to you. *All* of it can go away. You can be happy here."

I kept my temper. "In exchange for?"

Annalee sat up. "Removing your 'pride' flag, ripping up those poppies, enforcing a more gender-appropriate dress code on Nathan. Stopping this pagan worship your friend 'Bryce' told us about. Paying your HOA dues."

"After what you've put us through?" I scoffed. "I think we'll just leave."

"No. Please, look outside." I raised an eyebrow and stood, walked to the window, and raised the curtain.

Several dozen people stood in the street. They were all adorned in white. Even the children were there. Everyone we'd met in Good Earth, standing still as marble under the cold moonlight, staring at us. They all smiled. I let the curtain fall. My stomach twisted. How dare they? My fingers trembled; I steadied my hand, torn between rage and fear.

"We need you," Annalee said. "Diversity helps us."

"Diversity on your terms," I said, returning to my seat.

"Just so," she said. "We need you to grow our community. I told you it is my deepest wish that Good Earth prosper. You are—will soon be—one of us, body and soul, and that means coming to us on our terms. Try to leave, and CPS takes Nathan again. A call from me will do it."

I looked at Andrew, and he nodded. We had no choice: the Lesser and Greater Mysteries were useless. The Oldest Mystery was now our only option. Ironically lucky, given it was the Equinox.

"We agree," I said.

True to her word, Annalee made a call on her cell. She then opened the door and gestured, and the crowd outside dispersed.

Within an hour, Nathan was back and in our arms, but he wasn't the same.

He wore ill-fitting jeans and an old t-shirt. His beautiful, long hair had been shaved to a buzzcut. His beautiful eyes were both marred by black bruising. We cried. As we did, Annalee sat, sipping water, smiling. My rage mingled with resignation. There'd be no other way out of this.

Andrew said, "If we conform, will that be enough to join your cult?"

Annalee sighed. "We aren't a cult. We're a family-community. We believe in ourselves, in the perfection of our creation, nothing more. Nothing so *pagan* as what your friend Bryce confided in us."

"Does everyone know," I said, "what he told you?" I knew the answer, and Annalee confirmed it. Nathan offered us all water to continue our negotiations with Annalee, and we all accepted.

Another half-hour of going over the full terms of HOA membership with her, and Annalee became tired.

Just so.

I picked up her glass and said, "Annalee, you were misinformed about what Andrew and Nathan and I are all about. We don't worship some hippy, neo-pagan god."

"I," she slurred her words. "That's not—what's wrong with me?"

"Eleusinian poppies," I said, gesturing to her glass. "A very special species with many properties. That's beside the point. Come." I stood and helped her up. She leaned against me, and we walked toward the basement.

As we did, I continued. "We wanted to co-exist with you. We have, after all, co-existed with society for over seven thousand years, though we've had to change our name every so often. Our Mother became the Poppy Goddess, and later Demeter, as we moved around. People have tried to stamp us out—the Sarmatians and Visigoths almost succeeded—but you can't really destroy something older than civilization. Nathan, the door."

Nathan opened the basement door.

I pushed Annalee forward and guided her face so she could see what waited below.

"You see," I said, "*Nobody* hurts my child, threatens my family, and betrays Her Mysteries, without facing consequences. Meet Bryce."

Her gaze fell slowly upon what lay down in the basement. On seeing the writhing, skinless thing, Annalee broke through her poppy-laced stupor to let out a final, rattling gasp.

Vivaldi's spring movement played in the back garden, which was abundant with color. Poppies mingled with lilacs and daffodils in overflowing beds. At the garden's center was a tower of poppies woven together by the stems. Several garden tables, recently filled with food and drink, were empty. The chairs that had been arranged around them were still filled with our neighbors, but they—the Ransom-Joneses (minus Annalee), Desmonds, Sheehans, Dodsons, and others—now faced the tower of poppies.

They had come to the party, had consumed our food, had taken in Her sacred essence.

And they now watched, paralyzed.

Nathan knelt before the tower. Beside him, Jace and Chase stood, each facing the other. Andrew stood next to the tower, our altar. I stood on its other side. We all wore green robes fringed with gold and lavender.

"Rarely," I said, "do we get the opportunity to allow an entire community into the Great Mysteries of Her, the Mother of Poppies, Giver of Harvests. Rarely do we have the means to perform the Oldest Rite, a showing of power and an offer of eternal abundance. Through the Oldest Rite, all are bound to Her secrecy. Nathan."

He looked up. "Yes?"

"Initiates usually sacrifice a pig to progress from the Lesser to the Great Mysteries. Yet now you have the opportunity to inherit your place by the Oldest Rite. Do you accept?"

"I do." His eyes filled with tears; his smile was ecstasy itself.

I nodded to Andrew. He pulled at a stem on the tower, and it collapsed. And as they fell away, the flowers gave birth to the thing which stood in pure light before our neighbors. She was beautiful: an effigy of the Poppy Mother, standing upright with her arms at a right angle, palms facing outward. The figure moved slightly.

Bryce, sewn into Annalee's still-supple skin, struggled. I sighed at the beauty of our creation. Exchanging Bryce's skin for hers, sewing him carefully into the taught hide, had been a labor of love. But worth every second of effort.

I shouted. "One betrayed the Lesser Mysteries, thinking it petty vengeance. And one used that information to harm an innocent. Together they are now bound, the unholy traitor wedding his flesh with the defiler of the innocent! With the blood of the defiler and the elixir of Queen Death, we anoint them." Andrew held a vase containing Annalee's blood and pomegranate juice. He poured its ruby contents over the effigy.

I nodded to Chase, who handed Nathan a dagger.

"When the defiler's blood mingles with the blood of the traitor of the Mysteries, and both soak the earth, She blesses us. Take the dagger, Nathan. May your aim be true: one strike, one chance to bind all who bear witness to her sacred purpose."

Nathan stood.

Bryce's frightened, bovine eyes widened, the whites expanding.

Nathan lifted the dagger.

Within a day we had an abundance of spring vegetables.

The neighbors are now bound by something more ancient than a mere promise. That and fear. They leave us offerings once a week. Good Earth no longer has an HOA, for Andrew and I are enough. The yards all overflow with poppies, which fill the air with their sweet scent. We had a rough start here, true, but with a little work and dedication to cultivating our garden, Good Earth has become such a lovely place to live.

And our flag still flies.

UN LAMENTO DE FLORES

A.P. THAYER

THE BELL CLANGS a second time and I shuffle out of the heat of the inner courtyard, the tiles shimmering from the midday sun. With my hand on the bolt, I take a moment to compose myself in the cool shade of the foyer, the other resting on my swollen belly.

"What is taking so long?" My husband steps from the gloom beneath the arches. He snaps his fingers. "Open it." I bow my head and pull the heavy wooden door open.

Sun pours in, obliterating the cool air, blinding me for a moment.

"Mister Alvarez, how good to see you again!" There is a smile in my husband's voice. One of the many he uses for others. I blink away the sunspots and wonder, briefly, whether I prefer the fake smiles or no smiles at all.

"Mister de la Torre," says the round man as he grips my husband's hand. The man from church. "It has been too long. Thank you for your invitation." He is several years older than my husband, with gray touching his mustache and temples and a paunch that only comes with age and status. He turns to me and inclines his head and I spread my skirts, about to welcome him inside, when a woman steps into view behind him.

Her white dress radiates in the noon sun, a blazing inferno of pure ivory that makes me blink even harder. The dress hangs off her shoulders, her skin light brown with a touch of gold. A splash of red, a poinsettia, rests above her ear, tucked into the curls of her dark hair. Large brown eyes peer out from strands that fall over her face and she smiles softly at me, like sharing a secret.

UN LAMENTO DE FLORES

For a moment, there is only the two of us, standing, facing one another, in a deluge of white and red petals, stirred up by a cool breeze.

"Woman, stand aside." My husband's sharp voice cuts through the hallucination and I finish my curtsy before stepping back and gesturing them into our home.

"Mister and Misses de la Torre, this is my niece, Alejandra. She is my charge. She is back from her university studies and, if it is not an imposition, I thought it would do her good to meet the lady." He gives my husband a knowing look. "I know there is much work to be done around the house with the baby on the way."

My husband, who cares only for the cattle sale, forces another one of his smiles and bows to Alejandra. "A pleasure, miss. Wife, you will show her around, won't you?"

I bow my head quickly. "Of course, husband."

"Good. Come, Mister Alvarez. My study is this way." My husband leads Mister Alvarez across the courtyard and out of sight, leaving me alone with Alejandra.

We stand for a moment, me attempting to speak, the words frozen in my throat as she watches me, before her lip curls just so and she releases me.

"Thank you for welcoming me into your home," Alejandra says in a soft voice and she steps into the sunlight of the courtyard. She glows in the sun, while I stay in the shadows, hunted. Her fingers trail over the vines growing on the arches around the edge of the courtyard and she flashes a smile of white teeth. "So beautiful."

I swallow, trying to work moisture into my mouth. "Of course. I mean thank you. What brings you to—but of course, your classes are over. How long have you been back? What did you study?" I am babbling, as if now that I am released, I cannot stop the constant stream of words. The heat of the courtyard grows, heavy with the smell of cempasuchil and honeysuckle, and I grow lightheaded. I want to be close to her. What is happening to me?

"Who does your gardening?" She glides between the flower beds, bending to smell each blossom. I blink. It looked, for just a moment, like one of the buds stretched out to meet her face.

I clear my throat.

"I do."

Her smile grows wider and she straightens, finally meeting my gaze.

"There is so much love in the growing of them. They sing with it." She takes a step toward me and I try to swallow.

"Can I offer you something to drink?" An excuse to get myself one. The air is syrupy and I can't catch my breath. She steps closer again and my heart rabbits inside my chest. She has to be able to hear it. She looks up at me through long lashes and all proper thoughts flee from me.

A burst of laughter from my husband's study echoes through the villa and the spell breaks once more.

"Yes, thank you," she says with a warm smile and she allows me lead her to the kitchen.

Mister Alvarez and my husband strike a deal. As part of it, Alejandra will come clean the house to ease my duties while I am with child.

She insists I recline in the courtyard, surrounded by my flowers, while she brings me drinks and fruit and tidies the house. I try to read, but her presence makes the words disappear on the page. No matter where she is in the villa, I can sense her. I can lift my finger and point to exactly where she stands. A lodestone.

At the end of the first afternoon, Alejandra asks, "Is there anything else you need, misses?" She looks up at me through her long lashes, her brown eyes large and burning, and I swallow. My heart races at the question but I can only shake my head, unable to speak. She smiles and I watch her go, regretting my silence.

The flowers in my courtyard are blooming.

At church, I find out more about her. The older women, bitter from their own marriages, hate her for her beauty and youth. Men covet her in that way they do all things that make them confront their weakness. They want her so they can break her.

"There's something wrong with that one," mutters Misses Salinas, when she catches me staring at Alejandra. "I hear her parents died when their villa burned down."

"She has spent too much time in the capital. Too much time in the classroom, not enough in a pew," mutters Misses Varela. "And I've heard she practices witchcraft by the moonlight, that's why she is so beautiful."

UN LAMENTO DE FLORES

I swallow my anger. I want to scream at them, but I have long ago given up doing what I wanted.

I excuse myself. The heat, I say, it's too much.

Alejandra catches me looking once more as the services end. She comes over and greets my husband and then me.

"Is there anything you need, misses?"

I am silent once more.

A week later, she asks me her question and I am prepared for it. I press a flower into her palm, a vibrant Morning Glory, trimmed at the peak of its bloom.

She lifts it to her lips, her eyes still locked onto mine, and then gives it a kiss. Something changes, and I find my voice.

"Thank you for your help, miss." I smile, a foreign sensation to my face, and she smiles back.

"Until tomorrow," she says, and she spares my having to come up with more words by leaving. She places the blue flower into her hair and I swear the blue of her dress changes to match it.

It is the hottest day of summer. I fan my blouse, hoping to catch a stray breeze, while the sun-soaked tiles of the villa radiate heat like an oven. There is no reprieve and sweat trickles down every part of me. In the distance, even the cries of the street vendors are muted by the oppression of the sun.

Alejandra is unaffected, though, and she makes sure I am as comfortable and cool as I can be, insisting I lay on a couch in the darkest room of the villa. I am powerless to resist her and with a firm touch, I am reclined. She leaves me in the less stifling shade and begins to hum as she moves around the rest of the house. I imagine her dancing as she hums, her skirts flaring as she spins, white and red petals raining down around her as she pirouettes.

I stand in the courtyard beneath an impossibly large full moon. It fills the sky above and bathes everything in a silver light. I am dreaming, but even as I recognize it, I become unsure. Yellow and purple Passiflora fill the air with their pungent fragrance and my skin prickles in a cool breeze.

Alejandra holds one of my hands, a young girl the other. My daughter. I am going to have a daughter. The certainty of it feels so natural. Alejandra nods to me and smiles before bending forward to kiss my cheek. I weep with joy. I so want to have a girl. I squeeze both their hands.

A soft knocking wakes me.

"I am finished for the day, Misses de la Torre," Alejandra murmurs. She leans against the door frame, silhouetted by the light of the courtyard behind her.

I nod. "Thank you, Alejandra. I should not have made you come. It is too hot to do anything today."

Alejandra straightens and takes one step into the room and I am suddenly very aware of the space between us. My skin tingles where she kissed my cheek in the dream and I lick my lips.

"Not everything," she murmurs.

My face heats. The spicy scent of honeysuckle presses in around me as the villa sighs. I want to fall into the space between us, to feel her hand in mine again. I brush stray hairs from my face and will myself to snap out of it, hoping the darkness will hide my trembling fingers.

"Thank you, Alejandra," I say again, a mantra to get myself under control. I make as if to walk her out, but she blocks my path. There are only centimeters between us now.

"Is there anything else I can do for you, misses?" She curls a thick eyebrow at me and my breath catches in my throat. Did I make a sound? Oh, Lord, let it not be so.

I clear my throat and push past her, gasping for air. "No, no, my dear. It's just the heat, and the baby . . . " I trail off and rush to the front door. As I put my hand on it, she catches it and presses herself close behind me.

Her lips brush my ear and I shiver. Her fingers trail up my arm to my neck and she pulls me around. Our faces are so close. All I can smell is blooming flowers and her sweat. I don't dare move. I don't want to.

She plucks the blossom woven into her hair, a rosy-tinted Laelia, and holds it out in her palm. The petals are wrinkled from a day in the heat, but they grow plump in her hand and the bud lifts into the air, spinning slowly. It floats into my hair and she pushes it in right above my ear.

"How did you—?"

Her fingers curl around the back of my neck and she pulls me in, my lips to hers, and she lets me taste her. She is all strength and blooming flowers and I am hers.

UN LAMENTO DE FLORES

As the heat of summer abates, ours burns brighter. We steal kisses, our lips hungry for one another's, beneath the eaves of the flower-filled courtyard. We find excuses to be alone for brief moments. A question about a piece of furniture. What groceries are needed. We brush fingers as she passes through the courtyard to another part of the house and the whole villa sings while my belly grows.

On the first full moon of autumn, she sneaks me out of the villa and we dance naked under the brilliant silver orb until we fall into each other, a tangle of arms and hair. She caresses my swollen stomach while the queens-of-the-night bloom around us, pale and bright.

She tells me she loves me and I bloom for her, too.

The next day, Mister Alvarez pays us a visit.

"My apologies, Misses de la Torre. I must speak to your husband."

Something twists in my gut. My husband and Mister Alvarez shut themselves off in the study. I hover nearby, hoping to catch anything more than the whiff of tobacco, but there are only somber voices, too quiet to make out.

Mister Alvarez gives me a shallow bow as he leaves. My husband watches him go and shuts the door.

"What has happened?" There is a surprising strength to my voice, even with the terror writhing in my gut.

My husband considers me for a moment before replying.

"Mister Alvarez has found Alejandra a husband. He regrets she is no longer able to help around the house here." He misunderstands the look on my face. He trails his fingers on my cheek and I shudder. "Do not worry, wife. We will find another."

That night I cry myself to sleep.

I dream of her again.

We stand in the courtyard, the moon high above, the flowers singing around us. Her fingers trace patterns on my skin and her lips brush mine before she whispers in my ear.

"Bring the ashes of the largest bloom in your garden to me.

Bring salt. Bring a broken tile from the courtyard. Pack some belongings and money with you. I will take all three of us from here." Her hand rests on my belly and my daughter kicks with pleasure. Alejandra's breath is warm on my ear and I shiver, missing her, missing her touch.

When I wake, I know it is more than a dream.

It does not take me long to gather the items. I pick a red poinsettia, like the one she wore when I first saw her.

I hurry to Mister Alvarez's house, but the guard are already there.

A half circle of them surrounds Mister Alvarez. He is wild-eyed and gesticulating. Blood covers his shirt. "She tried to burn my house down!"

"We will have to burn her body," mutters one of the guards, as two medics pull a stretcher covered with a white sheet from inside. The priest walks out after them, his holy book in his hands and disgust painted all over his face. He holds a bundle of dried flowers and bones, inspecting them.

"Filthy witchcraft." He tosses the totem aside. "A good thing you woke when you did, Mister Alvarez."

I flee, tears streaming down my face, until I am alone in our field. I scream out to her, wailing for her not to be gone, though I know she is.

The column of smoke from the village square blackens the skies and a thunderstorm batters the village for three days. When the storm clouds finally break apart, the village celebrates. The church bells toll and they dance in the street, eager to spit in the face of the devil and his dead mistress.

I clip flowers in the courtyard for a wreath. I will take it to our field.

"In my own home! And you didn't suspect her of anything?" My husband leans against one of the arches in the courtyard, a dangerous glint in his eye.

If I open my mouth, I can't be sure I won't break down again.

He steps closer, looming over me as I pick the largest sunflower. "I will have the priest come and bless this house." His voice is cold and expectant, but I remain silent. He crouches behind me and snakes his hand onto my belly. "To make sure she didn't do anything to either of you."

UN LAMENTO DE FLORES

I suppress a shudder.

After a while, he retreats to his study.

That night, she comes to me again.

Her touch is fire and I weep and gulp for air as I smile and she kisses me. She is not gone, not yet, but will be soon, she tells me.

"Do you have the ashes?"

I nod, unable to speak even in my dream.

"Good. I cannot complete the spell, anymore. You will have to."

I shake in her arms and she smooths my hair and holds me close. My girl kicks in between us, surrounded by our love.

"You are braver than you know. Trust in me and we will be together soon." I nod, my face in her chest.

As soon as I hear my husband snoring, I lock myself in the nursery.

I draw the sigils as Alejandra instructed me. She is with me, unseen, her hand on mine, guiding me. A pinprick of my blood, some of my spit, swirled with the ashes to make an ink. I draw, my finger the pen, and black lines mark the tile, like scorch marks left by a fire. As I draw the patterns, she whispers in my ear. A gust of wind, filled with the scent of flowers, swirls around the room.

My husband hammers the door with his fist.

"What are you doing in there?"

You have to hurry, she tells me.

The door shakes, hard. "Why is this door locked?"

Almost there. Almost finished. We will be together soon, she says, the three of us.

The door crashes open and my husband yanks me out of the circle. "What the devil is this?"

I scream. He hits me and the smell of flowers dissipates as I lose consciousness.

When I wake, he is dragging me behind the villa to the creek.

I beg for him to let me go. He doesn't listen. He hits me again and I fall to the bank, my head swimming, but I push myself up, try to lunge at him. He kicks me, his boot hard against my temple, and all strength leaves me.

"Please," I say. "My daughter."

He holds my head below the water until the world goes dark.

I wake in our field. The symbols are burned into the dry grass of the meadow, with me in its center. The queens-of-the-night are shriveled. The air is dry and stale. I am alone.

My husband tells the other villagers I, too, had been a witch and I had tried to give our unborn daughter's soul to the devil. I had drowned myself in the attempt. So he said.

I weep for my unborn daughter, and I weep for Alejandra and I weep for the incomplete ritual, but I have no tears for myself.

A few nights later, they find my husband hanged in the middle of the courtyard. No one notices the scuff marks on the tile from where he had kept trying to stand.

Mister Alvarez's villa goes up in a conflagration the night after. Neighbors say they could hear him screaming for forgiveness as the fire consumed him. The priest drinks every cask of red wine in the rectory shortly thereafter, drowning himself in the sanguine liquid. The cattle herds have grown emaciated, and the orchards are rotten. The river has dried up. Only one thing grows in the whole of the countryside. A single blossom of red in a field of dry grass.

I weep over the single poinsettia every day and during the night, I exact my revenge.

INCIDENT ON A SOCIAL PLATFORM

J. DANIEL STONE

"If you listen to fools, the mob rules"
—Black Sabbath

"SOMETHING DANGEROUS IS going to happen," Arrow said to me.

I only half believed him, as he was known for emotional ramblings. Angry old goth just past the age of thirty, stuck in a mindset that being chaotic could still get him ahead. That may have worked when we were adolescents, back when the world was less connected. Today we're bound by the noose of cell phones and hooks of social media; a technological thruway of online rampages, cancel culture and political correctness. Millennials have aged out; Gen Z controls the social culture now, and somehow boomers, the political.

"How dangerous?" I said, opening a can of PBR.

"Hate that piss drink," Arrow whispered.

"It's all we can afford," I retorted.

"Wish we had better jobs."

What jobs? I wanted to say. *You haven't written in a year, and I've barely drawn.* We were both suffering from a tremendous creative block and blamed the other for it. Inevitably, when you're with a romantic partner for a certain amount of time, excitement is replaced by routine, reward hormones traded for complacency. The insanity that brought us together had wilted. And it seemed to take all creativity with it. This is the circle of life.

Instead of arguing, I draped a luxurious black blanket across my shoulders and kept my thoughts to myself. I was always cold in the morning, especially after being up all night. We were on another one of our famous benders, furiously bored and overthinking *everything* as we paralyzed our brains with drugs and embalmed our organs with liquor.

But it was not time wasted.

Somewhere deep in the recesses of ketamine and alcohol, I found focus; inebriation made me want to be creative again, and so I dusted off my sketch books, dragging a number two pencil across it without sober inhibitions. Tendrils and spirals, small bones in my hand aching since it had been so long. I showed Arrow my work, was quite proud of it being I hadn't drawn since the pandemic, but all he did was quickly glance at the round jawline and black eyes—the indistinguishable countenance—unable to break himself away from his cell phone.

"When you going to give that up?"

Arrow grabbed my t-shirt, ripped the collar he pulled me so close. "It's too early for your bullshit."

Anyone who wanted to be kept up to speed with the spooky, kooky, queer and all-around weirdness of New York City, Arrow was your man. His goal was to earn a blue check mark on his social media only allotted to proper famous people. I was used to it by now, as he'd been obsessed with social media since the day we met. Actually, social media was how we found one another. As much as I loathe the addiction, sometimes these platforms work well for the anti-social and socially awkward, bringing together people who would not normally know how to carry on a conversation without first introducing themselves behind a screen.

"You hate that I love these platforms, but you were once on them."

"And look at us now, the happy couple."

"It's so easy for you to unplug, but for the rest of us, we like to remain *informed*." Arrow got very quiet, but the intensity in his eyes told me he was serious. "These are volatile times. Abortion rights are dead and they're coming for gay marriage next."

"And here I thought you were talking about one of your infamous Twitter wars."

"Henry, please." Arrow's pale eyes were glazed in cell phone light. "You're not understanding me. Society is on the brink of a collapse, both socially and politically. We're once again in a place where we're looking over our shoulders. But I can change that."

"You're not going to change politics or culture by being glued to your damn phone. You wonder why you can't write anymore."

"There was once a time where people like us would get arrested just for holding hands in public."

"It's not going to happen again."

"We'll see about that."

It didn't take much to get a rise out of Arrow, and it showed in the studio we shared in Brooklyn. Every window was broken, the floor littered with clothes, CDs and random ephemera; the walls were slaughtered with strange cursive that swooped like bats—depending on the hour you looked at it—that he claimed came to him in dreams. For every hole he smashed into sheetrock with his fist, he covered it with a black pillowcase or a magazine cutout of the heavy metal bands we blew our ear drums out to. But today I sensed something different in Arrow, he had a mean gleam in his eyes, and his mouth downturned into nothing like a frown.

"No matter how far we've come, it'll always be us versus them."

"That's usually how life goes."

Arrow scoffed. "And you wonder why I'm on high alert?" He threw his cell phone across the room; I saw it crash into a pile of paperback books. "Can't look at it anymore."

His tone was detestable, mood even worse. I lit a cigarette for Arrow and myself, then put my hand on his thin leg, slowly grazing my nail across the carnival of ink. I saw colored constellations and astrological glyphs. It was as if his skin was the personification of his disastrous hobbies: esoterica, the rejected cultures of horror and heavy metal. Where he got the money to pay tattoo artists was beyond my comprehension; Arrow had connections; somebody always owed him a favor, somebody always wanted to create alongside him.

"Do you wanna go to bed?"

Cigarette smoke slowly crawled out of Arrow's mouth, lips wet and welcoming for a kiss that I was sick of wanting. He rested his hand against the windowsill, gazing into the endless spiderweb patterns in the broken glass. It was a simple summer day and the sun seemed to pour into our apartment like syrup. I suddenly had the energy to go outside, take a morning stroll when the air was the freshest, just me and Arrow against the everchanging world, the world he so desperately needed to recognize him.

I looked at him again, saw a spherical point of light land in the crystal lens of his cornea, then run down his face like a yellow tear. He was seeing something out there on the barren street that I could not; somehow, I knew it was bad. *I'll do something about it*, he said to himself, thinking I couldn't hear him. But I heard everything Arrow ever said, sleep or awake, that's how much I loved him.

"I'm not tired," Arrow suddenly said. "But I'll cuddle you if you want."

"No," I said abruptly. "What're you planning to do?"

I saw Arrow's ears wiggle; surgical steel piercings danced darkly. The black hair that he tucked behind his ears fell across his countenance like rain. I noticed that my hand instantly covered my lips, but it was far too late. I'd planted an insidious idea in his head. He looked at me, completely serious, sharp features full of too much makeup. I saw imaginary smoke wheel out of his ear drums, and if I closed my eyes hard enough, I could see into his overwrought brain, throbbing dangerously as his next misadventure came to be.

"I thought you'd never ask."

Arrow disappeared for six weeks. No texts, no calls. The only reason I knew he was alive was through social media. Hyperbolic posts derived from irrelevant insanity; nothing made sense, but that was part of Arrow's malignant charm. As much as he was addicted to that little LED screen, Arrow also averted its laws with palindromic sentences and ambigram typesets so that only very few could understand him; a big fuck you to our linear culture.

In his absence, I spent my time lazing about our apartment, Vitruvian man incarnate, waiting for my boy to come home. I attempted to break the uncreative cycle, do something different with my life. Another sketch, then one more; same face veiled in darkness, eyes so black they had an unnatural sheen; its features were no different than my own or Arrow's. What jarred me the most was that I never drew studies of the physiognomy—surreal and unsettling imagery was my only talent—so to see how my hand had gone in a new direction allowed me to feel less depressed about my directionless life.

INCIDENT ON A SOCIAL PLATFORM

But then something happened. Even if I forcibly took my hand and made it go in a different direction, a tugging pain would overtake my tendons—the small bones of my fingers and wrist— and bring me right back to these faces. So many that I hung them up on the walls, faces of abyssal madness and cantankerousness, faces that looked at you more than you could ever look at them. The abyss incarnate; eyes swathed in so much shimmering lead they made one feel as if they were being watched.

When my drawing had had enough, masturbation kept me sane, as I was physically incapable of being with any other man but Arrow, despite gay culture's open-door policy for sex. Arrow had my heart caged; my libido arrested. He was the most mysterious person I'd ever met, and his dark whim kept me completely on my toes. I never knew what Arrow was going to do next, and that was the part I liked the most.

On the morning he showed up on our doorstep, Arrow was profuse with sweat and stunk like dirt. His hands were black, and the fingernails that I was used to seeing painted in random bright colors were caked with mud. The Mötley Crüe crop top that was normally too tight on his torso was ripped through the center so that I could see a fresh sunburn blaze about his nipples. He had a cigarette between his lips and a vial of ketamine behind his ear; daubs of powder sparkled on his upper lip.

"Where the hell've you been?"

"I'm going to be Instafamous."

"Yeah right," I rolled my eyes so hard I saw a blue flash of light.

"I told you that something dangerous was coming, and I was right."

Arrow rushed past me. Emotions quarreled deep within the recesses of his eyes. I wasn't sure what he'd done, or what he'd seen, but his freakish presence frightened me. He brought himself back to our window, traced the labyrinthine cracks that blazed in the pink light of dawn. Then his head turned fast; I saw one hand grab the vial behind his ear, as the other stamped out the cigarette on the exposed brick wall. His entire body quivered, not that it was cold out, but it was from the multitudinous faces on the walls.

"Masks?" Arrow asked.

"No."

"You drew them; tell me what they are."

"I don't know."

Arrow's mouth was so close I gave in and kissed his lips. But that was not the end of it. The kiss led to my hand grabbing the back of his neck, pulling him closer. I ran my fingers through the black silk of his hair, our tongues slowly searching the other's mouth for secrets and lies. We never found it, never needed to. Our connection was not superficial like so many gay male couples that dominate social media. We were outsiders in that our sex was explosive since day one, and it still was three years later, even with our mental connection being off.

We kissed again, deeply; it was almost as if Arrow's tongue was reaching into my body to collect my soul. Arrow's pheromones swam up my nose as the flavor of his saliva sizzled across my lips. I tasted ketamine in the back of his throat, and all the cigarettes he'd been smoking. I couldn't stand how perfect it felt, how right his mouth felt on my own. A metaphorical fire ignited between us.

Then something unsheathed itself inside of me, a feral thing that wanted what it wanted. *I love you*, Arrow said. *It's always been you*, as I slid my pants off and wrapped my legs around Arrow's thin naked waist. The moment he entered me, I knew I wouldn't be satisfied until my belly was slimed with white ribbons of liquid. *You're so warm*, he said into my ear as he bit it, his lips suddenly red as candy apple syrup. And then it was over. Arrow's head rested on my shoulder, rapid breath slowly descending to decadent sighs.

"That was too good," Arrow said.

"Tell me where you were."

He was silent, flicked some dirt off his fingers, which landed near me. I smelled altars, and something like hops; a blend of herbs and spices wrapped into deliquescent incense. Arrow got to his feet. He was incorrigible, a newly made mad thing filled with piss and venom. Incapable of being calmed down until he was good and ready, I let Arrow have his freak out. Throw stuff around our place, flip the bed as if there was something under it that he desperately needed. *So many faces*, Arrow roared in a new voice I wasn't familiar with, one that bayed as high as a wolf, but was somehow laced with the deep bass of a subwoofer.

"I'm going to change the world."

INCIDENT ON A SOCIAL PLATFORM

It was pitch black when he took me out. But the sweltering summer day had bled into nightfall; darkness oozed all over New York City as if it were a living thing. I felt it stick to my skin, humidity like syrup that could not be washed clean. We were headed east, away from the white noise of Manhattan, skyscrapers jutting out of the horizon like LED spikes, whereas the tenements that banked the shorelines remained squat and decrepit.

Despite being born and raised here, the sight never ceased to amaze me. Manhattan glinted no matter what angle you looked at it, and the powerful glitz within it filled the mind with thoughts both good and bad. We doubt ourselves; we believe in ourselves. We take risks, we get rewarded. We bleed. We crave. We don't know if tomorrow will come, so we live our lives as if today will be our last.

As we entered the black static known as the borough of Queens, I knew Arrow was not leading me anywhere fun. The town had no name, not one that I could pinpoint on my phone anyway. *Found it by mistake*, Arrow said under his breath. I walked a few paces behind him, slowly taking in the things that I could see, and couldn't see. Yes, there were still portions of the five boroughs that remained untapped and unscathed from big business. Yes, there were still places so desolate it was hard to imagine that just a mile away was a burgeoning metropolis, and dare I say it, necropolis in some ways. This place was one of them.

"It feels different here," I noted aloud.

"That's because you're used to your hipster Brooklyn paradise," Arrow said with disdain.

It was a warehouse district that hadn't been used in quite some time. Everything was in disrepair, scarred by rust and aching with abandonment. Timeworn brick and blighted buildings showcased where people must have once lived or worked. I saw heavily boarded windows and overgrown brush bulging out of doorways. Graffiti plagued most edifices, and a nearby swamp was slowly eating the foundation of one of the warehouses. I could see how it slowly was pulling away from the foundation, sinking irritably. It looked like the earth was taking the land back that was wrongfully taken from it.

The air was crisp with the ghosts of diesel fumes and grease vapors. It filled me with basic fear, but at the same time the silence somehow made me brave. I could think here, safely, without all the interruptions from the internet and the never-ending noise between my ears. Clarity came to me in rare form. I wanted to draw, but there were no sidewalks or blacktop streets, and obviously nowhere to sit. I used my cell phone light to see things up close—garbage at my feet, broken furniture, cans piled like stalagmites—and moonlight to guide my eyes the rest of the way.

"Be careful," Arrow held my hand. "Hypodermics all over the place."

"I'm only wearing Converses."

"If you shut up and listen to me." Arrow released my hand and grabbed my neck, digging a fingernail beneath the skin. "I'll get you through. And then you can sit and doodle."

"I don't *doodle*."

Arrow released my neck, then twined his fingers within my own. The touch of his hand instantly deleted all thoughts of his being mean. I've been marveling at this power Arrow had over me since the day we met, and I do not think I will ever figure it out. When they say 'love can make people do crazy things' I finally understood what they mean. I was just going to keep on following this boy, and do crazy things, because I was simply in love.

"Those things you've been drawing," Arrow's face was bright with moonlight. "Do you know what they are?"

"I don't think much about them."

"Well, you should, because I've seen that face before."

"I thought the same thing when I drew them."

"Rather narcissistic of you." I could tell Arrow was not kidding.

"It's called facial pareidolia. Our brains make us—"

"I need to post a story." Arrow interrupted; another Twitter war and Instagram whore wanting attention I imagined.

"What would you do without precious social media?"

Arrow stopped walking, touched the side of my face with the nail he dug into my neck. "You're so beautiful, Henry. But I wish that beauty reached your brain."

His flower petal lips upturned into something not like a smile, showing off his small teeth that were too white for the number of cigarettes he smoked. And then we were off again, approaching a warehouse, or factory, I couldn't tell from this distance. But its outline seemed to punch a hole into reality, disperse light or eat it as does a vacuum to dust. Just this huge structure born from metal and mortar, now on its death bed from lack of upkeep and volatile weather patterns.

INCIDENT ON A SOCIAL PLATFORM

"This is where I saw it."

Through the small black entrance, once a door but now rubble that forced us to climb into a hole no bigger than a cupboard. The sill gave in to my weight, sent me falling onto shrapnel, pebbles and shards of stained glass. Arrow helped me up and put one finger on his lips to signal to not make a noise. He was very serious, as if we were going to scare someone, or something, away. But there was nowhere to lurk, as far as I could see, as moonlight filtered through the slatted boards, illuminating the huge space so that I saw it was mostly empty.

"It's just an empty warehouse," I said. "Why do we gotta be quiet?"

And then a sudden pain on my arm, a pain I wouldn't think was Arrow's little white hands, until I saw his fingers trembling, multiple rings biting my skin. *There*, Arrow whispered into my ear. I looked to the right, directly where his eyes pointed, but couldn't see more than ten feet in front my own face it suddenly became so dark. I heard a faint noise, rustling like rats burrowing into a garbage bag, or a rake gathering leaves. I focused my vision, waiting for my eyes to adjust.

"I got it on camera last time. I told you I'm going to be instafamous."

"What is it?" I whispered?

I made Arrow sit down and show me what he was talking about. For once in my life, I found myself impatient as he, felt myself almost wanting to rip the phone out of his hand he was taking so long. But that's only because I was three beers in; Arrow bought us an expensive IPA with an alcohol by volume content that was three times the normal amount of bodega beer. My head was swimming, and my stomach was reeling with . . . not excitement, but dread.

"Play the damn video."

"Only if you swear to keep your mouth shut."

"Pinky promise."

"This is going to change everything."

Arrow licked his lips, pulled a cigarette out from behind his ear and fired it up. I finished my beer and added it to my shelf of collectable bottles and caps, a side hobby of mine when it came to limited edition brews. Arrow motioned for me to sit on his lap; the red mini skirt and crop top of the Zodiac I was wearing turned him on. I knew he wanted to rub his hands on my smooth legs. The act of boys wearing girls' clothing was another middle finger to the establishment he continuously rejected.

"Don't get off my lap when you see it. Understand?"

"Yes," I said with consternation under my breath.

He brought his phone in front of us. The camera roll was loaded with all sorts of pictures, from selfies to nudes and screenshots of social media arguments, to videos of Arrow just roaming the streets of New York City and talking into the screen as if he was a haunted tour guide. I had never investigated Arrow's phone before; you don't do that when in a trusting relationship. And seeing this now was like a gateway into a perturbed brain, one that felt new to me again.

Arrow clicked his nail on the video of choice. An unexpected static and white noise hit my ears like the televisions of my childhood. That was something I thought I'd never see again on screen. And then it was just that town in Queens, a long black ribbon of road, population zero, maybe one. Arrow's heavy breathing wormed into my ears; he was oddly silent, slowly dragging the video through the same path he took me, until I saw the full panoramic view of the old building.

With the advanced lens, I was able to see what my rudimentary eyes could not. The inside of the warehouse was not as empty as I once thought. While time had been cruel to it, water rot ceiling and crumbling floors, there was a certain charm to the dark decadence that filled that space. A DJ booth was in the far back, and a broken disco ball rained little blades of light down onto floor. There was a makeshift bar and unnamed taps that still had foam about the nozzles.

"Was this some kind of—"

"I don't know."

"Mausoleum?"

"Definitely not."

"So then?"

"Looks to me like some sort of event space."

Then we both went back to the video. Arrow's thighs were tense against my buttocks; he wrapped his skinny arms completely around my torso ran his hands under my skirt, feeling for my dick and balls. But I could not pay attention to his touch, as I was too glued to the screen. There was a presence, opaque like a big piece of dust hovering over the camera lens, thus I found myself biting my nails, just waiting for it to be brushed away. *Anyone there?* Arrow's voice was thin and weak in the video. He was scared.

"Do you see how this will change the world?"

"There's nothing there."

"You dumb fuck."

Arrow turned my head back to the screen with one hand. It was almost all white now, as if he'd pointed his camera directly into a car's headlight. But it was short lived, as the glowing white dissipated, I saw the outline of a figure, two arms and two legs, neck torso and head like any human, except that I was able to see through this thing as if it was made of tissue paper. I held my breath, while at the same time trying to figure out if it was male or female, but as soon as it turned its cavernous face towards Arrow's phone, it was gone.

I didn't dwell on what I saw. No point in trying to figure out what was real and what wasn't. It would be far too easy for me to blame drugs, or my own superstitiousness, because reality is not as black and white as we are conditioned to believe. Arrow tried to pull thoughts out of my head relentlessly, query after query like an investigative journalist. He'd never been so inquisitive with me, never so interested. I thought that I finally had become the center of his attention, until he threw a fit and declared me mentally catatonic when I refused to budge.

"You really want to get on my bad side," Arrow growled.

Sleep came intermittently. My dreams were ferocious, pale battering rams against the back of my skull. Their intensity fueled my insomnia, and as each day crawled by, the exhaustion had me irritable, but somehow inspired. I lay awake in bed, staring at our small window with all the intricate cracks, the sun spitting little gobs of fire unto my skin during the day, and brilliant marbles of moonlight at night.

Arrow remained emotionally distant, but physically close. He talked to himself more than ever, which was not surprising given his frustration. My guess is that being I refused to indulge him, he felt alone; or that this was the prelude he didn't expect, given he was so addicted to pushing cultural change with social media. How could he not think anyone would question what they saw on the video?

I reached my hand beneath our dirty mattress; several things brushed against my fingers—safety pins, wallet chain, baggie of ketamine—but when I found my pencil, I began to draw. Three sketch books were filled in less than a day. That same hollow face lolled in the corner of my eyes. No reason or rhyme for it. A face so devoid of emotion and human features, I knew that I would never make sense of it being our brains make us see familiar objects in completely random shapes and designs.

"Some ghosts never exist in physical form," Arrow was standing above me, skinnier and fiercer than before.

I removed my face from the sketch book. "What do you mean?"

Arrow's eyes were buried deep in his cell phone. "Death is not the only reason ghosts exist."

He pointed to his Instagram, which had garnered a few thousand more followers. *Posted a quick snippet on my story*, Arrow mouthed to me. His pipe dream as king of the unknown, emperor of the empaths, was starting to take shape. I felt jealousy bubble inside my stomach, imagining all the messages he was receiving from boys who wanted to sleep with him; all the fights he was taking part in that would introduce him to endless amounts of people he could keep in his back pocket for later ramblings and anti-social connections.

"Lucky you, more distractions."

"You'll thank me later when I create a new social movement."

"Which is?"

"That we're not *alone*."

"And what's that going to do for the world?"

"You still don't get it, do you?"

The sky was almost too clear the next night. Every star was closer to the earth than they should have been. I traced their patterns with my hand, connecting the dots and drawing phantom faces. Arrow watched me do this with childlike fascination, while the same time recording this candid moment for another one of his Instagram stories. I got rid of my social media years ago, so my presence on his was a mere stain in the landscape of electronic connections being I had no handle they could snoop.

"It's the politicians and the religious that need a humble lesson."

INCIDENT ON A SOCIAL PLATFORM

"And you think your little ghost hunt will have them pay attention to you?"

"I wonder if you see what I see in your drawings," Arrow stopped recording, and was back to filling his nose with ketamine and his lungs with tobacco.

"Where are we going?"

"To check it out again."

"I don't feel like going back."

"You don't get to choose. When you start becoming original, I'll let you lead. Until then, you follow me."

Light from the west dazzled across Brooklyn. But the more east we headed, the world became darker. The train ride to Queens was literal hell, humidity once again so thick I felt it grip my face and twist, take hold of my skin and lick. The subway station was overcrowded with yuppies, bums, gays, and hipsters, even for a Friday night. How many of them were heading to Queens, I'd never know. By the time the train arrived, the miniskirt I was wearing nearly slipped off my hips, and the high-top converses were soaked all the way through.

Arrow pulled me by my mesh crop top, hooked his arm in mine. *Stay together*, he whispered. I didn't recognize where I was, didn't pay attention to the train stops due to the noise inside my head being so loud. But there were some vaguely familiar elements, starting with the desolation and mounds of trash, as if people were using this place as their personal junkyard. Then I saw a trail of hypodermics winking, alongside a very huge carpet of broken glass.

There was no point in which Arrow didn't film. I saw him post story after story, taking his viewers, or soon to be "fans" on this adventure. Whether it was the way that this town shapeshifted or how it personified abandonment, Arrow was going to put this place on the map. I saw the same warehouse in the distance, laved in starlight. Its boarded windows looked as wet as my own eyeballs, and the large doorway seemed to shape itself into a malicious mouth.

"Do you see it?" I asked Arrow.

"Shh."

It was a huge face, and not one that my brain wanted me to see. It was an actual face, one that throbbed, thrived; one that bent the foundation of the warehouse, forcing the mortar to crack and its steel bones to creak. *Take this*, Arrow handed me his key with a big bump of ketamine on it, to which I snorted it without hesitation. The drug dripped slowly into the back of my throat, partially numbing my epiglottis. But in no time, it began to take effect, flowering into my bloodstream and dissociating my inhibitions. I took the free ride on this dark wave of adventure.

"You see it, because that's exactly what you draw."

"That's not how it works."

"I'm an artist, Henry. I know what I'm talking about."

"You're only a writer. And now wannabe influencer."

"I can interpret all forms of art, because I respect it."

We slid into the gaping maw. I felt this great sense of coming back to square one, but at the same time being somewhere completely different. I followed Arrow, swirled slowly about him, as if I were a satellite and he the rock to which I was gravitationally bound. The same slatted light spilled throughout the warehouse's insides, all bones and dust and endless trash. Arrow lit a cigarette, then pulled us into a corner that was so dark I could not even see my hand in front of my face.

"I'm about to go live," Arrow said. "They're waiting."

"Who're waiting?"

"My audience."

He placed his cell phone on a wooden beam, using the bashed wall as its fulcrum. Then he pressed record. Time somehow did not want to move. The only reason I knew the clock was ticking was because the Instagram live feed was beginning to fill. People commented immediately. *Just a black screen* and *Bullshit* is what I made out immediately and I couldn't help but agree. What we were doing was social suicide, not social influencing. That was until I heard the noise again.

Same muffled rustle, far away but at the same time so close the sound crawled onto my outer ear. Maybe not the sound at all, but the thing that preceded it. I looked back at Arrow's phone, keyboard warriors conflating arguments of their own, against one another but also in tandem with the live feed. A lump surged in my throat, because I was finally feeling something again, and it wasn't anything that I associated with good. It left me thirsty, my eyes dry and my pulse surging into my ears.

Because I saw it.

The real thing.

No longer hominid as my brain would have liked me to

recognize, but something greater, a process too big to capture on the small screen or translate from my primordial eyes. Not shadow, not even any true sensation; just void. It reminded me how black holes sit in space, a spherical tear in the fabric of the universe, serving as an area of nothingness that eats everything around it. This thing was certainly eating my sanity.

I blinked to make sure I wasn't dreaming. Each time I did I saw a mouth ringed in endless vacuum. Then I heard ding after ding, the sound of Arrow's followers growing. Word of mouth was the best form of marketing these days, especially within the interconnected world of technology. Then he started to laugh, and I wondered what was so funny. When I turned, I saw black tears welling into little bright beads on his chin, and the kohl liner around his eyes slowly fading.

I felt his heat close in on me, body to body; Arrow was holding me in place, wiping away the blood that fell out of my ears in rivulets. *It's mine*, Arrow whispered. *It's all mine.* That's when my own cell phone began vibrating, texts from everyone I didn't care to talk to, asking me if I was okay, if I was being kidnapped. Their worry was proof that they believed what they saw. But their worry pained me because I wasn't sure I even saw what I saw.

No point in trying to rationalize.

Reality is transient, as is our own lifespan.

LAVENDERS

YAH YAH SCHOLFIELD

IT'S BEEN SAID that any man of means in lack of a wife is surely in want of one. He's got no excuse if he's wealthy, handsome. Certainly, this creature wants nothing more than to be caught and owned. Otherwise, if he is too ugly or too poor of or disreputable origins, he is to be pitied. Poor thing, what a shame.

I am neither handsome nor am I repulsive, neither grandly rich nor pitiably poor. I am simply Michelangelo, a single man. If I look at myself from a distance with a stranger's unbiased eye, this is what I see—a solitary young man, white and bloodless and drawn into himself, dark eyes and dark hair, a sullen and listless expression. This man lives alone on a quiet street. His bungalow—inherited, they say, from his dearly departed mother, poor boy—drips with bougainvillea and is shaded by many a black tupelo tree. His garden is neat and fragrant, predominantly Hidcote blue lavender and peace lily. Nosy neighbors and observant passersby alike might spy him through the filmy gauze of curtains settled in an armchair, nose hidden in a book of poetry, or else sitting at his baby grand piano, playing mournful sonatas by Bach and Chopin. He keeps to himself. His neighbors call him shy.

So desperately do I wish to be this man, this shapeless and awkward stranger. I want to be the reflection, not the source, but the mirror *is* distorted, and anyways, I cannot see myself in fine silver.

The truth of me is this. I *am* Michelangelo and I am alone. I am not white, though I am light enough to pass for it, my mother's Black genes lost somewhere in the coil of my hair, the fullness of my mouth. I've been told I'm the spitting image of my father. Though I appear to be like most men, I am nothing like anyone I've ever known. There's something lurking inside of me, a foul thing that makes me queer and untouchable. I crave, endlessly, the curve of a man's neck, the decadent sheen of sweat on the brow, the jaw. And of course, the hands, the wrists, the powerful legs, their pumping, pulsating veins heaving with begs, begging to be pierced, bitten and lapped, the jailed juice my own desire.

I am cautious of my hunger. There are others like me—monsters, inverts—who let their desires run rampant and let themselves go wild with lust. I've seen these sorts of men, how they prowl the streets, noses twitching and lapping at their lips like common dogs. Shamelessly, they flash their teeth in darkened bars, teasing and taunting at their prey until the men follow them into alleyways, stairwells and bathrooms. I'm not like these men either. Fear of discovery makes me vigilant with myself, and I lock the wicked thing deep inside of me and cool it with the arts. Poetry helps. Whitman and Baldwin and Hughes, though sometimes they too can bring heat to my neck with their terrible, irresistible visions. Music is better—nothing tames the beast quite like a chorale. The thing settles in my belly, lulled to sleep by piano, by the unending busy work of scales, reading sheet music, or writing music of my own when the old standards just won't cut it.

And yet there are times when my desires are not so easily sated, times when my body burns with want and my vision blurs from how much I need. I loll in bed, writhe and gnash my teeth. I roll my eyes and claw at my skin, the itch right beneath the surface too strong to be soothed by Chopin. When this happens, when I feel I might literally split apart from hunger, I go out into the night.

I bear myself in daytime. I have my distractions, my tidy home to keep and all my twee curios that amuse me. A skin condition and a general aversion to sunlight keeps me indoors, the windows darkened with drapes. It is lonely, but I don't mind it. I take my solitude with the practiced reservation of a man long imprisoned, a man to whom the sun is but a fleeting memory. So it is, so it is, I tell myself, and go deeper into my home, into another room to doze or read or play a little music.

At night, there are no excuses, no distractions. I go out dressed in featureless clothes, a plain black overcoat and boots, matching leather gloves and a dark scarf wound tightly around the lower half of my face to conceal my mouth, my horrible teeth. I go into the city where there is much too much temptation, men in bars and men twisting in the dancehalls with their lady loves. Through red and greedy eyes, I watch them dance, how their move their hips, how easily laughter comes to them, how smoothly they can grab one another's shoulders. If fate were kind, if I were anyone but myself, I would go into these places and stand with these men, drink beer and grab shoulders, laugh at bawdy jokes with the same boisterous voice as them. Instead, I stand at windows, my sullen face reflected as a strange beast with sunken eyes and cheeks, mouth-watering for things it will not permit itself to have.

I walk the streets. I keep my hands in my pants pockets so no one will see them twitch, and whistle to myself, *Ode to Joy* then the opening chords of *Fur Elise*. Warm yellow streetlights brighten the way. Posters encouraging young men and boys to enlist in the war surround me, billboards with uniformed men gazing optimistically at nothing, signs screaming *Do your duty! For your country!* I do not think so much about the words as I do about the men with their Leyendecker looks, chiseled jaws and bright eyes that look right through me.

I've not fallen far enough to find companionship in alleyways, so I find my way to a bar that promises good jazz and liquor. The bar's dim and moody, candles arranged artfully on each of the tables, and lights positioned over the stage and bar for extra ambience.

There's a Black man crooning up on the stage, a song I don't recognize but like immediately. Something about gay places, women with traces of joy, about sad looks mistaken for love—*I guess I was wrong. Again, I was wrong!* I take a seat at the far end of the bar, far from the other patrons. When the bartender asks me what I'd like to drink, I order my usual.

"A Bloody Mary, please," say I, and thank God for the dimness of the bar because the heat on my neck and cheeks is enough to reduce me down to nothing. Are they looking at me? What sort of mean thoughts is the bartender forming about me, and do the people at the other end of the bar think lowly of me for ordering such a "fruity" drink? Has even this small thing implicated me? I straighten my back and square my shoulders, harden the line of my wrist so I don't look so damn foppish. I blink and clear my throat, avert my eyes and unwind my scarf.

LAVENDERS

I am my mother's child entirely. Her hands, at least, are mine, long and graceful with pianist's fingers. She used to joke that my father all but stole her from a jazz bar, him an uptight and stringent white man bowled over by her smile, the way she played. My warmest memories of her are the ones in which she's playing piano for me, winking at me, teaching me my scales. The uglier memories also have her music as a score, I'm afraid—swing music blaring brazenly from her Victrola after a bloody fight with my father, the discordant noise of a piano being taken apart key by key. I remember her aging, her fine hands curling in on themselves. Mine, at least, will never wither, the delicate orchids never wilting.

The bartender returns with my drink, and I let it sit there in front of me, a prop more than anything. I've got a sensitive stomach, most foods and drink making me retch if they so much as touch my tongue. This ungodly mix of alcohol, tomato juice, tabasco and celery is sure to ruin my belly, but it's better to be seen with something near you than to sit at the bar drink-less, gazing around the room like a predator looking for its prey. I keep a hand on the glass and listen to the man singing. His repertoire is melancholy, romantic. One moment he weeps about his blues, the next he reminiscences over a lost April. Naïve, I think to myself that this might not be so bad an evening, that it'll be enough to hear music and go home. No blood needs to be shed, nothing regrettable needs to be done.

But then *he* comes in. I lose my breath; my eyes grow wide. His is a vision, a perfect Arrow Man, the jaw and hands and dazzling eyes that smolder in the dark of the bar. From the way he's dressed, to the way he looks around the place, unamused and bored, I guess he's one of those beatniks. Even clothed in black and thick glasses, shrouded by disaffection and that practiced moue, the beauty of this boy astounds me, his nose and mouth, his hair curled boyishly around his ears.

My stomach clenches. I tremble. I reach for my drink and a take a long, slow sip, grabbing at anything that'll distract me from the ever-loudening pounding in my head. *Need it, need it, need him*, my body cries. I watch the man from the corner of my eye as he scans the room. I turn my head, just an inch, just for one more look at him, and our eyes meet. Hellfire runs through me, from the tip of my fingers to my loins then out through my toes. My mouth dries. I flex my hands against the bar top before quickly stuffing them back into my pockets.

YAH YAH SCHOLFIELD

He comes to me, and for one brief, terrible moment, I think that I've tricked him somehow, hypnotized him into doing my bidding, but no. He is clear-eyed and curious as he takes the stool next to me. He discards his jacket and orders a drink, some heady masculine thing that he knocks back with a grimace before ordering another.

"Cold night, huh?"

His pliant mouth, his strong hands, the scrub of his beard against my smooth face. I am weak in the knees, weak in the spirit. I want to take him into my mouth, like communion, feel him on my tongue, lust and hunger merging into one carnal need to bite, to devour. I smell the blood pumping hot in his neck. I lick my lips and fall to my knees and take all that I am given.

II.

Come morning, the taste of the beatnik's blood is hot and rank as halitosis in my mouth. Shame binds me to the bed. My desperation embarrasses me, how ready I was to take anything and everything he could've offered. I did not kill him, I don't think. Even in my lusty haze, I knew to stop before draining him or ruining him altogether. My mind, a petty punisher, shows me images of all the times I did not stop, all the times that I let my hunger rule me, all the men I've sucked and emptied and left as husks, men I've made into monsters.

(Fabio, one of them was called. He was fair-skinned and eager, and when he held me in his hand, I felt he held all of me, all my memories and evil thoughts. When I woke from my daze, he was lifeless and breathing and almost ash, and I ran before I saw him become nothing.)

The sun rises. Light trickles in and around the curtains, just enough to make shadows in the corners but not enough to hurt me. I watch the light dance as memories of the night previous come to me. One good thing about my nocturnal hunting is that I only have to do it every so often. The right man, the right vein, will keep me sated for weeks on end. I recall a few months ago, nipping the flesh just behind a sailor's ear, his hands traveling down the line of my back. His blood kept me for a while, and often, when my urges feel strong enough to break me, I remind myself of his smell, how he groaned when I bit into him, like my soiling him was the greatest pleasure he ever had.

LAVENDERS

The beatnik will be more than enough. Even in my disgust at myself, I'm happy as a cat with cream at the thought of his mouth upon mine, his hands and wicked tongue. He will wake—dear Lord, let him wake—to find himself covered with curious bites at his wrist and neck, strange bruises where I gripped and held fast, and spirit-willing, he will move on. Keep writing poetry, find a nice girl to settle with, have two and a half cheery, apple-checked babies.

(I am no fool. I know he is a man like me. I imagine him with a wife, with children, and even with those chains, he will fly to the nearest alleyway, find the prettiest thing and take and take. Poor thing, I think. For shame.)

I rise, try to pull myself together. The house is not so beautiful without daylight, but I make do with lamps and light fixtures. I go through the house and click each of them all until the place is bright, then settle down in my library to waste a few hours. It used to be my father's study, but what he studied in here I don't know. He wasn't an intellectual man—reading was effeminate, book-learning was for sissies. What a mockery I make of him now, curled up in my cozy chair, Lorca's *Ode to Walt Whitman* warming my lap. I drift in and out of dreams; James Baldwin visits me in one, teasing me with French poetry. I slip stems of lavender into his tooth gap, but I force myself awake before my mind sullies the beauty of the moment.

The day passes slowly. In summer, I'm confined to my rooms, reading and writing. Occasionally, I'll get the idea to change something in the house, and I'll pull out the furniture catalogs and scry through them until I realize I cannot and will never change a thing in my mother's house. At best, I'll refresh the flowers that sit in the antique vases, though always the same genus and color, always the same arrangement of fronds.

My father was a wealthy man, proud and self-serious. His affair with my mother was his one and only act of impulsivity—a loosening of his tie, if you will. My mother said to me once that she made him feel lawless. There was never any joy in her voice as she repeated his words to me, never any private pride. Only shame, a slight curl to her lip that showed me what it was like to be Black and visible. The unbroken mirror showed animals; maybe it's best if my reflection is skewed?

Anyways, I don't think they loved each other. My mother, at least, loved me, and she proved it in little ways that seem grander now that she's gone. She bought the house we shared with hush money from my father and built up the garden walls to keep us private. She instilled in me from youth the understanding that no matter what showed on the outside, on the inside I was *her* child, her Black child. My pale face in her dark hands, her deep eyes my first and only mirror.

Did she know what kind of man she raised? She must've, must've realized I wasn't quite like the other children, even before my turning. She was sensitive to my tenderness, my fragile nature and later, once I returned from a trip down south to visit some relatives even more drawn and closed off than ever, she had to have had ideas. Oh, but Mother was gentle; she drew closed the curtains and pulled me in tight, her precious boy, not so precious.

III.

The phone rings at three o'clock, and I know before answering who's calling. I smile and say, "Charlie Yewman, you've got a lot of nerve calling me before sunset."

Charlie laughs in response and my heart flutters to hear it. Charlie Yewman is my best and only friend, and I think I'm his best and only as well. We cling to each other, or I cling to Charlie, and he tolerates me and patronizes me with these friendly phone calls.

Charlie's a good man. There's no other way to describe him, his easygoing nature and his big laugh. Like me, he's shy of others. The war's made him nervous of the outdoors, shellshock turning this massive man jittery. If you loosen his tongue with whiskey, he'll tell you stories from Germany about gunfire, the POW camps, and all the men he's seen die. He remembers their names, our dear Charlie, and insignificant details about them that have stamped themselves onto his brain. During thunderstorms and on the Fourth of July, he keeps his house lit like Christmas.

"Really, though, Chuck, what's convinced you to call me so early?"

"Ah, loneliness if you can believe it," he says. "Got tired of watching the ol' boob tube, and wanted to see how you felt about dinner."

"In general? Positive. My place or yours?"

"Mine." After a moment, he says, "After sundown of course. I think the sun's going down around six."

LAVENDERS

I rarely leave the house lest I'm out hunting, and Charlie's good fun. He's kind to me, asks no hard questions, and doesn't mind if I don't eat. I harbor suspicions about him—I think he might be my sort of man, lavender-colored, though I'll never summon the courage to question him about it. It's enough to hear how he talks about the soldiers he once knew, their fit bodies and wise-cracking mouths.

"Any port in a storm," he once told me, laughing, though I knew, and he knew that I knew that some ports were more favorable than others.

"You'll come then?" Charlie asks. His voice is so quiet and meek. I think of him less like the big, burly man he is, and more as a tender, shrinking thing. I think of his hand reaching out to me through the dark, and I reach back for his.

Charlie's waiting for me at the window when I walk up to his house at seven. The sun's hidden her face behind some houses, and it's dark enough for me to not worry about the eyes of neighbors. Charlie opens the door for me before I can ring the bell, slips me in as secret as a mistress. We wait until we are well inside to shake hands. He claps my back with his powerful paw, and smiles in my face, squeezing my shoulder. Charlie asks me about my day, and I tell him all that I did, though I'm sure it's as uninteresting and unvaried as usual.

He brings me to his living room (cluttered, busy with magazines and books), and we sit in Charlie's overstuffed armchairs to half-watch the television. An old drama is playing—Audrey Hepburn and Gregory Peck in black-and-white, tearing around Rome.

"So, Michelangelo," he says after a while. "Keeping yourself busy?"

"Oh, you know." I smile. "Doing this and that, poetry and sonatas. I'm thinking of writing jazz."

"Careful now. You start playing that Negro music, and the whole neighborhood will get suspicious of that nose of yours."

"My nose?" I put a hand up to the offending organ, realize Charlie's teasing me, and laugh. "Oh! Really, Chuck, nobody sees my nose enough to form any opinions on it. It could be a *bat's* nose for all they know."

"Well, you *are* something of a bat, aren't you? Cave-like dwelling, half-blind, nocturnal . . . "

"Since when did you become so knowledgeable about bats, Charlie Yewman?"

He shrugs and says, "Who's to say I'm not one myself?"

I look at him carefully, and he looks back. After a quiet moment, he goes back to watching the movie. The silence that holds us is uncomfortable, strained. I see the red rising on his neck, just above his collar, and I wonder if it's his own blood or something he took off another man. How does he like them, my dear Charlie? Lithe and swanny, long necks and delicate features? Does he like them strong, muscled, men in suits or in leather or uniform?

On screen, Hepburn is drunk. She mumbles about never having been alone with a man with a dress on, never mind with her dress off. She quotes a little bit of poetry and spars, gently, with Gregory Peck about the line being from Keats or Shelley. Charlie breaks the silence and asks me, "Which one is it anyway, Shakespeare? Keats or Shelley."

I say, "I've no clue." Which is true enough, though mostly I'm distracted by thoughts of Charlie's boys. Do they come to his room? Does he overcome his fear just enough to fetch them for himself? When he bites them (*if* he bites into them, if he's queer in the way that I'm queer), do they groan and twist in his powerful hands?

The movie blurs in front of me. Hepburn cuts her hair short and steals a Vespa, kisses Peck over and over and over. By the time the end comes, Hepburn and Peck making vague but grand declarations of affection, I am drowsy. I cover my mouth as I yawn and apologize to Charlie for my lackluster company.

"I fear this has been a real snooze of a dinner. No food, no drink, and not one of the guests had the class to sing a little something."

"Oh, that's fine. Really, it is, Mikey. I don't go for singing much, anyway." Charlie quiets, considering something, then he says, "Do you think *you* might play for me though?"

"*Me*? You want *me* to play something?"

"Yes. I have a little . . . Well, it's not as grand as the ones you're used to, I'm sure, but there *is* a piano in the other room. Come on, I'll show it to you."

Charlie leads me to an adjoining room, a small drawing room

outfitted with disorderly stacks of books and overwhelmed with furniture. It's dusty and stale, closed-off smelling, but to the right of the room, obscured by a ghastly floral sofa is a dark brown upright piano. Charlie lifts the cover from off the piano and shows me the keys, yellowed with age.

"I didn't know you played, Chuck."

He ducks his head, bashful, and says, "I don't really. My ma, she tried teaching me some things, nursery rhymes and hymns, but I never had the head for it. Hands were always too big, not quite gentle enough. The best you can get out of me is 'Mary Had a Little Lamb'." Charlie takes a breath, looks at me sidelong. "I wanna you hear, Mikey. Sometimes I hear you, the music coming from your house at night when you prop a window open. It's the loveliest thing in the world, and it always sounds like you're playing for somebody." He catches himself, blinks rapidly, and clears his throat. "Play a little for me, Mikey? Please?"

The back of my neck burning, my stomach roiling, I take a sit at the piano bench and position my hands over the keys. "What would you like to hear?"

"Anything, Mikey." Then, after a moment, Charlie says, "Swan Lake. I'd love to hear you play that one piece from Swan Lake."

I cannot remember the last time I've played for anybody. My mother, maybe. I used to put on shows for her, little concertos in the parlor to amuse her, but they never felt like this. Never like how it feels to sit in Charlie's dusty drawing room, hemmed in by his possessions. I play for him, the beginning notes of Tchaikovsky's *Swan Lake*, the introduction in *moderato assai*, building and building the music, slowly, gradually until it fills the room entirely. I feel as if I'm being flayed alive, my own traitorous hands the ones that hold the knife that peels back the skin. I play for Charlie, and with each note, each chord, there is a confession. There is love and desire, a need so infinite and endless it threatens to unman me, if I were ever a man before. The surge of feeling makes me dizzy. *He* makes me dizzy, my Charlie, the way he watches me so quietly, so intently. I find myself regretting the beatnik, not only for the violence of my lust, but because he wasn't Charlie, because it wasn't his hands around my waist or his wicked tongue playing along my neck.

At the end of the song, my breathing is heavy, strained. Charlie's eyes are wet with tears, and he weeps quiet and controlled. His tears, those delicate pearls dripping down his face . . . All of me seizes. Thoughtlessly, impulsively, I kiss them away, the salt headier than any blood that has ever touched my lips.

"Mikey . . . *Oh*, Mikey . . ."

His hands, undeniably rough from countless years of hard labor and gun handling, are lambs against my cheek. He holds me, and I allow myself to be held. For once, the heat that courses through me does not destroy; it lights, it warms. Charlie kisses my fingertips, my palms, my wrist. It's a horrible mouth, I know it, full of horrible teeth that've committed atrocities, but it's good on me and good for me. Good when this bloody man is shedding tears and kissing me oh-so-chastely, like I'm a storybook maiden and not a creature as vicious as he.

I make love to him, on purpose and with purpose. I shall not repeat the words that we said, nor the looks that we exchanged, but I will say this: in the dark of night when I am usually crushed by my loneliness, ruined by desire, I am held fast and warm and sweet things are told to me. Charlie rises at midnight and pulls open his curtains, moonlight spilling like silver over us, the moon's gaze as peaceful and mindful as the gaze of God.

"Do you remember the sun, Michelangelo?"

I hold Charlie's head against my belly and say, "I remember going down to my aunt's house in the summer, the sun shining through the little windows. I remember missing it too, afterwards, when it burnt me."

"Fighting in the daytime, the sun beating me red, I thought I'd never want to be so hot again," says Charlie. "Being cold is worse. I miss sweating, almost."

"Almost, Charlie Yewman?"

He lifts his face to me so I can see his smile, his cruel canines, but also his tears. From above, looking down at this dear man, my heart rends itself in two, and I find I do not miss the offending organ.

"Yes, Michelangelo, almost. There *are* things better than sunlight."

QUEEN OF DIRT'S END

OLIVER NASH

EUCHRE STUMBLED THROUGH the sticker-plastered doors of the Dirt's End Pub on some half-friend's slurred recommendation one hot and neoned night in the nausea of August on the South End. The bouncer slid his sticky hand off his crotch, moving to card Euchre, but when he saw their dead-eyed drunken weariness he shook his head and waved them past like a bad smell. Euchre—*they* to friends, *he* or *she* or *it* to the violent and ever confused public—scoffed at the thick crowd of strangers. Here's where I'm supposed to get laid, they thought, yeah fucking right. Last time I take a recommendation from a guy with a name like CoCan't.

Euchre leaned by the entrance. The DJ was dressed in black leather and chains, and there was a cage atop one of the tables. Oh, great. They did not come here to be ogled by old leather gays—no motorcycles outside though, which, well, in the South End you don't get one without the other. Crowd looked normal, though. An old TV was playing a special on that meteorite that hit some poor fucking apartment complex; took off some old lady's leg; put a hole through five floors.

The bartender, a pretty, probably queer girl—so that was a good sign—fixed them up with a double shot of Rumplemintz.

"What's your name?"

She laughed, but then her eyes narrowed, trying to see if they—despite their crop top and other twink accouterments—were hitting on her or not. She decided no, or at least such attention would be no threat.

"Marilyn. Yours?"

He told her.

"Sounds made up."

They'd hoped for some flirtatious edge to that remark, but there was none. On these lonely nights Euchre felt like a cryptid hunter, searching for the perfect beautiful and scary woman who wanted somebody like them. Who would enjoy breaking someone like them. Another day, in another life, Euchre had known and been known by a few of this caliber, North End business-types who thought their use and abuse of Euchre exemplified some werewolfish double existence alongside their corporate careers, but actually, as far as Euchre was concerned, made all too much sense. That was before the undeniable urge towards fem clothes made them too visible in the gastropubs and oyster bars, the liberal hangouts sardined with law schoolers and the tech rich. Mostly they were pursued by men who saw their androgyny as invitation, and were themself a little guilty, felt a little fake-queer for rejecting these men.

"Do I even ask about the cage?" they said, "Is it like, I dunno, a strip club?"

She ran her fingers through her steppe of bleach-yellow hair.

"Nobody's gonna pay you to get in it, I'll tell you now."

The woman dancing in the cage had no tattoos. She was of the new type, Euchre decided, those who had no generational aesthetic, and instead cannibalized fashion's past epochs. Euchre was only twenty-eight, but they felt old. Used up, watching this woman in her frayed white dress and truck stop chest harness, her mall-sourced studded choker with a heart at its apex, her plastic elf ears—elf ears?—and her black pits of eyeshadow, and, the crowning detail, that which turned Euchre's attention into lust: her hair. Great, thick ringlets of rust red-brown, more volume than her upper body, stretching down past her waist, shoved and thrown and whipped to the beat of some DIY ear splitter remix. She was short but had presence, rattling the bars of the cage and screaming, pressing her mouth between steel and scrunching her face into a benevolent snarl. In it, Euchre saw the vivacity they'd lost around age fourteen. She looked toward Euchre and smiled once and maybe they imagined it but it made their heart skip.

Euchre had been told by college students on the internet that, being non-binary, everyone who wasn't straight should have the same potential to be attracted to them. In practice, this was not the case. Most women Euchre approached were lesbians, and most lesbians sought a certain anatomy. This was not to say all. But most. So they didn't hold their breath.

"Her name's Elita. We used to go to high school together, actually," said the man next to them at the bar, taking a drag off a cigarette.

"Uh. What?"

"She changed. Did you, did you know that can happen? Viruses get in your brain and shit? Oh, have you heard of how you can get fat from a fecal transplant—" Euchre tuned the man out until he returned to a comprehensible subject. "But hey, are you—"

"Not gay." Well, maybe a little, Euchre thought, and I mean, look at me, but it's a lot simpler to say no.

His look of exaggerated, drunken surprise made Euchre want to peel either theirs or this idiot's skin off. He coughed, spat, put his cigarette out against the bar. He told them to talk to her. Said she's a slut, now. Used that word: slut. The man laughed and clapped them on the shoulder and it was a strange, pitying kindness, including Euchre in his locker room bullshit, putting a bad taste behind their teeth. Not bad enough not to go, however.

Euchre downed a glass of water and did a line in the bathroom, careful to comb back their dirty black hair into something not too feminine. It was an impossible ghost to have on your shoulder, this self-panopticon of how people perceive your gender, of if stares come from lust or hate or indifference, of if you're presenting the correct cocktail of gender markers to make this person like you, see you as what they want to see you as. They saw, in Elita, a live-live-live! attitude, and so they tried to affect that. They enlarged the holes in their crop top, let their shorts lay half over one hip with the belt spearing outwards, smudging what little makeup they had on, letting themself really feel the blow. It was a mistake they'd made before, trying to seduce somebody by becoming them, but the problem was they really wanted to become them on some level, to be the world's girlfriend, fae and happy, and not just a failure of a man.

Her face lit up when she saw them coming toward her table, as if they knew each other. Her attention was a force majeure. You forget, Euchre considered, that people can actually be magnetic. They wanted her smile and her teeth on their neck.

"Oh my god!" she said, voice raspy, lilting up and down, pulling you in and back out with the changing of tone. "I absolutely love your top. And the eyeliner! Very chic. Very cool."

"Oh, I love your dress," Euchre fumbled.

Elita leaned forward on her elbows. Each finger supported a thick, silver ring. The tips shook, and her eyes moved a little bit side to side.

"I think I might adopt you tonight," she said, and her friends looked horrified. They were much older than her.

"Adopt me?" Euchre tried not to let their excitement show.

"Only if you take your medicine," she said, with a low-register laugh that led you into her good graces and then cut. She pulled Euchre down to sit at the table with a tug of their shirt and a single, infinitely warm brush of her fingernail against ribs. "I'm fucking with you. Ah! But you should. I just, *just* took mine, and Maneki couldn't handle it—"

"Hey!" Maneki said, "It tastes like rat poison."

"Take it with coffee," another said, all black clothes/skewed beanie/bold stares down Elita's dress.

"I have this slip at home," Elita said, ignoring everyone but Euchre, making them queen of the validated: gender, sexual, personal. "I think you'd look so good in it. You need a stylist, I think. You're too cute to—just take it, yeah? I don't want to be out of sync with you."

She looked serious in a cute and intense way, putting her hand on Euchre's arm and tapping out a line of tiny, gray crystals onto her palm.

"Molly?"

She nodded with excitement. "It's my favorite," she said.

They bent down to snort it and Elita said "uh-uh" and made them lick it up, its terrible chemical taste, the attempt to taste her skin through it, the buzzing and waves of warmth and suddenly, a few minutes later, sneaking out the back, the friends abandoned, the amazing feeling of their skin against the hot night air and their skin against skin and them, running, holding hands and guzzling ciggies and singing and kicking over trash cans and yelling at cars and kissing, finally kissing, up against a dumpster in the industrial park. Kissing on ecstasy is, well, *ecstasy*. Within and through their lips it was palpably electric, and each motion was divinely ordained and in the streets and in their mind there was just the word: *yes*.

Yes-yes-yes!

And the two stumbled into her apartment, up five floors of

stairs out of ten. It was nice to run. To throw yourself up steps like a kid again.

Unlike Euchre's, her apartment was a nest of thrifted maximalism: tchotchkes and fake ivy and posters and mirrored tile and color. She skipped across the chipped cherry wood floors and bent over her laptop, swishing her hair back and forth to the music before it started. Euchre usually hated gothy hyperpop shit, but then it was gorgeous, it was just perfect. She turned around, smile fangy and shaking. They danced.

"C'mere," she said, "Ah! Oh my god, Euchre. Oh my fucking god. You're so fun."

Euchre cried but it was normal because they were on ecstasy, so she wouldn't know how much she made them feel like who they were inside. Euchre felt like one of the girls, maybe. Something like that, and Elita crossed the distance with predatory swiftness and grabbed them and shook, digging her fingernails sweetly and painfully into their arms.

One second they were dancing, the next she pushed them back, stripped them, stripped herself, leaving one long wet biting kiss on their sweaty collarbone, them attempting to internalize the sight-sensation of her cool torsioned body, and she brought out her cheap lace and adorned them both. In matching ripped lingerie, Euchre felt beautiful, and they looked into her eyes and knew she wanted them, and if she hadn't it still would've been perfect, and they were dancing again, and then she pushed them down onto the sagging red couch and straddled them and Euchre thought, here, this is it, I should say something, but for a long while she just bounced and pinched and hit and screamed in their ear and sighed with pleasure at the music and the company and god damnit. They were sure as hell rolling.

"What's this?" Euchre asked, yelling above the music.

They held her bony wrist up to the light. Thin strands of undulating black snaked below the skin, disappearing below muscle somewhere up the arm.

"You're silly," she said, "Do you really care right now?"

Euchre found that they did. On a quick inspection, in the light, through the pain-pleasure and the drugs, there were a number of these wormlike strands under her skin: flanking the carotid artery, encircling one breast, sweeping across just below the jaw as if a subcutaneous scar from a slit throat.

In the haze of that moment—the heat making them more delirious, maybe, than the drugs—they laughed because the worms in her skin looked like hair in a drain, all clotted up and randomly stuck.

"What's so funny-funny-funny?" she asked.

She choked them, and Euchre lolled their tongue out and went limp and they both broke into hysterics.

"I was just gonna ask," Euchre said, "If this is all okay. I don't want to presume, but like, I don't want to take advantage of anything or . . . "

"No it's fine! *Don't* worry. I do this literally all the time now. Wait—"

"What?"

"Are you saying you want to fuck me?"

"I mean, yes."

"Ha, I knew it. I figured you out."

And Euchre said "No shit!" and there were hysterics again.

Her voice came from the entire room at once, oscillating back and forth with the music. Everything was sensation. Speaking felt amazing; every word sizzled and buzzed. Syllables, like candy. Like a fizzy sweet drink in hot, hot August.

"Let's take a bath," she said, and led them into her room to grab towels from a nest of fabrics atop her bed, and they were naked again, and the worms weaved close and deep in the skin around her spine and that was certainly not normal. Maybe ringworm? Or, I don't know, Euchre thought, it had to be some kind of parasitic *something*.

"I'm gonna run the bath," she said.

Left alone, Euchre's attention slipped to the patch of wood nailed into the ceiling, and the circle of charred floor below it, hastily and not completely covered with a blanket. When they lifted it up and touched the edge of the black sear, their hand went numb and didn't stop being numb.

"Euchre!" she yelled.

They wiped their hand in frenzied worry against the bed but could not feel it at all. There was nausea, now, below the euphoric. They ached and shivered. Quickly, they entered the bathroom. Once molly started going south, Euchre knew, you only had so long before the weight of serotonin syndrome guillotined down. Euchre still wanted to get fucked. If Elita had some parasite or if there was a hole in her fifth-floor apartment, somehow, that was her business.

Elita's head peeked crocodilian above the bubble bath. They could only see her eyes: bright green in black-eyeshadow lava fields.

"What are you doing?" she asked, her voice muffled. "C'mon in, okay sweetie? Be good for me."

Her tone was sweet but slower now. Euchre supposed she was feeling the come down as well. Her mane of hair lay haphazardly in and out of the water, soaking in bubbles and oil. Her eyes narrowed. Euchre liked feeling like prey.

They stepped forward, stood at the edge of the tub.

"Elita?" Euchre asked.

"Yes?" she replied, elongating the word as a breathy, so-simple-it-doesn't-fail seduction. Her hand rose out of the water and rested with sharp, black acrylics against their leg.

"My hand is numb, I . . . "

"Hmm?" She ran the nails up hard enough that they would leave trailing evidence for tomorrow, ran them up and grasped Euchre's cock, really, finally, Euchre thought, and that was the word, *cock;* Euchre liked it because it made them just a body, animalistic and ownable. Her fingertips were cold, and Euchre was vulnerable. She touched them like she was touching a person, not a man, as her nail traced the paperish skin around the central vein of it. "What's that, honey? Baby? Is your hand numb? I'm *so* sorry."

Euchre grunted. "No. Um. Yes. It is."

"Get in the bath," she commanded.

"One thing—" Euchre swallowed, and she goaded them slowly into the bath, her hands cradling their face above water. She held their face with sharp nails. "What are the burn marks in your room? What's with the hole in the ceiling?"

She cradled them fetalesque in the water which sloshed back and forth, their gangly too-long body on top of her.

"Ask nicely!" she said, "Call me, oh, hmm, let me choose. Mommy. Call me Mommy and I'll tell you."

Euchre wanted to, sure, of course they did, who were they kidding? But they were really concerned about the worms and the burn and the hole in the ceiling. This situation had taken on an absurd quality. They dipped their head lower into the water, tasting soap, feeling the currents against their legs.

"What happened in your room?" And then, ". . . Mommy?"

She raised her head back and up and her sharp teeth grinned behind a beard of foam. The currents were strong. Their mind was hazy, heavy. The heat lulled them. They felt like they might pass out. Visions flashed of dying of heatstroke, drowning. The currents were strong. But, currents, in a bathtub?

"A rock from outer space fell through my ceiling. Isn't that funny?"

Euchre slurred their words. Something dark swam below the water. They could hardly feel it. Sleep approached.

"Wheresh . . . wheres-is . . . "

"Where is it? Oh, silly thing. Silly toy I absolutely just *had to* bring home, I hid it under my pillow."

She tilted their head up and brought them choking upwards for a kiss and bit down on their lip till they tasted blood and her hair was a cowl/a cave/a shroud around them, and something too thin to be a tongue parted their lips and entered and was gone and they felt the water writhe and shift slimy like the bacchanal orgies of mating snakes, and there was the taste of blood and sweet perfume and sweat and spit and as they lost consciousness Elita was saying "good toy, good toy" over and over as she jerked them off and at the moment of climax something swam inside there as well.

Euchre woke gasping in their bug-infested apartment. Out the open door of their trashed room, their other roommates were splayed out in the remains of last night's party: Fluke and Skua and Ceps and three strangers. There was pizza and beer cans and a bong long turned carapace-brown. The only neat thing in the room was the rolling tray and the pocket mirror next to it—both licked clean.

They got up, head aching. Euchre stumbled past the TV playing a nature documentary; nausea overtook them at the sight of millions of bugs, all those skittering legs, the segmented bodies moving like liquid.

They vomited into the dirty dishes and then swallowed six ibuprofen, two glasses of water, a cup of coffee, and, finally, testingly, a single piece of bread which, as they feared, triggered the vomiting again.

QUEEN OF DIRT'S END

They tried to rest up before work, but the headache wouldn't let them, just made them cold, so cold, so they wrapped themself in every blanket they had and did not go to work that day. They had to have blacked out, dreamed some of the previous night—only, their hand was still numb. Jesus, they thought, I gotta get my shit together. One of these days I'm gonna get baited by some mugger's honeypot and come home without teeth. Or with syphilis. Did people still get syphilis? Euchre found themself shivering in the dark heat of their blanket cocoon and mulling this question over in their head, staring at the stitchwork, the perfectly anonymous and fine stitchwork of their comforter, the same one they'd had since they were twelve. People had to get syphilis. It didn't just not exist. Diseases, like, ingrained themself in your DNA. Or RNA? Or, maybe, yeah, that was it, they went dormant. You can't just stop inoculating cause the rates are low. Anti-vaxxers are fucking stupid, Euchre said, tottering back and forth, muttering to themself. They sniffled and listened to the air conditioner.

On the sixth day of not going to work, Euchre could no longer access the digital schedule and they knew, without recovering, it would be maybe a month before they ran out of money. At around five, Fluke opened their door and let in a painful assault of sunlight and Euchre recoiled shivering like a Dollar Store Dracula.

"Are you okay, dude?" Fluke asked.

"Not really."

Euchre wondered what time it was. They'd lost their phone.

"Sick or withdrawals?" He asked. No accusation, no fear. Just a question.

In a house like theirs, in the South End, you stored Narcan in the pantry and did not mince words about things like this. There were plenty of idiots in the scene, but those who did not value their life were always outlasted by those who did, those who had long since become the type of people who'd ask you to pick up clean needles like honey dearest might ask for milk.

"Sick. Really, really sick. I have chills all the time. The only thing I've been able to eat are the instant breakfast mixes from Skua's shelf, the ones you stir into milk, and even that only once a day. The light hurts my eyes. My stomach is always in knots. My muscles ache—"

"And you're pale," Fluke said, mercifully brushing past Euchre's theft of Skua's food.

"I'm always pale."

"No, I mean, you are *pale*. You look like you bled out and by some miracle are still walking around."

"Thanks, Fluke."

"We're just worried."

"I can't go to the doctor. I don't have insurance. So don't suggest it."

"I think Ceps has Medicaid, you could ask her—"

"Don't think they give you a plus one," Euchre rasped.

"Just let me know if you need anything, okay? I've got some leftover antibiotics, and we've got ibuprofen, and some other random pills n' such from that job that Skua—"

"Thanks, Fluke. I will."

"All right, All right."

And Fluke was gone. Why couldn't they just meet a nice girl who would both leave welts on their ass and also stick around longer than a night or two? If that girl could avoid giving them a terrible STD or whatever this was, that would be a bonus. Euchre reflected that all sensation was judged on context. The ache of the welts would be lovely; this ache was agonizing. What is love by night is revealed to be obsession, or lust, or self-destruction by day. Or vice versa. One's first time on cocaine is adventurous; one's thousandth is depressing. They missed Elita, even as they could not deny their failing body.

Euchre draped a blanket over the TV and set it to the lowest brightness, turned their head in the opposite direction and listened at a low, low volume. This amount of light would be safe, they thought. They didn't want to see their own skin. Their arms. The places in them that squirmed with what could be the pains of a bad flu mixed with coke weaning, or could, they could hardly consider, be worms.

The stories about the meteor had ceased airing by this point, and Euchre could not bear to open their phone and feel the sting of it to check old articles. There was no way to track her down. They waited and waited for any inkling of it, anything that might direct them to her again, but by eleven they were too tired. They backed up towards the TV, eyes shut, until they had to open them and turn around or they were going to trip on the swells of trash.

QUEEN OF DIRT'S END

They moved quickly. But not quick enough to miss the strand of black beneath their wrist, the coiled living something there. Frantically, they checked every other part of their body that they could see, angling a dirty mirror to scout all their rail-thin flesh. It was just the one. They hyperventilated. This is going to be okay, they soothed, I caught it early. I can just get rid of it. Euchre, tottering naked in the dark, pressed the tip of a pocketknife against their wrist, and could feel the fragile machinery inside. With one final breath, they cut in a millimeter, just the barest amount, not even enough for blood to seep through—

The worm shot up their arm with a rush of pins and needles. They tried to track its path but lost it once it rounded the armpit and disappeared somewhere within their chest cavity. Where the worm had gone they felt better than better. Like the ecstasy was kicking back in, all the way up that left arm. Something *like* ecstasy. They got horny for the first time since that night. A peculiar thought occurred to them: maybe I can tire out the worm. Maybe if I make it run long enough, my immune system can get it. Behind that, even unthought, was the hope that if the worm was chased, it would keep leaving behind its pleasure trail. They wanted it. They knew that it was maybe poison, maybe terrible for them, that they could be making it worse, but they wanted it very, very badly:

What worked once would work again.

They found it easy to stab holes across their chest. This time, they were not so careful. Euphoria set their eyes shaking, and streaming globules of blood seeped out of the rapidly expanding network of wounds all fine and pretty, like red stars in a gray sky. The worm dashed and dove and tumbled. It was like play. And soon their entire body, toes to temples, was awash with pleasure that deadened thought.

They dressed in their fem clothes, the regalia of the half of their gender long denied to them: ripped stockings and white underwear that was not built for their anatomy, makeup scrawled on like a teenager, and, finally, Elita's white dress. It smelled like her. Euchre inhaled and found that they could smell with a richness they had not ever before been able to. They smelled her sweat, the sweet ichor of it, the pheromonal slurry of it, and knew that nothing would ever smell that good again: layers and layers of want and beckoning musk.

They turned on loud music. They touched themself and then

caught themself in the mirror and stopped suddenly, cock grasped in trembling, veiny hands. Blood shone through the dress. There was this sense that everything was wrong, and this sense squirmed below the knowledge that everything was all right just fine. Hours passed and days passed. More than ever, more than in just a shallow kink way, they desired to be used, to give themself up wholly and completely to anyone who would have them. To Mommy or mistress or God or whatever she wanted to be. They wanted to leave pieces of themself inside others. But the dress. The blood on the pleats. Whose dress was it? Why did they have it? Who had given them this gift? This need?

Three syllables came like benediction: El-i-ta. *Elita.*

They needed to find her, to pay penance for this protracted, full body gift. They brushed their long hair straight. They shaved. They put on deodorant—rose scented—and perfume and moisturizer and shaved their legs, all in service of perfect, plasticine femininity.

Euchre walked slowly and happily down the hot miasma of their street, barefoot and feeling every shard of glass and bottle cap, all the dirt and dog shit and slimy runoff through the grid of the fishnets around their toes. Euchre reflected dimly and distantly on how very silly their roommates were, with all their questions, clustered around that dirty table.

"Are you okay? Where are you going?"

"This reminds me of that thing on the news."

"Your roommate looks like shit. Sorry, man, you look like shit."

"They're non-binary."

'Well, *they* look like shit. You look like you're gonna drop dead, pal."

What were their names? Euchre wondered. They frowned. Everything was so fuzzy. That was okay. That was just fine—just fuzzy. They considered fucking the roommates—since when did they want that?—but one at a time. Somewhere warm. Somewhere wet. Something like a bathtub. A hot tub. A pool. The ocean. El-i-ta's bathtub was so safe and warm and good, they thought. Every shard that pierced their foot was like a finger slipping in some sensitive place, and the runoff was spit from a lover, but there'd be no pleasure like Elita's manic, beatific voice. Rasp and lilt and *love.*

QUEEN OF DIRT'S END

So many sirens out tonight. They rounded the sidewalk and shot through the woods, leaving all those stinging red and blue lights behind. They passed by people that smelled amazing, two girls fucking in a briar patch, and smiled stupid at them and they smiled back and that was good and all right. They felt awake. A man kissed a man against the chain link fence to the playground that penetrated the woods and smiled, both, at Euchre. There were helicopters, somewhere.

At the Dirt's End Pub, there was no bouncer, and the staff wore masks. No band, either, or DJ. Cherilyn the bartender was yelling at a couple making out aggressively on her bar but would not get close enough to physically make them stop.

Cherilyn saw Euchre and frowned. "Oh, Jesus fucking Christ. Another one?" She raised her voice. "Look at the news! You people need to go to a *hospital.*"

Nobody listened, so she took a bottle of vodka and left, exasperated. Euchre laughed and laughed. It was funny-absurd to see somebody walk off their job. Funny-happy, too, because it meant that Euchre could walk behind the bar and mix themself *any-thing* they wanted. Mmm, but the worm smell in the bar alone near sated them. They drank a rich blend of mint and cherries and tequila and eggs, pregnantly craving.

"Yo man, personal space, yeah? I'm trying to enjoy my G&T and you're harshing my private cube," a man at the bar said, shrugging someone off. "Ey, you wanna pour me a drink? Since that—I'll be nice, I'll be progressive—that young lady fucked off to—"

"Sure," Euchre said, grinning.

"Don't I know you?"

"Hmm, maybe."

"Wait, wait, you're Euchre. Yeah man! We played euchre together at my niece's birthday block party, I called bullshit on your name . . . last time I get that fucked up on a Tuesday at 4pm. I mean, not really," CoCan't said.

A voice crackled out from the TV that now had a stiletto buried in it:

An outbreak of parasitic infections has overwhelmed the Christ Kenoma Hospital's . . .

The bar was thronged with slow and slippery people moaning and singing and laughing. What a good crowd, Euchre thought.

"I remember," Euchre lied. It was better, their brain said, to be friendly. To keep *all* your options open.

"Love the get up, man, really. If I liked dick I'd be all over you."

The National Guard has cordoned off 189-E, 189-W, blocking all access to the North End . . .

"You're sweet," Euchre said, "But I'm looking for Elita. Maybe later."

CoCan't picked one probing hand off his cheetah print jacket, dropping it back into the slosh of people like a used napkin. He wiped a trickle of milky residue from his nose.

"Oh, Elita! I know her. Do you need her number?"

"Address, please," Euchre said, handing CoCan't a tall glass of bubbly alcohol they'd poured at random.

"You Casanova. Got a boombox and some roses hidden up that dress? Gonna serenade her through the plague? Say, you look a little sick yourself. Little out of it, buddy boy," CoCan't slurred.

"I'm not sick."

"Oh, okay. Man, I'm drunk."

Cases reported to have flown through Chicago Midway and LAX. No known treatments. CDC advising you to stay at home, close your blinds. If your loved one shows signs of increased libido or sensitivity to light, please lock them in a room without weapons. Unrest is anticipated. Protests are . . .

There were fires in the streets now. Euchre was drawn to the heat, but the light repelled them. This was the case with the others, so that masses of writhing bodies crowded against trashcans and the sides of cars, coming as close to the flames as they could while remaining in the relative dark. Euchre wanted to join them, these people like bugs, these people who are elated roaches hiding behind the fridge, but Elita's apartment was not far. They added writhing in the street to their vague and long list of things to do after.

Police cars shot past them in the industrial park. Thick columns of black smoke spiraled out of the factories, and the police seemed very worried about that. How silly, Euchre thought, smoke is *supposed* to come out of factories. Euchre tried to reconcile the two visions that appeared in their head. In one, they are a child in a cafeteria. They stare at the girl's table and wonder how freeing it must feel to wear a dress. Stare at the way that even through the bog of puberty they maintain a blunt grace that Euchre cannot find in the boys, or in themself. In this vision they tell their parents about this and get their hair ruffled, because they are finally getting interested in girls. In the second vision, they are an elephant-sized hexapod in a field of red grass and fractal trees. The sulfur in the wind means rain is coming, the year's Big Storm, means it is Euchre's time to be endowed. They lie submerged on their chitinous flank as their mother endows them with worm.

Euchre was both child and hexapod, sure, but mostly Euchre was the bloody-footed, beautiful and happy thing that walked the city at night and sang out for Elita. Euchre existed as body and blood in a dress that wimpled over their shoulders and no longer made them feel like an ersatz crossdresser.

The front door to Elita's complex was busted open through a failed barricade. They entered and smiled because they knew this high would never end. This was life without death. This was the panacea: comedownless joy. In the hallway, four naked people were dead with gunshot wounds or blunt caves where their foreheads should be. Three people rolled on top of them, laughing and kissing and fingering each other.

One kept saying: "I love you, I love you, I love you."

Another would reply: "Can you feel it? Can you feel the grass?"

And they ran their fingers through the rancid red carpet turned brown with blood. And they blew kisses to Euchre. And they did not judge them. And that was good. And all right.

Elita's door was closed but not locked. Inside, a powerful smell: sweet, meaty, sulphury, minty, ozone. It was flooded up to their ankles, warm dark water covered in bubbles and saturated with unidentifiable, biotic specks.

"El-i-ta? E-lita? Eli-ta?" they called, and giggled because they sounded like a husband on an old TV show.

Her record collection floated like lily pads, with roaches and mice frantic and trapped upon them. Nature is beautiful, Euchre thought.

"Euchre!" she replied, from the bedroom, her voice watery, and when she spoke she did so with more than one voice. Euchre never wanted anyone else to say their name, for it would be pale imitation.

Two corpses floated face down in the bedroom, partially digested, tendrils of worm wrapped around their torsos.

"Where are you hiding?" they asked.

"I'm under the bed, silly," she replied.

That was silly, Euchre thought, and waded closer, and the tendrils snaked around their legs, probing, and then decided they were family, and let them go. With a heave and a huff, Euchre upended the waterlogged mattress. There was Elita. Green-eyed Elita, Elita that made them feel not so much like a boy, Elita that gave them worm, unjudging Elita, Elita lying on her side, curled up against a black sphere cracked open like an egg, worms emerging from her pores like meat from a grinder, a moving wall of worm surrounding and keeping some of the water out, she attached unbreakably to it. She smiled and her lips were putrescent purple and oh, so pretty.

"I missed you," they said.

"We don't even know each other," she replied, kindly, as if in awe.

"I don't want to know you, I want to love you."

"Do you love me?" she asked.

"Can I kiss you?"

"Only if you take your medicine," she replied, and giggled with all those voices of hers, and behind her dilated eyes was real care. Euchre took the worms into their mouth and settled down with her, into perfection, into happiness, into themself, and tasted the sweetness of her rotting, meat-soft lips.

DAUGHTERS OF EVE

HOLLY LYN WALRATH

IT'S DARK—ALWAYS DARK. We play a game where I tickle the skin of her back, which is so delicate, downy, and expansive. She flickers out of existence for a brief moment—her body blinking into the ether—and my hand pauses in the air. I don't break character, not for a second, even when I realize she has vanished.

This is what they cautioned us against in sex-ed class, where the boys are separated from the girls, why they told us it's safer not to do it at all. But they never explained the details, so I sweat in the dark, my lips dry, convinced she's disappeared completely and will never return. I am so terrified.

When she comes back, her body slowly reforming in the darkness like the dots of jelly we made in science class with a dropper, I unclench my jaw and slip back into my character, whispering in a deep voice. I am a knight, a king, a football player. Sometimes I am Link from Zelda, or Hercules, or Jack from Titanic. I trace the stillness in her spine, the wrinkles on her elbows, the curve before her hips. She wears faded gray underwear. I wear pajama bottoms and a shirt.

Sometimes we do this after swimming, and we are both wearing clammy bikinis that draw goosebumps on our skin, and we have to cuddle under the comforter. On Halloween, we are witches in black rags and black lipstick. She paints a third eye on my forehead and tells me I am evil. We are listening to CDs on repeat, howling black metal. Afterwards, we read a book to each other or tell each other secrets.

I finally break the habit of chewing my nails. I grow them long for her, paint them the soft pink of morning sun.

You can die if you flicker and never come back. This is the unspoken rule. Or maybe you're not dead. Everything they tell us in school is that we are worth nothing but the price of a corpse. We watch documentaries about girls like us on the streets. The documentaries say words like rape, prostitution, beating, abuse, drugs. The point is to scare us straight. We watch the news about the boy left for dead, tied to a fencepost. I wonder if he flickered too.

Kissing feels boring at first. We are real actors who want to be good at their parts and memorize the right lines. Kissing is part of the point; it would be unrealistic not to kiss.

I think of the first girl I kissed in the secret of my parent's closet, the safest place in the house where you might go to hide when a tornado is barreling toward you because there's the bedroom door and the bathroom door and then the glass mirror door of the closet and then utter darkness even in daytime.

But our kisses are not like that first kiss either. They are longer and less furtive. Our kisses are not like the kisses I will receive from boys, and later, men. I chew on her lip like I do on my own when I am nervous, and she flickers again. This time I taste it. There's the salt of her mouth and then a transitory tang of almonds. When she comes back into being, her smile in the dark is upside-down.

We are fifteen. We are supposed to be under the control of our parents. We crawl into the attic and walk along the boards above the fluffy pink insulation and try not to fall, if we did our legs would get stuck in the ceiling of the dining room below. Her brother likes to play with Barbies too, but this is our world. We sink our dolls out in the lake. We cast spells under moonlight in the driveway with chalk but nothing comes of this.

At night, we should be exhausted enough to sleep through the darkness, but we aren't.

At night, I pretend to be someone else so that she will let me touch her.

Over her underwear, my fingers are a shovel. She writhes

suddenly and blinks out so hard that I am shocked for a moment, and yet, I feel extremely powerful, almost superhuman. Would this work on boys? I don't think so, when I really consider it. She comes back slowly, first the impression of her body in the bed, then an outline of herself like a doodle, then skin and bones, and when she opens her eyes she turns on her side with her naked back towards me.

I go downstairs and put my soiled pad in the trash, wrapped tightly in its wrapper so the dog won't get at it. Her house backs up to a lake and outside the back door I can hear her dog pacing, so I open it and he stands, his massive black hulk waiting for me to come outside and pet him, so I do. The night is cool and gleaming. I run my hand over his black fur. He is a big dog with sad eyes who is overbred so he's big enough to lean against me and knock me over. We walk out in the backyard, and he stays beside me, a reassuring manifestation. I look up for my stars—Pleiades. They have been mine since I learned to look for stars. But it's not the right time of the year and the moon is bright so I can't see the edges of the horizon where the lake begins and the trees end.

For a long period of time my hand is all there is. It aches. I grow tired of the endless monotony of my hand. I begin to think my hand will fall off, that it will divorce my arm and go to the other place itself. I am bored. I don't know how to stop wanting her. I try to make my hand work on myself, but it doesn't seem to want to. I don't know what is wrong with me and I'm too young to know there's nothing wrong at all, except that maybe we should talk more.

There are boundaries to this game. Kissing is allowed as well as rubbing of her breasts as long as my hands are over her shirt. Sometimes this is enough to make her flicker and whine, then laugh in a fake girlish laugh because she's always the girl and I'm always the boy even though she's better at the boy voices. It's better to be the boy though, the boy is the one with the power. I kiss my way down her panty line. I pull back the fabric with one finger. She's pretending to be a popular girl who we both know. She's good at mocking them. We've been at this for hours without a single flicker. I'm getting tired, really tired, because it's so late and we spent hours watching movies with her little brother pelting us with popcorn and me coughing from a cold, which annoys her mother, and me not wanting to go home so I called my mom and argued her into letting me stay. I just want to get the game over with. So, I slip my tongue under the elastic of her underwear. She stops talking. I taste almonds. Her skin is surprising to me because it's wet but not as wet as it should be, and her hair is so tender. I think, yes, at last now she will leave and go to the other place. But she doesn't. She stays solid and I can feel every tense line in her body. She is so quiet. So I stop. She doesn't say anything and neither do I. I've taken a misstep, and it feels like being ripped apart—there's my hand over there on the carpet, twitching in impatience—there's my leg on the other side of the room, jittering and restless.

Later, she will tell a boy at our school what I did. She will say it like I did something wrong, like there's something wrong with me.

He will ask me if it's true. I won't know what to say, so I will say nothing. I neither confirm nor deny the high school rumor of our breakup. Except the way people say it is like this: You had a Friend Breakup. I accept this explanation and get a new best friend. This time, a boy. They seem safer. When he has sex with one of the baseball players and the boys follow us home, wanting to beat him up if not for my presence, I will feel a little jealous, but I will be brave enough to tell them to go home. I know how to mess with their control. I will start to tell them the most revolting things I can think of, like how they fantasize about fucking their own mothers, like how I bet their penises are shriveled and tiny. Disgusted by the fact that they suddenly find *me* disgusting, they will leave us alone.

I will think, *I could've told everyone.* I could've gone to school the next day and said how she was one of the invisible girls, how she was disappearing at night and going to somewhere else, somewhere I just wanted to be too and what was so wrong with that?

But I don't, I didn't. I still can't.

I stare at her back. She falls asleep. I roll over and cry in silence, pressing down my own engorged heartbeat until I can't hear it anymore.

DAUGHTERS OF EVE

I can't remember whether I flickered out the first time I made love to a man. Maybe I did. I remember clearly that he thought he was in when he wasn't and that I was giddy afterwards because losing your virginity is a big deal. I didn't tell him at first that I wasn't a virgin, not really, but I was still glad, perhaps because I could be the girl for once. I didn't tell him stop because I thought this was the way to the other side, and I was curious. But I don't remember if I ever went to the other place that first time. I didn't think about it then either because I pushed down the memories of my high school girlfriend so hard that maybe I didn't remember.

Later in life, I finally became aware of my own flickering when my boyfriend gave me head, or when I was alone with the vibrator I asked him to buy for me. When I flickered out, I just went into myself. I couldn't remember much about that place. It was like slipping into a cold pool, one that is past its prime, with algae and little fish at the bottom. I thought of the pools in Narnia that went somewhere else. Another world.

My boyfriend came to like this about me, my occasional lapses in being.

Now that I'm in my thirties, young women discuss flickering online in public spaces. One admits to seeing an impressionist painting when she flickers out, like she's standing in the middle of a lake muted with Monet colors. Another sees ghosts. *They can't pass back into our world*, she says. It's more common for women to be like me, flickering out for just a moment and not remembering the other side. This is supposed to make me feel better, but I just feel numb.

We are learning more about what the other side is and how to get there. There are whole majors and PhDs for this kind of thing now. We go to rallies. We stand in front of murals painted with dark swaths of emptiness that represent the other side and we take selfies. We make cardboard cutouts to represent the women who never came back. Who flickered out and decided to stay on the other side. The cardboard is pasted with photographs. More and more of them line the streets each day. I walk around them to get to the bus stop. I try to memorize their faces in case I ever see them again.

But I am married to a man so it's kind of a moot point. When I go into my daughters' room, I watch them sleep like every mother. One has a shock of red hair, the other curls her toes in her sleep. I tell myself I will teach my daughters about the flickering. I tell them I will teach them consent, given and received. I hope their flickering will take them somewhere more beautiful than this world. At night, my husband brings me to that other place, but I don't remember afterwards where I go, just that I love how it feels. He tells me I smell like almonds.

I go into the bathroom and wash my hands, meet my eyes in the mirror, and wonder if there's another me on the other side who wants to get into this world.

IF DILLON BELIEVED IN ANY KIND OF GHOSTS

PAUL TREMBLAY

DILLON **WAS AN** event coordinator at Northeastern University, and he couldn't miss the Wednesday dinner-hour reception for a visiting Pulitzer Prize winning photojournalist. After work, Dillon drove the two-and-a-half hours to Lake Winnipesaukee by himself. He alternated listening to '80s new wave and no wave music and reviewing the few details he knew about his boyfriend Peter's family in the albeit unlikely case he would be quizzed. Peter and his family had been at the rental since Saturday. Dillon being invited to the lake house was a big deal. He wasn't sure if their relationship was ready for the pressure of meeting and then staying with Peter's daughters and his mother for a day and a half. Dillon thought of their *relationship,* now going on five months old, as an entity wholly separate from himself, so he could be more objective when considering where it was going, where it could go. Peter's and Dillion's fifteen-year difference in ages was another regimented block of time that would at some point become an unscalable wall. Somewhere on the drive, the sun set in the woods surrounding I-93.

The rental property's steeply pitched and rutted driveway was long enough that Dillon questioned if he was at the right place despite Peter's dryly worded text that, "the driveway was challenging." At bottom of the hill, trees parted for the lake house. They'd left the outdoor lights on for him, but he couldn't make out property details beyond there being two other structures huddled near the main house: next to the parked cars was a small bunkhouse he would later learn they did not have access to; on the opposite side of the graveled parking area was a square, squat roofed structure that looked too solidly built to be a simple storage shed.

Dillon parked. His engine ticked as it cooled, an odd-timed drumbeat beneath the swelling laughter coming from inside the lake house. He gathered his bags, swatted mosquitos whining in his ear, walked across the gravel lot, and fought the near undeniable urge to drive back home.

It was a little after 10 PM and Dillon let himself in after a polite knock on the front screen door, which set Peter's small dog Gizmo barking and scurrying to the be the first to greet him. Dillon said, "Hi, Giz," and scratched the brown terrier-mix's backside. The dog pranced, twirled in circles, and led Dillon through a brief, cramped hallway into a rectangular common area.

Peter and the three women were sitting on the same half of a long table and had been in the middle of a boisterous card game. Dillon's nervous instinct was to tell them to keep playing, don't mind him, and he would go to his room, wherever that was. Peter, never Pete, was a fifty-one-year-old white man, tall, lithe, had effortless shaggy salt and pepper hair and worried blue eyes. He wore a red tank top which showed off his sunburnt neck and arms below the bicep. Dillon said, "Wow. Were you going for a farmer's tan?" and everyone laughed.

Peter shrugged affably, said, "Glad you made it, Mr. Fancy," a reference to Dillon's work attire, and greeted Dillon, who was a full head shorter, with a hug and a peck kiss. The women eagerly queued up for introductions and hugs of their own. They were hyper friendly, too happy to see him, and the intensity of expectation heightened by his being the only sober person in the house.

Peter's youngest daughter Abby had recently graduated from college and was, if Dillon remembered correctly, living with her mother for the summer before a planned move to Portland, Maine. She sported nose rings and tattoos on her forearms, and she had straight hair dyed jet black and a lighter-hued, more piercing version of her father's eyes. Abby shouted, "You've missed so much!" and led Dillon to an open seat at the table. The chair was wicker and creaky and felt like it he might fall through it if he wasn't careful.

Peter grabbed Dillon a beer from the kitchen. Above the table a dangling light fixture had a cluster of small moths and flies in its orbit. On the table, a deck of cards had been dealt into four abandoned piles, and in front of Peter was a page of yellow lined paper scored with his rough scribbles. The excitement and nervous introductory chatter quieted until Dillon said, "That driveway is no joke. Especially in the dark. My little car almost didn't make it."

Abby said, "Right? And if you couldn't tell already, the place is totally haunted."

Dillon made a show of looking around the room. A space leaning into its rustic, cabin style, there were zero traces of modern updates, but the interior didn't feel or look neglected. There were wood and clapboard walls, exposed ceiling beams, wooden floors pitched in spots. He couldn't see it fully now, but there was an elevated deck out back with great views of the lake. Adjacent to their table was a sitting area with two small sofas, one tucked under stairs that led to a loft. A fireplace separated a small kitchen from the sitting area.

Dillon said, "Obviously haunted."

"Do you believe in ghosts?" Abby asked.

"Yeah, why not. It'd be cool to see one, right?" Dillon tried to sound playful, but he was aware what he thought of as playful often sounded deadly serious to others.

Abby mangled a joke about Peter glowing ghostly white with his shirt off.

"Your words are hurtful," said Peter.

Brianna was the older sister; Dillon couldn't remember if there was a four- or five-year difference. She said, "Please, no ghosts. It would not be cool to see one. I won't be able to sleep. Again. It's so scary upstairs." Brianna was taller than Abby, her face fuller, rounder. Her long, wavy brown hair tied into a loose ponytail. Brianna lived just outside of Washington D.C., was a senator's aide, and her being able to make Peter's annual daughter's week on the lake, a tradition he'd maintained since his amicable divorce from their mother fifteen years ago, had been in question.

Peter's daughters being closer in age to Dillon than Dillon was to Peter was something he already knew, but to see it sitting at the table was jarring. Dillon wondered if Peter was thinking the same thing. Dillon flashed him a side-smile. Peter returned it, then dropped his head to the scoresheet, flipped it over, and wrote everyone's names at the top.

Abby continued with the haunted house riff. "Me and Bri might crash on the couches down here instead of the loft. But then we'd have that sketchy picture staring at us." She pointed out the painted portrait of a young man in a jacket and tie. The sisters had already built up a story about it being a memorial painting for the teenage boy who had drowned here. Dillon understood the urge to create a mythos for the place. Being surrounded by house full of other people's stuff, their hidden stories, was innately creepy.

Peter normally didn't talk about ghosts, and as far as Dillon knew, didn't believe in them, but he said, "If we see any ghosts, blame Nana." With the one word, Peter's mother Cindy was transformed into his daughters' grandmother. "She rang the forbidden ghost bell as soon as we walked in," Peter continued.

Nana was in her mid-70s, her short, thick hair, entirely gray. She said, "What? I'm the one that has to sleep by myself in the bedroom not connected to the rest of the house." Her defensive indignation was both joking and real, a trait he recognized in Peter.

Abby pointed out ornate brass shelving, made to look like climbing ivy, affixed to the wall behind and above Dillon at a height where one might normally install a light fixture. A silver hand-held bell was on the lower shelf, on the second shelf was a strange wooden sculpture of a head with exaggerated and smoothed out facial features that reminded Dillon of an Easter Island statue.

Dillon said, "Yeah, that's messed up. Don't ring the ghost bell, Nana."

"Hey!"

Brianna, perhaps wanting to change the ghostly subject, said, "Peter saw a bear Sunday morning on his walk with Gizmo."

Dillon said, "I guess I'm not leaving the house then."

Peter said it was no big deal. He and Giz were walking back up the paved road that led to a large community campground and a few minutes before being back on their driveway he heard crashing through the woods and turned to see a large black bear about one hundred feet away, loping in the opposite direction. Peter admitted to half-running, half-walking with Giz to the driveway, but they were never in danger.

Abby read from her phone, "Black bear attacks are rare, but

they almost always involve a dog, the dog owner getting attacked after trying to intervene to save their pet."

Peter said, "Sorry Giz, I would've thrown you at the bear like a hand grenade if I had to."

The women shouted at him. Dillon joined in. Abby left her seat, scooped up the sleeping, confused dog and hugged her tightly.

Peter was in Dad-mode, a mode with which Dillon was unfamiliar but found endearing. Peter gathered the cards and announced they would restart their game of hearts. Dillon asked where the bathroom was. Nana said, "Are you gonna send him to the outside shitter," and broke up laughing, a wheezing and tears-squirting, contagious laughter that infected the rest of the room. Dillon pointed at the oversized wine glasses and said, "Maybe I should have some of that," and finished his beer. Brianna was the first to compose herself and explain that main bathroom was next to the front door, or he could use the outhouse next to the gravel parking area. Dillon said, "Oh, that's what that small building is? No thanks." Peter, somehow personally affronted on behalf of the Airbnb rental, denied it was an outhouse. Abby insisted that if the bathroom was outside then it was an outhouse and that this one was "totally haunted, too." Peter said an outhouse was a shack over a hole in the ground, what they had was an actual half-bathroom, flushing toilet, and it was nicer than their inside bathroom, plus there was also a washer/dryer inside the well-constructed dwelling. The others mocked his use of *dwelling*.

Dillon said he'd explore the *outhouse* during daylight hours and made his way to the bathroom by the front door. While inside he heard the women's excited stage whispers and laughter. He knew they were giving Peter their early verdict on him, which sounded overwhelmingly positive. Peter had told Dillon his daughters hadn't liked his long-time partner Christopher very much by the end of their near ten-year on-and-off-and-on again relationship. Peter always spoke carefully, as if every word would be etched on someone's final record. He'd described Christopher as loving, kind, and patient initially, something for which he'd be forever grateful. However, it was that gratefulness that tied them together longer than was healthy as Christopher had become intense, exacting, and resentful in ways that were difficult to parse and, in the end, impossible to reconcile. Dillon assumed Peter was seeing or reliving the ghosts of his past now that he was here with his family.

Dillon returned to the table. Abby fetched another beer for him, and she asked him if he wanted a weed gummy. Dillon declined. Peter dealt a hand, restarting the hearts game.

Unprompted, Nana leaned on the table and said, "Hey, Dillon. When you were in the bathroom. Did you see any—" she paused and waved a hand, "—spooky light when you walked by the shower?"

Everyone quieted. Dillon looked around to room for a tell that this was the setup for some joke. The others looked as confused as he felt. Dillon said, "No. I didn't notice anything."

Nana's conspiratorial, expectant grin faded. She said, "Inside the shower drain, you didn't see any, like—" she paused, looking for the right words and not being able to find them, "—um, orange balls?" which set off more drunk, red-faced laughter from everyone. Nana said, "Hey?" and "What?" and by the end of the group laughing fit seemed genuinely hurt by the wisecracks about how many gummies she'd eaten and her needing to be put to bed. Nana attempted to defend herself by explaining that when she got up in the middle of the night to pee, she saw orange balls of light in the shower drain.

Dillon asked, "So ghosts, bells, outhouse, orange balls: now am I all caught up on what I missed?"

No one else admitted to seeing orange balls but they did enjoy saying and using the phrase the rest of the evening.

The next morning Peter was up early to take Gizmo for a walk. He tried in his preternaturally noisy way to not wake Dillon. Dillon considered joining him, but instead stayed behind, and sat on the rear deck, soaking in his first views of the lake with the new sun rising behind the house. Their house didn't have a sandy beach. There was a wooden dock with ladders that jutted an L into the lake. Offshore outcroppings of glacial boulders peeked their tips above the still water. Loons called sporadically. Houses dotted the woods across their corner of the lake. Dillon was surprised at how close neighboring cabins and camps were to their property and was oddly disappointed. He also was embarrassed as the whole lake must've heard them laughing, shouting, playing cards well past midnight. Dillon was an only child of parents who were supportive but emotionally reserved, as though they were always being judged. Dillon knew this was true about himself as well, and he didn't like it.

He went back inside and sat at the long table, gathered the cards, and played solitaire. Solitaire was a vacation game, after all. He enjoyed the quiet as he didn't have to be *on* for anyone, and he hoped the time would recharge his social batteries for the hours ahead. As fun as the previous night was, it was also exhausting. He wondered how the day might go without the aid of alcohol and gummies.

The sisters were sleeping upstairs in the loft and Nana in her bedroom off the deck. Nana was the next person to get up. She whispered, "Good morning," to Dillon as she shuffled by on her way the bathroom. Dillon returned her good morning and apologized if he'd woken her. She insisted that only her bladder had woken her up. Dillon was nearing the end of a solitaire game he would lose, and he thought about offering to make coffee when Nana whisper-called, "Dillon? Can you come here for a second?"

Alarmed, Dillon instantly thought the worst, that Nana was confused, that she needed help. He hadn't heard her fall. Was she having chest pains?

She called out his name again and said, "I need to show you something."

Dillon said, "Okay, yeah," He walked slowly and softly to the front of the house, thinking she had found a giant spider or something, and whatever it was, he didn't really want to see it. He turned the corner to the short hallway and Nana had a half smile on her face that eased some of his anxiety. She pointed into the bathroom and said, "I didn't dream it and I wasn't seeing things. They all thought I was losing it."

Confused, Dillon knew that she was referring to something previously discussed but he didn't know what it was. His nerves sputtered with cross-wired instinct telling him he shouldn't go inside the bathroom, shouldn't look. He sidled past her and crept inside a step or two, afraid to go too deeply into the bathroom. A shower stall was on his right, the sink and wall-length counter ahead, the toilet tucked past the shower stall.

Nana said, "Do you see it? In the shower drain?"

Dillon pivoted right, leaned his torso into the shower stall, looked down, following directions as though he was her exploratory drone. Below the metal cover, the white PVC drainpipe below glowed with orange light.

Nana stepped into the bathroom, behind Dillon, peering around him. "You see it, right?"

Dillon laughed. "Yeah, holy shit, I see it."

"I knew I wasn't crazy," she said and wacked him playfully on the shoulder. "They all tried to make me think I was crazy. You're my witness." There was mirth behind her words, but also, a raw relief that was heartbreaking.

Dillon said, "Orange light balls. In the drain." He snapped a picture with his phone.

Nana asked him to send it to Peter and he'd send it to her. Nana added, "You said you wanted to see a ghost, right?"

"I did say that."

There weren't orange balls of light, per se. The PVC pipe itself was glowing orange. They both stared, luxuriating in the unease and wonder of what shouldn't be. They whispered *what* and *why* and *how* questions because whispering was appropriate, until Nana asked, "Should I ring the ghost bell again, send it away?"

Dillon shook his head no, which meant *why would you want to send this away*, yet another part of him meant *don't, because you might call up something worse*. Then Dillon noticed that above the shower stall was a squat rectangular window and sunlight filled it, and puzzle pieces quickly fit together in his brain. He wasn't asked for an explanation, but he said the rising sun at this time of day and probably only this time of day must be hitting exposed pipe near or under the foundation. The explanation, immediately plausible, landed like disappointment. He'd metaphorically rang the ghost bell and sent the wonder away.

Dillon scooted around Nana and went outside to verify his theory. There was about a foot of space between the frame of the house and sloped earth under the bathroom. He imagined at night it was a dark space that a raccoon or another critter might fill. He wondered if the space was purposeful by the owner, perhaps to help with water runoff and snow in the colder months.

Dillon ducked back through the front screen door and said, "Yeah, it's definitely the sunlight hitting the piping."

Nana had already left the bathroom and started making coffee in the kitchen.

IF DILLON BELIEVED IN ANY KIND OF GHOSTS

The weather was perfect. The sisters got up late, ate breakfast and studied and dissected the drain photo as though it was the famously frauded Loch Ness Monster or Bigfoot snapshots, and then they went on a long kayak trip that lasted most of the afternoon. Nana kept to herself mostly, reading a book in varying locations. Dillon explored the property, including the loft, which was indeed creepy. A place in which he would not want to see a ghost, he had to admit, with its four twin-sized beds tucked like hiding children under and below the eaves. Out back, he walked the sloped gravel path, past the parked cars and to the locked bunkhouse, which was painted the same shade of forest green as the main house. He found the disputed outhouse to be to Peter's description. The half-bathroom was narrow, but the white clapboard walls were clean, and the toilet was new. It was too nice to be a part of the haunting, he decided. Dillon and Peter played cribbage on the deck as they ate cold cut sandwiches and salad for lunch. Their conversation was warm but guarded, as though honoring the significance of this briefly shared vacation and what would come next for them. Dillon couldn't help but compute and extrapolate their future ages. When Peter would be Nana's age, Dillon would be in his late fifties, and what would he and they look like then? Dillon won three cribbage games to Peter's two, and he felt guilty and apologetic for a reason he couldn't explain. When the sun moved out over the lake, raising the temperature on the deck and in the house, they floated on plastic rafts in the water. The lake was busy with boats and jet-skis, stirring the water into small waves that nudged their rafts apart. Gizmo, confined to the deck with Nana, whined when a jet ski buzzed by. The daughters returned and eventually joined them in the water. The lake bottom was sandy until Dillon was about waist height in water, then it turned mucky with silt and decaying weeds. Dillon didn't complain, but his careful steps were obvious. When Peter and the daughters commented, Dillon said liked to see where he was stepping and that he was more of an ocean guy. Abby joked that Peter's and Dillion's relationship was doomed. Brianna called her younger sister a brat and splashed her. Later, they drove into the town of Meredith and had an early dinner at a touristy place on the lake harbor. When they returned to the house, they resumed playing cards and drinking. The conversation, as it was all day, was easy, but not as raucous and carless as the previous evening, and everyone turned in for the night much earlier. In bed, Peter told Dillon how happy he was with him there, and Dillon said he was happy to be here too. Peter kissed him, said that Dillon was a big hit with the girls, and rolled onto his other side.

The next morning everyone was up with the sun. After hugs and shared laurels of *it was so good to finally meet you* the daughters and Nana piled into Nana's mini-SUV and left.

Dillon and Peter watched and waved as the car crawled up the wood-lined driveway. They hugged, shared a kiss, and then, standing an arm-length apart from each other, with Gizmo restlessly sniffing and circling around and between their legs, Peter sheepishly stared at Dillon long enough for Dillon to say, "What?"

Peter said, "They're the best, right?"

"Oh, yeah. Your mom is a hoot and Abby and Bri are fun and very sweet," Dillon said, still more in shock than he would care to admit that his boyfriend had adult daughters.

"But they're a lot," Peter added.

"Yes, they kinda are."

Peter smiled and seemed relieved at the honesty. "I'm going to take Giz on her walk before I have to set up for my stupid zoom meeting." Peter was an editor of educational texts for Addison-Wesley and this supply-chain/printer issues meeting was an emergency one. Dillon thought about joking that Peter do the zoom out on the deck while wearing his tank top, but didn't, and he didn't know why he didn't.

Peter produced Gizmo's leash from his back pocket, like a magic trick. "Come with us?"

Dillon said, "No?" and shrank away a step or two. "I'm sorry. Is that okay?"

"It's fine," Peter said in that jokey, put on upon way that meant the opposite.

Dillon said, "I'm a little hungover. I might go back to bed. Or make coffee. Or do both."

"Yeah, okay. But we're kayaking later, right? No getting out of that."

"Only if I can dunk you into a vat of sunscreen before we go."

"Deal."

They kissed again, then walked in opposite directions.

IF DILLON BELIEVED IN ANY KIND OF GHOSTS

Inside the lake house the sudden emptiness and stillness was a thick mist. If there was an undercurrent of happiness or contentment to what he was feeling, and there was, it was overwhelmed by the surety that he would build a life with Peter, one he feared would be too brief because of Peter's age, and an empty, formerly shared space would be Dillon's inescapable destiny.

Dillon meandered to the other side of the living room table and grabbed the ghost bell's handle. He lifted the bell off the shelf and rang it. It was jarringly loud for its size. The ringing clouded out all the space in his head, and he roughly dropped the bell back onto the shelf. He looked around like a caught, guilty child. The wooden statue stared back at him. A dog from a neighboring lake house, a large one by the sound of it, barked twice.

He next inspected the living room shelves and walls, studied pictures of the family who owned the place. Their unfamiliar smiling faces were as inscrutable as the wooden statue above the bell. It occurred to Dillon that if the house were full of photos from Peter's prior fifty years of life, the images would be equally as enigmatic. Dillon tried to find a photo that matched the haunted teen portrait above the fireplace, but he couldn't. He next considered going upstairs to the loft but decided against freaking himself out any further. If Dillon believed in any kind of ghosts, they were like the silent pictures and keepsakes that filled this lake house, their messages and meanings beyond reach or forever lost.

In the end, he chose the kitchen and a coffee pot over returning to bed. With the water near a boil, there was a sudden flurry of sounds coming from the drive, or starting just beyond the drive, but approaching the house. Gizmo barked frantically, high-pitched, and desperate. There was a crash of snapping branches. Peter yelled but was not yelling any words.

Dillon looked out the kitchen window, wooden frame and fogged glass occluded the view, but Peter was between the bunkhouse and outhouse, his back turned to Dillon, his arms held above his head, and in front of him, approaching quickly, the bounding shape of a black bear with Gizmo barking in its orbit.

Dillon dashed to the fireplace and grabbed a cast iron poker, then ran through the living room to the front door, and on the short run he considered grabbing the bell to make noise. He flung open the screen door, rushed past the front stoop and onto the lower edge of the gravel walkway.

A handful of rushed and elevated steps away, on the near edge of the parking area, the bear had Peter on his back and was squatting on his legs and chest. Peter sputtered muted grunts and moans, like he didn't have any air left, and he struck awkwardly at the bear's head and brown snout.

Dillon yelled at the bear in attempt to scare it away and he approached while swinging the poker, which suddenly felt as small as a wooden switch in his hand. Giz was nowhere to be seen.

The bear reared up and brought all its weight down on its front paws, which landed on Peter's chest. There was a terrible crack, a whoosh of released breath, and Peter's arms twitched, then fell. The bear reared up and punched back down again two more times. Peter didn't react. The bear nosed Peter's head once, then stalked over Peter's limp body and toward Dillon, its head swinging low, as though ashamed of the mess it found itself in.

Dillon backed away, swinging and jabbing the poker, thinking he had to get to Peter, to help him, and his instant plan was to get the bear to follow him out back or even onto the deck, then Dillon could double back around the house, or cut through it, then help Peter into one of their cars or into the outhouse and call for help, but the bear blocked his angle to the back yard, was herding him, cornering him, and Dillon had no choice but to retreat inside the house. Dillon fumbled the screen door open, it let fall shut. The clattering sound goosed the bear into a forward charge, and as Dillon swung the wooden front door closed, he saw a flash of Peter stalking down the gravel path almost to the bear. Peter was lopsided, his head and left shoulder hung grotesquely, and the bloodied middle of his chest was all wrong, caved in, cratered, and in his right hand he held a large stone. By the time Dillon processed what he saw the bear crashed into the front doors, juddering the entire house, splintering the door frame at the lock.

No matter if the bear was on the stoop, Dillon reached for the doorknob to open the door to make sure that he had seen Peter upright. He needed to see Peter's face. But then there were two roars, and Dillon froze.

Both roars had not come from the bear. One roar was from further away, but was louder, and its raspy bass jumped octaves without hitting the ones between and was more menacing because of its lack of pattern, reason.

Dillon backed away from the door. He called out Peter's name twice. There was that roar again, the one that sounded like it started from a place deeper than the bottom of the lake. He stumbled into the bathroom and into the shower stall. Because of the window's height and proximity to the front door, Dillon could only see the gravel lot, which was empty of Peter's body, and the woods beyond. He could not see the scuffle happening on or near the front stoop. Claws scrabbled on the cement, the bear knocked and bumped into the door and the frame, low growls, a braying roar, then a repeating thudding sound that turned soft. Dillon imagined the rock in Peter's hand pistoning down onto the bear's head. Was that possible? Was any of this possible? The impact sounds morphed into a wet squashing. The bear stopped growling.

Dillon turned away from the window, so his back was against the shower stall. Down by his feet, the drain glowed orange like it had the prior morning.

There were careful, approaching footsteps on the gravel outside. The footsteps were clearly being made by two feet and not four. The shower drain's orange glow cut out, went dark. A hand scratched at the other side of the bathroom wall, behind Dillon's back. Then that roar, that not-bear roar, and it lowered, settled, an idling engine, a dangerous purr of impossible, ragged breathing. Dillon held his own breath.

The two-legged footsteps restarted, this time walking away from the house. The shower drain glowed orange again. The careful crunching steps stopped with a crash to the gravel. Dillon looked out the window. Peter's motionless body sprawled in the lot where the bear had left him.

Dillon dialed 911, reported a bear attack, and remained in the stall. He watched the glowing drain dim with the rising sun.

DEPARTURES

CARMILLA VOIEZ

NODDED AT the polished woman, whose cravat resembled a noose, and gathered my passport and tickets while a machine spewed out my boarding pass. A stiff wheel screeched, escalating my sense of dread, as I maneuvered my carryon suitcase between meandering travelers. Head bowed, I felt rather than saw the cold eyes and twisted mouths of the horde, appraising me, judging how far from social norms I strayed, and whether violence was needed to correct my course or eradicate me completely. The battered leather of my flight-bag nestling against my leg, I wobbled on the ascending step of the stuttering escalator, gazing at Jun's ageless buttocks. Cold comfort. She was three steps ahead, hovering in my field of vision, but untouchable. When the torment of airport security was behind me, I would grab a glass of warmer comfort while waiting for the Barcelona flight to be called.

I scanned the queue. Bored businessmen and irritated parents mingled with smiling heterosexual couples who linked arms and leaned against each other. Each arduous half-step was an agonizing slog across hot coals. Jun stretched her delicate fingers toward me. I turned away, pretending not to notice, afraid to attract attention.

Nylon strips of fencing herded us toward conveyor belts and the groping hands of airport security, like cattle to an abattoir. I unlaced my boots, tugged rings from my fingers and dropped them into a black tray, wishing I could tear out the pins that would instigate an inevitable body search—a memento mori of the time before I learned how to conform.

Bladder weighing me down, I stepped through the bleeping archway, beckoned by rubber glove and malevolent sneer. The butterfly touch of a thumb grazed the cluster of nerve endings between my thighs. I stifled a gasp and cursed my involuntary dampness. Hands swept down one leg, then the other. Cheeks burning, eyes moist, I collected my belongings. Jun's pale hand covered her cupid's bow lips as she hid her amused giggle. Perhaps she considered it payback.

I hurried toward an image of feminine conformity—the circle of a featureless face above a triangle representing a wide-hemmed knee-length dress few adult women had worn since the 1950s. Two women leaned against a wall of basins. The one facing me arched a thin eyebrow. Painted lips wrapped around the phallic neck of a liter bottle of vodka. Lascivious, pornographic, flouting rules with impunity, daring me to protest with a disdainful stare reminiscent of a young Greta Garbo, the dazzling star who lived authentically, unapologetically. A dangerous role model, I learned two decades ago when a splintering thigh bone dragged screams from my lips. The woman's stare followed me. Her left eye twitched and her hands curled into fists. I locked the stall door the moment Jun slipped in behind me. As I wiped the urine-soaked seat, I imagined kissing the stranger's wide mouth, tasting the seminal liquor on her tongue, knowing she would be more likely to tear my lips to shreds than return my desire.

"She's straighter than a ghost's steps," Jun whispered. "You've never had reliable gaydar."

"You can talk," I said.

She shrugged.

I sank onto the toilet and relaxed my pelvic muscles. Voices floated into the stall, mispronouncing Ibiza as *I-beef-a*. I stifled the laughter bubbling in my chest. Gorgeous or not, that woman's stare was a challenge. Long after my bladder was emptied, I waited, hoping they would leave before my flesh merged with the seat, and I would be forced to peel myself from the gaping wound.

"Afraid of your own shadow," Jun said.

My turn to shrug. At least *I* was alive.

"Get the fuck out of here," a woman growled.

Was she talking to me? Did she think I leered at her through a crack in the door? I imagined her kicking it open and pounding my face into the toilet seat, grey matter spilling like yolk from my cracked skull.

"Show us your passport or what's under that fugly skirt, you pervert. No men allowed."

Not me. I hid my metal-pinned and skin-grafted limbs beneath baggy jeans and a long-sleeved t-shirt. I had packed emergency shorts in case the heat became unbearable, but no skirts. I always felt fraudulent in dresses and skirts. Thankfully, the days of burning women who wore trousers were behind us.

The intruder remained silent.

"The fuck I'm gonna let you hide in one of them stalls and spy on us. This is women only, you hear me?"

The thud of flesh hitting tiles. I shrank against the cistern, pretending I did not know what was happening beyond the inadequate shield of the stall door. It was not my problem. I had fought and lost my own battles, and who had intervened to help me? No one. The crowd laughed as I rolled across the concrete, arms wrapped around my skull, legs curled into my stomach, cheering like they had when Samuel Luiz was kicked to death by thirteen men and women last year. Like they did when . . . no, that memory remained too painful.

Jun hissed and punched my shoulder. She was not the only entity to express annoyance. The stern faces of my heroes condemned my inaction. The muscles in Forster's throat protruded like tentacles. Her pale eyebrows merged with the creases above her nose as the self-proclaimed roaring-dyke ordered me to open the door. Her face melted and became an obscene jellyfish, bulbous translucence threatening an excruciatingly painful sting, but I was more afraid of the flesh and blood women than my conscience. I shook my head to dispel the phantom. My treacherous mind created another.

This time, Taylor-Stone's pout denied me that beautiful gap-toothed smile while her sharp Cockney vowels urged me to keep fighting, but that was not the message I wanted to hear, and the faces of lesbians who preferred safety to heroism were unknown to me, invisible, and unavailable to offer prudent counterarguments. Hating my heroes and their harsh judgment more than I despised my cowardice, I remained out of sight.

"What's going on in here?" A new voice, deep but female. Likely a security guard, taking control of the situation after witnessing the violence and intimidation via one of the ubiquitous closed-circuit cameras. When the attackers had been escorted out, I heard muffled sobbing and opened the stall door.

A yellow ribbon of liquid pointed accusingly as a smudged face peered up from a floral huddle of fabric. I dodged the line of urine and approached the woman, who seemed to merge into the wall and floor, unable to understand why the security guard left her sitting in her own filth.

"I'm sorry," I said, reaching across the chasm. "I wanted to help . . . "

The woman shook her head and tried to slide up the tiles before legs buckled beneath her and she splashed back to the floor. She eyed me cautiously, as if trying to decide whether trust might incite further violence before extending a large hand and allowing me to pull her to her feet.

"What a way to start a holiday?" Her cheeks blazed.

"Where's your suitcase? Do you have any clean clothes?" I asked, unable to inquire about her injuries without accepting some of the blame.

"My boyfriend has it. I waited until I really needed to go."

"I'll find something." I pulled a pair of shorts with an elasticated waist from my case, hoping they would be small enough for her slender hips.

The woman bent over a basin, scrubbing the trails of mascara which ran from her swollen eyes.

I recovered a handbag from the corner of the room. "Is this yours?"

She nodded. The door opened and an older woman glared at us, dragging the wheels of her luggage through the puddle. I looked away to avoid cowering at her discomfiting stare and caught the more nuanced look of the transwoman in the mirror. Words of self-justification rose in my throat before I tamped them down. In reapplying her warpaint, she had removed any trace of fear. How many times had this woman faced bullies who perceived her difference and hated her for it? Her eyes communicated both anger and resignation. She did not want my advice, would hate me for suggesting she hide herself from the world, and I knew I had no right to question her choices. We may have shared the umbrella of an acronym, but we were not the same, and when speaking might have helped her, I had remained silent. I was nothing, not even an ally. A coward, desperate to rid myself of guilt in exchange for a pair of old shorts. I stared at her, wishing I was half as strong.

"Bruises fade. Denying my true self is more painful." Her mascara wand a conductor's baton, emphasizing the point. "An odd choice of battlefield, though."

Not the hill I wanted to die on. The whoosh of a cistern flushing. I had forgotten the older woman who emerged from a stall, washed her hands without catching our eyes, and left. Washing her hands of us and everything we represented, I suspected. Hatred came in many forms and was older than dirt. I wanted to share what had happened to me and Jun, but I felt the unburdening might be misinterpreted as a who-had-it-worse competition, and while it was only bruises this time, who knew what wounds this woman hid beneath her floral patterns. She had not pulled on the shorts I offered. Were there patchworks of old scars on those long legs?

"I should go. Dave will worry," she said.

"Can I buy you a drink?"

"No."

Not *No, thank you*, just no.

I stuffed the shorts into my case and followed her out, blushing, ashamed of my relief that we would not sit together in a public place, forcing me to endure the charnel-house glares of other patrons. Their combined judgment—guilt by association. Was that why no one stood between me and the people punching and kicking me? And why no one saved Samuel Luiz in his final minutes? Or did they believe we both deserved our beatings?

I had been young and naïve when I moved to the city. Eighteen and welcoming the new millennium of enlightenment. Our rights had been won in the twentieth century and were now enshrined in law. We were no longer the pink-triangle wearing outcasts queuing submissively outside deadly showers, but full members of a healthy, diverse society.

At university I heard tales of painful coming-outs, but when I introduced my Chinese girlfriend to my parents that first Christmas, they claimed they had intuited my burgeoning sexuality when I was thirteen. Smiles, congratulations were given, and photographs taken to display their latest liberal fashion accessory to like-minded friends—their fabulous lesbian daughter and her ethnic minority girlfriend—proof of how progressive they were. Their acceptance robbed me of the traumatic rite of passage that bonded my peers, and my relief was tainted with resentment. Clearing that hurdle so easily, I believed everyone would embrace, or at worst tolerate, my sexuality. I was wrong.

The transwoman approached a scrawny young man with a weak chin and prominent nose.

DEPARTURES

"Protect her," I told him as I passed, knowing no one else would.

Jun strode beside me as I followed a tiled pathway between gaudily colored seats and potted trees. The departures board gave ninety-minutes notice for my flight. I headed to the bar and sat on a high stool with a whisky and ginger. I could justify the actions of the bathroom bullies—label them the angry generation that politicians ignored and whose legitimate rage was merely misdirected towards those with even less power. My parents, eyes shadowed by resignation, said similar things as they wheeled my broken body from the hospital, shrouded in black, but I needed my anger, and used my sharpened sense of fear to stay safe. Hidden.

It happened twenty-one years ago. I was out and proud. Jun and I had been exclusive for a year, but we argued that night because I did not understand why I could not join her that summer and meet her parents.

"Not everyone finds life as easy as you," she said. "I haven't told them I'm gay."

"When will you?" I asked.

Instead of replying, she fled toward a beautiful blonde girl gyrating provocatively on the dancefloor. Jealousy burned my chest as the blonde whispered something in my girlfriend's ear.

I was more than half-cut as I staggered from the nightclub in pursuit of Jun and the slim, blonde beauty on her arm. A honey trap who steered them into an alley, eager for a taste of my Asian peach, or so I had believed.

The departures board flickered, and a forty-minute delay suffixed my flight. I bought another over-priced drink. My head was not numb enough yet. Did the barman nod too knowingly? Was my mask slipping? I glanced at the other patrons, shriveling from their accusing eyes. If I made myself small enough, would they tolerate me?

The shadows in the alley coalesced into five men. My fear spiked, and I stepped in front of Jun, shielding her tiny body with my alcohol-fueled frame; a hero in a white vest top and blue jeans— very James Dean.

The blonde shoved my shoulders, laughing. I landed on all fours. Adrenaline shook my arms, preparing me for fight or flight. I chose the latter, grabbing Jun's wrist and knocking the blonde on that pert little arse.

They caught up with us near the taxi rank.

I paid for my drink and skulked back to the elevated seat and matching table. Floundering on the edge of my pedestal, I resisted the urge to swallow the liquor in one gulp and buy another. The familiarity I had sensed in the barman's acknowledgement unnerved me, and I knew intimately that crowded did not mean safe, not for people like me.

Back then, before I knew better, I expected someone to intervene on our behalf. I recalled how the mob's laughter reminded me of hyenas as they gathered around weak and isolated prey, preparing to feast.

I tipped my glass, but only a single drop of amber slid onto my tongue. I wanted more. When I glanced up, four faces were angled toward my table. On a nearby couch, a man and woman had their tongues down each other's throats, but no one paid them any attention. What gave them the right to examine me like a specimen in a lab? A blackened tongue flicked across dry lips, suggesting ghoulish hunger, while hollow eyes feasted on my discomfort. I heard or imagined growls of dyke and pervert. I lurched to the bar and ordered a double, promising myself I would stop after this one.

A fist connected with my jaw and left cheekbone. I hit the ground and curled into a protective comma. My fingers tentatively explored the right side of my chin, but searing pain prevented me from pushing it back into its rightful place. Boots and trainers rocked my body, stamping, kicking, shattering bones. I could not escape the flurry of vicious blows, shielding my head with my arms and my stomach with my knees, rolling across the concrete but not rising from it. Even if I had wanted to fight back, the feet were too swift to grab, their targets too random to predict. When it stopped, I rolled onto my hands and knees. Blood filled my mouth. My hip shook, the intense pain in my thigh numbing the rest of my broken body. Jun's face peered at me through a forest of legs. She stretched out a pale arm, mottled with blossoming bruises.

"Help me," she mouthed.

Fear and pain anchored me to the spot. It would have been less terrifying to jump into a live volcano than crawl the three meters that divided us. I watched as the light in her eyes was extinguished.

Was this a memory, or was it happening again? It had happened a thousand times since that dreadful night. Each time I was lifted from the carpet, my fingers would check my jaw, expecting the same looseness, the same blinding agony. Even after the doctor told me they were flashbacks, they felt too real to disbelieve.

The barman's hand cupped my shoulder. My spine vibrated against the cushioned back of the same couch the heterosexual couple had occupied. How long ago? Had I missed my flight?

"How long was I . . . "

"A few minutes. Paramedics are on their way."

I tasted blood. "Did someone hit me?"

He pursed his lips. "No, you collapsed and bit your tongue."

I struggled to sit up, but his hand weighed me down. In my periphery vision, I glimpsed the bathroom bullies sniggering, planning their attack, drawn to the stench of my fear. I imagined the Garbo-lookalike pulling a half-empty vodka bottle from her handbag, felt the impact and heard my skull crack as she smashed it against my temple. I loathed the brain that created technicolor horror movies from every anxiety that flickered through my mind. Two decades of palpitations and panic attacks had stolen my will to live, yet I became jelly each time it portrayed a new way I might die. Exhausting.

I shrugged the barman off and pushed myself to a seated position, spitting out blood and saliva. "I'm fine. This isn't the first time."

"Epilepsy?" he asked.

"PTSD."

His eyes promised understanding. Whether empathy or personal experience, I welcomed the solidarity he offered. Those dark, slightly hooded eyes, arched brows, and the whisper of shadow on his chin—did they still call it designer stubble—seemed familiar. A sad smile emphasized his sculpted cheeks. I had seen him before, somewhere. Running, crawling, drenched in sweat and tears and blood. Or did he simply resemble that twenty-four-year-old, whose beautiful, kind face had adorned *Justicia Para Samuel* posters? His image was ubiquitous for months before people packed away his memory, knowing that it would not be long before another victim was thrown on the pyre of heterosexual rage, forcing them to unpack their still raw pain and convince an ambivalent world of their humanity. The Pride marches I was too afraid to attend. The petitions I refused to sign unless I could do so anonymously. Hiding terrified while a woman was humiliated, slapped, shoved, and intimidated by two others, knowing that the ounce of courage I needed to stop the attack had drained out of me with my screams twenty-one years ago. Only when invisible did I feel safe. Strangers' stares gouged holes in my flesh. Crimson poured from my wounds, but the hue of my blood did not convince them we belonged to the same species. Instead, they saw only my muted rainbow and kept stabbing, determined to destroy the non-conformity I represented.

He did not tell me his name, but Samuel, or whoever he was, sat beside me until the medics arrived, to the chagrin of other patrons. After whispering my explanation and getting a clean bill of health, I shuffled out of the bar, dragging my baggage behind me.

Eyes focused on the floor, I returned to the tiled pathway. Jun lay before me, staining the tiles with her blood. I yearned to curl up by her side, hold her frozen hand, shed hot tears. With Herculean effort, she twisted her throat to face me. I saw her broken face again, her desperate confusion, her fear, and the knowledge of imminent death dulling her jet eyes. I could have saved her. I should have, even if it meant sacrificing my life. The pain would have ended, and maybe she would not have suffered the same survivor's guilt. My beautiful Jun. My truth. Her lips trembled with shallow breaths too weak to carry the words she tried to form. I put my ear against her mouth. "Don't try to save her. You're weak, useless. I pity you."

Save who?

Jun vanished.

I scanned the room, eyes grazing over the bent heads of readers and the angry faces of those whose path we blocked, whose eyes expressed a visceral hatred out of all proportion to the momentary delay. Me and my bloody truth. My overwhelming shame. I stepped aside, apologizing. Heads turning to keep me in their cross hairs, they shuffled away, discomfort written large on each scowl. Eyes devoid of understanding. Canines bared in hateful snarls. They wanted to obliterate me and my toxic presence; a disease they were terrified of catching. Blood roared through my eardrums, pumped by my sprinting heart. My torso swayed as cruel laughter flooded my mind. Memories threatened to fell me. If I let them in, they would swallow me whole. I flailed on the edge of madness, searching impotently for something, anything, to ground me. Jun's arm reached through a primeval forest of legs. The only light in my darkness. Bitter and accusing. Face as cold as the moon, reflecting my agony.

'Not now,' I thought. 'Please.'

Then I saw her. The transwoman had been cornered again. The bathroom bullies and two men surrounded her as she held paper coffee cups: one in each hand. She did not see me, but her terror pinned me in place. Where was airport security? They had a duty of care, not me. Mine died with Jun. Where was her boyfriend? I warned him he must protect her. How dare he foist that responsibility on me? Why was no one helping her? Why did no one protect Jun . . . or me?

My flight was called. I was tempted to run toward the gate—I wanted to help, but . . .

Jun's face filled my vision. A scarlet orb pulsed within the cracked cavern of her eye socket. "There's nothing you can do," she said.

Samuel shoved her aside. "It only takes one person to stand up. That person should be you. You know what will happen if no one stops it."

Icy lips sealed my mouth, filling my nostrils with the stench of death and decay, coating my tongue, choking me. Jun's beautiful face ballooned into a giant purple bruise. "Don't be a hero. You're too weak. Too broken."

I gazed at her, wishing she were with me, wanting things to be different. If I had not pressured her that night; if I had been patient, understood and respected her decision, she would never have left with that girl. If I was stronger than my pain, I could have crawled to her, shielded her body with mine, until the police arrived.

Impotence and grief wove the dark shroud I wore. I deserved no better. Rather than fight back, I had perfected the illusion of normality, stamped out my queerness. Invisibility and metal pins held me straight. My ephemeral privilege depended on both. Maintaining it meant denying parts of myself, but it kept me alive. Shame and fear held me prisoner. I knew there was nothing wrong with loving other women; no religion could convince me otherwise. I was ashamed because I did not save her. Afraid that any public display of affection or solidarity would summon those laughing, biting, kicking hyenas, and next time they might finish the job.

Legislation was powerless in the face of such deep-seated hatred, especially when those paid to protect us turned a blind eye. Whenever my fearless peers raised their rainbow flags, a darker rainbow hovered above our heads like the sword of Damocles.

"It only takes one person to stand up."

I wanted to, but I was afraid.

Something moved beneath Jun's eschar skin. A distended lump burrowed up her cheek. Pale skin rippled and swelled, pulsing with life that was not hers. Gelatinous darkness pushed between her bleached eye and socket. She prodded the protrusion before capturing it between her thumb and forefinger. Her lower lid gaped as she dragged a wriggling maggot from her eye and tossed it to the floor. My stomach somersaulted. I diverted my gaze. Her fingers wrapped around my forearm, grip unnaturally tight, distended fingernails piercing my skin. Something alien moved within my flesh. I felt its interminable progress through tendons and muscles, consuming me. Bile burned my throat. If I pushed her away, I would be left with nothing, so I yielded, knowing I owed what remained of my miserable life to her sacrifice.

"You'll miss your flight. Someone else will step up, someone braver. It's crowded. Security everywhere. Don't take a beating for a stranger."

I grabbed my case and ran, not towards the gate and its promise of safety, but at the group of bullies and their victim, bulldozing through clusters of people too oblivious or uncaring to intervene. Curses and complaints of bruised ankles followed in my wake, but they did not know real pain, and I hated them all. Nihilistic anger replaced my fear as I crashed through the crowd. The internal pressure of my rage built until I imagined exploding, tearing the terminal apart with shards of bone and clumps of flesh, destroying the false sense of safety that suffocated the air, piercing throats, eyes, and hearts. I imagined a Jian sword in my fist, visualized slicing my way to the bullies and showering under arcs of their blood. Why stop with the bullies? The uncaring onlookers deserved my wrath. In the darkness of my despair, I slaughtered them all before falling on my blade and gaining peace.

But there was no sword. Only me. My voice. My fists.

Jun's hands were a steel vice clamping my cheeks, forcing me to stare into the abyss in her eyes. I drowned, unable to rise from her pain, her death. I belonged there. We should have died together that night. Juliet and her Romeo.

I tried to prise her away, but ribbons of her putrescent flesh clung to my fingertips, and I was afraid those delicate, desiccated bones would snap. Jun begged me not to leave her again, told me she needed my eternal suffering. It infused her, tethered her to my side.

"I'm sorry," I said, pulling away.

The predators were hypnotized by their power. Shark-eyes glared at the frightened woman. Fingers twitched, threatening violence. Clenched jaws sharpened the men's chins, which bristled with barbed cacti needles, promising pain. They were barely human. Caricatures of rage.

"Run," Jun said.

Not this time.

I pushed between the bathroom bullies, entering the circle, taking up space. It felt amazing, empowering, that shedding of decades old terror. I stared at people, barely past their teens, not demons created by a treacherous mind. Adrenaline coursed through my body, making me feel invincible, immortal. I was no coward; I was a god. The fear that created the scaffolding for their hatred, the threat of their violence, seemed obvious now I did not share it. Their anger was primitive, mine divine—righteous.

"Get the fuck out of my face!" I jutted my chin towards the largest man. "And you two, attacking women in bathrooms. Where do you get off? Safe spaces for women! She's got a bloody boyfriend. I'm a lesbian, but I wouldn't touch either of you stupid, hateful twats with a bargepole. You don't even know how to pronounce the name of the island you're flying to."

I was rambling. Their gaping mouths assured me that none of them had a clue what I was saying. They considered me mad. Wondered what I was capable of, calculating how significant a threat I posed. I did not care. As the man's fist hurtled towards my face, others stepped forward, pulling the bullies away. I did not know whether my words had emboldened the crowd, challenged their ambivalence, or just drawn their attention, and I did not care. I missed Jun so much, even now, but I let her go. My hand was empty, and my love was free. I had clung to her for too long.

My name crackled over the tannoy. A final warning. If I did not reach the gate soon, my luggage would be removed from the plane.

"I have to go," I told the woman, whose damp eyes sparkled with gratitude. "My flight's about to leave."

I darted past the reluctant security guards who finally appeared, pulling my bag behind me—featherlight now—and ran towards gate nine.

BORDER TOWNS

JAMES CATO

TODAY, **LIKE ON** most weekdays, a man named Gael stalks me home on the train. I switch cars at the second stop to avoid him, but minutes later he's behind me again. If I turn to stare, he's facing his feet, short black hair kicked up in tufts like crabgrass.

I'm not afraid of him. But his persistence makes me uncomfortable. When the rail doors rumble wide at my stop, he gets off and tails me to my car. His shoes scrape behind mine, their rubber scuffles deafening, until I reach my Corolla in the shady corner of the lot.

"Hi, Tyler," he whines at last.

I meet his shiny eyes and plain face. His expression is slack; the way someone looks when nobody is looking back. I respond hello. He shifts his weight, picking the seam on his pocket, tongue moving in his mouth. The silence becomes unbearable but I don't encourage him. Early on, I made that mistake—small talk, pleasantries. We don't have anything in common and I have no idea why or when he began stalking me.

"Did you have a good day?" he asks. Pained, wistful.

"Yes," I say. Truthfully it chugged along like a protracted breath, a slow wound, leaving me thin and deflated by afternoon. The coffee shop isn't nearly so pleasant a workplace as it seemed when I moved here. Plus, my housemates got me drunk last night, leaving me with a hangover today. I open my car door and stick a leg inside, making a polite but firm statement.

He doesn't budge. "Did you sell lots of drinks? Did you figure out something to write in your stories?"

"No."

"Inspiration will come soon. You told me you like to watch people unlike yourself to get ideas. And places. Things out of the ordinary. Did you notice anything like that today?"

"No. Not today."

"We both have that problem. We watch what we can't have. You told me you live in a border town, right?"

"Gael, I have to go," I say. I have a hard time confronting people. There's something childlike about him. Or doglike. It's sad. He watches me in the silence born between us, planted in front of my car. He taps the hood with one finger, a hunter checking his traps. When I finally drive away he wanders in my dust, tongue punching the insides of his cheeks like insults are fighting to break free.

My house has been gutted by the time I arrive home. I live in a house of artists. Fry, a dioramist, has hollowed the walls and laid strips of insulation in a swirling pink fiberglass ocean through the entire living room. He's pooled the stuff in ripples and in the middle sits a frog propped in a tiny model boat.

I hang up my coat and pick up a box with my name on it. Under the packing tape it reads, *Love, Mom*. My package is full of books. A post-it atop the stack labels it *Inspiration* with a smiley face. Even my mother knows I'm dogged for ideas. Sometimes gifts hurt.

"Fry, you've ruined the house," I say. A hole where the ceiling fan should be. Rectangular pits where there should be light switches. The entire house hollowed of its thermal lining. Fry squats by his installation, photographing it by light of sunset. The frog smells.

"Inspiration struck," Fry says, squinting through the lens. "The whimsy of a pink ocean. The frog Cecily's cat dragged in. The water like clouds, like fairy dust, but there is danger. Asbestos, lost in a turbulent sea. I'll put it all back, don't worry."

I stick my hand in a hole. There's two feet of empty space between the wafer-thin drywall and the siding. "Be quick, please. Something nasty could move in. We live behind a swamp for god's sakes."

"That's what *I* said!" calls Heather, the sculptor, from the kitchen. "God knows what'll creep through our house! I keep picturing a muskrat forcing its head through the vent. How was barista duty, Ty?"

I set down my novels and follow the voice. The women of the house, Heather and Cecily, sit around the kitchen table. Heather is working clay with her hands into a faceless figurine, which she'll place in the swamp to join her small army. Cecily, who we are all in love with, snips letters and images from magazines into a pile—a collagist. I tell them about my day of steaming silver machines and warm ground beans.

"Want to move out to the patio?" Fry interrupts. He stretches, brown ponytail like a whip. "My knees hurt. We can cook hot dogs over the fire pit for dinner."

We migrate outdoors, Fry and I balancing the cooking materials, Heather with her clay man, Cecily carrying nothing with perfect posture like the letter *L*. She has these disarming amber eyes against her dark hair and looks so good in anything that she can truly experiment with fashion. Today it's a quilted jacket she made from baby bibs. The only thing she wears consistently are her rainbow crocs. I wonder, if I described her in a story, if she would notice. Sharp chin, high-breasted, glabrous legs.

"You didn't get to finish telling us about your day," Heather says, patting my arm. "We like hearing about the real world. Something inspiring about it. The schedule, maybe."

"Funny how I'm the one barren of inspiration," I say, watching Fry with interest as he fearlessly eats an uncooked hotdog. "Gael followed me to my car again. I tried being short with him but he did not get the message."

"That poor thing," says Cecily. She parts her shirt collar to flick at a hanging button.

"There must be something wrong with him," Heather sighs.

Fry blows life into the kindling so flames nuzzle the logs. "Dude deserves to get popped. Hit him once in the jaw and he'll back off."

"Fry!" Heather scolds. "The man is fricken' mentally ill!"

"Love a girl who isn't afraid to say *fricken*," he says. "For all we know he wants Ty chopped up in his fridge. Do you think he's into you or something, Ty?"

I shrug. Gael has never said anything implying romantic interest. "I'm not afraid of him. But he does make me uncomfortable. I'd get a restraining order if I could."

"Getting one of those, as a man? Harder than drowning a snake."

"If he makes you uncomfortable you should tell him to leave

you alone," Heather says. Her palms crush the clay face to make a nose. "Even if he only wants a friend. Your own comfort comes first."

Cecily agrees. Fry hands everyone wieners and we squeeze buns tight to their skins. I bite down and lukewarm juice shoots into my cheeks. We watch the swamp from the safety of our patio, the greased ground glinting, cattails nodding with the movements of animals, Heather's clay people rising from the muck. Our fire whirls, looking for a way out of its pit.

"If he doesn't back off after you talk, hit him," mumbles Fry through two hotdogs.

"Chubby bunny," says Heather.

Cecily brings out beers and we sit till the sun becomes a pink hint. Cecily's cat, named Cheshire for now, ambles out of the kitchen with her. None of us think the cat should be allowed outside, but it makes Cecily happy to let it wander and we all want to make her happy. She changes Cheshire's name every few weeks. When she asks if we like the new name, we say yes and mean it. But a few weeks later, the name changes again.

We laugh louder with more alcohol, flirt shamelessly. Fry and I pee together off the deck as the girls cry about the nastiness. I hear his stream patter the ground, then hear mine join. He slides a hand over to spank me. Heather squelches into the yard to place her new figure by the reeds and scoops a fresh wad of red clay from the water line to dry for tomorrow. She pauses for a moment and pulls something heavy from the earth. It's a boot full of mud.

"Someone's been in our yard," Cecily hums in a spooky voice. We laugh, but it's true.

Later that night, someone crawls into bed with me. I don't stir, in a fog of drunkenness, but register their hips digging against my ass. I hope it's Cecily. The thought rouses me, if only slightly, until a firm hand pulls me gently against a hard penis. It's Fry. I don't mind. Heather slept with Fry once or twice, maybe more; Cecily hasn't hooked up with anyone, and neither have I—though not for lack of trying. I wiggle against the organ and the floating hand crawls to my chest, where it cups the swell of muscle there. It remains until I fade again into sleep.

Sometime later, I wake. My eyes snap open and I'm up,

thudding through the gutted house to drink water. Fry's body remains curled beneath the duvet. Nothing more involved than touching took place before he, too, fell asleep. I frown at the insulation in the living room as I pass. The frog's stretchy skin has ballooned, filling with gas.

I jump. A ridged body presses against the sliding door in the kitchen, startling me with its panting grin—a coyote. Its snout grinds against the glass. Cheshire hisses from the table. Coyotes often visit the patio at night. They stare at Cecily's cat from outside the way Cecily's cat stares at the frogs from inside. Lingering on something they want but can't have, unable to abandon their fixation.

In that way, they're like me.

I rush to the door, waving my arms. The mongrel trots away as if less scared than sympathetic. I return to the table, inspecting Cecily's work-in-progress left there. Cheshire whisks his tail. A stack of chopped magazines sits beside the collage. One has been forgotten spread-eagle to the side. I pick it up to stack it with the rest and find photos of myself hidden beneath. Dozens of them. Old photos from albums in my room. Childhood vacations, graduations, old relationships. My face has been cut out of each one.

Cecily invaded my privacy and destroyed my property. I should be annoyed. But really I'm excited. I smile to myself. We drink tea, play games, and wear nothing but underwear. We lose our wallets and find them; we kiss each other on the lips and talk about the books we're reading. We bring home donuts and forget stale bread in the cabinet and let dishes become Mount Everest in the sink. We share clothes and mugs and bodies.

I pause, alarmed, at a sound upstairs like a giant bird shuddering in a box. I hope Fry hasn't weakened the foundation somehow. He took insulation from every room in the house for his project, including my own—there's a section of floor trim removed, a slot above the hardwood. He also messed up the wiring because my lights and outlets no longer work. The rubber boot sits on the porch. The clay men shift in the fog. When I return to my bed, Fry's gone, perhaps to banish this affection to a dreamy space left unsaid.

"You make me uncomfortable," is the phrase I repeat. "You need to leave me alone. Stop following me." My tone, I hope, is fair and measured. Maybe even sympathetic.

"Why?" asks Gael, again. He hovers on the sidewalk near the train station where I've chosen to confront him. I didn't want to wait until we were alone in the parking lot. "What did I do wrong?"

"You make me uncomfortable. You follow me to my car, and you pepper me with questions about my writing, my job, my friends. I'm asking you to stop." My leg shakes a little.

Gael gazes, first at my eyes, then at my jittering leg. His cheeks pucker. It strikes me how relaxed his body is. Knees slightly bent, one hand in his pocket. The other holding a to-go coffee. Like this conversation resembles any other he's had today. After a long time, he settles on something to say. "What is it about me you don't like? Tell me, and I'll change."

"You make me uncomfortable. We don't have anything in common."

"Tyler. You don't ask me about myself! If you did, you would grow to like me. This is the trouble. You collect matters from the fringe. But you could touch if you like."

I hesitate, weakening. I need this to end. "No, Gael. I'm sorry. Your stalking of me . . . it's wrong. Please. Why can't you just stop?"

"I don't know why I'm following you," he whines, face contorting. "I can't help it. I see you on the train. I want to be close with you. I thought I could become your friend, help you with your writing. You need inspiration."

I shake my head. He couldn't have known anything about my writing when he started trailing me. I hold strong. I tell him no when he asks me for another chance. I tell him he needs to leave. When he says we'll still take the same train from the city, I acquiesce. "You can say hello," I say. "But nothing else. No more conversations. No more following."

He shrugs, says goodbye. He forgets his coffee on the railing when he wanders off to wherever he goes. He pressed a smiley face into the Styrofoam with his fingernails. I shake the jitters from my leg.

Afterwards, I don't drive home; I drive to the abandoned town of Woodcliff. It was once a border town to Columbus not unlike my own. We selected our neighborhood for its seat on the lip of rural swamp and urban bustle. Muse for the artist. A lookout. Woodcliff is all that returned to the earth. I nose my car through a tunnel of leaves on a sinuous street, seeking something to spark my creativity. I'm getting desperate.

Though the neighborhood is fenced with a slinky of razor wire up top, I know a spot behind a grain silo where the chain links have been cut and peeled out. I park and duck through the opening. I pass rows and rows of condemned homes, wandering toward the gymnasium, the largest structure yet unexplored. All my published stories were born in places like this. Romance in a flooded basement. Hide-and-seek in Uncle Hoarder's house. Saber-tooth skull fossil breaking through a kitchen window during a mud slide.

I'm not ready to face my roommates yet. If I went home, the day would be a complete wash capped by drinking. I've failed to write a meaningful word for six months. My housemates all have booming socials. Fry gets commissions for taxidermies; Heather sells vases; Cecily has patrons that fund her enough to live on her collages. I pray Woodcliff will stick to me, collect, form into shapes for stories. In a new place, words become moons circling my body. So I'm trespassing on an abandoned Planet Fitness.

It's easy enough. I walk straight through the front entrance. Someone has already done the work of breaking a boarded window and unlocking the glass doors from inside. I try slamming it, just to hear the sound, but the soft-close hinge slows it with a hiss. Ferns thin as feathers nod in the corners and a skylight lets plaque-colored beams into the room. Otherwise, it's barren as a cave. No equipment, no graffiti, no furniture. The shattered window gapes across the room. Trees and bushes loom uncomfortably close outside, too close, as if peering in.

A book sails through the hole.

It lands with a booming echo, slides along the porcelain like a hockey puck.

I run. Adrenaline springs my legs back through the front door. It's been years, since such fear has coursed through my muscles, like a pheasant flushed from its bush. I flash through streets plowed by tree roots. When I make the edge of the town I scurry along the fence until I find my hole. Police check Woodcliff for intruders. Highschoolers ransack the homes and light fires. There are fresh treads behind my car. Six books make a smiley face on my windshield.

Inspiration reads the post-it note on my wiper. *From Mom.*

This time, I can't shake the trembles in my leg.

Cecily speaks in a husky voice to her relatives on Zoom in the kitchen. She speaks two languages in two different voices, the Arabic lower and more serious-sounding than her English. I check the package from "mother" to confirm it's still on the table. It is. The books placed on my car, and the one thrown through the gymnasium window, did not come from inside this house. This was no practical joke of Fry's.

Gael knows where I live.

It's not surprising, really. He knows my car. I've never seen his. He could have tracked me from the train station weeks ago.

Fry whistles down the stairs, carrying his newest diorama. He nods at me, setting the piece on the coffee table above yesterday's project. He's placed a live leech on a miniature figurine outside of a tiny clapboard house. To scale, the leech is dog-sized. He mixes green and grey dye into resin to pour into a mold for water in the fake swamp.

"Fry, he knows our address." While I retell the events of the afternoon, Fry begins shooting uneasy glances at the package of books.

"Dude, you should take that box outside," he warns. "What if he dusted them with fentanyl or something?"

"I don't think so. He's done nothing aggressive until today. Until I confronted him."

"What's going on?" Heather's scrawny profile slides through a crack in the door. "Fry, I thought you were going to clean up that insulation and that poor dead frog. Remember? It's gross. I thought for sure it'd be gone by the time I came back inside. I've been working on my figures for literally six hours."

"No way! He's blowing up like a basketball! The photos get cooler and cooler!"

Cecily sticks her head in the room and makes a shushing motion. We shush.

I fill Heather in, whispering. "Tyler, you need a restraining order," she hisses.

"I don't even know his last name," I sigh. "Couldn't tell you his ethnicity either. He's vague-looking. Tan with black hair. Italian, maybe? Persian, Greek, Hispanic?"

"Take a photo next time you see him. Turn that in. Also, there are those old sisters who sit on the porch all day across the street—Mary and Gillian. Let them know to keep an eye out for people dropping off packages."

I promise to do so.

"Maybe this is it," Fry posits. "I mean, you told him to fuck off this afternoon. It pissed him off. He'll cool down."

Fry's hypothesis brings me some relief. We eat dinner on the patio but leave Cheshire inside—dinner is later today, and the stalks hammered into the bog rattle with activity. I consider Heather's idea to use the old ladies across the street as watchdogs. The swamp peopled by clay men looks deeper than the slate sky right now.

"Maybe you should read that book he threw at you," Cecily murmurs. Her outfit today is a plastic rain poncho cut in half to expose midriff. She sits sideways in her Adirondack chair so her long legs extend off the armrest like a diving board, rainbow crocs dangling from her toes.

I'd left the book where it had fallen. It was a self-help book.

I don't see Gael at all the next day. But when I return home from the coffee shop, a small package is soaking up rain on the front stoop. I take it inside, gather my friends.

Inside are seven tarantulas wrapped in tissue paper.

"Did you see a man place a box on our porch today?" I ask Mary and Gillian.

They look at each other, pass the glowing dot generously called a roach back and forth, trading puff for puff. They shake their heads.

"Please try to remember. There was hate-mail in that box. I think it's from a man of slight build, tan skin, mild features. Short spiky hair."

"Another hippy?" Mary snorts. "We remember everything. No skinny man stuck that box on your porch."

"You the working man?" Gillian asks. "You're the only one who ever leaves. You pay their bills? Or do mommy and daddy fund their special art projects?"

"Look, please. They make fine money. Fry sells taxidermies of animals dressed in human clothes he wires together from roadkill. Heather sells—anyway. I'm begging. Can you keep an eye out for someone like I described?"

Mary and Gillian throw back their baggy heads and cackle. They kick off from the porch railing to rock violently in their wicker chairs. "We don't like to stir the pot, but," Mary says.

"But that housemate of yours set that box there," Gillian nods.

"The pretty one, wears weird clothes."

"She always manages to show off her handsome little body, though!"

The next day FedEx delivers 64 ounces of wolf urine with my name on it. After that, twenty extra-absorbent vomit bags. Six slabs of pig skin for practice by tattoo artists. I start leaving the boxes on the porch. 1,000 live crickets chew holes through their cardboard prison and escape into the swamp. Though many of the gifts arrive by USPS, FedEx, and Amazon, Mary and Gillian swear they catch Cecily setting new terrors onto the stoop. They seem to relish their new nosy mission.

"Saw Ms. Hot Stuff again," they whisper, beckoning me from across the street. "She put a plastic bag behind the screen door. That fashion of hers. Today she had on a mini-skirt covered in yellow buttons and a sweatshirt with a spike on the hood."

Would Cecily torment me like this? She cut my face out of my pictures, hid them for her own use. Creepy and invasive, yes, but of a different magnitude. I attempt to write a story about our household but falter, unsure how to characterize her. Fry slips into bed with me again, then once more, always after I'm asleep, never for sex. When I wake, he's gone.

Except for one Wednesday night. Wednesday night, he's shaking me awake, looming by the foot of the bed. The bedside clock reads 03:43 in polygon red. His cheekbones press against his tightened face, eyes white as a spooked horse. His claws dig into my arms, pulling me downstairs, his forearms coated in foul-smelling fluid. His mouth hangs open, whickering.

There's so much blood on the kitchen floor. I see the smear where Fry slipped, red handprints on the counter where he climbed to his feet. The glass sliding door is wide open. Cheshire's tail lays severed in the mess. Coyote prints make scarlet stamps on our patio. They devoured Cheshire right in the kitchen. Dozens of figures stand just outside the door, one even hunched in the viscera with orange clay-pile legs. There are craters in the swamp where someone undid Heather's hard work. Each figure wears a paper mask stuck to its soft clay head. My own likeness, sliced from photos by the expert hand of a collagist.

My housemates hold off on calling the police by my request. We're in no immediate danger, I tell them. All Gael did was open a sliding door and move some statues. The coyotes did the rest. As for the faces—he might have scoured the web and printed pictures from the Facebook accounts of my aunts and uncles. We peel my photos from Heather's sculptures. Cecily doesn't cry about the cat, reacts mutedly. Cheshire is the last name it will ever have.

"Do you think . . . no," Fry after Cecily retreats upstairs.

I regard him with apprehension.

"Do you think she'd mind if I used the tail in a diorama?"

Heather blinks. We send Fry upstairs to sleep it off.

"Sorry about him," she says.

I shake my head, smiling despite myself.

"Fry and I are dating now, official. So I'll probably be saying sorry for him a lot more."

My jaw hits the floor. "Since when?"

Heather smacks my cheek lightly. "Don't look so appalled. We've been sleeping together every night. You foggy writer-types never notice anything. You just live in your mind, don't you. Funny, because Cecily says writers are creepy. Watching and waiting for your own work-overs like starving scavengers. She's wrong about that."

I congratulate Heather, thinking a delicate conversation might be in our future. Fry can only snuggle me for so long before she finds out. I'm not the only inattentive artist in the house. For now, I usher her upstairs with Fry to sleep, offering to place her art back in the dug-out swamp for her. She doesn't protest.

Secretly, I want time to probe. Footprints in the peat near the holes dug under the clay statuettes take the profile of crocs.

Over the next few days, Cecily begins to frighten me. Weekend meals together feel menacing, like cult death rituals, rather than opportunities to woo her. First Feeding, Second Feeding, Third Feeding. I fell for her, *hard*, obsession at first sight. Now I expect something loathsome.

Until she comes downstairs one evening wearing jeans and a t-shirt. A neon polka-dot hairband is all that distinguishes her from a random sample of young professionals. Heather adjusts her glasses. Fry pauses his preoccupation—prodding the frog with a hammer to see if it will pop—to admire the outfit a bit oafishly.

"I know," Cecily sighs, collapsing into a seat. "I'm bland. All of my favorite personality-outfits are missing. Even the crocs. I suspect I've left them around the house buried under blankets or something. Maybe Fry got drunk and stuffed them into his laundry sack. No accusations, obviously. Only hypotheses."

"You look great!" Heather says. I stand up as if wire-shocked. I stride into the kitchen, dig around in a drawer, find a penlight. A muffled *What's going on, Ty?* reaches me from the living room but I ignore it. I pass by and Fry gets up too, hammer swinging by his side, keen as a dog to follow. *What is it?* I lunge up the stairs, two at a time, and shoulder-ram my bedroom door. There, in the unplumbed gap between my floor and the wall, a human leg attached to a multicolored croc slithers back into the hole.

It can't escape before Fry and I dive on it. I feel Gael's leg hairs screaming through my fingers, foot throbbing to kick us away, not strong enough for our combined weight. Gael's moans echo down the shafts in our house and I hear scrambling below—I pray Heather and Cecily have cops on the phone. When we fish him out of the wall, he's wearing Cecily's clothes. I aim the penlight at his face and his pupils dilate, collecting the light.

"Hey, Tyler," he whimpers.

"Hey?" Fry roars.

"Are you angry, Tyler? I know you're angry. I was just trying to help. With your writing. You know? Like, you watch everything. You think about things. The girl you like. But you needed to experience something. Something personal. Now you can write. I know you better than them, I've been so close to you—"

Gael steps forward and Fry's hammer slams into his jaw. It doesn't knock Gael out, but it does knock him down. Fry is terrified, riled up. Dangerous. Mouth on the floorboards, Gael keeps talking, cheek sunken. "Closer than anyone. If you saw how close I could get, you might try to get closer to me too. We're so similar. We're watchers. We watch and we reshape ourselves. We're not doers. I wanted to change that for me. For *you*. Beside you in bed, I knew we'd done something tremendous."

His lips wipe drool back and forth as they move. I see him for what he is, finally, and I scream. Fry's hammer jumps at the sound, again, a rabbit, defensive. Self-defense. The police agree when they come. When Gael is gone, I cannot again trust the swamp bounding this house as mine. Not the city, not the neighborhood. Fry uses the boot on the porch as a pencil cup. We tell him he shouldn't wear a dead man's shoes. A small creature dislodges itself from the clay and walks into the reeds. Soon I am gone too, recalled to a solid place, one of comfort, my mother's house, so familiar all of it touches me without my noticing. I am completely enveloped in it.

WHITE MEAT

LUCY A. SNYDER

SPARROW AND I had just started making out on the sofa when my iPhone buzzed and played "9 to 5." Mom's ringtone.

I gently pushed her back. "I should get this . . . gotta finalize Thanksgiving stuff."

She gave an exaggerated sigh and shook her head. "I *swear* that woman has nookie radar."

I winked at her. "Nah. Just epic bad timing. She used to call right when I was taking a shit."

"Ew." She snort-laughed. "TMI!"

I picked up my cell. "Hey, Mom. What's up?"

"Oh, Julie, I'm so glad I caught you!"

I winced when she said my deadname. I'd come out to everyone but my family as nonbinary, so it wasn't her fault. But I hadn't told her yet because I dreaded the long, frustrating conversation that was sure to ensue . . . and then she'd turn around and deadname me anyhow. Ignorance was an easier pill than casual disrespect. I knew I'd have to tell her soon, but it seemed like trying to rip off a particularly large, sticky Band-Aid.

"So . . . " The single word was infused with unspoken anxiety. "There's been . . . a change of plans. For tomorrow."

"Oh? You need us to bring extra mashed potatoes, or chairs, or . . . ?"

"Well, no. You . . . you won't need to bring anything except yourself." Mom took a deep breath before she continued. "We'll be going to Grandmother Claudia's estate instead. It's . . . best if Sparrow doesn't come with us."

"*What?*" I looked over at Sparrow, whose puzzled frown told me she'd overheard just enough to be confused. "Yeah, no, that's not happening. If she can't go, then I won't go."

"Honey, I know this is a big, big thing to ask—"

"It's a *ridiculous* thing to ask. I'm not about to leave my own fiancée alone on Thanksgiving."

"Oh. I didn't realize you two were . . . ."

I tried to swallow down my growing anger. "I told you I got her a ring."

"I . . . I thought you meant, like, a friendship ring. Not an *engagement* ring." Her tone was half-helpless, half-accusatory. As if I'd somehow lied to her, when the reality was she refused to listen.

Apparently my face had turned red, because Sparrow sat cross-legged on the couch like a yoga teacher, pantomiming breathing in and out slowly.

So I inhaled, exhaled, and tried to get the conversation back on track: "Why on Earth do you want to go to Claudia's, anyhow? Was Mephistopheles all booked up, or what?"

My mom choked back a startled laugh. "Julia! Be nice."

"Seriously, why?" Great-grandmother Claudia was 85. Old age had not softened her in the slightest. Her mind was as sharp as a shark's tooth and her heart just as warm.

"She's threatening to suspend my share of the trust. Normally I could make do, but Chuck left me with his medical debts and—"

"Wait, she's *what*? Why?"

"She's angry about Quinton's arrest."

My heart jumped at the mention of his name. For a second, I felt him grab my shoulders, his fingers slithering across my ribs, his breath hot in my ear as he giggled nasty things about my breasts and whispered the violent things he planned to do. *I'm gonna tie you up and cut holes in these great big meatbags of yours and fuck all your holes.* I thought for a bad second I was going to throw up, but the feeling passed.

"She's mad that he's finally facing some consequences? Seriously? And how is that your fault?"

"She thinks I was wrong to try to put him in therapy, then kick him out when he refused." Mom's voice carried tremendous strain but was barely above a whisper. "She thinks your 'early development' was the problem and that I should have sent you to boarding school instead of sending him to 'some female head-shrinker'."

"Are . . . are you joking?" My fury rose into the stratosphere, and my vision started to tunnel, going dark at the edges. Sparrow leaned over to put a comforting hand on my knee, but I barely felt it.

"I'm not, honey," my mom said. "I wish I was."

"What am I to her?" My voice shook. "Just a pair of boobs making her poor angelic Quinton do the devil's work?"

"No, honey, of course not—"

"Then why the *fuck* is she mad he got arrested for serial rape when she didn't say a goddamned word after he harassed me for months in my own home and then tried to assault me? Why wasn't that the last straw for her, too?"

"She's just old fashioned, honey. You know that."

"And how were you supposed to do anything but get him away from us? He was sixteen when Claudia guilted you into taking him after his parents died. The damage was done. You were in no way qualified to undo it. He'd already raped at least one girl before he came to live with us."

Mom inhaled sharply. "He what?"

"He bragged about sodomizing a girl in the recreation center. *Graphically.* He laughed when he talked about how much she cried and bled."

"Why didn't you tell me?" Her voice had that helpless, accusatory tone again, and I had to muster all my reserves to keep from screaming at her.

"I *tried.* You didn't want to hear it. I told you he was harassing me, but you blew it off as him being 'rambunctious' and grieving his folks. You didn't listen until you found him on top of me."

Mom didn't say anything for so long that I thought the call had dropped.

"I'm so sorry, honey," she finally said.

"Well, apparently Claudia isn't, so I'm not really feeling Thanksgiving at her house."

"I know, and I'm sorry about that, too . . . but she *demanded* that both of us be there, or else. I'm really over a barrel here. I know this is a huge, huge ask, but if I have a chip to call in . . . well, I'm calling it."

Sparrow flashed me a football timeout signal, so I told my mom to hang on for a minute and muted the call.

"I didn't hear everything," she said, "and don't think it's the healthiest thing to do . . . but if you feel like you really, really, *really* need to go eat dry turkey and endure terrible religious lectures at your grandmother's, I can go hang out at the Orphan Thanksgiving my thesis advisor is hosting at her house. It's no big deal, honest."

"Are you *sure*?" I asked.

"Absolutely." She leaned in and kissed the tip of my nose. "After all, there's Christmas, and I fully intend to spend the next fifty Thanksgivings with you."

Later that night, as we were going through the walk-in closet helping each other pick out Thanksgiving outfits, Sparrow said, "Your grandmother's place is kind of out in the boonies, isn't it?"

"Waaay out in the boonies, two hours north of my mom's house," I said. "The nearest towns mostly dried up when the big sawmill shut down in the 70s. Her nurse has to drive Claudia a hundred miles just to get her to her doctors, but she won't move. Heaven forbid she abandon the ancestral family estate."

"Are you and your mom taking one car?"

"Yeah. She'll drive us up after I get to her place."

"Hmm . . . " She paged through my shirts, looking thoughtful and uncertain.

"Whatcha thinking?"

"OK, so . . . please don't take this as criticism, but I couldn't help but notice that you got pretty worked up when you were talking to your mom."

"Yeah, that's true." I shrugged. "It dredged up awful memories."

"So, what happens if actually being there is super-triggering and you really need to get out of there . . . but you can't?"

"Well, if things get really bad, I can fake a migraine and hide in a bedroom until Mom's ready to go home. Or I can walk down the road to the old gas station and drown my feelings in a cup of the world's worst coffee until she's done."

"What if her car won't start?"

"She has AAA."

"Okay, but what if nobody's available because of the holiday? We should have a Plan B for me to come get you in an emergency. And we should have some kind of code in case you can't talk or text freely."

I paused. "Have you been binging true crime documentaries again?"

"Yes . . . but that's not the point."

"So the point is . . . ?"

She gave me sad puppy dog eyes. "A code would make me feel better?"

"OK, sure. I can . . . rave about the food, I guess. Like if I texted, 'Wow, this cranberry sauce is off the hook!' you'll know I need you. But I won't, because I'm not making my bestest girlfriend drive three hours to the middle of nowhere just because I'm having a shitty holiday."

She smiled at me. "Well, as your bestest girlfriend, it's my job to worry about you, and having a plan helps me worry a little less."

When I got to Mom's house in my tiny hometown the next morning, I discovered she'd eaten half a THC gummy on top of her anti-anxiety medication and was wobbly, distractible, and chatty. In other words: an obvious road hazard. I talked her into the passenger seat of her aging blue Honda Accord and took her keys, then the wheel.

Mom's stoned, I texted Sparrow. *So I'm driving.*

LOL oh no, she replied. *Drive safe.* ♡ *U.*

We weren't on the road very long before my mom started fussing over my appearance. I knew it was bound to happen sooner or later, but I'd been hoping for later.

"Why didn't you wear your nice green sweater dress? You look so pretty in that. Grandmother likes it when you wear dresses."

I adjusted the collar of my charcoal blazer under my seatbelt. "I haven't owned that outfit in years. And Sparrow thinks I look nice in this."

Mom continued as if I hadn't said anything: "And your hair is so *short*. It makes you look like a boy. If it weren't for your bosom, nobody on the street would have a clue you're a girl."

"Well, sometimes I wear a binder to fix that." The words were out of my mouth before I could think better of them. A half-second later, I figured it didn't matter because she wasn't listening anyhow.

But my response actually seemed to register this time, and she blinked in confusion. "A binder?"

Might as well dive in. "It's like a tight tank top, or sports bra.

It squishes your boobs down so they're less noticeable under clothes. It doesn't hurt, at least not for me."

My breasts were fun for Sparrow—she could fit her entire head in my cleavage—but disappointing for me. Practically every woman I knew could orgasm from breast stimulation, but mine weren't wired for that. Sparrow was convinced that my tits were a locked vault of pleasure, and she could figure out the combination if she kept trying. I didn't have the heart to ask her to give up. And maybe time would prove her right.

"Why on Earth would you want to wear something like that?" Mom looked aghast.

"Because I don't actually want to look like a woman. It doesn't fit me. It feels like we all got lined up, and the boys got cool sneakers, and the girls got cute Mary Janes, but they gave me a pair of clown shoes that trip me and keep falling off my feet. Everyone keeps telling me these clown shoes would be nice if I just tried hard enough. I'm sick of it. I'd rather go barefoot."

"Well, *nobody* really likes being a woman," she replied dismissively. "But it's like taking out the trash: you have to do it anyhow. Not liking a thing doesn't get you out of your obligations."

Wow, but there was a lot to unpack there. I wanted to say, *Actually, the trans women I know are pretty thrilled* but I knew that was certain to start a tedious argument with her.

So I focused on her second comment: "Why does being born with girl bits have to be an obligation? Why can't I just be a human being and live my life in a way that makes me happy?"

"Well, I just worry about how people will see you. Employers —"

"My boss is fine with who I am," I retorted, then tried to take a calmer, gentler tone. "I have a stable job. I'm about to get married in a few months. My future looks as bright as anyone's my age."

"Well, it's not like it will be a *real* marriage."

I gripped the steering wheel and stared out at the flat gray expanse of wintry highway, giving myself a moment to keep from yelling at her.

"What do you mean by that?" I asked as evenly as I could manage.

"Our church would never —"

"*Your* church. Not mine. Your pastor's prehistoric opinions haven't concerned me for close to a decade. Sparrow's church is 100% onboard with our marriage."

"But it won't be legal in a lot of places."

"Mom, I love you, but you have *not* been paying attention. Last week the Senate advanced the Respect For Marriage Act. It protects same-sex marriages, and both parties voted in support of it. They hardly ever agree on anything, and they agreed on this! Biden's certainly going to sign it into law. Most people are totally fine with it."

"But not everyone."

"And *those* people are small-minded, hateful bullies! They don't need you doing their dirty work for them. *Honestly.*"

At least I'd managed to not swear at her. My therapist was gonna give me a high-five for that at my next session. Nonetheless, my mother fell silent, and when I chanced a glance over at her, she was staring down at her purse, her mouth a thin clamped line of dismay.

The car didn't have working Bluetooth, so I turned on the radio to fill the empty space between us. Some station was playing Christmas music, so I left it there.

Mom was silent just long enough for me to get lost in thoughts about a recurring database problem at work.

"I couldn't stand it if you mutilated yourself!" she blurted out.

I jumped in my seat and nearly swerved us off the road.

"What?"

Mom started crying. "You . . . you have such a lovely figure. I would just *die* if you destroyed the gifts God gave you."

The gears of my brain shifted out of SQL to work on the puzzle of her statement. The gifts God gave me? Oh. Boobs. She meant boobs.

For fuck's sake, I thought.

Aloud, I replied: "I don't want top surgery. I'm not even gonna take testosterone. I don't identify with being a woman . . . but I don't identify with being a man, either. I'm nonbinary."

My words seemed to sink in. She stopped weeping, rummaged through her purse for a Kleenex, and blew her nose.

"So it's just your clothes, then?" she asked hopefully.

I nodded. "Basically, yes. Just my clothes. And my name. I'd prefer that people call me J. instead of Julia."

"Oh. Well, that's not so bad, then. Clothes aren't permanent."

I relaxed in my seat. The conversation had gone a lot better than I was afraid it would. Perhaps this Thanksgiving wasn't going to be complete torture after all.

WHITE MEAT

Mom got increasingly anxious in the last half hour of the drive, when the land turned from barren cornfields to hills and sparse forest to signal our drawing closer to Claudia. Her knee was bouncing, and she kept fiddling with her phone.

When we turned onto the private blacktop road that led up the hill to Claudia's estate, she said, "You didn't tell her about Sparrow, did you?"

"No. I can't actually remember the last time I talked to her." Anytime I called, her dour fiftysomething German assistant Mr. Eisenstreng answered, and he seldom put her on. He was the third Eisenstreng who'd worked for Claudia; the first was his grandfather, who her industrialist father recruited after WWII. Apparently the Eisenstrengs were once nobles in Bavaria, but their land and wealth burned in the first war. They'd vainly hoped to make their family great again in the second. Claudia never addressed whether the grandfather was a Nazi, but it seemed likely. His grandson was absolutely the kind of man I could imagine wearing a fascist uniform.

"I do send cards for holidays and her birthday," I said.

"Good," Mom replied. "I haven't told her, either. I don't think it's a good idea for her to know. She's not broad-minded like I am."

I bit back an unhelpful remark. "Does she think Sparrow's my roommate, or what?"

"She doesn't know about her at all. Claudia assumed you live alone, and I didn't correct her." Mom paused. "It's best that she not know about the nonbinary thing, either."

If it were anyone else, I'd have figured Mom was projecting her own discomfort. But in this case, I agreed with her instincts 100%. "Gotcha."

Mom and I were sitting in awkward silence with Mr. Eisenstreng in the dark, wood-paneled parlor, waiting for Claudia's personal nurse to bring her down, when the heavy front doors opened.

"That will be your cousin," Mr. Eisenstreng said. Like his father, he'd spent his youth in German boarding schools, so while his English was perfect he still had an accent.

There was such a strange, dark inflection in the way he said *cousin* that made me look toward the door—

—And I froze when I saw my nightmare stroll in, flanked by two burly blond teenagers who had to be his twin younger brothers, all grown up in the seven years since I'd laid eyes on any of them.

This isn't real this isn't real this isn't real, I prayed.

"*Quinton*. It's *you*." My mother's voice and her smile were tight as the springs in my vintage wristwatch. "How . . . how can you be here?"

"He's here at my request," Claudia announced regally as her nurse helped her down the broad foyer staircase. "The judge is a friend, and he granted Quinton a furlough."

Mr. Eisenstreng stood up as the nurse escorted Claudia past the brothers, who were still shucking off their coats. All three were wearing suits as if they were going to church.

This was too much. No. I was *not* eating dinner with Quinton. My hands shaking, I pulled out my phone, unlocked it, realized I was too rattled to form a complete sentence, so I just started typing out "sauce" in a text to Sparrow.

Mr. Eisenstreng swooped over and plucked the phone out of my hand.

"Hey!" I jabbed at the green "send" arrow as it slipped from my fingers, but I didn't know if I got it or not.

"Madame Claudia requires all guests relinquish their phones for the festivities." Eisenstreng turned to my mother and held out his hand. "I shall need yours as well."

"I can't abide people fiddling with those tiny idiot boxes," Claudia said as my mother reluctantly handed over her cell. "Staring at nonsense instead of paying attention to the people around them."

And that's when I dissociated for a little bit, quietly leaving my body while Claudia made more pronouncements and the cousins exchanged strained small talk with my mother. My memories of the following hour are pretty fuzzy. The next thing I remember clearly was sitting at the dinner table, staring across the silver platters of food at the interlocking bronze triangles of the valknut ring one of Quinton's brothers wore on the index finger of his right hand.

Was he just into Viking stuff, or was this worse? I glanced at the other twin, who sat beside him . . . and saw a black paracord bracelet emblazoned with an enamel Confederate flag peeking from under the cuff of his white dress shirt. Shit. Both brothers sported nearly identical fashy high-and-tight haircuts that had gone out of style for practically everyone but alt-right jerkoffs.

"Can I help you, ma'am?" The brother in front of me had noticed me staring. I couldn't quite read his expression.

Heat rose in my face. I didn't think of myself as nearly old enough to be a 'ma'am' yet. "Um . . . do you see a plate with thighs or wings?"

"Dark meat?" Claudia exclaimed. "Heavens, no! I will *not* have an inferior cut of fowl served at my table."

I love my mom, I reminded myself. *I'm doing this for her.*

The one saving grace in all this was that I wasn't sitting where I had much chance of making eye contact with Quinton. We were one the same side of the table, but my mom (who kept whispering apologies and entreaties to stay calm) was between us. Claudia sat at the head of the table with Quinton to her left, and Eisenstreng at her right. The brothers sat by the German.

An empty plate and wine glass sat at the end of the table to my left: Claudia kept that seat reserved in honor of her father, who died in 1955 when she was just 18. A lifelike oil portrait of him in a gray suit hung on the wall behind the chair, glowering sternly for eternity. Anyone in Claudia's chair had the illusion that he was sitting at the table. In years past, I'd never been able to decide whether it was touching or creepy, but now I was definitely leaning toward creepy.

As dinner was winding down and her house staff were clearing the table, Eisenstreng helped Claudia up out of her chair, then went to the bar table in the corner to gather glasses and a bottle of brandy.

"I'd like to propose a toast," she announced after Eisenstreng had poured everyone two fingers of liquor. "First and foremost, to honor the settlers who rescued this beautiful land from the savages."

"Jesus Christ," I muttered under my breath.

My mom gripped my leg as if to steady me. "Be pleasant." Her voice was barely audible.

So I forced myself to smile as Claudia extolled male ancestors who'd taken their plantation money and run north after the Civil War to re-invent themselves as industrialists. When she finished her tribute to her father, Eisenstreng said "Hear, hear" and we all drank.

I'd only had brandy once or twice before, but it seemed to me that this was unusually bitter. My head started to spin as I reached for my water glass to rinse the taste out of my mouth. I realized I'd been drugged or poisoned right before I lost consciousness.

I woke tied to a wooden chair down in the brick-walled wine cellar. My vision was fuzzy, and I had to blink several times before I could make out my mother in the chair to my left and Quinton past her. Claudia stood beneath the yellowish light, leaning heavily on her cane. The twins stood beside her; they'd taken off their jackets, ties, and shirts and stood there in white tee shirts. One of them held an Aquafina bottle. Their shoulder muscles and biceps looked like halved bowling balls. Eisenstreng was off to the side, examining a rack of dusty wine bottles, fiddling with a loop of the rope he and the brothers must have used to tie us up.

"Are you back with us, Julia?" Claudia asked.

"Whatdafaaa . . . " I groaned. My tongue felt thick and sticky.

"Well. Now that she's awake, I expect we can get started. I do apologize for this inhospitality." Claudia didn't seem very sorry. "However, you have left me no choice. Our country is at a critical moment in history. The descendants of the pioneers who founded our great nation are being pushed from their rightful positions by the spawn of immigrants. This must not stand. All white families of good blood must stand strong against this dark tide."

Christ, she's gone full Nazi, I thought, still trying to work up enough spit to loosen my tongue. I twisted my wrists against the nylon ropes binding me to the hard armrests. The knots didn't budge. Had Eisenstreng poisoned her mind, or had she always believed in this toxic white supremacy bullshit?

"Healthy families are like trees," Claudia continued. "Good roots build a strong trunk that grows mighty branches. But if a twig becomes diseased, the rot can spread. Threaten the whole tree. They must be treated or pruned."

She paused to stare down her nose at us. "The three of you are infected twigs, and I cannot allow you to ruin our family."

Claudia cleared her throat. Eisenstreng silently moved from the wine rack to stand behind Quinton's chair.

"Grandson, I had high hopes for you when you were born," Claudia said to Quinton, who gazed up at her blearily. "And I share some of the blame in how you turned out. I should've removed your parents the moment I found out about your father's perversions, but I didn't. At least I did so in time to put your brothers on the straight and narrow. But you? What were you thinking, going after white girls from good families? There's no talking the prosecutor into a plea deal. He *wants* a big trial, and it will disgrace the whole family. I can't allow it."

Anger cut through some of my drug haze. I knew better, but a tiny part of me expected that with me sitting right there, she'd express some kind of dismay about what he'd done to me, or his most recent victims. But no. She was mad because he'd *embarrassed* her.

"Ahm surry," Quinton mumbled drunkenly.

"I know," Claudia told him pityingly. "You're so sorry that you'll get drunk, go out to the switch willow by the pond, and hang yourself."

Quinton's slurred "What?" cut off in a strangled gagging as Eisenstreng whipped the length of rope around his neck and began to throttle him.

I gaped, shocked. On dark nights I'd imagined strangling Quinton myself or setting him on fire. Surely seeing him die would cure my nightmares. But this? Watching him strain and struggle and go purple in the face because Claudia was embarrassed? I only felt sick.

"Oh my God, stop!" Mom shrieked at Eisenstreng.

"Hush!" Claudia barked. "I'm cleaning up your mess. I trusted you to straighten this boy out, and you failed me. You failed the whole family. Tonight, you realize that Quinton is gone, and go looking for him. You find him hanging from the tree. In your grief, you take too many of your nervous pills. The boys find you dead in the guest suite tomorrow morning."

Jesus Christ. *Jesus fucking Christ.* I struggled in earnest in my chair, trying to find a weak spot in the wood or the ropes, but everything was solid. I was stuck.

Meanwhile, my mom was straight-up panicking, moaning, "No no no no no . . . ." A sound like an animal caught in a trap.

The twin who held the Aquafina pulled a tan bottle of prescription pills out of his pocket and walked toward my mother.

"Don't fight this, ma'am," he said. "I don't want to hurt you."

"If he does, the county coroner will courteously omit any recent injuries from his report." Claudia's eyes glittered. "I've bailed him out of financial misfortune, and he knows to respect my favor."

"Leave her alone!" I croaked as the twin took hold of my mother's chin to force her mouth open. "Stop it!"

The other twin strode over to me. "Calm down."

"No! Fuck you!" I had to stop this. *Somehow.*

He pressed the cold steel tip of an air-powered injector against my neck. Burning chemicals jetted into my flesh.

"I'm not asking," he said.

I slowly woke in an aggressively pink room. I was still in my Thanksgiving outfit, shoes off, lying on my side facing the wall. The first thing my eyes focused on was the hideous wallpaper. It had a garden-y pattern on it, but I couldn't tell if the fuchsia curls and whorls were supposed to be flowers or leaves. The background color was unpleasantly fleshy and reminded me of cow udders. I decided I hated it.

"Gross," I whispered.

A man cleared his throat behind me. I sat bolt upright in bed . . . and was hit by an intense wave of nausea. For a moment all I could do was close my eyes and focus on not barfing.

When I was able to look up, I saw that the Odinist twin sat in a ladderback chair beside the closed door.

"Where's my mom?" My voice was a dry squeak.

"Body's in the downstairs guest room." He fiddled with his valknut ring instead of making eye contact. "In the morning we'll call 9-1-1."

I wanted to scream, but I didn't have the air. I wanted to cry, but the tears wouldn't come.

"You fuck-faced Nazi bastard," I whispered.

"We gotta do something about that nasty mouth of yours." He still didn't look at me. "Grandma Claudia don't like it. I don't like it. It's not ladylike."

"I don't care."

"Well, you're gonna care. She's gonna make sure you learn to dress and act like a lady so you can find a proper husband. You owe it to our family and our race to make white babies. We can't let the mud people outbreed us. So you're gonna stay here and get taught until Grandma is satisfied."

WHITE MEAT

This was absolutely too much. I felt myself start to dissociate again.

"No choice, huh?" I said numbly. I felt as though I were talking to him from the bottom of a deep, dark well.

"Sure, you got a choice." He reached into his suit jacket pocket, pulled out another bottle of pills and tossed it into my lap. "We ain't *that* hard up for women. One of the cousins can take up the slack. You're kinda old for breedin' anyhow, if you ask me. Not that I'd mind trying. I figure overall you're only a five, but that rack of yours is definitely an eight or nine."

With a shaking hand, I picked up the bottle. Oxycodone.

"Take the whole bottle, and you won't wake up." He stood. "I'll come back in the morning, after the cops deal with the bodies. Be sweet and you get breakfast."

He left the bedroom, locking the door behind him.

I slipped out of the bed. My body felt numb, as if it were a rubber doll that I was puppeteering at a distance.

"I'm *not* staying here," I told myself. "GTFO."

I tried the door to the hallway to confirm that it was definitely, solidly locked. There were two other doors in the room. One led to a small walk-in closet, and the other to a half-bath with a sink and toilet. I got a drink, washed my face to try to wake myself up a bit more, and started assessing my situation. They hadn't taken my wristwatch—it was 6 P.M. and still Thanksgiving—nor my wallet. My shoes were on the bare hardwood beside the door. But my phone could be anywhere.

A single, narrow window lurked behind pink frilly drapes. A gibbous moon illuminated a short drop to the slate roof of the floor below. Beyond, I saw a path to a trellis I could climb to the ground. Thanks to my childhood explorations, I knew that there was a gap in the tall iron security fence where a stream entered the property a few hundred yards away. From there it was a straight shot down the road to the gas station.

After some fumbling and shoving—I could only vaguely feel my fingers—I got the latch to slide open, and to my surprise the window wasn't sealed shut. But it was *super* narrow. I could get my head through, and if I breathed out I might be able to squeeze my shoulders through. But no way was I going to squish my boobs down enough. There was just too much flesh.

After trying for several minutes to wedge myself through to the chilly darkness, I backed out and stood gasping and lightheaded in the middle of the room. If I'd just had another two or three inches of space . . . .

I suddenly realized that the left arm of my button-down felt wet beneath my blazer. I took the jacket off. The lower half of my shirtsleeve was sodden with blood. I'd snagged my elbow on a jutting nail that ripped right through three layers of fabric and tore a pretty big hole in my skin. The knockout drugs still had me numbed far more than I'd realized.

My brain churned as I went into the bathroom to patch myself up with old Band-Aids from the medicine cabinet. Maybe there was something in the closet or dressers I could use to get the molding off? Something I could use as a screwdriver or prybar?

I riffled through the drawers and shelves as quietly as I could, pulling out anything that seemed even remotely useful. When I was done, all I had was a roll of duct tape, a small hand-cranked flashlight, a random assortment of letter openers, and a stack of old framed photographs I'd pulled out of the way so I could rummage the junk beneath.

The glass of the top frame was cracked, the long shards shaped like the blades of butcher knives.

A terrible idea formed in my mind, one that I tried to push away as I set to work on the window frame with the letter openers. But as the cheap steel blade of the last opener snapped in my hand, I realized that an awful plan was better than none.

I don't really remember squeezing out the window, creeping over the roof, climbing down the trellis, and stumbling across the estate to the gap in the fence. All that has the fuzziness of a nightmare.

But I do remember Sparrow's horrified face in the beam of the flashlight as she ran up to me on the dark road. Her hands covered in the blood shining darkly on the duct tape strapping hand towels tight across my chest. How she shrieked, "Oh god, oh god, what did they do to you?"

Five days later, the fever from my infection broke. I woke from nightmares to find myself in a hospital room back in the city. My bandaged, flattened chest felt like it was on fire.

Sparrow dozed in the companion chair.

"Hey," I croaked.

She stirred, opened her eyes, and smiled at me. "Hey, Sleeping Beauty!"

Her offhand endearment stabbed me through my ragged scars, and I started to sob. "Don't say that. I'm no beauty, I'm fuckin' mangled. And I let my mom die."

"Sweetie." She came to my bedside and took my hand. "You didn't kill your mom. Her sick, awful family did that. And you're still beautiful in every way that matters. I love you for *you*, not your body parts."

"Would you love me if I was a worm?" I sniffled.

"*Sweetie*. This is heartfelt stuff. Stop undermining."

I smiled in spite of all the pain. "I guess you got my text?"

She shook her head. "I messaged both you and your mom, and after no replies I got worried and drove up. Nobody answered the gate intercom, so I parked at that gas station you mentioned, checked for you inside, then started walking down the road by the fence to see if I could figure out a way in. That's how I found you."

"Thank you." My head was clearing a little. "Do the police know?"

She nodded grimly. "Granny Homicide didn't count on the cops searching the whole mansion. First they found the scene in the basement, and later about a dozen bodies walled up down there. So they arrested everyone."

"Holy family history of violence, Batgirl." I paused. "You *sure* you still want to marry me?"

She gently kissed my forehead. "I'm in this for the long haul. But I'm *very* glad that you're in counseling."

I laughed weakly. "Me, too."

§175

MAXWELL I. GOLD

THROUGH BIZARRE TEMPLES** built with parchment and burnt words, codified by unreasonable nomenclature, whose restrictive bailments kept us locked away, colored and contextured by orientation and love; here the paragraphs were taken down as if an unholy commandment written by gods that were never ours.

The words themselves put down not in ink, but the blood of so many like us, the Queen-Goddesses who fell in the stone streets where the blue-bald thugs laughed at their glitter and gold; the Yellow Stars and Pink Lights who burned underneath the cigarette and concentration of neon flames by the fires of progress. All tenants wrought by words which were never meant to, but still linger like the ghosts of yesterday.

The ruined Temple of Nomenclature, bodies of signifiers spilling out of the Cosmic Bath Houses, scattered across the stars not only for the world to see but confined inside our closets where the fingers of new corporate gods hoped to press us further, deeper; the words of their awful prayers forever codified as if we *never-were* or *never-could-be*.

Though, this was for the Queen Goddesses, Yellow Stars, and Vogue-Mothers who damned the commandments of an old world that never wanted them in the first place, who cried in languages of
love,
    rage,
       and light;

§175

to leave behind not ruins of a nameless temple, or phrases that beg
to categorize, conflate, and ascribe meaningless affirmation to
existence, but throw into the pyres of Someday, the bodies of old,
white gods who never knew
    the love,
        rage,
            and light;
                to deconstruct the universe with their final cry,
    Down
        with
            175!

THE MIKVAH

ZACHARY ROSENBERG

AS MY LOVE and I bathed in the mikvah, our people in the *shtetl* were slain.

Yakub and I had come to the mikvah for purification and cleansing. His eyes had met mine, his voice murmuring my name with tenderness: "Elijah." His voice filled the silence in the cave, my name a prayer on his lips. His fingers brushed my arm, a gentle caress that left me wordless. His eyes lingered upon mine, rich and dark above that thin and knowing smile.

It lasted an eternity. It lasted only a moment. I turned to the mikvah awaiting us, the pale blue of the waters swaying and lapping to reach our feet. The pool had been long blessed by the Rabbis of our small *shtetl.* This small strip of Russia was where we had lived for centuries. It had been nearly eighteen hundred years since the great exile by the Romans and we had settled here, creating our *shtetl,* our home. Throughout all those years, our people had come to the caves deep in the woods, where the women first came to the mikvah so they might perform *teivilat keilim,* the ritual washing of vessels.

Over time, the mikvah grew to expect our people's visits, to hear our troubles and to help relieve the burdens of our lives with its renewing waters.

The mikvah was where the inhabitants of our *shtetl* came to wash themselves for purification, liberation from sin, from plague, and from our own imperfections. I held Yakub's hand as we stepped into the cold, clear waters, peering downward to the abyss where azure merged with onyx. Into the depths we gazed as we prepared for the cold, synchronized as one. We said our blessings at the first immersion, sinking into the pool.

THE MIKVAH

The mikvah knew us, as it had known so many of our people. It received us with joy, celebrating our feelings and celebrating our return. This land was ancient, waiting for our people when we arrived harried and chased almost a century ago. The land embraced and received us, accepted our blessings and rituals. The land has ever rejoiced for our love in all its forms. Our people knew of us and our love. Not only did they expect it, they encouraged it.

Outside the cave, in the *shtetl,* men on horseback rode through the streets, armed with steel and a hatred over eighteen hundred years old. They consigned our people to the grave, some laughing for the joy of it. Some knew of the sin in their actions, staining their hands in carmine so that not even the mikvah could wash it away.

All around me, the waters quavered and shuddered, a frigid embrace that beckoned Yakub and me lower still on our second immersion. We washed the impurities from our bodies, the shock of the cold taking impurities from our souls.

Submerged entirely, peering at one another, we were cleansed together. Pure, as back in the *shtetl,* our neighbors' blood dirtied the earth and rusted upon the blades of our tormentors. All Yakub and I knew at that moment was one another. Clean and pure as one in the mikvah's embrace.

"Elijah." He mouthed my name in the water, the smile bright on his smooth face. We lingered there before we surfaced, sucking in breaths as cold as the waters that licked at our chests, all while torches pressed to the synagogue and sparked the roaring, crackling fires.

Consuming all we had built, centuries of life and tradition. We, in our ignorance, were not there to see it. We committed ourselves to this ritual together, and so I was not there to die alongside my brothers and my father. Perhaps the mikvah forgave me, as we took our third and final immersion within the cool depths.

Perhaps there was nothing to forgive.

Once we left the pool, Yakub retrieved his clothing, binding his chest anew. Some might say his pride in his identity was sinful, a revocation of the roles that *Hashem* had shaped him for. But in his heart and soul, Yakub was a man and his name sounded all the sweeter for having chosen it himself. The mikvah rebuked him not, nor did it rebuke me for loving him.

Those were not the sins we meant to cleanse this day, for they were not sins at all. The mikvah shivered behind us, delighted at our visit. We silently promised we would return soon, loving it as we did the land. This pool was old, perhaps even older than our people's many thousands of years. It still felt like it had been waiting for us for so long.

We dressed as one, leaving behind the water and the cave. We were in time to see the purge of our *shtetl,* a reminder our people had never known a home that could not be taken from us. Lost in our ritual cleansing, we had not known the attack had occurred. Lost in us, the mikvah had not felt it either.

Ashen pillars of smoke against the sky filled our gaze, orange tongues licking over the trees. I glanced back towards the mikvah, vainly seeking a reason for the injustice we now beheld.

But Yakub was already moving, sorrow and fear pushing him to bravery. I shouted his name, desperate and despairing as I ran after him. The mikvah had cleansed me of the sins of greed, anger and indolence. It could not take my fear.

To my shame, part of me wished to dash into the woods, to hide until it was at an end. I pictured the men on horseback with their crazed eyes, their hands locked on curved blades dripping scarlet droplets of life to the thirsting soil. I witnessed their hatred, more intense than the flames consuming our *shtetl.*

My hatred encompassed hundreds of graves, a thousand exiles, a million oppressions. Wherever we have been driven, our footsteps were marked in the blood of the kin we were forced to leave behind.

Whether they flew the Roman eagle, or the Tsar's banners, they were the same. They came to take from us, to exile us, to murder us. We were unwelcome lambs grazing upon what they viewed as theirs, a herd to be culled. They killed Jews and lovers alike, nothing but hatred driving them on.

They turned our homes into abattoirs. The wails of children calling for parents carried over the crackle of the fires, ignored by the laughing wolves who rode across the *shtetl's* sodden earth. The empty eyes of those I had known for my entire life are glossy reflections of lost mortality. Our synagogue burned, the door barred and pounding with screams carrying out. Yakub saw it and his eyes fixed with a courage borne of madness.

I ran with him, through the wheeling mob of horses, jeers, and shouts. I knew my love's intent. Only death would stop him. The man before the synagogue chuckled at his work in affixing the bar upon the pounding door, the flames spread out along the rooftop.

Yakub caught the man as he spun. His fist took the man in the skull and our ravener fell like a tree, his head striking a rock. His eyes remained wide, a seeping pool of darkness joining our people's blood underneath him.

"Elijah, help me!" Yakub shouted. He was not shouting for me to save him from the cullers. He had no thought for his own safety, working at the heavy bolt upon the door. I joined him, weeping for fear of the death around me. The smoke stung at my eyes, my lungs rebelling at the ashen intrusion. I coughed. I wept. I stayed. I pulled.

The wood splintered, coming loose, and the doors swung open. Men and women hurtled out in a flood, holding children and sucking in the clear air that they had never expected to taste again.

Our tormentors remained fixed, blades and pistols at the ready. Robbed of their sport, they chortled still. One grinned through a thick beard, a bear's leer.

We were not lambs. We were men. This was no cull of a surplus horde. This was robbery, an attempt to steal what was ours. It was the attempt to drown our claim to this land with blood enough to wash us away.

They were not Romans. They were not knights. But a pogrom was a pogrom all the same.

"You fight." The man with the beard laughed. His eyes glittered inhuman above wolfish teeth. In his hand was a curved blade, wet with stolen life. I saw a dead butcher lying beside a farmer, their blood mingling in the earth and perhaps upon that sword. The men chuckled at their compatriot's assertion. "You killed one of ours. That is murder." He stepped to Yakub, his sword teasing the air.

"This is our land." Yakub did not answer the charge. His eyes blazed defiance and I feared our life together would be measured in naught but moments more. "Our land. Our home."

For centuries, we had been taught we were a people without land. We took an existence where we could, though sermons demonized us and authorities sided with our tormentors. We had been perhaps tolerated here in Russia. Tolerated, but never truly welcomed even as the 19th century drew to an end. In these ancient woods, we had allowed our blood and sweat to conjure illusions of belonging.

I thought of the mikvah with its silken cold water. Our mikvah, blessed so that it might renew us. Our way was forgiveness. But only after *teshuvah,* of repentance. The look in this man's callous eyes revealed contrition was as foreign to him as mercy.

His sword came out, opening a wide red smile on Yakub's chest. Yakub flinched, the bindings revealed. His hand clapped to the wound, but dark rubies bled through to spatter against the ground. His blood joined that of our people's own, the same as countless places we had dared to believe would be our safety.

The next blow opened my shoulder. I tried not to scream but could not smother a yelp. My blood joined Yakub's on the ground, swallowed by parched soil.

The survivors stared at us mutely, wearing expressions of horror. Some coughed, weakened by the smoke we had delivered them from. Yakub's head tilted high with defiance, though he trembled through the pain. I was at his side, my hands upon his shoulders. Flames roared about us, bringing down all we had built while I stared in the eyes of oppression.

Eyes that had remained the same since Rome. Since Byzantium. Since France. Now in Russia, where oppression still refused to stay its hand. Our blood now mingled with the land below us.

I felt the land respond. Far from me, I felt the ebb and flow of the mikvah call. Through the rage and hate, it soothed me. Through the pain and fear, it lulled me.

I heard no words in my head, for land could not speak, though the rumble of thunder overhead and the sudden downpour of rain released by heavy clouds that drowned the fires in our *shtetl* told me that it could weep.

The land had welcomed us. The land had heard our blessings upon it. The cold rain cleansed my wound, soothing as the waters of the mikvah. No transient intruders were we.

I stared into the eyes of the man before me. "Have you not killed enough?" I asked in Russian as the blood ran from his saber. "Is this not enough?"

He delivered the answer of all oppressors: "Never."

The land's discontent suffused my very soul. Looking at Yakub, I could tell he felt the same. I drew strength from him, he from me. I linked my hand to his, grasping tightly and wanting only to feel his skin to mine. Desire and carnality had no home in our hearts, but our love would be neither broken nor separated. So I held his hand all the tighter, though the man before me tapped his blade upon the ground. "Will we be sufficient?" Yakub asked then. The notion of martyrdom was as old as our people, as old as the land we stood upon. He mirrored my thoughts, speaking my words through his lips.

"Hunt us. That should satisfy you, no? We took your fun from you. Take us, end your cull. Hunt us and let our people live and rebuild. We will offer you more sport than helpless women and children."

Yakub chanced upon their sadism and his gamble was rewarded. The men looked amongst themselves, speaking in their native *Balachka* dialect. Their laughter carried again, the bearded man with the saber stepping forth through the muddy ground with no reverence for the lives he had spilled there.

"Agreed," he said, merriment dancing like stars across his eyes. "Jews are one thing, but?" He gazed between us, a knowing smirk spreading over his face. "Those like you, we will take a special joy in hunting." His sword flicked to the woods, away from the *shtetl*. Yakub caught fluid in his throat and spat upon the ground at the man's feet. With a Cossack's fury behind the beaming grin, the man tapped his sword upon the ground, careless for the land beneath his feet as the people whose blood drenched it.

"I am Kristov," he said. "So you abominations know whom to beg from."

"Swear that the rest will be unharmed," I said, only Yakub's hand in mine giving me the strength to challenge this man. He shrugged, snorting like a bull as the rest barked out their contempt. "Swear to me."

Kristov shrugged, apathy driving him more than mercy now. "I so swear," he said. "I shall warn you, no man nor woman eludes us for long. We shall give you a start and then we shall find you and make the sport of you that was denied us here. We have seen men like you before, obscenities before heaven. We take special delight in sport with you, beyond other Jews."

The land shivered beneath my feet, telling me I could trust this man to keep his word. That was all I wanted. It was all we needed. I saw in Kristov's eyes the mirrored arrogance of our persecution and I vowed my vengeance then.

I felt the mikvah call to me. The mikvah invited me to bring sin and impurity to it so it might be washed clean from this world.

I would. Yakub and I would bring them together. I brought his hand to my lips, uncaring who saw. I brushed his smooth fingers against my mouth, never leaving Kristov's gaze. I challenged him and he would respond.

We set off from the *shtetl,* with no time to mourn our dead friends and neighbors. The men were resting their horses, sending us off with merry waves and pantomimed cuts with their blades. They were the hunters, we were the harts. They hunted us because we were Jewish, because we were men who loved one another.

We had nothing save for one other. Save the land beneath us.

Save the mikvah calling us back. The land was with us, offering to guard us. The trees thickened about us, the branches and leaves tightened to grip us in a concealing embrace. We walked through together, stealthy and silent without even a stray noise to cost us our lives.

No light pierced the thick canopy ahead, the wind rustled the trees so that their song drowned away the meager noises we made. I looked into Yakub's eyes, afraid and devoted all at once. We had come here many times, he and I walking from our *shtetl.* Not only to be cleansed, but to savor the perfection of the land with its trees and flowers.

I held him every night, cradled against me. Even when his blood was on him, he could never be impure to me. "They might find us." I could not help but to voice my fears. "They might find us. If they do, they'll kill us."

"Then we would die together," murmured Yakub. His smile was fearless and bold, a sun to scorch away the shadows of doubt in my heart. He spoke our tongue, the language of our ancestors, reminding me of what we had kept through nearly two millennia of oppression. "But we will not, Elijah. They cannot even take our lives. How can they take what we hold dearest? Our people. Our love. Our *names.*"

He had chosen his name himself, casting off his old one like a shed cloak. His name was his prized possession, his identity inseparable from him as I was. I whispered to *Hashem,* not afraid I might die for death's sake.

Only afraid that I might miss decades ahead with this man before me. The land shuddered about us, informing me that it would not let that happen. These woods were old. They had their own traditions, long predating us. Their vows were to be taken most seriously.

THE MIKVAH

We crept through the forest, no sunlight piercing the fortress of vegetation above. We did not take the path back to the cave, knowing that our pursuers would be lurking along the roads.

We heard the braying of horses and the cracking of whips. Men shouted, their voices the thick rage of men who could not taste enough blood, drunkards thirsting for one more drop. If we died now, nothing would prevent them from leaving and returning to the *shtetl* a week or a month or years later to take more lives.

It was a terrible burden we bore, to end their rapacity here. Yakub and I shared it gladly as the land beckoned us forth, deeper into the embrace of the foliage.

That way, Yakub turned his head, the sound of hooves thudding upon the ground drawing us closer still. I followed him close as the men stalked us through the underbrush.

Some had dismounted, perhaps eighteen in all that I had counted among the carnage. Eighteen with guns and swords and horses against a people armed only with faith and fists, the brave soldiers indeed. They had no reverence for the land, nor the forests and hacked with cruel blades through leaf and branch. The land trembled, but it held firm for our sake.

We led them deeper into the labyrinth, to the maze of flora. Yakub turned his head at last, directing me so that I might know his intent. I knew it without need for a gesture and turned myself with him. We walked through the forest, the sounds distant behind us. The crack of twigs heralded the arrivals of the hunters, the land shuddering as their swords left scars on the wood around them.

Hoots and jeers accompanied their pursuit. We were helpless, unarmed, destined to be nothing more than pleasant memories of sporting chases. We turned in the direction of the mikvah in its cave, we went faster, with the wind at our backs to urge us on. We went, filled with hope the land would not betray us.

On, we went. Each step was accompanied by the anguished thrumming of my heart in my skull. Through the connection of blood to the land, the mikvah reassured us. Whatever spirits had possessed this land would not desert us now.

I saw the cave, a black maw in the woods. The men behind us had caught our trail, hooting and jeering while Yakub and I passed into the mouth of the cave. There was the mikvah, just as we had left it. Always did it wait, inviting the return of our people. Before it had been a mikvah, it had been nothing more than a pool in the cave before a rabbi had come here and said the words so this site may be blessed. The land could have seen us as strange people with strange blessings. The land and the pool could have seen us as intruders, as Kristov and his men did.

But the land and whatever spirits dwelt within had been flattered and accepted the blessings, accepted us. One might even have called it a conversion. We welcomed them as they welcomed us. Our lives were difficult, but happy. We managed, connected in spirit to our people all across Europe, Asia and the rest of the world. We celebrated our rituals, so that they might bind us as one.

Never once had we forgotten to include the land itself.

I could hear the hunters behind us as we walked to the end of our mikvah. The pool's waters lapped at our feet and I felt its concern for us. Yakub knelt and washed his wound in the waters. The blood trickled into the pool, vanishing instantly, the mikvah drinking the same blood the soil had tasted. I mirrored him, washing my wound with cold water and allowing the mikvah to purify the injury.

The mikvah tasted my blood and no longer was it merely sympathetic. No longer was it simply worried. It was angry, wrathful.

I often wondered if we had defied our scriptures when I was younger, for it was the first of all commandments that we should have no other before *Hashem*. But the land and the mikvah were not gods, meaning we were in no violation of our law. They had been there before we were, to welcome us. They protected us now.

The Cossacks were clambering through the mouth of the cave. They came in a single group, laughing and whooping to congratulate one another on a hunt well completed. Their reward was before them, the leader, Kristov, stepping forth with his saber at the ready. But as he stared at us, a brief confusion lit the eyes above that thick beard.

For he could see our wounds were healed. My clothes were torn, but the skin had knitted closed, pale and smooth. The mikvah took our sins from us and renewed our flesh as it renewed our souls. My smile grew upon my face, Yakub eyeing each of the men. "Our people are safe?"

"We want sport. Those like you always provide it," Kristov said, though there was no arrogance in it now. He looked about with his men, the cave suddenly spacious enough to accommodate all of them. But when he turned around, there was no more mouth to the cave. The entrance was sealed, like a clever spider shutting its burrow to disallow escape from the insects.

"I am Yakub. And he is Elijah," my love said. "I do not care for your begging. I tell you only so you may know we have names. That you have never taken *those* from us."

"What magic have you worked?" One man shouted as he pounded at the stone wall that had been a passage to safety but moments ago.

"Magic?" I asked. I squeezed Yakub's hand. "There is no magic, nor *Kabbalah* here. There is only the land you have trespassed upon. The mikvah wishes to answer for your transgression.

"Let us see what you are without your sins."

The first man lost his footing. He fell into the mikvah with a sudden shriek. The pool was growing, expanding. Kristov's eyes widened as he turned with an awful howl of terror. He laid into his own men with his saber to take himself from danger, bonds forged of hatred and bloodlust being most fragile indeed. He fought his way to the wall, all while the ground crumbled away to reveal the waters beneath.

The mikvah called them in. They backed away, they screamed pleas and prayers to us as though Yakub and I might have delivered them from what they had earned, knowing only with the instinctive fear of the wicked to avoid the mikvah. They fell into the water, screams muffled by the suffocating embrace of the waters.

Kristov clawed at the cave wall, pounding at it so hard that his blood stained the stone. Yakub and I watched. My heart was softer than his, for Yakub's was filled with a wrathful satisfaction. I was not beyond pity, for all their crimes.

Sin is a word in the old tongue of our people, for what has gone astray. Mikvahs purify, helping to renew and to find the right path. But when one is nothing but sin, there can be nothing that remains when the mikvah has had its say.

Kristov surfaced briefly. He had no more thick beard on his face. Nor did he have flesh remaining. Below him, his fellows twisted in the waters, their bodies pink and raw as the mikvah took their sin from them and found nothing beneath.

Kristov moaned and beckoned to us, seeking to cast his hate or to beg for salvation.

The flesh sloughed from his bones, taken into the depths of the pool and devoured, consumed to become nourishment for the land about him. The mikvah feasted ravenously upon him, and he sank within.

Glutted upon sin and hate, the mikvah receded to become the pool we had bathed in but a short time before. The cave opened to allow us our exit. The waters were clear, cold, and sweet, with no sign of even a drop of blood or a mote of flesh.

Yakub embraced me tightly. I murmured to him how scared I had been, and he held me with a hand to my hair. He understood, he always did. It was at its end now. We had to return to our *shtetl* and rebuild, to care for our dead and even bury the one man Yakub had killed. Our people would be safe now. Our love was safe.

For a time.

I knelt first and ran my hands into the waters of the pool. The mikvah responded, flowing about the limb, cool and sweet. It knew, having feasted well. I prayed to *Hashem* again and faced Yakub. There was no sin in the deaths of men in self-defense or to save others. We were blameless for their ends.

There was no need to submerge anew. And so, with my love's hand in mine, we departed the cave and walked down the path with the land shuddering in its protective delight all about us.

A FAMILIAR SONG

MATTHEW BLAIN-HARTUNG

IT **WAS THE** song which stirred him from the deep, melodic vibrations accompanied by a squelching, suction noise. Thoughts ripped loose from the heavy sludge, followed by limbs, the slurry sliding away in rippling sheets. The water itself quivered as sensation trickled into eight tactile arms and traveled upwards to his brain, electrical charge gently prodding his consciousness.

Pop, thwap, pop.

Three tentacles peeled loose from the rock underneath; he had been anchored to the seabed, awaiting . . .

Awaiting now. Awaiting him.

A few thoughts floated by on the gentle current, the deeps flowing over delicate skin, tickling each sucker in a playful gesture.

—mangy poofs, not on my ship—

He was a sailor, born for the high seas. This much was certain, of course.

Yet he also scuttled along the bottom, a denizen of the deep. This fact, too, was curiously certain. Doubts flooded in, threatening to overload a spongy, oblong head; yet his mind simply pushed them away, siphon pumping outwards with innate perfection. Water flowing in, water flowing out; thoughts flowing in, thoughts flowing out.

—I'm tired Ivan, tired of lying all the bloody time. Tired of—

—not my son, not in my house—

Prying each limb from his stone bed, he began to probe the surroundings, instinctive responses spooling forth with ease. The tip of each tentacle tapped the seafloor, grasping the rubble and sifting through the sand, nerves aflame. Satisfied, he gathered up oxygen—an influx of sea rippling over shuttering gills—and was off, propelled by brute force and liquid physics.

He could see clearly, but how? More thoughts flowed in, arriving with the rapid flow of water racing across bulging eyes: it was dark down here, on the seafloor. Dark and cold and deadly quiet.

Death, death, a watery grave.

High above, a commotion rattled his senses, clicking and clattering, not unlike ivory dice rattling in his old copper cup. *Four snakes*, that had been his vice—loose-lipped ship hands huddled in a crude circle, drenched with rum and sea-spray, thirsty for the other's coin. He had won some and lost more, but mostly he was the one who couldn't say no.

—Yes! Just say yes. We'll disappear at the next port—

—Hey Tev, where the bloody hell are those two, anyways?—

He froze, eight legs stiff with tension, before retreating backwards, crouched low in the silt, swimming slowly to avoid casting up plumes of sand.

<danger in the deep. danger in the deep.>

The warning rushed in with the next influx of seawater, mingling with the thoughts of the sailor, but sticking like barnacles to a hull, even as others were washed away. He heeded the advice and dug into the gloom until the chittering had faded.

Again, he probed his surroundings, and again his body responded instantly to the information gliding across dexterous limbs. Safe—and nearly there. Salty brine flooded in, bringing with it spikes of confusion and trepidation; salty brine flooded out, spouting the fears of men back into the watery depths.

This was the spot. The body arched out of the muck, its swollen belly rising towards the surface, the tattered remains of a woolen shirt coated in a slimy, emerald sheen. He could spot the anchor and seagull tattoo, clumsily drawn upon the left-bicep. The ink dazzled his vision, a glossy black against pale skin, pearly white and bloated, stretched tight and floating with a grim buoyancy. Iron manacles pinned its hostage to the seafloor, arms and legs sunk several inches deep, the dull metal poignant in its careless efficiency.

—no listen, it's not what it looks like, let go of him—

—at least spare him, Cap', for Christ's sake, spare him, promise me you'll—

A FAMILIAR SONG

A swell of emotions flood in, stronger and more viscous this time, the consistency of blood cooling on a salted-crusted deck. Sorrow: bitter and ice-cold. Regret: sinking like an anchor. Pain: as sharp as his father's dagger, still hanging loosely from the leather belt.

He'd been thrown overboard—weighted down, his body tossed into the sea like a sack of putrid oats. Eight arms scurried closer, tiny suckers gripping water-logged pantaloons, traversing across a bare chest, and crawling toward the head. Ah yes, now he remembered. The crooked slash gaped like a fleshy canyon: frayed and tinged a stormy blue, deep enough to expose a pair of vocal cords. He never could keep his voice down, could he?

—any last words, Solly?—

—I'm keeping 'is dice, ain't lucky but pretty little bones—

—just cut 'em Cap and be done with it—

—get out of my home, Solomon, take your demons and leave your poor mother—

—making me sick just looking at those two—

—quiet, we need to be more careful. Wait, seven hells Sol, someone is coming—

Water flowed in, and water flowed out, his siphon pumping without conscious effort. Time swirled alongside the lazy currents, never quite linear but eventually making its own way across the barren landscape. And so, with time, these memories too were diluted by the sea, the slicks of blood on deck washed clean by moonlit waves. Eight limbs pulsated with contained energy, the urge to swim more pressing than man's grief.

Yet, another desire tugged at his mind; another reason to escape from his frozen repose.

<he lies near>

Primal functions grabbed the reins, and he was content to swim without care until his arms touched down on the seafloor. For a moment, he thought that he had circled back to his own ghastly corpse until his stomach lurched violently, realization dawning with cruel certainty. He hovered above, suckers gently prodding—but this skin was that of another man, noticeably darker even as it floated suspended in the depths. One tentacle traced the curving lines of a snow-capped mountain rising from the sea, the setting sun balancing directly atop the peak. Ivan's tattoo, drawn onto his chest like an ancient talisman, had been the source of admiration among the crew, its artistry a raw source of beauty on a ship renowned for its blubbery stench.

That same skin was now mottled with blue veins, begging to burst forth. He tread carefully upon such delicate tapestry, just as his rough hands had done so many times before; exploring with a feather-soft touch, relishing a sensation shared only with the dead man. And he closed his bulbous eyes as two limbs found the base of his lover's neck, wound even deeper than his own, plunging inwards to expose a glossy white spine.

—no, no! It was me, God-dammit, spare—

—Solly, do you really think settling down in a port-town will change a damn thing?—

—Welcome aboard, kid. My name is Solomon but you can call me—

The left side of Ivan's body was floating higher than his right, the manacle having slipped from one delicate wrist; as the current ebbed and flowed, the corpse appeared to lunge upwards, one hand outstretched, fingers taut and splayed wide, reaching for the surface.

The same bone-chilling chattering sounded again, much nearer this time.

Clack, click, clack.

<danger. danger above.>

Clack, click, clack.

Like the sound of rusty iron closing around Ivan's wrist.

His pliable form squeezed beneath the distended body of his lover. One eye spied the enormous, arrow-shaped squid as it pulsed through the water, slicing through the water with deceptive speed, razor-sharp beak clamping down on lingering prey.

Swoosh, click, swoosh, clack.

As the mud settled back to the seafloor, silence returned to drape itself across the seabed. Floating upwards for a moment, he settled back down on the man's chest. The deep thrum of his own heart and the rhythmic passage of water through his gills lulled the sailor towards sleep; just as dreams of dry land began to descend, a new sound shattered his tranquil rest. An echo—deep and resonant—traveling through the dense water slowly and with otherworldly purpose.

The tips of each of his arms twitched as though caught in an open flame; yet his body was not responding to danger or fear, but of longing. Intertwined within the darkest currents of this sea, it was a haunting call—hopeless, doomed, but unrelenting. A familiar song. Before he could extend even a single arm in recognition, the sound was gone, leaving behind only tremors of desire dancing upon his skin.

I loved him, he thought. And the memory did in fact float by, Neptune's final gift.

—*Yes, Solomon. I love you too.*

Water flowed in, and out, and back in again—but the song did not return. It didn't matter, he had already made up his mind. His body consented with grace. His heart, after all, was never in doubt. Tentacles tracing over lovely curves one last time, he pushed off into the depths, leaving behind only an inky cloud, a funeral veil for love lost at sea.

IMMACULATE

MARYSE MEIJER

THE IPOD IS DEAD; it played all night. Amie plugs it in so it can charge before class. He puts on a brown skirt, cream-colored tights, boots. He doesn't look in the mirror. Dressing, doing his hair, choosing a lip gloss is like programming a computer: you tell it once what to do and then it just does it, every day, forever, until you tell it to stop.

He eats a stringy fried egg on toast. Greg, the stepdad, says nothing, stomach bisected by the edge of the table as he reaches for the coffee. Amie blots up margarine from the top of the bread with his napkin. The light in the kitchen is astounding. A roach rests on its back beside the trash can. The chair legs have made brown pits in the linoleum; the stove is still black from when Amie's mom used to burn the pans. But the mail is in a tidy stack on the counter and there is always milk in the fridge. Amie smiles at his stepdad, but his stepdad never looks up.

After school he goes to the library downtown to see how his site looks on a different screen: it looks beautiful. The main colors are black and white, with the name SKeLeTaL DeATh WhoRE in a drippy red. Thousands of people visit every day; it's *the* top site for Nadir, more popular than their official page, with a huge library of photos, the most accurate archive of tour dates and biographical info. But what Amie is known for is his immaculate records of the band's hundreds of songs; he's even corrected the band's own lyric sheets. GallowsCock says it's a gift, maybe even a sign of a kind of genius, but for Amie it's effortless: every scream appears to him as clearly as his own calm thoughts. It's a connection he's never had with any other band; he doesn't question it. Some things just are the way they are. He scrolls through the day's comments, types a few replies; behind him, eyes. He turns, tucking his hair behind his ear. Morgan and Alicia stare, hands wrapped around neon smoothies, looking for a table. Alicia is a senior, like Amie; Morgan graduated last year.

Hey, Amie says.

Morgan turns, quick, her gaze darting over Amie's face. Hey, she says.

What's up?

Morgan and Alicia exchange glances.

Nothing, Morgan says.

She's engaged, Alicia says. Morgan holds up her hand: a ring with an infinitesimal diamond glitters on her finger.

Wow, are you pregnant?

Morgan's whole body jerks, as if shot through with electricity; her smoothie bounces in its cup.

Where did you hear that?

Nowhere, Amie says with a smile. I can just tell.

Well, yeah, actually, she says, flushing bright red. Three months.

That's great, Amie says. I'm pregnant, too.

Morgan and Alicia blink in tandem.

But you—don't even have a boyfriend, Alicia scoffs.

Amie shrugs.

Was it an accident? Alicia asks.

What do you mean?

I mean . . . did you plan it?

Amie considers. No, he says.

Did . . . someone . . . rape you? Alicia presses, leaning into Amie; Morgan emits a small, shocked snort.

No, Amie says, smiling.

Is it someone who lives here?

Is who someone who lives here?

The father.

Amie just sits there. Morgan looks at her phone.

You're, like, seventeen, Alicia says.

Maybe we could have a party together, Amie says to Morgan. A baby shower or something.

Um, Morgan says.

We actually can't talk right now, Alicia says, tugging the hem of her crop top over her soft white waist. We're kind of in the middle of something?

Yeah, okay, Amie says. It was nice running into you. Congratulations, Morgan.

Morgan dips her head lower over her phone, her hair cutting off her face. Bye, she mumbles.

Amie walks home swallowing a giddy laugh. A drug store looms on his left; he goes in, buys a pregnancy test, ginger candy, a bottle of vitamins. The cashier clears her throat. Amie thinks of the diamond on Morgan's ring, the sudden double knowledge of his pregnancy and hers, a knowing like wildfire burrowing into his skull, sent from somewhere inside that tiny cold stone.

In the yard Chrissy rubs against the fence. Her owners, who sell prescription drugs to Amie's classmates, never let her inside. So she sleeps in a little hole in the dirt. Years ago, Amie was scared of Chrissy, because she's the kind of dog everyone thinks wants to bite people, but it was Chrissy who jumped over the gate in the driveway and barked so long and so loud the police finally came to Amie's house to see what was wrong, and they've been friends ever since.

Hey girl, Amie says. Hey sweet one. Chrissy pants. Hungry? he says. Chrissy licks the fence. Amie lifts his skirt and presses his hips against the rough wood. Chrissy pulls her head back, shakes her collar. Amie gives her a piece of cheese, then all of the cheese, in one fat yellow roll. Chrissy chokes a little before swallowing. You're okay, Amie hums, as Nadir screams on repeat: A *fucking graveyard/ that's you.*

On the site one of the regulars, GallowsCock, writes about his obsession with fucking his ex-girlfriend's mutilated corpse. He's thirty-eight and lives with his grandparents and is on the site almost as often as Amie, chronicling his obsession with his ex. *I just hate her so much,* is the title of his latest post. *She's lucky she lives two states away because if I ever find her I'll have a field day with her body, I will turn it into an amusement park of pain!!!!*

IMMACULATE

Every description of torture and necrophilia ends with at least three exclamation marks. Amie gets on his thread and says, *sorry to interrupt, but* and inserts the photo of the unwrapped pregnancy test along with a vomiting face and a screaming ghost. *Holy shit, is this for real?!* GC types. Everyone is so excited and surprised; there are jokes about eating the baby, burning the baby, sacrificing the baby, sending the baby to Satan for Christmas, etc. Amie rubs his stomach.

At dinner he is careful to eat lots of protein and veggies. I'm sorry, I think something stinks? Amie says.

Greg sniffs, makes a face. I told you to take out the garbage.

Amie chews a stalk of broccoli. I know, I'm sorry, but it just makes me sick to my stomach.

Why?

I'm very sensitive to smells right now.

Right now?

I think it has something to do with my uterus, Amie says with an apologetic smile as he tips a square of chicken onto his knife. Greg hides his face in a glass of milk, collects his plate, empties the trash.

The night Amie discovered Nadir he was standing beneath Jared's bedroom window, where Jared and some other boys were lumped around a desk, watching videos. They clicked on Nadir's song about the holocaust orgy; a close-up of XK's dark mouth smeared in fake shit filled the computer screen as he chanted in a deep scream: *fuck the pits/dick stuck in maggots/scraps of flesh/for Nazi faggots.* That was when the first pattern—jagged gray circles churning through an infinite, pulsating tunnel of a color Amie could not name—shattered his field of vision; he could feel the music entering his body, not through his ears or eyes, but starting at the back of his head, at the crown, which burned, as if a finger of fire had poked through his skull. He gasped quietly, frozen with joy beneath the window, as the music and its aura or whatever poured through him. *Oh,* he thought: *it's you.* Inside the house, one of the boys pretended to barf; another cut the video short. Jared said it was stupid music only poseurs and freaks would like. Amie fell out of love with him instantly. He went home and downloaded Nadir's entire oeuvre and confirmed that the first pattern was no accident. Each song had one, and Amie saw them all, huge shivering shapes strobing and collapsing beyond the beats in that unnamable landscape Amie was somehow expected to contain: *make room,* the music demanded, that tongue of fire striking through his head to his chest to his guts, torching a path for this infinite catalogue, and he did make room, he gave it every empty space he had.

He pats concealer beneath his eyes, plucks his brows. The hair iron heats up. His mom used to brush his hair when she was high, talking with a cigarette bouncing on her lip, ash smudging Amie's scalp. Amie liked to be touched by her, but his mom never seemed to realize it was him she was touching; he was just there, like a cat or a wall, to absorb whatever spilled out of her mouth. His dad had been living somewhere else; Amie rarely saw him, though he heard his voice through the phone, screaming into his mother's ear: *How dare you, cunt, slut, bitch, loser, whore.* And then there was just Greg, who never spoke about what happened but at least stuck around; he'd always been the kind of person who followed through, even on mistakes, but just barely.

Amie irons his hair and makes sure nothing is stuck in his lip gloss. At school, everyone stares. He goes to the bathroom. The stalls are full, so he waits. In the mirror Amie slouches against the wall. She is objectively a beautiful person, he knows. Amie hasn't posted a photo on his site; no one knows his real name, or how old he is, or where he lives, and no matter how many times people ask, he doesn't answer. Everyone, online and off, has a different wrong idea about Amie, in addition to their right ideas, which Amie accepts, even encourages. It's okay to float on the surface of other people's expectations, he thinks. The surface is pretty interesting, too.

In the last stall there is a spot of blood on the floor, probably from someone's period. He touches the blood with his pinky. He never uses the school bathrooms to piss or shit. He just holds it. He wraps his fingers over the top edge of the wall adjoining one stall to the next, leaving a little red mark on the metal. From outside, someone could see his hand and his feet but nothing in between, like something being censored. He unspools toilet paper from the roll, coils it into the toilet, and flushes.

IMMACULATE

How are you? Alicia says at the sinks, looking Amie up and down.

Great, he says, waiting for her to move so he can wash his hands. After a second she shifts slightly to the side. Amie squeezes beside her, turning on the water. Their arms touch.

Does your family know?

Amie rubs his fingers beneath the faucet. It's fine.

What do you mean, it's fine? What's fine?

Amie shrugs. Everything, he says softly. During lunch he sits on the front steps of the school and watches the traffic in the parking lot while Nadir screams about paramedics fucking the mutilated bodies of car crash victims. The song is called "First on the Scene." If a baby can hear everything its mother hears, then it might be a good idea to play death metal nonstop throughout pregnancy; that way, the baby would come out of the womb unsurprised by how ugly life is, and how funny, in a way. He tilts his face to the sun, eyes scrunched closed. Wind skips down the concrete. Everyone knows he is pregnant, now. Every person in the school.

The weeks go on. In spring Nadir releases a new album, *Fleshgasm*; Amie transcribes, as usual, all the lyrics, which takes hours and hours, because typing through the visions is almost impossible; the new music makes incredible shapes, patterns and colors he's never seen before, all edged in gold; he watches and listens, absorbed, engulfed, the album on repeat, pulsing through the room. He's asked if other people on the site see the same things he sees; they don't. But they all agree that the music is beautiful, which is impossible for their friends and family to understand. People think the point of the music is to be as violent and hateful as possible, when really that wasn't it at all, Amie blogs: If humans were just bodies, and bodies were just these insignificant, stupid things, you wouldn't think about death or murder or violence or gore at all: a dead human would have the same significance as a crushed bug, and Nadir wouldn't bother making music about it, because things that don't matter are boring. But Nadir knows that being in a body is the most insane and incredible experience there is; and that what's inside a body, and what happens when the inside is exposed to the outside, is art. There's more than one thing to say about death, Amie writes, more than one way to die, which means there is more than one way to live, because as you're dying you're still living, it's just a part of what it means to be alive, and what it means to be alive is to experience the savage but sacred excess of existence, which is what Nadir's music worships and glorifies. So their music isn't as nihilistic as it seemed; maybe it is actually even more beautiful, more truly *good*, than other forms of music that only talk about things that everyone already likes and understands, like love or friendship; maybe it makes sense out of things people forget to make sense of.

Amie posts his little essay. By the end of the day it has gathered hundreds of black hearts. His ears are sore from the constant rub and noise from the earbuds, but he can't stop listening. There's too much to see. His favorite song is about a serial killer on death row; when the killer is asked if he has any last words he describes, in detail, his filthiest cannibal rape-murders. But he's cut off when the executioner turns on the electric chair, and everything turns bright, bright blue: *No one cries/when you FRYYYY YYYYYYYYYYYY*

Morgan's in her room with Alicia, drinking iced tea while getting ready to go somewhere. Amie leans beneath the open window, one shoulder against the rough stucco, a dead bush poking the side of his leg. They talk about their dumb jobs, community college, Alicia's asthma. Morgan's hand trembles on the mascara wand; the wand jerks.

Shit, she yelps.

What is it?

Nothing, I just felt it for a moment, Morgan says, wiping her eyelid with a tissue.

Does it hurt?

It's weird.

You can really tell now, Alicia says, giggling at Morgan's belly. Your bump is super cute.

Ugh.

No, seriously, it is!

It's actually not, Morgan says. Her phone pings; she squints.

What?

Morgan shakes her head. Nothing.

Alicia grabs Morgan's phone, grimacing when she sees Amie's name.

Ugh. Just block her.

I don't want to be mean.

It's not mean if someone is being a complete psycho.

It's not really her fault.

Alicia rolls her eyes. That stuff with her parents happened, like, four years ago. She can't expect people to feel sorry for her forever.

Morgan dips a brush into a pan of green shadow, pinning one eye closed with her pinky. But, like, she's the one that found her mom like that, you know? In her actual *house.* I just think it must be kind of hard.

Everyone's life is hard.

Morgan blinks at her reflection. I guess.

Well, whatever, Alicia says, pulling her hair off her neck. She needs to stop stalking you.

Morgan's phone pings again. She turns off her phone, wincing. Ow, God. Makeup is swept back into bags; the girls leave the room.

Amie touches his stomach. His baby can punch around all it wants, he doesn't mind. He slides around the back of the house, glancing at Morgan's mother through the kitchen window as she covers a chicken with a sheet of foil. He's spent so many afternoons inside this house, listening to pop music and doing his nails or looking through magazines while Morgan's mother poured soft drinks and cut up Little Debbie cakes. He skirts the concrete lip of the tiny pool, where he'd watched Morgan swim, back when they were eleven, twelve, knees tucked against his chest, the sun hammering the water as blood wormed its way from his nose to his chin; he didn't even know it was happening until a drop hit the water and Morgan screamed for no reason. It was a luxury, he thought, to scream like that, to bleed only as much as you could stand to lose. Kneeling, Amie holds his hair back and spits into the deep end; his saliva floats, like the laughter from the open window.

A remarkable thing about Amie's body is that its thighs don't touch. Not even now. Pregnancy has not put a pound on it. Why don't you gain any weight? they say. Do you throw up? Are you engaged? Are you going to college? Aren't you a virgin? Alicia waits in the corner of the bathroom, her shoulder against the wall, arms crossed beneath her flat chest.

Is it a boy or a girl? she asks.

In the cavity of your mutilated thigh/I see myself/a fucked-up eye, Amie whispers to himself.

Morgan's mouth falls open. What?

Amie laughs. Oh, it's a surprise! he says, and the words, when he says them, sound like glitter, they burst into the air and fall over the girls in the bathroom, and he walks through the sparkles and out into the hall, there is no fresh air in the entire school, the baby needs to breathe, so he goes outside and unwraps the headphones from his iPod.

He texts Morgan to ask how she's feeling. Morgan never writes back. He switches to email, Facebook, instant messenger. Eventually Alicia texts him. Amie's eye skips down her words as he scrolls: *Pathetic, help, desperate, attention* etc. Amie stretches his arms above his bed, yawns. Turns his head to look out the window. A bird pecks on the glass, hard; a crack immediately darts across the old glass, like a shot of lightening. Why do you have to explain what's happening to anyone? You don't even have to explain it to yourself.

There are blue balloons lining Morgan's driveway. Amie follows them to the backyard, where tables have been set up, piled with gifts in blue paper, blue-frosted cupcakes, and blue punch. There are a lot of people from school, of course, but also people Amie doesn't recognize, relatives and people from wherever Morgan and her boyfriend work, all dressed up. Alicia and Jared are sitting by the pool, their back to Amie; Alicia whispers something in Jared's ear, giggling and squeezing his arm. Amie smiles at whoever looks at him, standing in the middle of the lawn with his gift clasped in front of his flat stomach.

Hi Ms. Jordan, Amie whispers, and the mother smiles wide and says, Why Amie, it has been a while! Amie leans into her embrace. If Ms. Jordan is panicked about her daughter getting pregnant or married so young Amie can't tell. She just looks happy. The mother grabs Morgan and ushers her to Amie, saying, Look who's here!

Hi, Amie says. I got this for you.

Um, thanks, Morgan says flatly. Morgan's mother takes the box.

Isn't this wrapped so pretty! How sweet you are, Amie. And you look so grown up, gosh.

Amie smiles. Ms. Jordan squeezes Amie's wrist before scooting off to put the gift with the others. Morgan crosses her arms.

Who told you about the shower?

No one.

Morgan raises a brow. No one . . . ?

I just heard. I texted you.

Look, you kind of need to be invited to these things. You don't just . . . show up. There's limited, like, food and everything.

Oh, I won't eat anything.

Okay, but that's not really the point.

I just figured . . . since we were friends . . . and we're both expecting . . .

Well, the thing is, we're not.

I don't know. Seems like we are, Amie says.

A fine mesh of perspiration spreads over Morgan's chest, partially darkening her yellow dress.

Amie, do you know how to take a hint?

What hint?

A bird flies straight into a balloon, popping it. The guests gasp, then laugh. I don't want to deal with this right now, Morgan says, hands fluttering near her face. I'm really, like, overwhelmed.

Sorry, Amie says. But I'm so happy for you.

At the pool, Alicia glares at Amie, pulling her feet out of the water. It's funny that Alicia acts like she owns Morgan when Alicia didn't even know Morgan until the tenth grade. Amie leans forward, almost on tiptoe, fingers whispering against Morgan's elbow.

Good luck with everything, he says.

Amie does a post about all the times members of Nadir have passed out on stage. At every concert they beat the shit out of each other, themselves, the audience, or they let the audience beat the shit out of them. They start fires, piss on people, destroy their own equipment, throw trash and shit. They get banned from entire towns. GC brags that once he hit Nadir's bassist in the face with a beer bottle; others claim to have chewed flesh from the band member's arms, torn clothing from their bodies, been thrown against walls. *If I died at a concert, it would be the biggest honor of my life!!!* The tone of these accounts is rhapsodic, accompanied by cell phone photos and video clips. Amie spends the entire day sorting through the chaos, cropping images and zooming in on the details to be re-posted in an enormous collage: Wrists and arms and legs gouged with corkscrews, slit with razorblades, bodies sprawled on the dark floors of graffitied bars, most of them in Germany. The collage takes on the shape of one of Amie's soundscapes: there are patterns everywhere, weirdly soothing. He gets lost. Everyone looks the same—either they don't feel anything, or they feel too much, on purpose, he's not sure which. But it's beautiful.

A loud knock on the door. Amie is in the kitchen, laying two long slices of pickle onto a piece of bread. Greg gets up from the couch, opens the door, then shuffles heavily to the kitchen.

Someone wants to talk to you.

Okay. He licks a drop of pickle juice from his finger. He has to turn sideways to get past the stepdad; still, their bodies touch. At the half-open door Amie glances through the crack; it's Jared, hands shoved in his pockets, his trashy Honda idling at the curb. Amie steps out onto the porch, closing the door gently behind him.

You need to stop trying to contact Morgan, Jared says.

Amie shrugs. Okay.

Yeah, because it's really freaking her out.

Why?

Because you're acting like a weirdo. He keeps shifting his weight, moving his hands inside his pockets.

How so?

Jared blinks. Everyone knows you're lying.

Amie cocks his head. Oh, really?

Yeah. You don't even look pregnant, you look—like a fucking skeleton.

Amie laughs. I know. The baby is really small.

Jared rubs his face with both hands. Have you even gone to a doctor?

Why would I go to a doctor?

Because that's what you *do*. Jesus. It's like you don't even know how it works.

I don't need a doctor, Amie says.

Jared looks over his shoulder, caught between wanting to leave and wanting to say something that will force Amie to say something that makes sense. Amie leans his head against the doorframe.

What's really on your mind, Jared?

Shut up, he snaps, then pauses before lowering his voice. Just—what you've been saying is so fucked up. You need to understand that.

What have I been saying?

That I'm—that I'm the, fuck, that I'm the—father, he scoffs, rubbing his head with shaking hands.

Who said that?

You! *You* said that.

Huh.

Stop smiling, it's not funny.

I'm not smiling.

I never even touched you, Jared says.

Amie stands there. Jared shakes his head.

This is bullshit.

Amie sighs. Do you want to know?

Know what?

Who the father is.

I don't fucking care.

I know, but I just figured it out.

You what?

I just—I know now, Amie says, and then laughs. He gets on his tiptoes and puts his mouth against Jared's ear, breathing right into the hole. Jared jerks away. There's something about how weak Amie looks and how he doesn't seem to care how weak he is that makes Jared want to hit him, but he doesn't, probably because he thinks Amie is a girl, which is too bad, because Amie wouldn't mind getting hit. It doesn't matter, he wants to say, everyone is free to do whatever they want, and that's the whole point.

You are literally insane, you know that, Jared breathes.

It's complicated, Amie says. But you'll see.

See what?

Amie shrugs. It would be nice, if you were the dad, he says. Because you're beautiful, you know? But don't worry. You're not.

Jared turns and jumps the porch steps; he wants to get as far away from Amie as he can, so he can take out his phone and tell everyone that the father of Amie's nonexistent baby is a death metal band.

Morgan gives birth to a boy and plasters Facebook with photos. Amie downloads one of the photos, blows it up, then prints it out. On the photo he writes, *He's amazing!! Congrats!!! Love, Amie.* Then he puts it in an envelope with Morgan's name in big curly letters and bits of blue ribbon along the edges. Then he scratches out Morgan's name and writes *Amie.* Then he scratches that out, too. He knows the baby is not his baby. He knows Morgan is not his friend. There's nowhere to send this beautiful envelope.

Amie will graduate in a couple hours. When he gets a job, when he moves away, when he starts life over somewhere new, what will the mirror say? Amie is a name a dead person gave him. Well, two dead people. It had meant something to them, but he isn't sure what; they never told him. He writes AMIE in bubble letters on the outside of his notebook. He has really nice handwriting, large, cheerful; he got straight As in penmanship in grade school. He gets As in everything. He retraces the letters, the lines making deep troughs on the paper. He shaves his legs, sitting on the lip of the tub and mowing paths into the cream with the razor. He does his arms, the pits, the upper lip. No nicks. Earbuds in. *Do you know who I am?* Amie sings, under his breath. He's always had a beautiful voice. He puts on his graduation dress, which is white with blue flowers, curls the ends of his hair so that it falls in soft waves over his shoulders. Out in the yard he can hear Chrissy slobbering at the bushes. He walks past Greg tying up the trash on his way out the door. Bye, Amie says. The door slams.

There are hordes of people in the auditorium, almost everyone he has ever known. Near the door Morgan is fussing with the sleeves of her robe; Jared is sitting on a folding chair, laughing. Amie tries to find his seat, according to a list handed to him, but he can't find an open spot; he scans the rows, solid with knees, caps, hands, stares. His name comes right after Alicia's, but there are people sitting on both sides of her. It's okay, he thinks; there is room in the back to stand.

Excuse me, he says, trying to exit the row, but his foot strikes another foot, and he falls, meeting the floor with his stomach, then his chin. Alicia gasps; someone laughs. There is blood in his mouth, sharp pain in his pelvis. He tries to breathe. A long silence.

Are you okay? Alicia asks, bending in her seat. Amie doesn't get up. His mother had lain, just like this, three years ago, on the floor of their kitchen, the only recognizable thing left of her head a single brown eye adrift in a sea of brain, an eye as wide as Amie's when Amie's father, his mouth around a gun, pulled the trigger a second time.

Amie, Alicia says, touching his shoulder, gentle at first, then roughly, panic stiffening her fingers. Amie's ears burn; his vision tessellates, black and purple, then white, then gold. *How,* he wonders, when there is no music?

I'm okay, he says, sitting up, slow, reaching beneath his robe. It's true: between his thighs he's completely clean—no blood, no water, everything where it should be. Safe. A teacher and some others gather around him, saying things. The room continues to roll itself into glowing folds; the music comes. *No one,* Nadir screams, *can destroy what is not meant to be destroyed.* Amie laces his hands over his belly, the gold soft, relentless. There is so much love inside Amie. It is growing all the time. And he is strong enough to keep it there, until it is ready, someday, to be born.

THIS IS NOT A GAME

VINCENT KOVAR

MARIUS HAS ALWAYS felt alone. He felt alone when he was the only kid in his class with such a peculiar name. His parents didn't name him Mark or Mike or Matt like the other boys in the alphabetical roll call. He wasn't like those other boys in a lot of ways. He still isn't but, in the intervening decades he had—slowly at first—met others: boys and guys and dudes and then men, so many men [*it's raining men, hallelujah!*] who were—are—even more flamboyantly queer than Marius had ever been.

After a few more ever-shortening years, the rain slowed to a sprinkle. Then finally dissolved back into a frustrated haze as an aging Marius slunk back into the shadows of the last bathhouse in the shrinking gayborhood. He'd no longer been ashamed of his identity but instead, repulsed by the flaccid and unrequited attractions of age.

Then came Daniel.

Onyx haired Daniel. Seven percent body fat Daniel. Daniel, whose tawny skin embraced a parade of friends while shunning so much as a hint of a freckle, slackness, or sag. Daniel, whose chest hair was still dark, spandex velvet drawn over bowstring muscles.

Marius gave these comparisons a great deal of thought and stretched the metaphors across the twenty one years that separated Daniel's thirty-second birthday from Marius's unfrosted, uncandled, fifty-three.

Daniel is sitting across the gym, in a plastic chair somewhere behind and to the right of Marius's unforgiving seat.

Never skip leg day. A good set of glutes makes everything more comfortable.

THIS IS NOT A GAME

They are sitting in a gym. The varnish and painted strips of the floor are long worn away. Only one of the four hoops that once perched in the positions of the cross remains, netless and several panes of the milkglass windows are poked through, the desert breeze stirring up hints of dust and mildew; sweat and testosterone; great, gulping sobs and the lifelong, acid tang of shame.

It is less a gym, really, and more properly a multipurpose room; a room among whose multipurposes have included sport yes, but also other assorted, gender-appropriate activities. Learning to walk with a swagger rather than a sashay [*and now you must sashay . . . away*]. It was a room for Bible study, a room for circled chairs of group "therapy," and maybe even for the odd non-denominational exorcism or two.

Marius wants a cigarette.

Daniel doesn't smoke.

Of course.

Except "vaping" cannabis.

Of course.

The young have even sanitized sin. Maybe that is what makes this surreal, definitely controversial experience attractive to Daniel and the other twenties to thirties. They are mostly post something and that post list is extensive: post-capitalist, post-Facebook, post-colonial, post-gender normative, post-hankie code, and post-most-everything Marius understands.

The multipurpose room's current purpose is hosting around forty people for a Nordic-Style LARP: a live action role-play which a slick website described as,

"A collective reenactment where participants (called "rehabbers") co-create the therapy, evangelizing, educational exercises, and challenges of identity of a homosexual-to-heterosexual 1970s conversion facility. The experience will explore questions of sexuality through the dual lenses of social construction and essentialism."

"Sam? Sam?" The speaker on stage jolts Marius out of his thoughts. Sam is the name of the character Marius is inhabiting for the next four days. Everyone in the room, from the rehabbers to the so-called counselors are play-acting using different names, often even different genders from their "outside lives."

The speaker's character, Hawley, is prominently displayed in black marker on a blue card inside a plastic holder pinned to a blue sweater. Blue is for boys, Marius remembers.

There is no such term as cis-gendered during the LARP but, of course, that concept wasn't in use during the 1970s. In the outside world, Hawley has another name and would—probably—identify as a female or female leaning gender-queer. Here, Hawley is a man, a hair slicked back with Brylcreem, belt buckled with a Texan star, country-brand jeans wearing man. Blue tag.

In the persona of Hawley, the rehabber radiates the kind of unstable bully aura that fills the room, a bully whose moods and actions are unpredictable. Hawley is a mix of oily charm and soft-voiced sadism.

Immediately upon Hawley's taking the stage, the chairs became more uncomfortable and no one dares to look away. His very presence is invasive.

"Sam? When was the last time you had impure thoughts?" Hawley prompts again.

This morning. In the woods on the way to orientation. With Daniel. Daniel who was reluctant but agreed when Marius claimed it was, "preparation. To get it out of our systems."

Aloud, Marius says, "a week ago-"

"That's a lie!" Hawley's voice jumps in volume, and *he* glowers down from the stage at Marius-*cum*-Sam with an expression that combines the lip curl of repulsion, the crunched forehead of judgment, and the bright eyed satisfaction of catching someone else in an obvious falsehood. Then Hawley smiled thinly.

Marius heard that the woman playing Hawley was a social worker in real life. What an odd role to play here. Did she choose it or was it assigned?

"Why are you lying? Wait. Before you answer, I want you to stand up, turn to face the group and list everyone you're lying to. Then tell us why you're choosing the identity of a liar."

Marius stands, surprised at his unsteadiness, surprised at the echoes his mind conjures from the multipurpose gym. *[Smear the queer! Smear the queer!]* Marius reminds himself he is a senior director of a billion-dollar video game company. He owns an electric sports car. *[Sissy]* He Just upgraded to a larger house with a bigger yard and a dual view of water and mountains. *[Fag]*.

We need to encourage our brother." Hawley goads the group. They begin. Murmurs at first then louder, louder even than his memories. Marius being chosen last for sports teams; snickered at when he asks the girls to dance.

Slowly, he is buoyed to his feet on acrid memories of Ralph Polo Green knockoffs. Marius turns, feeling the prickles of his face blushing.

"I suppose, I am—"

"You suppose?" Hawley's surprisingly masculine tones lash Marius. The group lets out a low, Pentecostal moan of disappointment and scorn.

"I am," Marius corrects. "Lying to myself."

"And?"

A sturdy woman in her early 20s with a short, severe haircut clutches a small cross on a chain like it was a string of pearls. [*Bulldyke*]

The slur is a whisper in Marius's mind and he is doubly disgusted at himself.

"And . . . God? I am lying to . . . God?"

"You sound unsure." The group shake their collective heads. Is that boy in the corner muttering in tongues? Maybe he is from the South. Who still does that? Others raise upturned palms to incandescent bulbs trapped in cages far above.

"I am lying to God. Yes." Does lying to God in a LARP count as a lie? Presumably God is familiar with the twenty-five page orientation PDF detailing that the organizers are not liable for damage, physical, spiritual, nor psychological and the agreement to abide by the gameplay rules, safewords, consents, and simulations. Rufus Wainwright joins Marius's mental Zoom call. [*If God had a name, what would it be? And would you call it to his face?*]

Wait. That's Joan Osbourne.

"And?"

And Rufus Wainwright sings Hallelujah. [*I've heard there was a secret chord. That David played and it pleased the Lord*]. Marius is just trying to please an amateur actor of unknown orientation, LARPing a character identifying as a man recently "converted" to heterosexuality.

"Myself. I am lying to myself and God."

"Is Sam correct?" Marius glances back to see Hawley in full-televangelist mode, arms wide. Creepy smile frozen firmly in place.

"No!" The sturdy cross-clutcher to Marius's right (her name

tag is blue and reads "Chad") shouts it so loudly Marius's gut spasms in a very unmasculine startle.

The crowd is in full tent-revival mode, re-enacting behaviors they are too young to have witnessed in person. They must have prepped with YouTube videos from the age of fake faith healing, big hair, and even bigger scandals.

"No. Sam, you're lying to everyone here. I want you to walk up and down each row and look each person in the eye. I want you to greet them by name saying 'My name is Sam. I am choosing to be free of homosexuality by admitting my previous choice was to lie.' Then ask for each person's forgiveness and offer to shake the hands of the men, and only the men."

Though he knows this is part of the orientation, Marius still feels an adolescent's combination of inexperience and shame. The person-by-person mini-humiliations will introduce him to the other participants while also solidifying their assumed identities.

The first is blue-badge Chad, who unfurls his hand from the cross long enough to give a reluctant shake. Chad's hand is hot, unnaturally hot, almost burning.

"I've lied to you, Chad." Marius intones his punishment. "I've also lied to myself and to God."

Chad jerks their hand away. Yes, it is easier if Marius uses the gender-neutral pronoun, even in his thoughts. [*It worked for Chaucer*].

"That's not right." Chad turns to Hawley and bawls out to the room. "He's not doing it right."

"Try again." says Hawley. Daniel is looking away, deliberately.

"My name is Sam. I am choosing to be free of the curse of homosexuality by admitting I lied."

Chad looks exasperated, like they are about to go full Karen and make a cell-phone call to the police. But they can't. All the participants' phones are in individual out-of-game cubbies in the "safe space."

Hawley says, "Close enough," and Marius moves on.

The exercise is tricky, like one of those party games where you have to read the word green off a purple card only sometimes the word is typed out in white. Each rehabber in the LARP may or may not have a gender identity written on the name tag different from their presentation. The red-blue color coding doesn't help. There are no transmen nor transwomen in the group reminding Marius that this simulation is, in itself, a type of privilege. To be able to play-act your torment requires a greater distance, a dose of assimilation, and a sense of safety.

Robin, wearing an anachronistic, Green Day t-shirt passes okay. "I forgive you," she responds. "For we are all sinners in the eyes of the Great God. May you open your mouth to the benediction."

Marius remembers not to shake her hand.

He suspects many of the character names have been anglicized. No one in the room is a Dishawn or Krishna or Pablo. Marius suspects John may actually be Jose in real life.

Marius does not meet John's eyes as they shake hands. The jet-black hair and soft eyes are reminiscent of Daniel, who remains aloof.

Keith, an attractive but very thin Indian fellow in a cowboy shirt and boots, shakes quickly and briefly as though more than a one-mississippi of touch could lead to further sin. *[two-mississippi, three-mississippi].*

Marius completes the exchange with Cat, a middle-aged woman playing at being a teenager—no shake—as well as a cis-gendered Rick. But then he messes up and sticks out his hand for Jennifer (a portly, bearded man with glasses) poorly portraying what was once called a "lip stick lesbian."

Jennifer flinches and lets out a tiny, over dramatic gasp. The worst though, is when Marius finally faces Daniel. Daniel who has somehow managed to make himself last. Daniel with whom Marius was a tangle of sweat and spit and other fluids not many hours earlier.

"My name is Marius and-" If the *ersatz* Jennifer was appalled by Marius's role-playing faux pas, Daniel is apoplectic. Though Daniel (his blue name tag reads "Jace") is silent, the furious look gushes volumes of judgment.

Don't use your old man glasses, people are looking.

Nobody cares what it used to be like.

I know you're tired but I'm going out. I'm bored. You're boring.

If you'd bought Bitcoin when you were my age, you'd be a billionaire.

When you were my age.

Daniel's age.

Marius's age.

Two lines that will never meet.

Hawley doesn't make them finish the ritual but instead, sighs and tells the group to circle their chairs around an open space. Marius kneels in supplication on the hard floor. Rehabbers create a circular wall of plastic and judgment.

About half the rehabbers, the "senior class," have been at the LARP a week longer than the rest. They lead the others in another forty-five or so minutes of "testimony" where everyone recites stories of sin from their character sheets.

Hawley repeatedly exhorts them to "open to the truth." The senior class doesn't need coaxing and immediately congeals into mob leadership of the group who all enthusiastically pile on.

Each player improvises how if they could fight against the sins of sodomy and lust and fellatio (Jennifer takes particular relish in describing her oral ministrations under bus-stop bathroom stalls) then surely, if Sam tries really, really, really hard, he can too. *[Smear the queer! Smear the queer!]*

When the circus of shaming ends, Hawley dismisses everyone for a period of free time before dinner. Marius picks up his character workbook. He can feel seeds of confusion and loathing taking root and recalling older infestations. He is half Sam and half himself.

He is both and he is neither.

Though the chalkboard just outside the double doors soberly lists the next hour as "free time," it is expected that the rehabbers will use the interlude to further develop their character arcs as guided by either one of the people playing counselors or one of the seniors.

Marius makes a line for Daniel, dodging the two color rainbow of rehabbers. Just as he draws near, Daniel spins and hisses, "Tinag! Tinag!" Then calls after Rick and John.

"Hey guys. Want to shoot some hoops?"

In the years Marius has known Daniel, the younger man has never spoken the word "hoops", let alone used it in context of what the couple referred to as the general category of "sports ball."

Before Marius can follow, Hawley appears right in front of him holding up a yellow card like a soccer referee. Or, is that hockey? Sportsball.

"Sam," Hawley says. "Yellow room." Then turns and leads the way.

THIS IS NOT A GAME

"Poor guy!" This comment comes from Cat, who squints at Marius's badge to make sure she correctly applied "guy."

During arrival, the rehabber playing Cat was wearing reading glasses but is currently avoiding them to be true to her character. Marius wonders how blind she really is. Then he wonders how blind they all are for agreeing to this bizarre experience.

"Maybe conversion just isn't for you." She seems nervous yet speaks brightly. Then she frowns as she follows how Marius's eyes dart to Daniel.

The yellow room is "out of bounds" for the LARP, a so-called safe space where rehabbers can drop their assumed identities for a time to "de-escalate" or work through issues using the "abstracted meta techniques" taught in the orientation.

As he closes the door behind him, Marius feels as though he has somehow broken the LARP with his violation of the TINAG convention. TINAG is the Alternative Reality Gamer's abbreviation for ``This Is Not A Game."

The yellow card turns out to be a ticket to a room covered in full-on, Charlotte Perkins Gilman, grimy yellow wallpaper, stamped in a bilious print.

Genuine panic accompanies a wave of nausea and Marius feels status as an older-man playing a Gen-Z game acutely. Everything is feeling less and less like a game and more and more like he's wandered into the Princeton prison experiment. Or, was it Stanford?

The creator of the LARP is already waiting, a man dressed in a black, gothic mix of non-denominational religious vestments and retro-fascist uniform. Marius wonders if the costume is reused for other LARPs set in concentration camps or *Handmaid's Tale* knock-offs. The man is not wearing a colored coded name tag so Marius assumes he identifies as a man both in and out of the game. The man appears to be in his very early thirties—like Daniel.

They are sitting at a table in front of the cubbies where the rehabbers' cell phones, wallets, and other out-of-game items are stored.

Hawley comes in behind him, closes the door, but does not sit.

"Sam, this is the Pontiff," he says. "He is both the designer and the spiritual leader of our movement." Hawley is speaking "in-game" so Marius plays along.

"Hello. Thank you for this experience. I am sure with your

guidance and the support of my fellow rehabbers, I can cure my sickness."

When he hears this whining plea for acceptance, Marius feels genuinely sick and a knot forms in his solar plexus. From behind him, he hears Hawley say, "we aren't here to cure you. A cure is not enough. You are all here to experience a full conversion."

Marius isn't sure where to look. Should he face the silent Pontiff or Hawley, who is speaking? He splits the difference, standing at an awkward right angle to both." I don't understand."

"You are holding the others back as well." Hawley continues. "Instead of being a father figure to Jace, you are expanding your self-abuse to him and causing real damage, permanent damage. Perversion aside, your age difference isn't a charming romcom, it's nearly pedophilia. You're a disgusting old man."

It takes Marius half a second to recall that Jace is the character that Daniel is playing. Then rage surges up inside him and he forgets the game.

"Who the fuck-" he starts.

"Sam, we know you anally violated Daniel in the woods outside rehab." The Pontiff says, every word woven into a lace of dark confessionals and warbling Sunday school educational films. [*Let's take the case of Jimmy Barnes. What Jimmy didn't know was that Ralph was sick, a sickness that was not visible like smallpox but no less dangerous and contagious, a sickness of the mind.*]

Wait. They called him Daniel. They used his real name.

Marius-Sam's vision pulls everything into fun house mirrors of distortion, then saturates everything with orangey-red before bleaching out to black.

Though he can see Hawley and the mysterious Pontiff, Sam has never felt so alone.

He wants to sleep but the screaming is giving him a headache.

The screaming stops when Sam feels a thick cylinder of something fleshy fill his mouth and throat. He can't breathe. He is suffocating.

Then Hawley says, "swallow, bitch."

THIS IS NOT A GAME

It's 6:30 a.m. when Sam joins the others outside in a recently mown field. The rusty metal of a soccer goal lies broken and collapsed at one end.

Hawley appears bright and freshly scrubbed though he is wearing a pair of vintage aviator sunglasses that hide his eyes.

"Who can tell me why we are up so early?"

Several of the senior class shout, military style, "To keep our hands off our morning temptation!"

Sam hears himself join the response. How had he known that? The moment of doubt squirms between his stomach and breastbone uncomfortably, then it passes.

The rehabbers are getting a "body orientation" lesson, to teach them how to properly inhabit their vessels.

In front of the group, Keith, the Indian guy, is being scolded for how he walks in cowboy boots.

"Those aren't high heels princess," Hawley mocks.

Everyone laughs. Sam laughs too. From the corner of his eye, Sam sees Jace turn away, visibly repulsed.

One by one, they all turn, as if on some imperceptible cue, isolating Keith behind a wall of backs. Several of the seniors and a few of the newer rehabbers spit on the dewy grass.

[*Tis an unweeded garden, That grows to seed; things rank and gross in nature. Possess it merely.*]

The unwelcome words float up in Sam's mind and he pushes them down into the pit at the center of his torso.

Hawley taps his shoulder and shoves a yellow-card into his hand. Both he and Keith are summoned back to the Yellow Room.

As Sam turns to go, he sees Jace laughing with John. They exchange some unheard comments and laugh again.

Sam imagines them both naked, twined together, laughing. He imagines John's thick tongue filling Jace's throat. They are disgusting. They are the ones that should be getting sent to the Yellow Room.

When they arrive at the door to the Yellow Room, only Keith is allowed inside. The Pontiff stands in the doorframe, preventing Sam from following.

Marius resents the young man, the creator and leader. He resents the Pontiff's youth, how he looks at Marius and sees only who the older man might have been.

The Pontiff's gaze silently counts off the wrinkles at the corners of Marius's eyes and mouth. The gaze quietly buries Marius's worth beneath the sedimentary lines that count down the decades on his forehead.

The Pontiff smiles as he closes the door from the inside and Sam can see that man has no teeth. The man's gums are black and, after the door closes, his breath leaves a noticeable smell of rot in the air. *[Things rank and gross in nature.]*

Sam shakes his head to clear the intrusive thoughts, closing a mental door but the smell of decay remains.

Sam assumes he is meant to guard the Yellow Room as the counselors use one of the approved meta-techniques to guide Keith to better participation. During orientation, Keith explained that his character—or was Keith the character?—had been bashed outside a queer bar and arrived at rehab covered in bruises.

"Sam? Are you thirsty?"

He turns to see Cat holding out a glass of cola. The glass is green and bubbled. His parents had a set when Marius was a kid. Very seventies. It's only after he's drank the whole thing that he notices the woman has none herself. Then, someone is screaming in the Yellow Room and Sam-Marius hears the hollow, meaty thuds of someone being beaten. He turns back to the woman but Cat is gone and the empty, green-bubble glass shatters on the linoleum floor.

He's begun to measure the severity of his food poisoning in toilet flushes.

Jace's head pops into the bathroom stall. "Are you okay?"

"Yeah," Marius replies. "Just something I ate. Or something." Marius decides to play along. TINAG. "Your name is Jace, right?"

Though Marius can't be positive, he is almost sure that it is the authentic Daniel, not the character Jace, who whispers into his ear. His Daniel. His ear. No TINAG nor role-play, no meta-game LARPing. The distance between Marius and his boyfriend melts, thaws, and resolves itself into the familiar scent and touch of Daniel.

"Meet me after lights out. At the back door to the gym." Then Daniel darts away.

It is the fantasy the LARP website promised, the moment when long lost fantasies of the guy you crushed on painfully and silently in High School says the forbidden thing his real version would never say. Blue tags do not love blue.

It's dark behind the milk-glass windows as Marius emerges from the bathroom. A cheap, plastic clock has been tacked up next to the ancient and unworking electric model behind its wire cage.

It is nearly, but not quite, lights out. A few minutes of anticipation. A few moments of drama. Marius stops.

Someone was screaming before.

Someone was being beaten.

He walks down the dim and dingy halls to the door of the Yellow Room. There is a clean circle on the linoleum, its circumference outlined by a smear and the tiniest, tiniest shard of green glass.

The air is foul.

Marius reaches for the knob, its brass almost worn away by the twists of a hundred hands. How long has the Yellow Room been as it is? Was the ironic wallpaper installed by the designers or is it a remnant of the original conversion crazies?

The air inside is worse, smelling of shit and whatever awful pus comes out of burst cysts. Marius had one of those. Daniel made him go to the dermatologist to get the entire thing cut out of Marius's shoulder.

He still had the scar.

Two hours ago, Marius had intended to come here to retrieve his phone and keys. He'd intended to leave Daniel and the LARP. He'd intended to see that, when Daniel came home, he'd find all his things packed into a van.

This is not a game. Marius thinks. My life is not a game. In another year or two, Marius would be over 55, able to retire but past the age when love would arrive in any form other than an hourly rental.

Being gay is hard. Being old and gay is monstrous.

But now, he knows Daniel's behavior was just part of the game.

As for the Yellow Room, though noxious, it shows no signs of blood or beatings. Like their mock-estrangement, the scene was just another plot point in the LARP narrative.

Marius nearly turns back but can't resist the urge to check his cell phone for messages. He doesn't remember which cubby is his, so he rifles through several. In the one labeled, "Cat" he finds a satchel. Again, he can't resist.

It contains an employee badge for something called the Queer Defense League, an organization Marius has never heard of. Cat's real name is printed across the top, Anne Marshall, and her title "outreach and intervention" is just below in a very unqueer sans-serif font. In the bottom of the bag is a vial half full of brown, viscous liquid. Drugs?

The bag also contains Cat's phone.

Remembering a trick Daniel taught him, Marius powers on the phone and uses the photo on Anne's badge to unlock it. Something about the way she spoke to him earlier sparks his interest. He can't say exactly what.

In the gallery of the phone are a number of photographs of newspaper articles and pages from academic journals.

They all feature pictures of a man who looks like the LARPer playing the Pontiff. They couldn't be the actual man, Marius notes, as several of the clippings date back to the early 1950s. The man never ages. The deep fake is brilliant.

A color image from the 60s shows the man's look-a-like in midstep between an old model black car and a cinderblock building. Someone has written, "Paperclip?" in pen across the lower edge.

Operation Paperclip. A secret smuggling operation by the United States to sneak out Nazi scientists after World War II. The LARPers not only reuse costumes but props and probably storylines.

The battery icon is near empty, and Marius also notices time on the tiny clock in the corner of the display. It is time to meet Daniel. Marius remembers to power off the phone and replace it and the satchel back in the cubby.

Just as he reaches the door, Marius turns back and completes his search of the other cubbies. The entire situation is fucked up. He re-resolves to get both his and Daniel's belongings and drive them home tonight.

The car keys are gone.

Daniel's cubby is empty.

THIS IS NOT A GAME

Marius jogs through the empty halls, circling around by the kitchen to avoid the dormitories. This is a game, he reminds himself. This is just a game.

This is part of it all, isn't it? This sneaking out? This escape room scenario? Maybe the two of them are supposed to run off into the night and drive to self-acceptance.

Maybe they'll be met at the gate leaving the facility with a hotel voucher and instructions for coming back for some kind of after-party breakfast.

Maybe.

Daniel will know. Without instruction sheets or user manuals, Daniel always knows.

If he does know anything about the plot twist, Daniel doesn't say when Marius meets him, meets the character Jace, that is, outside the gym.

Sam starts to ask Jace about what he found in the Yellow Room, about Anne, and the Queer Defense League, and the photoshopped pictures of an ever-young Pontiff tagged with a Nazi reference.

But Jace presses his finger to Sam's lips and then dashes off into the shadows.

Together, they sneak away from the main buildings and into the surrounding woods. At first, Marius thinks they are going back to their car but instead they wind their way through tall trees and ferns. Here and there small money trees flash their coin like seed pods yellowly and Marius is reminded of the wallpaper in the Yellow Room. He says nothing.

After a while, they arrive in a small clearing.

John is already there, waiting. John is naked and lying on a blanket. He is not smiling.

"They really let you have it yesterday, didn't they?" John says. It is not a question. He rolls over and the moonlight slides over his curved pre-forty buttocks. "Maybe now you'd like to give it to me." That is also not a question.

Marius is annoyed. He will not think of Daniel as Jace anymore, not here next to naked, young, gorgeous John. Marius drags his eyes away from John to confront Daniel and sees that his boyfriend is now also naked, clothes lying in a rumpled pile in the sparse grass. He hangs up his flashlight on a nearby pine tree and pushes Marius toward the other man.

Marius is angry. He feels abandoned and ashamed but he also knows the protocol of a three-way with two men better looking and much younger than himself.

He knows the necessity of following Daniel's wishes in sex. If Marius can't keep up, he will be left behind. Even so, he waits for one of the younger men to take the lead. Jace pushes him again, so forcefully that Marius falls onto the blanket and knows that this isn't Daniel acting now but his character Jace. Daniel is never so dominant.

According to the website and the rules laid out in orientation, sex isn't supposed to be real in a LARP but rather, one of the carefully consensual meta-techniques that function as stand-ins for the real thing. This is not a meta-technique.

No one brought any of the usual accessories for sex: condoms, lube, poppers. They use spit and determination.

Marius finds himself in the unfamiliar bottom role, Jace mounting him from behind. John kneels in front, thrusting himself into Marius's mouth. Awkward tangles of elbows and knees are transformed into *[Lambada. The forbidden dance!]* a narcotic against the pain of reality.

"Daniel. Daniel stop. It hurts." Marius calls back but then his mouth is full and he is choking.

He puts up his hands to push John away but finds no hips nor belly but empty air. Something like a whole, raw liver claws its way down past his larynx.

Marius opens his eyes and sees John standing on the other side of the clearing, still naked and erect but at least ten feet away.

From somewhere behind him, Marius hears Hawley.

"Finish off, then give everyone a turn. We want to make sure it takes this time."

The man from the Yellow Room, the Pontiff, walks out of the woods and begins to strip off his vestments. He smiles, and for a brief moment Marius the moonlight shines into the leader's toothless mouth. From between those rotten lips, the barbell pupil of a goat eye glares wetly back.

John opens his mouth, too, a Devil eye stares out.

Marius bucks and struggles to turn around.

Jace opens his mouth but, still breathless, Marius cannot scream.

Sam stands, pulls on clothes he doesn't remember taking off, and follows Hawley's flashlight as it bounces towards the facility. The tongue of light licks over a long lump on the ground.

As Sam passes it, he sees that the lump is the woman acting as Cat, the woman who tried to keep him human. But to be human is to be sick.

She doesn't move so he steps over her mortal, aging coil.

His fellow rehabbers line the path, faces fresh and youthful, full of potential. Full of God.

They are clapping and between the teeth of their smiles he can see the eyes of the Lord looking back at him.

Keith's face is shadowed with bruises and blood but through broken teeth, Sam is seen. Robin, Chad, and Denise watch him pass, three eyes each. Even Jennifer, beard falling away in scabrous patches to reveal taut, youthful skin; even she applauds and grins.

Not cured but converted.

Sam opens his mouth, lips pursed, and looks back.

Sam has never felt such belonging as he does at this moment. The LARPers sitting on the plastic chairs before him aren't like him, not yet. They don't belong. But they will. Sam is like those in the back row, young and connected. And they are like him. Robin and John and Keith and Jennifer and Jace. Jace will never leave now. Jace and he are one.

The songs in Sam's head have stopped and the isolating references to popular culture. He doesn't need to keep up by learning the new acronyms or downloading the latest app. Those in the back row don't see an older man, riddled with regrets. They don't see either his potential or his missed opportunities.

Through the eyes of the God, they see what he has become.

The varnish and painted strips of the floor are long worn away. Only one of the four hoops that once perched in the positions of the cross remains and several panes of the milk glass windows are broken. Sam no longer smells what the desert breeze stirs up.

Looking down from the stage, Sam scans faces of those seeking to find meaning in their individual identities. The new ones. The ones sitting uncomfortably in the plastic chairs with binary name tags of only red or only blue.

The God pulls back in his throat as Sam opens his mouth to address them.

"For many of you, this is your first LARP so there are two behaviors you need to adopt right now.

First, you are not here to be cured, you are here to be converted.

Second, this is not a game."

ON THE PRIMACY
OF OBJECTS

CG INGLIS

THE GREATER PART of the refrigerator door is covered in magnets. There are dozens of these, of varying sizes and designs. Stuck beneath the largest is a curling stack of receipts. Under another is the menu of a restaurant specializing in noodles. There is also a postcard, held in place by a round, red magnet in the center of the freezer's door. The grainy image is that of a sheep in a field, the animal's jet-black face offset by a cloud-shaped bloom of wool.

The refrigerator's cooling mechanism is old and inefficient. Its hum can be faintly heard throughout the apartment, a sound like that of a hive of working insects. Arranged in a tight, triangular knot on top of the refrigerator are three mismatched bottles of alcohol. Whenever the mechanism shudders into life, their rattled clinking is added to the drone.

A wide partition separates the kitchen from the living room. The overhead light is off, and the refrigerator, as well as the cupboards, stove, and sink are dulled by shadow.

One corner of the living room is illuminated by a standing lamp. Behind this is a window, and to one side a glass door that leads to the apartment's balcony. The city skyline is framed within the glass.

Seated on the couch is the apartment's owner. His young guest is sitting on the floor. Between them is a low coffee table. Here and there, the table's wooden surface is marked by faint rings where a glass has been set without a coaster. A bottle of wine and two fluted glasses stand at the table's midpoint.

"You know," the owner of the apartment says. "Growing up, I mainly lived with my uncle."

The apartment owner and his guest met less than an hour ago. So far, their time together has been pleasant enough. While not exactly attractive, the apartment's owner is at least clean, and neatly dressed. The young guest has spent other nights in far worse company.

"I didn't exactly have what you'd call a happy childhood. My mom and dad were the kind of people who should never have had a kid together. Eventually things got bad enough that I wound up living with this uncle of mine. He wasn't really my uncle, but that's what he asked me to call him. I remember when he came to collect me from my parents' house, he pulled up the drive in one of those old-fashioned luxury sedans. A huge boat of a car, with a gleaming black body and chrome details. The seats were real leather, and the dashboard was framed in real, imitation wood. I'd never sat in a car like that before, and when we drove off together, I remember feeling lucky. It was a truly beautiful machine, and he kept it in impeccable order. He had a thing about order, my uncle. He wasn't an easy man to be around, but given the state of things at home, it's not like I was in any position to complain."

The young guest laughs. The story isn't exactly funny, but the apartment owner's careful pause was designed to precipitate a reaction. The guest is seated on a plush, woollen rug. Behind him is a media unit, upon which is a record player, a glass vase, and a piece of metallic art in the shape of a gourd. Mounted on the wall is a flatscreen TV. Its surface reflects the light of the standing lamp and the outline of the apartment owner's body.

"He owned an old house way out in the country," the man continues. "A big place at the end of a dirt road. People back in town must have wondered how he kept his car so clean, driving in and out of there every day. When it rained, the mud in the driveway got as deep as my ankles. But whenever the car collected so much as a speck of dust, he had me out there washing it. There was a huge bucket by the shed that I'd fill up with soapy water. My uncle would toss me a rag and that was that. I'll tell you; I spent a lot of hours washing that car. A lot of hours."

The young guest is nodding. He is acutely aware of the rattling of the bottles on top of the refrigerator. The longer he spends in the apartment, the louder the noise becomes. The rattling sets his teeth on edge, and he wishes that the apartment's owner would do something about it.

He glances at the refrigerator, a white box covered in magnets. The shadows in the kitchen are very dense, like cobwebs, the young guest thinks, and frowns; the thought arrived as if from some point outside his head. He could use another drink.

"I didn't mind so much, except for the way the water would prune my hands. My fingers went all white and wrinkled. They looked like they belonged to some old man. I'd never lived in a place with a bathtub, and cleaning my uncle's car was the only time I'd ever seen them like that. Seemed like they didn't belong to me anymore. Not that it mattered, especially. My uncle kept me at it no matter what, until the job was done. Until he was satisfied. Then we'd apply the wax. That part we did together. He insisted on it. He'd show me how, his big hands guiding mine over the metal. God, I hated that smell. The smell of the wax. It stung the inside of my nose. Got into my throat."

The bottles on top of the refrigerator continue to clink and rattle. As another round of hot gas floods its condenser coils, the mechanism's fan jerks to a sudden halt. Inside the motor there is a short belch of smoke. The bottles fall silent.

The young guest exhales.

"Do you mind if I have some more wine?"

"Help yourself."

The bottle is tilted and a dark red line of liquid spills from its mouth and into the basin at the bottom of the glass.

"My uncle used to sit and watch me work. Sometimes he'd get to talking. He said the only good thing about having another body around was that it gave you someone to talk to. Before me, he'd always lived alone. He preferred it that way. He said when he lived alone, he could always be sure where his things were. Everything in its place, and no little hands moving things around the house without permission. He was a real believer in things. He said they had a tangible reality. He liked that phrase a lot, 'tangible reality.' In his view, reality was divided into classes. There was the reality of the mind, the reality of the body, and the reality of things. That was the highest level. Back then I didn't understand. To me it seemed like my body was real enough, and I told him so. But my uncle just laughed. 'You think your body's real huh?' he said, shaking his head and laughing. It used to bother me, him laughing at me like that."

"I think my body's real," the young guest says. The carpet is very soft beneath his legs. The room has taken on the stillness of the refrigerator. He drinks a little more, the wine bitter on his tongue.

"Of course, you do," the apartment's owner says. "That's only natural. You're young. Young and beautiful. But it was like my wrinkled fingers, you remember? The white tips of my fingers after washing my uncle's car. They didn't look like mine anymore. Well, now I'm older, and I can see lines like that when I look in the mirror. Time changes us. The body changes. It gets old, and it dies. It rots in the earth."

"That's true," the young guest says mildly. Inside the refrigerator, a drop of condensed water has appeared along the posterior wall.

"But things stay the way they are. They stay true in themselves. At least they do if we take care of them. If they're preserved properly. That's what my uncle meant by tangible reality."

"Makes sense."

"Anyway, that was his philosophy. I grew up hearing all about it. Some days all I wanted was for him to shut up, but when he really got going there was no stopping him. Talking about the body being impure, about the thousand ways it fails us. I used to get so sick of it. Besides, I've always found people more beautiful than things. Don't you?"

"Oh, definitely."

"But my uncle was right about one thing. We all age. Bodies decay. There's no getting around it. So, I developed my own philosophy."

"Oh yeah?" the young guest asks. "What's that?"

The wine glass is taken from him.

"Let me show you."

They enter the bedroom. Piece by piece, the young guest's clothes are discarded on the floor. The bed is situated beneath the room's only window. Passing through the blinds, the light of the city cuts the pristine sheets into strips. The fabric is cool on the young man's chest, and his belly. His back is striped with light. The muscles in his shoulders clench.

So beautiful, the apartment's owner thinks. So worthy of preservation.

ON THE PRIMACY OF OBJECTS

Climbing onto the bed, he wraps his hands around the young guest's neck.

The refrigerator is silent. All along its shelves, beaded water is pooling. In the freezer, a young man's head begins to thaw.

STRANGE ENCHANTED BOYS

CRAIG LAURANCE GIDNEY

THE BORDER IS weird and beautiful. There, at the edge, I watch time and how it changes things. I watch things be born, watch them grow. Then I watch them decay and die. I see plants go from seed to stalk, from stalk to flower or tree. And then I watch the petals brown and wither. I see trees grow from saplings to giants with branches like arms. Then I watch them die, split by lightning, smothered by vines, blasted with blight. I see the animals in spring, the rabbit and the deer and the raccoon. They spawn, live in the summer, mature in autumn and die in the winter. And I see time paint the most fascinating creatures of all.

Humankind.

It was Petunia, or Pansy or Peony that told me to stop watching them. It doesn't matter who told me. Names are not that important here, where we are, outside of time. I think all of them spoke to me about my habit, at one time or another.

They are like ants, said Petunia.

Pansy said, *They are callous and cruel and foolish.*

They are inferior versions of us, said Peony.

And she or they are right.

Like ants they build hills made of stone and metal and swarm over the land, eating up the trees and streams, and leave them tainted and twisted. I have seen them be cruel to those of their own kind. Cruel even to their own children, for no reason at all. They look like us if we were imprisoned by time. If we could age and rot from the inside.

STRANGE ENCHANTED BOYS

Just looking at time and its effects were no longer satisfying to me. I had to actually fall into it. Peony warned me against this.

The human world was full of treachery and sorrow. You will develop attachments to things that will wither away, she said. *Consider topsoil. It is made of impermanence itself. Everything that ever was is now dirt beneath your feet.*

I asked her, *What will happen to me, if I cross the border?*

She said, *You will change, in some way. I suppose. Or perhaps not. Only by doing it will you know.*

This last statement was as much a blessing as anything she said. Perhaps she wanted me to find out to satisfy her own curiosity.

I found a glade, a grassy area surrounded by trees. I saw oaks and beeches and elms, a few scattered pines here and there. It was beautiful there, especially at night. Stars there are different than in my world. Their stars cast light from dead suns. The stars in our world are alive and brighter. It's a lonely light, redolent of the death that surrounds things touched by time. I did not choose the glade for this reason. So I went beneath the canopy of trees, to a place not kissed by dead starlight. The ground was covered in bushes and vines of kudzu. The lack of direct light did not bother me. We can see in the dark.

I moved through the brush quietly. So quiet that the foxes and rabbits I passed did not notice my passing. Maybe they saw the quiver of a leaf, or a ripple in one of the muddy puddles. Where should I go? No place seemed right for my purposes. A willow tree looked promising until I saw the starlings nesting in the branches, momentarily hidden by the beaded curtain of leaves. A giant oak tree, ancient and gnarled, caught my eye but then I smelled the whiff of blight and the thousand and more parasites that crawled in its rotting heart. I found garbage in the wood. Man-made things that would never rot, things I later learned were crockery, plastic and metal. Things that kept their shape for ages even as the people who used them died. The blight of the oak tree was infinitely preferable to those things. There is strong magic in decay. There was nothing but coldness in these man-made instruments. It burned like frost when I touched them.

I finally found a place beneath a dogwood tree that was clear from disease and rubbish. The white blossoms glowed in the dark. They reminded me of Peony's gowns, which were white and made of petals and spider silk.

I thought to myself, *What form shall I take?*

This was important. Presently, I had many limbs of varying lengths and too many eyes to pass as human. They are skittish and judgmental creatures. So I plucked out my eyes until I only had two, and shed my wings and carapace. I shortened my mandible and grew hair on my head and face and shrunk my body down and sat beneath the tree and waited.

When daylight came, things awakened, and other things slumbered. White blossoms fell, landing on my head and around my body. I felt the worms burrowing in the earth beneath me and watched the birds flit through the air above. Animals crept out of the forest and investigated me. A raccoon stood on its hind legs and gazed into my eyes, waiting for movement of any kind. A bird landed on my shoulder and splattered me with excrement. A feral cat marked me with its scent. I stayed still the whole while, acclimating to the rhythm of time. Wind rustled leaves, but not the strands of my hair. I was both in and out of the stream of time. Things grew around me. Things began to grow *on* me—mosses and lichens. This did not bother me. The discomfort was a small price to pay for the pleasure of seeing the process of entropy.

There were no measurements of time where I came from. It was eternal twilight, pastel mauve and green, the other stars burning brightly in the sky. We danced and sang in that gloaming. At times, we would break off in pairs or threes for trysts that could last for eons—hours or weeks. We feasted on acorns and honey and dew, though we were never hungry. Our existence was endless and beautiful. We never aged and never died.

It was glorious.

It was boring.

One afternoon, after I had been beneath the dogwood tree for a time, two mortals saw me. By this time, all of the blossoms had been shed by the tree and were rotting on the ground beneath. Millipedes and cockroaches scuttled beneath the sickly-sweet sludge and birds nested in the boughs. One was male, the other female. Both were in their youth. The male was slightly taller and had hair the color of walnut bark and eyes to match. The female had yellow hair and a pleasant plumpness, like ripe fruit. They wandered around the area where I was before spying me.

"What is that *thing*?" The female pressed herself against the male.

He wrapped an arm around her shoulders. "Relax, babe. It looks like a broken statue."

He let go of her and walked to me and brushed off the layer of dogwood blossoms that had built up over me. "See?" He said, stepping away, "It's one of those cherubs. Can you see the wings? Or, should I say, wing?"

The female came closer to observe me. "Are you *sure* it's a cherub? It looks like a statue of a Greek god. Cherubs are baby angels."

He looked at me again, "Babe, I know what a cherub is. I'm not stupid. It does not look like a Greek god."

"I think it's Icarus," she said. "It's a grown man, definitely."

The male scoffed. "Whatever," he said and stomped off.

She followed him, saying, "I'm just saying what it looked like to me. You don't have to get all huffy over a stupid broken statue . . . "

I heard the crunch of their retreating steps. Of course, I could have moved. I could have spoken to them. I could have become a shape that both of them agreed upon. But to what end? The mortal perception of us is inaccurate at the best of times. They both saw what they wanted to see. Maybe, what they *needed* to see. To them, I was a broken ornament, abandoned beneath a dogwood tree. Such was the visual translation of my form.

Was I, in fact, broken? Both of them had agreed on one thing, though. I had only one wing. Where was the other one?

The next mortal I encountered was in the evening, a few weeks after. By this time, it was summer, and the humidity competed with violent thunderstorms. Things rotted in the heat, and fungus grew in the damp. The music of fungal spores is discordant and muffled. It's a song full of earth and decay. During that time, several spores alighted on my form and gilled tiers of mushroom grew where my broken wing had been. A man stumbled into the woods, beneath my dogwood tree. He stank of age and what I eventually learned was alcohol. I could read his thoughts like they were written in the air. To him, I had no wings at all. He thought I was a deformed lawn jockey, rusted over and the paint chipped. A week later, a group of teenaged girls came to try out smoking cigarettes in the forest. One thought I was a broken garden gnome, and another thought I the discarded part of a fountain that featured a pissing boy. They did not compare notes because they were—there were four of them—all preoccupied with their illicit activity.

I observed these two groups, the drunk man, and the disobedient teenagers, with fascination. Human life is so fragile and so finite. It is odd that they opt to poison themselves and shorten their time on earth. They are drawn to self-destruction. In the other world, we work and harmonize with nature. Our clothes are made of living things, and we spend endless hours frolicking with the gifts bestowed upon us. We are not apart from nature. We *are* nature itself. Temporal beings seem to enjoy and hasten their own entropy.

Perhaps that is the curse of being subject to time.

I stayed beneath the dogwood tree for a few seasons. In winter, everything went to sleep, and no human visited the wood. I watched as plants and insects died and rabbits, foxes and squirrels mostly stayed in their burrows and homes. I let snow cover my form and studied the bleak landscape. I learned to love the silence. Back home, winter never comes. Death never comes. Back home, we waltz outside of time. I briefly wondered if Peony, Pansy and Petunia missed me. They probably did not miss me. *Missing* is a byproduct of temporality. And what was time to me? Summer and winter passed like a day and an evening.

I first saw Maurice in the springtime. The dogwood blossoms weren't yet open. They were still green buds. I had considered returning home when he wandered into my orbit. By this time, whatever form I appeared in was weathered. I was covered in rust, my stone was corroded, and fungus and moss lived in every nook and cranny of my form.

He was the first human visitor in a while. He was tall and lean, brown-skinned and curly-haired. But I noticed his eyes first. They were *old* eyes, eyes that saw the truth. Deep brown pools that pierced any illusion I put up. He saw what I was, even if he did not have the language for it. The second thing I noticed was the way he walked. He moved like a dancer, as if the pull of gravity affected his body differently. His stance was effortlessly graceful. There was something deer-like about him.

Fearlessly, he approached me. He spoke: "Are you alive?"

I said nothing. I was just an observer, nothing more.

He put his hand on my body, right where my chest would be.

"Let's get you cleaned up," he said. And he removed the mushrooms. I saw that he could see my wings. I had both of them in his mind's eye. He left the moss, though. "I think you would like to keep that."

It was true. I could feel the life in the green mantling my body. He rubbed the substance of my flesh until it shone.

"Did you just smile?" he asked me.

Again, I said nothing. Words are imprecise things. They just symbolize what they mean. I felt his happiness, this child of time. So I sent that joy back to him. Back home, the emotions are controlled. When you live forever, nothing is wondrous since you've seen it all before. We are a cold people. Not much moves us and we bore easily. But this young man's emotional palette had nuances I'd never felt in my long, long life. I'd forgotten what joy felt like. What kindness was. The unending feasts and orgies of that other life could not compare to what this man radiated. I could see his emotions in his brown eyes, flecks of gold, silver and blue. I could taste the emotions, their sweet honeysuckle perfume.

Enraptured, I plucked his name from his mind.

Maurice.

It was a name that reminded me of sunsets and pools of moonlight in darkened glades.

I saw other things dancing in his mind. He loved his mother, viewed her as a goddess of strength and love. He loved the food she cooked, the collard greens and moist cornbread, the pungent chitterlings, and the tender braised chicken or pork. He loved spring and autumn.

Maurice lived in the moment. When he left, I *missed* him. It was a new sensation. Even if I did not see the others back home for centuries, I would see them eventually.

Ephemerality was a heady drug.

I was aware of things changing and dying at every moment, from single-celled organisms to plants to Maurice's skin, which died and shed even in that brief, enchanted afternoon. He left as evening approached, leaving me alone in the woods. I didn't think that I would see him again, so I placed a thought in his brain, a semi-precious stone, that would remind him about me. It would spark memory of me. I went through the flurry of his thoughts, and found he was more like the people back home than most mortals were. He had the same delicacy, the same love of the natural world. It was then that I found the word he had for me. He thought that I was an angel, which is a kind of divine being. He believed that I was a sculpture of some sort, not trusting his deeper instincts. He thought that I was made of some smooth black stone and could not fathom why I was left in an obscure part of the woods. Maurice was also open to random miracles and viewed the world with wonder. All of the visitors filtered the world through a cynical eye. That's why I appeared to be broken, one-winged, and cast off. Why they thought I was garbage. Only the animals and Maurice saw closer to the truth of what I was.

He returned a couple of days later. A cold spring rain had turned the forest floor into a muddy mess. I could sense the joy emanating from him even before I saw him.

"You've changed your position," he said when he saw me. He did not ask how or why. He just accepted it.

Something was strapped to his back, a carrying case of some kind. He lay the case on a nearby rock and opened it. He pulled out a curved wooden doll that had four strings stretched across the front of its body and placed it beneath his chin. He made it speak, pulling a long wand across the strings.

What language did it speak? None I had ever heard before. It was a language without words, sound without any meaning. And yet it evoked those nuances of feeling I found to be so intoxicating. Rifling through the stream of Maurice's thoughts, I realized that this was called music and he was playing a violin. We do not have music of this type where I come from. We have silly songs, made of nonsense words strung together. It makes us laugh and laugh. But the music this youth played was mournful even if it had moments of joy. The notes hung in the air like raindrops before they splashed down. The melody crawled through the air with the erratic flight pattern of a moth. Every collection of notes evoked a memory for Maurice, one that I could see reflected on the air around him. I saw his mother, with her dark brown skin overwritten with wrinkles. I saw the face of another brown skinned boy, his dark hair shot through with red curls here and there. I saw a building full of things called books, rectangles that held worlds between their covers. The notes curved and slashed through the air, a song of knives. Other times it perfumed the air. I could have listened to it forever.

But Maurice stopped playing.

All things in this world must end.

When he left, I plucked the resonance out of the air and placed it underneath my tongue.

Maurice came with his friend, the boy with the black and red curls. At first, I was jealous. It was a new emotion for me. I did not want to share Maurice with anyone else. The word *mine* echoed around, like a bat's call in the night.

Mine.

Mine.

Mine.

The boy with the red curls was named Elijah and he declared me 'creepy.' He did not see me as an angel statue. He saw something dark and ugly. Something grotesque and deformed. He saw a gargoyle. He told Maurice, "He has claws, for Christ's sake. How can you think that thing is beautiful?"

Maurice said, "Look at his wings. His face. His eyes are lovely. Look *closer*."

Elijah peered at me for a long while. The fangs and claws he saw melted away. The pinions of the gargoyle's wings softened. Finally, he said, "It is cute, even if it's ugly."

That seemed to mollify Maurice. I found that I was no longer irritated by the presence of Elijah. There was no reason why he could not be mine as well. The two of them spent the afternoon beneath the dogwood tree. While Maurice played the violin, Elijah drew pictures with a charcoal pencil in a notebook he carried with him. I could not see what he drew but I knew what was on his mind. Petals, trees, squirrels and finally, me. I'm sure that I looked like some nightmare creature in his scrawling. This did not offend me. After all, that was a part of my nature.

The two boys spent the summer visiting the dogwood tree in the forest. They spent hours in the sun-dappled place. Only Maurice could completely perceive me but Elijah had begun to notice subtle changes. He kept these observations to himself. The hours drifted by, marked by impromptu concerts. Sometimes the two of them were together without words. They removed articles of clothing until they were bare and naked in the sun. Laughing, they played with each other's bodies, devouring and suckling fingers, nipples and then genitals until they erupted in a sticky mess. I felt the wave of glory that emanated from their prone and resting bodies.

Maurice and Elijah were not the only visitors to the dogwood tree. In addition to raccoons and rabbits, I once saw a strange parade of men tramp through the woods one night. They were disguised in white sheets with pointed hoods, the white sheets decorated with red symbols that held no meaning for me. They prowled the night with flaming torches, stinking of aggression and unwashed masculinity. I could see the hate in their hearts. It broadcast above their heads in squiggly red lines. They ignored me, unseeing and blinded by their meaningless rage. In contrast to Maurice and Elijah, there was nothing but shame and darkness in them. They did not create anything. Maybe they could not. So they destroyed instead. The earth around them filled with fire. I called them the Desecrators, not knowing then that they had another name. The name they chose for themselves was more nonsensical than the silly songs from my world.

There came a time when both groups met. My beautiful boys and the Desecrators. It was inevitable, one of the rotten things about the mortal earth and temporality.

I was just observing. The seasons, the animals, the people. The passage of time. What was any of this to me? There is no moral code where I come from. No hate, but also no love. There is joy. That, we perfected. What were these people, these mortals, to me? I tasted the range of their emotions, from the loftiest dream to the most debased desire to harm. It was all there to observe. I could not weigh one thing over another.

Or could I?

The Desecrators came upon my beautiful boys at the worst possible time. Beneath the dogwood tree, next to the statue of me, was their sanctuary. They were not naked then. Only entwined when one of the Desecrators spied them. He was out of his disguise, a boy roughly the same age as Maurice and Elijah. Unlike them, he was ugly, a pale thing mottled with raw pink and bright red acne. I knew he was one of their number by the evil he befouled the air with.

He only watched from behind a bush for one hate filled moment before he scuttled off. Maurice and Elijah did not see him.

I could have warned them, I suppose. Fallen completely into the stream of time, into motion. Maybe that would have saved them. But my motion, my animation would end my idyllic moments, and that I could not bear.

My kind stay hidden. Our world, which exists in the spaces between the mortal world, is also clandestine. That's for a reason, which you shall later see.

Let the two brown boys have their moment away from the world now. Let them explore each other, endlessly. Away from all things that would spoil their love. Let them live in arousal, where every secret place on their bodies tingle. Let the music play and the ink flow on and on.

It did not happen that day. Nor the next.

It rained one day, so no one came to the dogwood for a couple of days. Summer was almost over. There was a faint chill in the wind.

Eventually, Maurice and Elijah met up again beneath the bare branches of the dogwood. It was a lazy summer day of sketching, both on paper and on violin. They were dozing when the Desecrators came.

I heard them before my boys did.

The group walked without grace, stomping on the ground beneath their feet. Birds chattered at their passing. There weren't that many of them. Maybe six men, only one of them hooded.

The hooded one said, "What you boys up to," slow and menacing like.

The one who'd spied them said, "They was doing buggery and cornholin'"

The hooded one said, "We can't have faggots here."

Someone else said, "Nigger faggots," and spat on the ground at their feet.

Both of my boys were shirtless. Their faces were overwritten with shock and horror.

The spy said, " I saw 'em going at it by that ugly statue. Writhing and panting like high school sweethearts!"

Elijah gathered up his shirt, and said to Maurice, *"Run."*

The six white men gathered around the two boys. I could see the murder in their eyes. The six men were waiting for a chance. They stank of hate. What does hatred smell like? Of rotting things.

I had just wanted to observe the forest, its animals and the people who came here. I wanted to gather stories to tell my ageless people.

I should just silently watch this play out, the way I watched the sun rise and set. The way I watched hawks grab rabbits and mice and eviscerate them in the trees. Watch as bones and offal fell to the ground to be covered up by leaves and mosses. What were these mortal things to me? Nothing. They meant no more to me than ants did to them. Watching them entertained me. That was all. Mortals were foolish and their lives were brief. What was any of this to me?

And yet I intervened anyway.

I pulled at the invisible seams that separated worlds. The world that moved through time and the one that stayed still. I unraveled the thread of moonlight and spiderweb and parted the gossamer wide enough to fit my two boys. I pushed them inside, out of time.

Then I turned on the Desecrators.

I burrowed through the sluggish dross in their brains. I punched through the veil of silver tissue that surrounded the huge pink mass of tissue that folded upon itself endlessly. They were like fungus shot through with streaks of blight. I felt their fear and their hatred and buried near the surface was all of the evidence of their crimes. The bodies they hung on trees, and the ones they burned with tar. I placed the fear and the rage into their smooth brains, had them tunnel through their thoughts and dreams like worms.

There those voices and images would stay there the rest of the Desecrators' miserable lives.

"Where are we?" asks Maurice. He frowns at the echo his voice makes.

Elijah places his hand on Maurice's shoulder. "I have no idea," he says.

The two of them crouch behind a yew tree. I remember that it will take a moment for their eyes to adjust to the dimness here. Now that they are here, I have no idea of what to do with them.

Should I just observe them?

Or should I announce my presence?

I opt to stay hidden for a while longer. I am invisible to them, wrapped in shadow.

Their eyes acclimatize, and I see them glance up from the forest floor to the canopy above.

"Those stars," says Maurice, his eyes wide.

"They're so big," Elijah says.

"They are as large as Ezekiel's chariot."

I am unfamiliar with the reference, but our stars *are* closer than theirs. They look like orb-shaped lanterns and not merely dots of dead light.

The two of them stand and move through the glade.

"Feel the ground, Maurice," Elijah says. He brushes his fingers on the forest floor. "It's as soft as carpet."

"Do you hear that?" Maurice pauses, trying to find the source of a sound.

I strain my ears. And yes, I hear it too. Bells tinkling in wind, bells made of hollow bone and acorn. It's a shivery, silvery sound, one that soothes and protects. And beneath it, laughter. Elijah startles at the sound.

It is in our nature to be hidden. As I experienced first-hand, people perceive us in different ways. Angel, or gargoyle. Our natural form is chimerical, with wings and fur and hooves. We have eyes, ears and noses in the wrong places, as they are unburdened with function and exist purely for aesthetic reasons. I was far from the only observer of the two youths in our midst.

"I think we're in Heaven," Maurice says after a while. They find a clearing, a circle of trees where the grass in the center is new and there are large stones where they could sit. There is a feast of berries and mushrooms and other sustenance tucked in a horn-shaped basket in front of one of the stones.

"You think we're dead?" Elijah does not seem to be overly shocked at this turn of events.

"I think those crackers killed us. And now we are here."

They sit on the largest stone, where they see our moon, which is larger than theirs, and has a golden hue. It sits in the sky next to the burning jewels that are the stars. The sky is the deep blue of the blackest sapphire.

We watch the lovers from the trees. Elijah lays his head on Maurice's shoulder.

They stay like that for a long while.

Then one of their hands reaches for a bright red strawberry that promises to be summer-sweet and full of juice.

It happens all at once. I emerge from the surrounding trees in all of my terrible glory. One wing of a dove, the other of a bat. Feet shod in hooves, my head that of a goat, my eyes red as embers. Hardly a heavenly host. Maurice, my Maurice, drops the summer fruit and screams. But that's fitting—if they eat the food of our world, they will be changed forever.

Then I cast a spell made of star shine and gossamer over them and send them to sleep. Others of my kind come forth and adorn their slumbering forms with flowers and pinecones. We watch them, our two brown and ebony princes in their nest of dew-sprinkled spiderweb.

How long do we keep them there?

Forever and a day.

Forever and a day later, I split a seam between the ephemeral and the timeless and into that fissure I placed my two boys beneath the dogwood tree. It had grown in that brief passage, the trunk thicker, the branches multitudinous. The blossoms were no longer just white. A blush of pink crept along the blossom edges.

We had woven a blanket of cobwebs and leaves for them, in which they were cocooned. I waited, also beneath the tree but also unseen.

When the sun rose, their blanket melted away. Magic cannot live long in this world.

Maurice woke first, and true to his nature, he knew that time had somehow passed. When he was with us, he startled awake sometimes and I'd have to rework the spell to settle him. Maurice gazed long at the tree, taking in its growth and its majesty. Elijah slept on, his breath slowly finds its tempo.

Then he looked directly at me. His eyes could not see me. But his heart did.

He took out the violin out of the case, which still had the residue of magic.

Then, still staring at my veiled form, he cast an enchantment of his own.

BODIES ON THE DANCE FLOOR

DAN COXON

NATHAN SEES HIM across the bar, nestled in the snug. His first thought is that he should be dead. Spangles is busy tonight, the dance floor bouncing to Sean Paul and Missy G, the bar thronged with sequins and stiletto heels and white shirts that glow like aliens under the ultraviolet light. He only glimpses through the crowd, but he knows it's him. He'd recognise that ridiculous quiff anywhere.

He makes a snap decision not to go over. They were never friends. There's a pleasure to be derived from seeing a familiar face, but Peter Barclay was never one of their circle. What was it they used to call him? He can't remember, but that's no great surprise— he's so off his face that he barely recalls his own name. For an office night out, tonight has gone off the rails surprisingly quickly. He blames Donovan and the smiley pills they shared in the bleach-and-piss stink of a toilet stall.

Barcladyboy. That was it. Simpson came up with it, the memory causing a smile to creep across his face. All his mincing and the stupid hair. They did laugh.

He's still grinning as he turns to walk back to the dance floor and finds Barclay standing next to him, summoned by the memory. His drink sloshes, coating his hand with a waft of alcohol fumes. He should thump the gayboy for that, he thinks, but he doesn't. Now isn't the time or place.

"I thought that was you," Barclay says, his face pale under the club lights. Was that eyeliner he was wearing? "I saw you across the bar, and I said to myself, 'That's Nathan Priestley, so it is.' You're looking well. Big night, is it?"

BODIES ON THE DANCE FLOOR

Nathan does his best to smile, waves the half-empty glass. He has to shout to be heard above the *thud-thud-thud* of the bass. "You could say. Office party. Got a bit out of hand." He waits, but Barclay just stands there, like he's expecting more. Finally, he asks, "And you?"

"I've been here a while," Barclay says, "just taking in the scene, you know? But Nathan Priestley, as I live and breathe . . . you'll join me, right? For old times? I've got a table . . . "

Before Nathan knows what's happening Barclay has him by the elbow, and he's leading—no, *dragging* him across the bar to the corner snug. He wants to say that he's busy, that he should get back to his colleagues. That he's surprised to see Barclay here, in the flesh, given the rumour circulating last summer that he'd offed himself, a massive overdose of painkillers and prescription antidepressants in a Holiday Inn in Slough. But he says none of that. Instead, he stumbles after Barclay, the flashing lights echoing the pounding in his head, the seed of tomorrow's hangover. The seclusion of the snug envelops them like a caul.

He doesn't know how long they've sat here. It's all blurred into one: the office party, the pub, the after party, now here, with Barclay, clutching a sticky drink in a padded booth. He might have been here for hours. His phone is in his pocket, but he doesn't get it out to check the time in case the outside world should impose on this bubble.

"So have you seen any of the others lately?" Barclay has been doing most of the talking, Nathan's brain mired in a drug-induced haze. "Davison? Simpson? Charlie Lake? They were the gang you used to roll with, weren't they?"

He wants to point out that no one says 'roll with' anymore, but his tongue is slow and thick. He shrugs, shouts "No" above the hurricane from the dance floor. It's not entirely true—he ran into Davison a few weeks ago, he's working for one of the high street banks—but it's easier than trying to explain. Barclay is leaning closer than he'd like, his breath hot in his ear. He can smell his sweat, the stale fug of alcohol, and something sweet beneath it all, like rotten fruit.

"Doesn't matter," Barclay says, waving his hand about in front of his face like he's chasing off a fly. "I'll catch up with them soon enough." At least that's what Nathan thinks he says. "You're here, anyway."

The hand settles on the table, the fingers resting on top of Nathan's own. They're surprisingly cold, but he finds he's unable to pull his hand away from beneath them, as if Barclay is somehow pinning him to the tabletop. He wonders if he might be having some kind of seizure. Whatever it was that Donovan gave him is still fizzing through his brain like a firework.

"Let's just sit here for a while, shall we," Barclay says, his lips brushing Nathan's ear. "We've got a lot of catching up to do."

They're playing the same Sean Paul song again. Its rhythm beats against Nathan's skull like a tattoo, and he almost convinces himself that it never ended, they've stuck it on an endless loop and no one has even noticed. He's sure he must be mistaken. These songs all sound the same when the volume's high enough.

Barclay's fingers are still on top of his. They don't feel so cold now, although he can't tell whether that's because they've warmed up or his own have chilled. The feel of another man's hand repulses him, but he's stuck in place.

This isn't the first time Barclay's hand has touched his. They were in Year Seven together, when they first came to Brookmere, and they had a couple of play dates before Nathan fell in with a different crowd. He remembers sitting on the beige carpet of Barclay's bedroom, a Monopoly board laid out between them. Barclay reaching out to move the boot and finding his hand instead, just for a moment, his fingers brushing gently, tentatively across the skin. They had been warmer then. They'd both known what it meant, but it was never mentioned. He'd met Simpson a few weeks later and that had become his social circle. The rugby lads—the quartet of him, Simpson, Davison, and Charlie—stealing beer from their dads' stashes, hounding the girls on the bus home until they gave them their numbers. That had been an entirely different world to the bedroom and the Monopoly board.

He'd never told them about him and Barclay, their stillborn friendship. When Davison started mocking him at break one day—mincing as he walked, one hand pulled up to his chest, the other flapping like that ridiculous quiff from his forehead—he'd laughed along with the others, joined in with the mimicry and the names.

BODIES ON THE DANCE FLOOR

If any of them noticed that he held back as they sashayed up the corridor together, they didn't mention it. He'd like to think he did it out of kindness, but he knows he was afraid they'd see something in him, some weakness that would mark him out as their next target—or, worse, as Barclay's friend. Nate and Barclay sitting in a tree.

The bar lights are strobing, and Nathan thinks he might be sick. His head is giddy with the booze and the pills, the thumping bass, the stink of Barclay beside him. If anyone from the office sees him now, or if word gets back to Simpson, somehow, through the gossip network . . .

"It's okay," Barclay says, his fingers sliding into Nathan's palm, his hand gripping tight. "Everything is different now."

He thinks he's been here a week, maybe more. Time has ceased to mean anything. The music still thuds against his ears, the lights still flash and dance, sending rainbow waves across the floor. In one hand he holds his unfinished drink. In the other, Barclay's fingers.

In all that time, he hasn't seen a single person from the office. There are still bodies at the bar, but at some point, they have lost all trace of identity. Faces featureless and bland, mannequins whirled around and around without end. The roar of their voices has become one with the music. He thinks he is holding his breath, until he realises that he isn't breathing at all.

When he looks at Barclay's face, he sees the coloured lights play across it, animating it with shadows, but otherwise it looks pale and still, a waxen image of the boy he once knew. The eyes are unlit, black holes drilled into his face. Those five fingers, so cold.

He sees everything and nothing. The music never ends.

DINOSAUR ON THE 18ᵀᴴ HOLE

KAITLIN TREMBLAY

"**T**HERE'S NO WAY that's what you actually think they're called," Max laughs, her lips twitching in that subtle way that somehow manages to make her mouth double in size.

"I'm serious!" I defend myself, stealing the briefest of glances her way before returning my eyes to the road in front of us. "That's what we called them all the time as kids."

"Goofy golf?"

"Yes!"

"*Goofy* golf?" Max asks again, this time with more emphasis in both tone and expression.

There are no cars behind us or in front of us for miles. Nothing but the highway, warmed by the early morning sun of the late summer. We do these drives out of the city because our condo is claustrophobic, all small walls and windows that don't lock. I don't sleep, which means Max doesn't sleep, which means by the early morning on the weekend, we're both frazzled and frustrated. The weekend drives are her idea. When the sun rises, we get into her car (trading turns on who has to drive) and roam around the county until the sun begins to set again. We try to steal a few hours of sleep when we get home, all limbs and blankets, and then the weekday hits and we pretend our life is normal. It's not helping my sleeping, but it prevents the monsters from leaking out of my head and into all the nooks and crannies of our small condo. It's easy to keep them safely tucked away on the open road, where it's too bright and we're driving too fast for them to lurk.

"Yes," I say very seriously despite my smile. "Because it's goofy!"

DINOSAUR ON THE 18ᵀᴴ HOLE

Max slaps her thigh. She is all giggles and joyful tears, and I shake my head, concentrating my eyes on the road. Even after all of our years together, her joy is still infectious.

"Well, what do you call it?" I counter.

Max wipes at her eyes, takes a steadying breath, and then gives me her most are-you-joking look. I can see it out of the corner of my eye. She absolutely cannot believe I am asking her this.

"Well?" I repeat my question. "If goofy golf is so weird to you, what do you call it?"

"Mini-putt!" she screeches.

"Mini-putt is like, I don't know, sure, a tiny little golf course. But what do you call it when the tiny little golf course has dinosaurs and is like a little village of weird, giant things?"

Max gives me a very serious look.

"Ioana, that's mini-putt!"

"No! Mini-putt is where I want to practice my serious putting!"

"Your serious putting?"

"But goofy golf is where fun and magic happen and where you go with your family to have a really cool get-out-of-the-city day trip or like when you need a break during a road trip." I will die on this hill.

Max is laughing so hard she starts to hiccup. She's waving her hands furiously, trying to calm herself down. It takes her a full few minutes, but her hysterical choking laughter does finally dissipate enough to where she manages words. I'm expecting her to take another run at my definition of goofy golf and I prepare to defend it.

But when she can finally speak again, she says, "Ioana, I need to know more *immediately* about how often you practice your serious putting."

I find a mostly empty bag of chips next to me and I throw them at her, causing her to fall right back into her hiccupping laughter.

"Oh, I'll show you my serious putting," I say.

I look at the exit sign we're about to pass, even though I don't need to. I know these highways by heart. I knew we were getting close, which prompted my memory and our entire discussion. "In fact," I say, signaling to switch to the exit lane, "we're right by the goofy golf course I used to go to as a kid."

A brief glimmer of concern shadows Max's face, asking without asking.

"I'm fine," I say. "Besides, nothing can get us at a goofy golf course. They're sacred."

Max smirks, an acknowledgment of my levity and mood. "Oh, you're on."

The course is fully automated, maintained by a family who have better things to do with their days but who can't be bothered to part with the roadside attraction. As we pull up, the T-Rex protecting Hole 18 looms in the distance, backlit by the sun, metal glinting like mirrors. It's all faded greens and oranges masking mechanical seams. Its mouth is open in a perpetual silent roar, its real roar activated only by a ball dipping into the 18th hole, a momentous end to a (hopefully) momentous game. Its teeth glimmer like liquid as the summer's morning sun already begins to warm the metal, and I'm surprised at how clean it is. The family that runs this place—the Burkes? Banks?—must keep it in good order.

"I wonder how much money this place makes," I ask, peering through the windshield of the car, and Max simultaneously shrugs and raises her eyebrows, like I must've lost my mind for asking *her* that.

"You're the business owner," I counter her expression.

"I sell croissants and flat whites out of a barbershop. Different world than . . . " Max pauses, surveys the dinosaur-themed roadside attraction, and says, "this twin-sized bed sheet brought to life."

She's not malicious. But she is getting uneasy. We've never made a stop before during our drives. She doesn't know what to expect. From the park or from me.

"Did you have dinosaur bed sheets growing up?" I ask, even though I know the answer already. The answer is canon Max.

"Sailor Moon, all the way" we both say at the same time, since Max's answer, down to the cadence and lilt of her voice is the same every time. This time there's a drop and, between the drop in her voice and the way her hands haven't moved from her lap, I know she's going to suggest I just keep on driving.

The parking lot is completely empty (a fact I am grateful for and clocked immediately—a single other car would've meant the spontaneous date was canceled). But I do a scan anyway. It's just us, the front gates, and the T-Rex looming over the metal fence. I know there's a Pteranodon, lifted up by a metal pole and flying high enough to be impossible to touch from the ground and low enough to be obscured by the small building housing the restrooms. That's Hole 14. And then there's a volcano at Hole 9. A large range, big enough to hide a kid or a crouched down adult. My stomach cramps at the thought of an adult crouching behind the volcano, and I do a quick series of taps against my thigh until the thought quiets and my stomach settles.

"C'mon, let's go," I say, killing the engine and popping my door open before Max either notices the compulsion or suggests we get back on the highway.

She follows me out of the car, eyes on the giant T-Rex.

We approach the automated teller that dispenses golf balls and clubs and I let myself think this could actually be fun. But then, as I take out my card, I hear a soft roar. One that is more like metal gears grinding and a stuttering tape machine playing than anything ferocious, but still, I swear I hear it, faint and muffled but unmistakably belonging to the T-Rex.

"Did you hear that?" I ask quickly, eyes scanning the parking lot.

"No." Max answers firmly, but not unkindly.

No? I think and feel my fingers begin their rapid tapping against my thigh.

"You good?" Max asks.

Am I good?

I tap out a sequence of three three more times and then nod.

"I really want to do this," I say. "I want something normal."

Max sighs, then nods. "I love that your idea of normal is animatronic dinosaurs and something you call *goofy golf*."

"I'm an artist, what can I say?"

We don't speak as we buy our tickets from the automated machine. Max is watching me and trying not to be obvious about it, but it's okay. The parking lot is big and empty, the pavement having pushed any possible trees off into the distance. The gate is creaking and while it unlocks when we punch in the code printed on our receipt, it takes a moment to shake off the rust and the cold and to fully stutter open. It's unlikely anybody is here (or has been in a while) and I've already confirmed our exits–or, in this case, our exit singular. The large, barbed wire fence surrounds the entire course, with only this one gate. Once we're in there and the gate re-locks, we're safe. The T-Rex doesn't roar again, so I let myself consider it was probably just my imagination (and as a set designer, my imagination is good at envisioning life and monsters over stillness). Or maybe it was my imagination in another way, the good, old-fashioned I'm-losing-my-grip-on-reality way. Maybe.

"You ready to get your butt kicked in goofy golf?" I ask, showing Max–or myself–that I am really, honestly okay.

Max takes the offer and smiles. "Then you won't mind going first and showing me how it's done?"

I know every detail by heart. There are giant fake turtles in the pond by Hole 4. Hole 7 is really difficult because the hole is behind a giant nest of wyvern eggs that sit dead center in the open course, obscuring a direct line of shot. The cave by Hole 13 is filled with spiders and I know intimately that you should never put your hand in there, that it's always worth the price of buying a new golf ball to avoid risking spider bites in an ill-advised rescue attempt. I know the spikes of the stegosaurus's tail at Hole 17 are great to bank shots off of, just as I know the palm tree shading Hole 5 is where you want to stand to avoid a sunburn (and the early July morning heat is already starting to build, stagnant in the park like breath in a paper bag).

It's a wonder I haven't brought Max here yet. Although before the attack, we never really felt the need to leave the city. The city was–is–our home. We have a one-bedroom in a high-rise condo, down the street from our friends, and a few blocks farther from our other friends. We have our grocery store, our bar, and our brunch spot. Max's cafe is in a small barbershop, a joint venture between her and a transmasc friend from college. The theater I work for is a few blocks down. Our world had–has–its own orbit in the city, an orbit filled with community, found family, extravagance, and love, and I never thought I'd want to leave that orbit. Then a strange man broke into our home and changed everything. The kind of random horror–a total stranger breaking into your place, no personal motive other than their own messed up need for power or control or greed or desperation–that they say so rarely happens (yet did happen) and now the city is a barbed wire cage full of eyes and hungry, carnivorous mouths.

Imagining monsters has gotten a whole lot easier for me.

The kitschy golf course is a stark contrast to the claustrophobia

DINOSAUR ON THE 18TH HOLE

of mine and Max's apartment, a small space that should feel safe in its knowableness, but instead is rife with all the ways it was violated and defiled. The balcony window, scalable because we are only on the fourth floor. The door with a singular lock against the constant flow of bodies in the hallway. The elevator that betrays the floor we live on and provides a haven from which to spy on us as we walk down the hall. At least the shadows here are pretend, driven by animatronics and a sun that is struggling to wake up.

"All right Ioana, show me those serious putting skills," Max says, gesturing for me to step up to the first hole.

I shake off the cloud that was starting to form (*I want this, I want normal, I want this, I want normal*) and assume my old stance, slipping easily and effortlessly back into it.

"This is goofy golf," I correct. "And while it's not serious, I will still kick your ass."

We play, me remembering my old tricks, the ways in which my brothers would taunt me and teach me, and Max slips from indulging me into enjoying herself. We miss shots, we flirt, and as the sun warms up and seeps into our skin, everything feels okay. Mostly.

Even though I haven't heard it again since, I struggle to shake the roar of the T-Rex at Hole 18 we heard as we approached the course. Max hadn't heard it, but Max also hadn't heard the window open, and she hadn't heard the footsteps on the hardwood in our living room. As we play and Max flirts, my brain is cycling the dinosaur's roar, an earworm that is trying to warn me to not let my guard down. I tap rhythms of three against my golf club when Max isn't looking. The gate was locked when we got here, there were no other cars in the parking lot, I remind myself. Nobody is here but us. But still, the dinosaur's tinny roar rolls around in my brain, a tune that won't let go.

Distracted, I shoot my ball into a water trap.

"I thought you were good," Max teases, eyes sizing up her shot toward the hole.

I begrudgingly go to grab my ball to a cacophony of taunts and good-natured jeers from Max. I crouch above the still-chilled water and as I reach into the tiny puddle to grab my ball, I see it.

A shadow.

A shadow that falls over my hand and then disappears quickly. Too quickly to be from the sun. I stumble backwards, eyes frantically checking my immediate surroundings. Just the water trap, the sun, and then–

There. A shadow, darting away from the waterfall of the third hole.

A shadow attempting to crouch behind the fake turtles at our next hole and my whole vision dips, blackness blurring like having stared at the sun too directly.

A shadow.

It darts, leaving the turtles and seeking refuge at the next hole, the palm trees.

A shadow.

A tall shadow, a quick shadow, a shadow that is darker than the rest and nimble in ways shadows aren't.

The shadow of a man, or the shadow of a monster.

Whoever, whatever, the shadow belongs to is quick and knows how to use the limited darkness of the early morning sun, slipping effortlessly into the palm tree's own limited shadow. Hiding from the sun, but still present.

I forget how to breathe. And then my heart beats so fast and hard I think I'm going to throw up.

I try to count my rhythm but can't.

The shadow moves and darts and belongs to nothing.

It snickers, a thing that can change shape, jumping from the palm tree to the wyvern eggs next.

It looks heavy and full, like it could be sliced with a knife. It doesn't look fragile and ethereal.

It's not a shadow.

The shape–the very real shape–moves and darts confidently, very unlike the man in our apartment, who lumbered and panicked.

This shape moves like it knows this place. Like it belongs in this place.

But now I can't see it and the sun is making me sweat.

I don't see anything other than dinosaurs and the golden morning sun.

My palms get clammy. The shadow did move, didn't it? The shadow did *exist*, right?

The sun is bright and fuzzy, gauzy with heat and the evaporating morning dew.

But I'm not certain. Still holding my dripping wet golf ball, I frantically scan the entire course. The heat of the morning makes everything feel out of focus, shifting what should be hard and solid lines of metal into fuzzy, dust-mottled hazes of familiar shapes. The dinosaurs cast shadows they shouldn't and the trees outside of the park feel hostile. There are pools of blackness that seem darker than the rest, shades of shapes that don't belong to anything I can pinpoint. The morning sun can't cast these types of shadows. Near the volcano range a flurry of shadows move like puppets, erratic and exaggerated, all arms and legs rushing about to find cover. Are there more people here? But there weren't any cars. The shadows continue to elongate and refract, bouncing to their own rhythm, ignoring the patterns they should follow if they were obeying the rules of the early morning sunlight. The shadows dance and twirl to a wind that doesn't exist and my stomach sinks even further.

I'm not imagining this.

We are not alone here.

And it's not that I'm scared of shadows. It's that I'm scared of what casts them.

I'm vaguely aware of Max trying to get my attention, but my lungs are galloping and my eyes are trying to tear through layers of early sunlight and shadow in a fervid attempt to categorize and understand and my mind is categorizing everything into threes. I try to analyze every distinct shadow I see. The one at the turtle lagoon could be the Frankensteined shadows of all the turtles together. The one below the palm tree could be from the way the walkway lights jumble, a balled-up mess of refractions instead of a hunched human ready to pounce. The wyvern nest casts its own strange sheen, bioluminescence from layers of black light painting and glitter, still faintly glowing in the daybreak. Did it always shimmer like that? Did it always make that *sound,* like knuckles cracking and forks scraping on plates. Everything is wrong. Everything is bright and then darker than it was before, and my mouth tastes like blood and I'm scratching at my left wrist where the bruises healed and I can't think.

Something is wrong something is here something is wrong something is—

There's a snicker like leaves being stepped on, the crack of tree branches breaking. The shadows all shiver and deepen, growing darker and larger even though the sun has passed behind a cloud.

Max is speaking but I can't hear her, my ears fill with the sound of branches breaking like bones, the leaves whispering malevolently. There is no sound except for the thunderous cacophony of nature contorting itself into new shapes, true shapes of monsters and ghosts and—

The T-Rex at Hole 18 loudly and distinctly roars, chilling my panic in a flash freeze. Even Max stops and looks toward the final hole. She catches my eye.

"I heard it," she says, and I could cry. I'm not crazy.

Why is the T-Rex roaring? It's only supposed to do that when a ball dips into the hole to get fed into the automated return system. Yet this is likely the second time it's roared now, counting the one from the parking lot. And this time, with the sudden stillness of the wind and the quietness enveloping Max, there's no mistaking it. The giant T-Rex reared its head, thrashed its tiny mechanical arms, and roared, a silly primal cry more cartoonish than realistic, but eerie and unsettling all the same. Someone is here. They have to be. Something is—

"Let's go back to the car," Max says. Practical. No. Not practical. Scared. But the car, with its diameter of very breakable windows and its tires that can be slashed and its gas tank that can be tampered with, is the opposite of safe. Going back to the car now feels like taking the bait, allowing myself to be reeled in by a monstrous fisherman I can't see. At least out here Max can turn a golf club into a weapon—like she did a heavy wooden candlestick— and we can give ourselves a chance at surviving. The shadows pull back and snicker again, shivering puddles of darkness. Not a somebody. A something. Then thoughts click together, gears finally turning after being greased.

The Burkes? The Banks? Whoever, it doesn't matter. They keep this place running, despite probably losing money on it every year. Why? Why would they do that? Unless this place, abandoned but not bulldozed, serves a purpose in its construction. Metal fences like prison bars. Animatronic dinosaurs rigged to roar in response to stimuli. All designed to keep tremathing in, to know where something *is*. Why keep this place running, unless this park is a cage?

"Ioana, the car," Max stresses.

"I can't."

My palms itch from sweat, my legs are jelly.

DINOSAUR ON THE 18ᵀᴴ HOLE

"Ioana—"

Sweat forms under my hair, hot and wet, and then is instantly chilled as something breathes heavy against the back of my neck.

I yelp and jump, nerves all fire and static, and swing my club. Max jumps back, avoiding the long edge of my putter, and she grabs my shoulders.

"Something breathed, my neck, I—"

"Ioana, breathe. I was right behind you. There was nothing."

But the breath, the cold.

"There was only me behind you."

The breath. The cold.

"There's only me."

No shadows between me and Max. No shadows, no monsters, no humans. Just me and Max.

"We both heard it," I say, grasping onto the T-Rex's roar, the only thing I know for sure is real—other than Max.

"Yes," she admits, and I don't know if I feel relieved or scared. "But," she continues. "Listen, Ioana, this place is old. It's on the verge of falling apart. Anything could've fallen into the hole and set off the dinosaur, yeah?"

Sure, but what about the shadows?

"Okay, look." Max steps away from me, and with a quick re-positioning of her putter, she taps a crabapple resting amongst a pile of leaves and twigs. The crabapple putters and rolls and stops near her golf ball. Similar shape. Similar weight. It could trick a mechanical dinosaur rigged to understand weight and nothing else. Max could be right. But what about the shadows? What about the shape I saw? What about how everything feels electric, and the slight breeze feels like knives and why are the shadows acting *so* weird if they're normal? My eyes burn and I scratch my wrist and then I manage to tell Max.

"I saw something," I admit. "At the next hole."

Maybe it's nothing. Or maybe it's my brain rewired into survival. Or maybe those are the same thing for me now.

Max doesn't miss a beat. "Okay," she says. She shifts her grip on her golf club to hold it like a sword. "Then let's go look."

Max leads the way, golf club in one hand and her phone out with the flashlight turned on in the other. The light from her phone bounces off the dinosaurs, causing the shadows to scurry back into their expected shapes. The dozens of dancing and entangling fingers and mouths from behind the volcano dissipate like dust, the phone flashlight revealing no monsters, just cigarette butts and candy wrappers. The palm tree isn't providing refuge for a man or monster behind its thick base, just worn-out AstroTurf. The wyvern eggs are stripped and pathetic looking, aged from weather and time. They don't shimmer and glow. Max doesn't speak, but simply looks at me, lets me point to a place where the shadows are taunting me, and then shines the light there. I watch as the shadows evaporate, extinguished and defeated, and we move on when I give a tiny nod. Like Gorgons, we turn every taunting shadow into stone, solidifying the laws of reality around us.

We check the entire park, behind every metallic dinosaur, behind every rusted geographical feature warped to fit the hole, behind every trashcan and table that lines the course. Sweat from the sun and the building humidity lines our backs, but we keep going, not breaking in the shade but dispersing the final remnants of the night. And we find nothing but litter, solar lights, and mechanical dinosaurs that somehow still work. No dragons or boogeymen or random strangers high as hell who saw an opportunity and took it. Nobody scaling a window and breaking glass and throwing punches before using those same hands to strangle. No humans, no monsters. Just me and Max.

Max, the person who didn't hear the stranger's footsteps in our apartment but who did hear me scream. Max, the person who grabbed a heavy wooden candlestick as a weapon. Max, the person who saved my life and who continues to save my life, even when it's under threat only from my own mind. I feel tired but my lungs are still itching, and my thoughts still feel like fire. Maybe I'm not ready for normal. The shadows feel like knives, and I still see them stretching their long legs toward me.

"I swear I—"

Max drops her club, its purpose as a weapon over, and walks over to me, taking both my hands. When I don't say anything else, she pulls me close and presses herself against me.

"I swear, I saw, it was a man or a shadow, he—it—was hiding behind the giant turtles—" The man in our home, standing tall behind our couch. "He, he ran to the palm tree." He lunges, pulling fists like knives. "I swear, Max, I swear, I—"

"Four things you can feel," she says. "Go."

I breathe in hiccups and my thoughts are static electricity, but

DINOSAUR ON THE 18ᵀᴴ HOLE

I find Max's voice, a golden thread in a maze of pain and fear and chemicals firing off alarm bells.

"Your hands," I say. I breathe. "Why are your hands so soft?"

Max smiles but doesn't say anything.

"Your forehead," I continue. I like when she presses her forehead against mine, like she's inviting me to step inside of her ribcage and to take a nap there, protected.

"My jeans. The tag is a little itchy."

I pause, my lungs calibrating and my thoughts slowing.

"The ground. The AstroTurf."

Max squeezes my hands, and asks, "Do you want me to keep going?"

My chest is hurting less and the thought of the dinosaur's roar making me spiral already causes me to flush with embarrassment. "No, I'm okay."

We stay this way for a moment, golf clubs discarded sloppily at our feet, the windmill of the course we stopped our search at barely spinning with the slight wind. It's quiet and despite the wide openness of the course, I'm safe. The dinosaurs and mishmash of out-of-date architecture all return back to what they've always been and it's just me and Max.

"You sure?"

"Yeah, I'm good," I say.

"Do you want to go home?"

I consider it. It's still early in the morning, the heat won't be unbearable for another hour or so.

"No." My body aches from tension, but I can't go home until my body is sluggish with exhaustion and my eyes close all on their own. Especially now that I know for a fact nobody, real or monstrous, is here with us. "Let's finish our game."

Max nods, kisses me with one last squeeze of my hands, and then we both pick up our clubs and resume our play. She puts on laughter and she flirts and she beats me handily despite my half-hearted trash talk. After our balls dip into the hole between the giant T-Rex's feet, the mechanical dinosaur roars its cheap, tinny roar and the sun blooms just beyond it, washing the cold metal in golden light. Max gives a warning look to the T-Rex, stretching out her golf club like a sword once again, theatricality telling it off for playing tricks on me.

I feel silly, but I feel more tired than anything else. I don't notice the shadows behind us, coming to a different life as the sun changes the shape of the course. I don't notice the way the wyvern egg seems to be lit on fire or the soft croaking of branches breaking. I don't notice the shadows parading behind us, a procession of quiet monsters. I am too tired, and Max's charm makes feeling afraid seem silly.

Max drives so I can sleep with my head touching the cold window, feeling the warmth of the sun, and smelling the leather of her coat, all reminders that, at least for this one singular moment, I am safe. Sleep comes easily, and Max's stare is lazy on the road in front of her, so neither of us notice the shadow that envelopes the T-Rex, that turns its oranges and greens to pure blackness, a void of light and heat, with nothing but the faint sounds of tree branches snapping like a song from inhuman vocal cords.

WISHBONE

MICHAEL THOMAS FORD

Thanksgiving 1985

"I always knew he was a fag."

"Like hell you did," Casey's grandmother said to her husband as she passed him the bowl of mashed potatoes. "You loved him in *McMillan & Wife*. In fact, you said you wanted to *be* him."

Casey's grandfather snorted. "Maybe if *you* looked like Susan Saint James," he said.

"It's such a pity," Casey's mother remarked. "He was so handsome. In the last picture I saw of him, he was practically a skeleton."

Casey poked at the turkey on his plate and said nothing.

"Who are you talking about?" his little brother, Alex, asked.

"Rock Hudson," Casey's mother said. "He was a popular actor."

"What happened to him?" said Alex, his mouth full of corn casserole.

"He died," Casey's mother answered.

"He got AIDS," Casey's grandfather said.

"What's AIDS?" Alex asked.

"It's what fags get when they—"

"Harold!" Casey's grandmother said, cutting her husband off. "He's eight. And anyway, this isn't Thanksgiving dinner conversation."

"You're the one who brought it up," Harold reminded her.

"Casey, have you decided where to apply to school?" Casey's grandmother asked.

"Not yet," Casey answered. "I'm still thinking about it."

This was not true. He had been thinking about it for a long

233

time. And he had already sent off three applications. All to schools as far as he could get from rural southeast Ohio. Schools in big cities. He thought he had a good chance of getting in. His grades were excellent. He'd played baseball and joined the school newspaper to make himself appear well-rounded.

His family wanted him to go to the local state school. He could live at home, they pointed out. Save money. Why go anywhere else when there was something nearby? Something familiar. Something safe.

"Don't know why you want to go to school, anyway," his grandfather said. "You can come work for your dad and me. People always need electricians. In a year you'd be making more than those guys spending four years in classrooms. It's honest work, too."

"I know it is," Casey said. "And maybe I will."

And since you're called Sparky and Dad is Sparky Jr., everyone will call me something like Sparkplug, he thought.

He knew his family only wanted what was best for him. At least what *they* thought was best for him. If he let them plan his future, he'd be married by 20, have a couple of kids by 25, and then spend the next 50 years living the same day over and over and over until he died.

He had other ideas about his future. The problem was, he wasn't sure how to get what he *did* want. Especially now.

He didn't really know who Rock Hudson was. But he'd heard a lot about him in the almost two months since his death. And what he knew was that Hudson was now the most famous person to die from AIDS and the first person that a lot of people knew personally to die from it, at least as much as you can know someone you've only seen in the movies or on TV.

He knew only slightly more about AIDS than he did about Rock Hudson. He was still not entirely clear on the details, and a lot of what he read in the papers was confusing or contradicted other things he read, but he knew that it seemed to be affecting gay men more than anyone else and that they were getting it from having sex with each other.

"Casey?"

Casey wasn't having sex with anyone except himself. But he wanted to. And he wanted it to be with other guys. Now, though, he was afraid that doing anything with another guy would kill him.

He'd seen the photographs of men who had AIDS. He'd seen the ugly lesions. The sunken faces. The haunted eyes. And now, whenever he thought about having sex, he saw himself looking like that too.

"Casey?"

"What?" He looked up and saw his mother watching him.

"I asked if you could drive some pie over to Mr. Gresham's house when you're done."

"Oh," Casey said. "Sure."

"I invited Luther for Thanksgiving dinner," his mother announced to the table. "But he said he was fine." She sighed. "He's gone downhill since Roberta died. Barely sees anyone. Least I can do is send some pie over."

Everyone agreed that Luther was most certainly not doing well, then returned to whatever it was they were talking about. Casey finished his plate and carried it to the kitchen. His grandmother and mother joined him, slicing up the pies and putting a piece each of pumpkin, mincemeat, and chocolate cream on a paper plate and covering it loosely with foil.

"Set it on the floor, not on the seat, so it doesn't slide off," his mother instructed as Casey took his letterman jacket from the hook by the back door and put it on. "And tell Luther we all missed him."

"I will," Casey promised.

He went outside and got into the beat-up '72 Ford F100 pickup that had been his present from his parents on his 16th birthday, and which he and his father had worked on together to get running more or less consistently. He waited a few minutes for the heater to start blowing warm air, then pulled out of the driveway. Twenty minutes later, he arrived at the Gresham house, where he knocked on the door and waited for old Luther to answer.

"Mom and Grandma sent some pie over," Casey said, holding out the plate. "Missy Durham and Sarah Branch," he added when Luther didn't seem to know who he meant.

"Sure, sure," Luther said, taking the plate. "Tell them thanks." He shut the door, which Casey stared at for a moment before turning and going back to the truck.

He drove home through the gathering gloom, not particularly anxious to get back to the house. His grandparents would still be there, his grandmother helping with the cleaning up and his grandfather and father sitting in the living room watching the

Cowboys/Cardinals game and shouting at the television. He loved them all, despite their narrow views of what his life ought to be, but sometimes it was exhausting being around them and the weight of their expectations.

At the end of the road, instead of turning right, he turned left and drove west toward Columbus. The city sat, like Oz, at the end of Route 33. He knew there were bars there where guys like him got together. Sometimes he thought about going. There were kids at school who went drinking in the city. They said they almost never got carded. Maybe, someday, he would go there and find out for himself.

For now, he drove until he came to the first rest area. There he pulled off and into the parking lot, taking one of the spots at the very end, away from the sallow glare of the sodium vapor lights. He left the truck running, for warmth, but turned the headlights off.

The restrooms themselves were set back from the lot, with a concrete pathway leading to them. The women's room was on the left and the men's on the right. There were two other cars, both parked closer to the center of the lot. One had someone sitting in the passenger seat. The other was empty. A moment later, a man exited the restroom and walked to the empty car, got in, and pulled away. Not long after, a woman emerged from the other side of the building and got into the remaining car.

Now alone in the lot, Casey asked himself what he was doing there. He asked himself this same question every time he found himself at the rest area, which over the past eight months or so had been perhaps half a dozen times. The first was after Kevin Dreyfuss at school had mentioned that a fairy had offered to suck his dick while he was taking a piss there. According to Kevin, he in return had offered to knock the fairy's teeth in and gotten out of there as fast as he could.

A couple of weeks later, Casey found himself in the parking lot for the first time. He sat in his truck for a couple of hours, watching men go in and out of the little concrete block building. Most were in there for only a few minutes. But some stayed far longer than necessary to do what they needed to do in there. When this happened, Casey found himself itching to go inside and see what they were doing. He kept telling himself that he would get out of the truck if the person or persons in question remained inside for just one more minute, then one more, then another, until inevitably they did emerge, and the opportunity was lost.

He had no idea of knowing what, exactly, happened inside the restroom. But the thought that *something* had both aroused and terrified him. He longed to find out for himself, but so far he had done nothing more than watch from the safety of the parking lot.

After that first time, he found himself returning a few weeks later. Again, he sat in the truck and watched as men came and went. Again, he didn't join them. It was on his third, or maybe fourth visit that he recognized one of the faces from a previous time. The man could have been one of his father's friends, or one of his friend's fathers. An ordinary man, handsome in an everyday way but not what most would call unusually striking or even memorable. And yet, Casey did remember him.

He watched the man enter the bathroom. He checked the time on his watch. Five minutes passed. Then ten. At fifteen minutes, Casey put his hand on the handle of the truck door but found he couldn't bring himself to open it. At twenty minutes, another man disappeared inside the restroom. Ten minutes later, the second man exited, followed a few minutes later by the first man.

That night Casey had jerked off right there in his truck, hidden in the shadows. He'd jerked off thinking about what the two men might have done together, what he might have done with one or both of them had he been brave enough to open the truck door and go join them. He'd cum hard, groaning, spraying his load onto his belly. Afterward, he'd cleaned up with a handful of Dairy Queen napkins, shoving the ball of soiled paper back into the glove box and slamming the door shut.

Thinking about that night now, as he again sat in the lot and wondered what happened inside the men's room, filled him with a peculiar mix of shame and desire. His cock stiffened inside his jeans, and he rubbed it while he stared out the windshield at the empty sidewalk. There were no cars there now. It would be safe to get out of the truck, venture into the restroom, see what it was like in there. Then, if nothing else, he would have an image to use when he was alone in his bedroom later, the door locked and his parents fast asleep downstairs.

He was opening the door when the shadows around the restroom door shifted, and someone appeared. Casey stopped, confused. No car had pulled into the rest area. It was still empty.

Yet, there was someone standing beneath the harsh light over the door to the men's room. It was definitely a man. But where had he come from?

The man turned and looked in the direction of Casey's truck. For a moment—very briefly—it seemed his eyes glowed a sickly yellow in the darkness. But that was probably just the light reflecting off glasses. That was all. Still, Casey found himself holding his breath until the man turned away and walked into the restroom.

Casey had an overwhelming desire to follow him. Again, he reached for the handle of the door. As his fingers touched it, the truck's radio blared to life: "We built this city on rock and rolllllll . . . !"

Startled, Casey pulled his hand away.

"Number one for the second week in a row," a DJ's voice said as the song faded away. "And I know most of you are still digesting your pumpkin pie, but the big daddy of the holiday season is just around the corner, so let's make things merry and bright with last year's biggest musical gift, Band Aid's 'Do They Know It's Christmas?'"

Casey turned the knob on the dash as the familiar drumbeat began, silencing the noise. He put the truck in reverse and pulled out of the spot, suddenly anxious to get away. Only when he was back on the highway, headed for home, did he turn the headlights back on, as if doing it any earlier would have brought unwanted attention.

When he got back to the house, his grandparents were gone and his mother and father were sitting in the living room, watching TV.

"How was Luther?" his mother asked.

"Fine," Casey said, heading for the stairs.

"Don't you want to watch *Magnum?*" his mother said. "It's a good one."

Casey didn't want to. But he also didn't want to be alone for some reason, or to make his parents think he was acting weird, so he sat down on the couch. He stared at the TV, barely paying attention as Magnum attempted to convince his skeptical friends that he really had seen the ghost of a boy swimming in the depths of the ocean while scuba diving.

Then Magnum turned and looked right at him. His eyes glowed yellow. "You want to suck my cock, Casey?" he asked.

Casey's parents laughed. Casey looked at them, horrified.

"I know you do, Casey," Magnum continued. "I see how you look at my chest. You want to see what's in my shorts?"

Magnum's hand slipped beneath the waistband of the tight shorts he was wearing. It went deeper. "Missy," Magnum said. "Brad. Did you know Casey thinks about sucking my cock?"

Casey glanced again at his parents. Their faces, bathed in the glow from the television, showed no traces of shock or surprise.

"Did you know he thinks about me bending him over and putting my cock inside him?" Magnum growled.

Casey stood up. "I'm tired," he mumbled. "I'm going to go upstairs."

"But you'll miss the end," his father said. "Don't you want to see how it turns out?"

"You can tell me later," Casey said.

"I saved you the wishbone," his mother said.

Casey stared at her. "What?"

"The wishbone," she said. "From the turkey. So you can make a wish when it dries. You always loved doing that when you were small. Usually, your daddy cuts through it when he carves the turkey, but this year he missed, and I saved it."

"Oh," Casey said. "Well, thanks."

"Think about what you want to wish for," his mother said. "You've got some time until it's ready."

Casey went upstairs to his room, where he shut the door and sat down on his bed. He had no idea what had just happened. Maybe he was getting sick. Or had food poisoning. But his stomach felt fine. It was his head that was a jumble of thoughts and feelings.

He took his shoes off, changed into a pair of sweats, and got into bed. He picked up the comic book on his bedside table—*Crisis on Infinite Earths #8*—and tried to read it. But the words disappeared from his mind as soon as he read them, and he couldn't focus on the images, so he dropped it on the floor and shut his eyes, hoping it would help.

It didn't. Leaning over the side of his bed, he reached underneath and felt around for the magazine he had hidden there. When his fingers touched it, he slid it out and picked it up. He held it in his hand, staring at the cover. It was the October 15 issue of *Star* magazine, the gossip rag his grandmother picked up in the checkout line at the Big Bear supermarket when she did her weekly shopping. She often passed them along to Casey's mother when she was done with them.

The magazine had Rock Hudson on the cover, and a substantial portion of the contents were devoted to a history of his career. Casey had taken it from the coffee table and brought it to his room, curious about the man who was so much in the news. But he'd also felt embarrassed and had hidden the magazine as he might have an issue of *Playboy* swiped from his father's stash in the garage.

He opened the magazine and turned to the photos of Hudson. He'd looked at them a thousand times already, searching them for something he didn't even have a name for, something that might tie the two of them together, perhaps, some clue as to what made Hudson—and by connection Casey himself—the way he was. Mostly, though, he enjoyed looking at pictures of a youthful, handsome Hudson, so beautiful before disease destroyed him.

That, Casey didn't want to think about. Because if the disease could ravage someone as handsome as Hudson had been, what could it do to an ordinary man? Or maybe it was Hudson's beauty that had been his downfall. Maybe the virus fed on desire. Maybe it knew what men like Hudson and Casey were and wanted to punish them.

He turned the page and looked at his favorite photo—an image of Hudson from one of his many films. In the picture he looked so young, so alive. His brown eyes seemed to look directly into Casey's soul. Staring at them, Casey became lost. He grew tired, and then he slept, and dreamed.

He was in a men's room, standing at a urinal. Beside him, Rock Hudson was taking a piss. Casey looked down and saw that the actor was hard.

"Go on," Hudson said. "It's okay."

Casey reached out.

"Not with your hand," Hudson said, pushing his hand away. "With your mouth."

Casey hesitated a moment, then dropped to his knees and parted his lips. Hudson thrust his hips forward. The head of his cock slid inside Casey's mouth. It was warm, the skin slightly salty. Casey looked up. A pair of jaundiced eyes looked down at him. The warm brown was scaled with sickness, a sticky film covering the irises. Hudson grinned and a fly crept from the corner of his mouth.

Casey sat up with a gasp. He was in his own room. The glowing green numbers on the clock on his bedside table showed the time to be 3:27. Then he felt the wetness on his belly, put his hand down there and came away with his fingers sticky. He brought them to his mouth and slipped them inside. Only then did he notice the two small, yellow moons watching him from the corner of his room. They blinked and disappeared.

Saturday, November 30

The inside of the men's room smelled like disinfectant and cigarette smoke. The cinderblock walls were painted a nondescript gray, and the light that filtered through the narrow, frosted windows along the top did little to brighten it up. Four urinals lined one side, with four sinks opposite them, and the concrete floor between them was littered here and there with wads of brown paper dropped by men who missed the garbage can or just didn't care about using it. Further in, three stalls with open doors loomed like caves.

Casey walked to the urinal closest to the stalls and unzipped. He pulled his dick out and peed, staring down at the pink triangle of disinfectant as his stream spattered against it. He half-hoped and half-feared that someone else would come in while he was there. But by the time he was done, he was still the lone occupant. He remained at the urinal for another minute or two, then felt self-conscious about it and tucked himself back into his pants and zipped up.

He walked down the row of toilets, pushing each door open and peering inside. Each stall was more or less the same, but he investigated each one as if it might hold some unexpected surprise. He had reached the last one when he heard voices.

"Hurry up, now," a man's voice said. "Do your business so we can get back on the road."

A boy ran inside, followed by a man. As the boy rushed into the first stall, Casey slipped into the third. He shut the door behind him and slid the latch shut. Then he sat on the toilet. He felt ridiculous being in there when he didn't even need to go, but he didn't know what else to do.

As he waited, he looked at the walls of the stall. They were metal, painted the same gray as the restroom walls. A dispenser for toilet paper was affixed to the wall on his right. On the wall beside it, someone had drawn an arrow in black marker, pointing to the dispenser. Puzzled, Casey leaned over and looked more closely. The arrow appeared to be pointing to the back of the dispenser. But why?

He put his hand on the metal box and pulled. To his surprise, it came away from the wall, attached to it by metal clasps on either side. The roller that held the toilet paper in place was still there, but behind that was a circular opening in the wall. By taking the toilet paper out, the hole was fully revealed. If the dispenser and paper in the center stall were also removed, there would be a view between the two.

Above the hole someone had written in small letters: SAT 11PM.

Casey heard a toilet flush. Hurriedly, he put the toilet paper back in place and slipped the cover back over it. The door to the first stall banged open, and he heard a small voice say, "All done!"

"Wash your hands," a man's voice ordered. This was followed by the sound of water running for a moment, then the click-click-click of paper being pulled from the dispenser. Then the restroom door was pushed open, and Casey was alone again.

He removed the dispenser cover and set it on the floor, placing the toilet paper on top of it. He stared at the opening in the wall, at the words written there. 11 PM. He looked at his watch. It was only a little past noon now. He wondered who—if anyone—would be here at 11. And who had written the message? Drawn the arrow? He felt as if he'd figured out a secret code. But surely others had too. How many? And what went on between the men who came there knowing to look?

The restroom door opened again, announcing a new arrival. Casey heard footsteps. Then the door to the middle stall opened as someone went inside. Casey held his breath, staring at the hole in the wall. He waited, wondering if the occupant would remove the dispenser on his side and, if he did, what Casey would do in response.

There was a gap between the bottom of the stall wall and the floor. Glancing down, Casey saw a work boot visible there, the generic brown kind common to so many working men. A pair of jeans was pushed down, puddling over the boot, and when he bent a little further down he saw an expanse of white skin covered in dark blond hair.

He raised his head and looked at the hole in the wall. In his pants, his dick stiffened as he imagined the faceless man beside him reaching over to open his side. When, a minute or two later, he heard the sound of toilet paper being pulled from the roll, his heartbeat quickened. But then there was the flush of the toilet and the sound of pants being pulled up, a buckle being fastened, the stall door opening. Then the restroom door squeaked, and he was alone again.

He replaced the dispenser on his side, opened the door, and slipped inside the center stall. A moment later the dispenser in there had been removed and he was staring at the opening from that side. There too the message had been scrawled in black marker: SAT 11 PM.

He covered it up again and left the restroom. Outside, it was snowing. He walked to his truck and got in. He sat for a while, watching the restroom door. Several cars came and went. Several men went in and out. None lingered. He wondered if any of them, like him, were curious enough about the arrow on the wall to look behind the dispenser. He wondered if any of them, like him, were thinking about coming back at 11 PM to find out what might be waiting there for them.

Monday, December 02

"Was Macbeth fated to die?"

While Mr. Nevill waited for someone to answer, Casey watched Kevin Dreyfuss draw the AC/DC logo on the white toe cap of the brand-new black Converse Chucks he was wearing. He had already drawn the KISS logo on the right one. Now, he used a black Sharpie to fill in the thunderbolt between the letters of the band's name on the left.

"Well?" Mr. Nevill said impatiently. "Did any of you actually *read* the play over break?"

"The witches predict he'll become king," Jen Price said.

"They do," Mr. Nevill agreed. "But what about his death? Do they predict that?"

"No," Casey heard himself say. He looked away from Kevin. "But they kind of talk him into it."

"Explain," Mr. Nevill said, but the smile playing at the corner of his mouth suggested he was pleased with the answer.

"Well," Casey said, "they give him predictions that make him think he'll be okay. Like the thing about no man born of woman being able to defeat him. It makes him think he's invincible. It ever occurs to him that Macduff wasn't born the usual way, and it's Macduff who ends up killing him."

"Thanks for ruining the ending," Kevin said, making the others laugh.

"Casey is exactly right," said Mr. Nevill. "But did the witches really trick him, or did they try to warn him, and he just didn't listen?"

Before anyone could answer, the bell rang.

"We'll pick this up tomorrow," Mr. Nevill said. "Now, get to lunch."

Casey walked with Kevin toward the cafeteria.

"Cool Chucks," he said.

Kevin laughed. "An early Christmas present to myself," he said. "Made a little cash over the holiday doing odd jobs. Trying to rough 'em up a little so they don't look too new."

As they passed the boys' restroom, Casey said, "I'll catch up with you."

"Enjoy your alone time with Rosy Palm and her five sisters," Kevin joked, holding up his hand and wiggling the fingers.

Casey ducked into the restroom and then into one of the stalls. He unbuckled his belt, lowered his pants, and sat down. As he waited for his body to do its thing, he found himself looking at the toilet paper dispenser affixed to the wall. There was no arrow drawn there. No graffiti of any kind. The janitor, Mr. Blix, made sure of that, scrubbing off any defacements as quickly as they appeared.

Casey reached over and tried removing the cover of the dispenser. It remained in place. He pulled again, but nothing happened. He wasn't sure if he was disappointed or relieved.

As he was finishing up, he heard the sound of whistling, accompanied by the noise of something rattling on the tile floor. Mr. Blix and his mop bucket. Casey flushed and opened the door.

"Hey, Mr. Blix," he said as he stepped into the room and went to the sink to wash his hands.

The whistling stopped. "You were playing with yourself," a gruff voice said.

Casey looked up and into the mirror. The janitor had his back to him and was moving the mop back and forth across the floor beneath the urinals.

"What?" Casey said.

"Playing with yourself," Mr. Blix said again. "Jerking off. I can smell it." He sniffed deeply, then laughed.

"I wasn't—" Casey said.

The janitor turned. His eyes sparkled dimly, gold coins in his dark face. "Smells like death," he said, grinning.

Casey fled into the hall, his hands still wet. Behind him, the whistling began again.

Saturday, December 07

Casey looked at his watch.

11:27

He was probably too late.

He hesitated at the door to the men's room. Remembering the sound it made, he pressed gently, inching it open as slowly as he could. It made only the slightest of squeaks as he slipped inside.

There were two cars in the parking lot besides his own, both already there when he pulled in. He almost hadn't come. Had told himself he wouldn't come. But as the numbers on the clock in his room ticked past 10:00 and kept going, he couldn't stop thinking about the arrow on the wall, about the promise of someone being there at 11 o'clock on a Saturday night.

But would he be there on this particular Saturday? A cold, dark, snowy one on which everyone else was tucked inside trying to stay warm? Given the choice between waiting in a cold room smelling of piss and smoke and lying in bed warm beneath a quilt made for him by his grandmother, what man would choose the former?

But Casey had been unable to sleep. When he closed his eyes, he saw the words written in black marker. When he tried to think of something, anything else, all he could think about was a faceless man standing on the other side of the wall, stroking himself while Casey pressed his eye to the hole and watched.

And so now he was here.

No one was at the urinals. And two of the stall doors were open.

But the third, the one at the farthest end of the room, was shut. Casey walked towards it, unsure what to do. As he got closer, the sound of muffled grunting seeped from under the door. He stopped, his heart pounding. He looked at the open door of the center stall, considered going inside. Then he heard a voice.

"Shoot inside me," a low voice said.

More grunting followed, faster and harder.

Casey crouched, peering beneath the stall door. He saw two sets of feet, both facing the rear of the toilet. One pair was wearing ordinary scuffed-up brown shoes like he might find in his father's closet. A pair of green corduroy trousers pooled around them. The other—the ones closest to the door—were sneakers. Black ones. On the toe, a familiar logo was inked in black marker. AC/DC.

"I'm gonna cum," a voice said. "I'm gonna cum in your faggot ass."

Casey's heart stuttered. He tried to stand, grew dizzy, felt himself slip on the slushy floor. He fell on his side.

Inside the stall, the sounds ceased. Casey scrambled to his feet and ran. He hit the door, heard it squawk in protest, then pounded down the sidewalk to his truck. He got in, fumbling with the keys as he kept his eyes on the restroom door. He was going to start the truck and get out of there before he was caught. Then something made him stop. Was it possible that it *wasn't* Kevin in there? He knew this was more than unlikely. He'd seen the shoes.

But still, he wanted to be sure.

And so, he waited. If Kevin did come out, and if he did see Casey there, did it really matter? After all, Kevin was the one who had been in the stall. The one who should be ashamed. Not Casey. Casey had only been curious.

Five minutes passed and no one emerged from the men's room. Then five more ticked by. After fifteen minutes, Casey began to wonder if he had imagined what he'd seen. Then another car pulled into the lot, and someone got out. Casey watched as the figure walked through snow to the restroom, disappeared inside, and came back out a few minutes later. The man got back into his car and left.

Something wasn't right.

Before he could talk himself out of it, Casey got out and walked quickly back to the restroom. He went inside, stopped, looked around. The doors to all three stalls were open. He bent down, looked beneath them, saw nothing.

There was only one door to the men's room. One way in and

out. The windows did not open. If anyone had exited, Casey would have seen.

He walked to the first stall and pushed the door all the way open. It was empty. So was the second. He stopped in front of the third, the one Kevin and the unknown man had occupied. His hand trembled as he pushed the door, which swung inward.

This one too was empty. Then Casey noticed the shoe. Just one. It was on its side to the right of the toilet. A black Converse Chuck. He leaned down and picked it up. On the toe cap the KISS logo was drawn in black marker.

Casey dropped the sneaker, turned, and left the restroom. He went back to his truck, got inside, and put his hands on the wheel to stop them from shaking. He stared at the doorway to the men's room. Kevin hadn't come out. He was sure of it.

He fumbled in his pocket for the keys, started the car. The engine sputtered to life, and he backed out.

As he sped down the road to the highway, he glanced in the rearview mirror. In the glass, the full moon reflected back at him. Then he looked out the windshield and saw it hanging above the road, a thin, silver sliver in the clear, black night. He looked again in the mirror and saw it there, round and full and yellow. Then the moon doubled, becoming two moons that slowly moved away from each other until they were a pair of eyes. The sound of whistling broke through the hum of the engine.

He turned on the radio. Mr. Mister's "Broken Wings" filled the cab. He turned it up as loud as it would go, singing along, drowning out the whistling as he raced for home.

Friday, December 13

The Genny Cream Ale wasn't helping.

Staring into the bonfire, Casey tried to forget about the dreams. He'd been having them more and more frequently since the night he'd walked into the men's room and found Kevin's shoe on the floor of the stall. Dreams where he was the one wearing the scuffed-up brown shoes and the green corduroy pants. Where he was the one with his hands pressed against the cold cinderblock wall of the men's room while Kevin stood behind him, whispering in his ear that he was going to cum.

Kevin himself was missing.

He hadn't been at school on Monday morning. Nor the next day. He hadn't been at school any day that week. Most people assumed he was sick with the flu that had been going around. Finally, that afternoon when school let out, Casey had stopped by his house, on the pretense of dropping off some homework assignments. Kevin's mother, who answered the door, had accepted the papers without comment. Casey had told her to tell Kevin he hoped he felt better soon. She'd nodded in response, then closed the door.

Casey took another long drink of beer. He'd thought coming to the party at Sheila Erikson's house might help, or at least make him feel less alone.

"You hear about Kevin?"

Casey looked up. Trevor McIntosh had come over to stand beside him. He took a swig from the bottle in his hand.

"Heard what?" Casey asked.

"They're saying he ran away," Trevor said.

"Why?" Casey asked.

Trevor grunted. "Cuz he's queer."

"What?" said Casey. "Why would you say that?"

"Heard they found some stuff in his room," Trevor said, as if this explained it. "Videos or something. Magazines. Gay shit. His dad told him to get the fuck out. Guess he did."

Casey wanted to say that this wasn't true. Then he thought about what he'd seen in the men's room. What he'd heard. So, he said nothing.

"Oh well," Trevor said. "If he is, AIDS'll get him anyway. He held the bottle he was drinking for up and shook it. You want another beer?"

"No," Casey said. "Thanks, though."

Trevor walked back towards the house. Casey remained by the fire. Had Kevin run away? Part of him wanted to believe this was true.

He never left the men's room.

The voice in his head whispered the words. Then it laughed. The laughter grew, filling his ears. He tossed his beer can into the fire.

WISHBONE

Saturday, December 21

When Casey put his hand in the pocket of his coat, he realized that he'd put the wishbone in there. His mother had handed it to him earlier in the day. "It's dried out," she said. "Time to make a wish."

But Casey hadn't been able to think of a wish. He hadn't been able to think about anything except the restroom and getting there before 11. Hadn't been able to think about anything else all week.

Now he was seated in the third stall. It was almost 11. Several men had come in and out in the half hour he'd been sitting there, but none had stayed. He worried that none would. Then he worried that they would.

The door opened and closed. Someone walked to the center stall, entered, shut the door. Casey held his breath. Then he heard the sound of metal scraping. The dispenser cover being removed.

He had already removed the cover on his side but left the toilet paper in place. Now, he reached over with trembling fingers and took that out too. Only the hole was there now, unobstructed.

A single eye looked through, green like summer grass. It blinked.

"Show me," a man's voice whispered.

Casey stood up, fumbled with the buckle on his belt. He unzipped his jeans and lowered them along with his underwear. His cock, already hard, jutted out from his body.

"Stroke it," the man ordered.

Casey did, wrapping his hand around his dick and pumping it slowly. The eye blinked.

"Tell me what you want," the voice said.

Casey didn't respond. He couldn't find the words.

"Tell me what you want," the voice said again.

Casey stared into the green, unblinking eye.

"Tell me."

Casey cleared his throat. He tried to say the words.

"Tell me."

"I want you inside me," Casey whispered.

The eye blinked shut. When it opened again, it was yellow. Casey stared at it. His hand continued to stroke himself. He couldn't stop.

"Unlock your door."

The eye disappeared, and Casey heard the sound of a latch sliding open. Then he saw shoes in the gap beneath his own stall door. They were brown, scuffed.

He reached out and slid the latch of his door to the side. The door swung inward. A man stepped in, closed the door behind him, locked it. Casey looked into his face, but saw only the eyes, glowing faintly.

"What's that in your hand?" the man asked.

Casey looked down and saw that he was still, ridiculously, holding the wishbone. "Oh," he said. "Nothing." He started to slip the wishbone back into his jacket pocket, but the man stuck out his hand. Casey hesitated, then held the wishbone up. The man gripped one side in his fingers.

"Make a wish," he said. "Then let's see whose comes true."

Casey pulled. The wishbone resisted for a moment, then snapped in two. The man held up the shorter side. He grinned. "You win," he said.

Casey looked at the man's face, which now shifted, becoming something familiar. A face he'd seen before in the magazine hidden beneath his bed.

"Turn around," the man said.

Casey obeyed. He placed his hands on the wall, feeling the roughness of the blocks, the coldness of the winter night that had soaked into them. Behind him, he heard the sound of a zipper. He closed his eyes.

He felt fingers spread him open. Heard the sound of spitting. Then there was pain as the man entered him. Casey gasped.

The man leaned forward. Breath, strangely cold, caressed the back of Casey's neck. The man's mouth found Casey's ear, a sweetly-sick scent like rotting fruit escaping his lips.

He began to whistle.

A BARBED QUILL

CRAIG BROWNLIE

ON AN AUTUMN NIGHT in 1992, Charlie Flynn walked into the lobby of the Macklowe Hotel on West 44th Street and considered the front desk. After a few minutes, the concierge stepped from behind his podium and approached, "Looking to check in, Mr. Flynn?"

Charlie had a show running at the nearby Belasco, so the recognition did not catch him off guard. He nodded and accepted an arm of support.

"If I may say so, Mr. Flynn, you should take care of yourself. You look like you could use a good night's rest and we have the room for you."

Charlie leaned away from the concierge. He had at least twenty years on Charlie. "Where's home . . . .," he leaned in to read the nametag, " . . . Paul? Queens?"

"Brooklyn, Mr. Flynn." The concierge used the shared confidence to move Charlie a little forward.

"Nice place with a wife and 2.3 little ragamuffins?"

"Four, Mr. Flynn. The youngest is a boy and he's . . . "

"I'm sure he's a pill, Paul." Charlie took Paul by the arm and lead him across the floor to the nearest alcove. "I've recently left a paradox, Paul. Have you ever been in a paradox?"

"Who hasn't, Mr. F? Like they say, when you come to a fork in the road, take it."

"I put the car into park and stared out the windshield. You understand my dilemma, Paul." Charlie came to a decision. "Want to see something luscious?"

Paul held up his hands in a definite no, which stopped nothing.

Charlie removed his corduroy sport coat and passed it to Paul. Then he tugged his t-shirt until Paul placed a calming hand in the way.

"Please, Mr. Flynn. We've already had the two leads from *Anna Karenina* in here tonight trying to have it off behind the potted palms."

Charlie clicked his tongue and said, "All right." He turned his back and added, "The neck is loose so tug the back down a bit."

Paul did. After a minute he said, "Who did this? Do you want me to call somebody?"

"Have you ever written anything, Paul? Maybe with a pencil which broke before you finished a thought? These bruises are the punctuation at the end of my sentence because I didn't have any ink left to write with."

"If I ever raised a hand to my wife, her brothers and her cousins would kill me, Mr. Flynn. You need somebody who'll protect you."

Charlie took the jacket back. "Signing up for the job? I didn't think so—part of the short list of men who've let me down. But don't worry. Not from a boyfriend. I don't even know their names, but let's not tell anyone tonight. I recognized a face or two from something nice I did once.

"Instead, why don't you walk me over to the front desk. We'll find me a nice room with a good lock on it where I can try to sleep." As they walked, Charlie said, "I feel like a penthouse tonight, Paul."

"Do you need a toothbrush or anything?" asked Paul, gesturing at the empty space where Charlie's suitcase ought to be.

Charlie jingled a pill bottle in his coat pocket, "I have everything I need."

Paul stopped them ten feet from the front desk, "You're not planning something stupid?"

"I'm never stupid with pills."

Charlie kept his word. Two hours later, leaving the bottle unopened on the nightstand, he stepped off the penthouse balcony and plummeted to his death.

Eight years earlier, the School of Theatre at Northern Appalachian University held a memorial service for Professor Spaulding right before fall semester. Charlie sat in the back row of the chapel surrounded by those who dreamed of jobs backstage, onstage, and front of house.

A BARBED QUILL

Frank arrived late and stood in the aisle until Charlie shoved over to make room. After frowning at Charlie, people greeted Frank with warmth.

"Your summer?" whispered Frank after settling in place.

"All right, I delivered pizzas."

"And worked on your suntan, it looks like."

"Your internship?" asked Charlie. "You managed a suntan too."

"Awesome. I spent the last week in the Hamptons. My boss's place. Gift bags for the interns." Frank reached into his shirt and displayed a gold chain. "Did you have any classes with Spaulding? What a dick."

"Did you have class with him?"

"He taught sophomore acting until he got sick. I looked forward to it but then he walks in the first day and gives me shit. Not only me. Then I heard how he'd forced anyone going for a theatre degree to resign from the Gay Alliance."

"We have a Gay Alliance?"

"They meet off campus." Frank bit a fingernail. "I swear the old queen drove the queer right out of anyone he suspected of 'leanings.'" After a few moments of quiet, Frank asked, "How'd he die? The gay plague?"

"He wasn't gay," said a nearby freshman. Wilting under the gazes of Charlie and Frank, he added, "Was he?"

Outside afterwards, Charlie mingled.

"Did you hear Alan Landru is coming here?" said Frank, reappearing by his side.

"To teach? You must have heard wrong. He can't be taking over for Spaulding."

"He's not. They have somebody coming in from Columbus. 'We do provincial' should be our motto."

"Still . . . Landru? Really? He's a big deal."

"You'd think so. He's been doing this thing for years where he heads out to some boondocks university and tries out new work on the young bucks. He's directing the second play this semester. Maybe he'll teach a class on playwriting. You'd like that."

Charlie stood in the wings of the proscenium stage. Landru sat out in the audience. Most roles had been cast for the season, but the school had scored a major coup by having the Pulitzer Prize winner spend the semester as a visiting professor. He merited a special open call three weeks into the term.

Tearing his eyes away from the seats, Charlie scanned his monologue again. Around him, the other upper-class actors wandered aimlessly and mouthed speeches silently. The seniors expected to be cast. For the juniors like Charlie, the audition would have to suffice as their brush with greatness.

None of them had seen a script for Landru's play. Charlie had chosen a Christopher Durang monologue because it felt absurd without being sycophantic. He watched as Landru dismissed the first two actors when they launched into pieces from his plays. Both rushed for the exit and could be heard screaming outside before the stage door slammed.

All around Charlie, actors tossed aside their plans and rapidly rehearsed new monologues. When the stage manager called for Frank, he whacked Charlie on the back as he passed. "Break a leg," hissed Charlie. Frank majored in arts management, but he could not resist the chance to stand in the room with Landru.

Frank nailed it. Landru had what he needed and urged the stage manager to rush the rest of the actors.

Charlie's left leg had fallen asleep as his turn arrived, so he did not mind when Landru yelled out "Cigarette break!" and walked out of the theatre.

Charlie looked at the stage manager, Mindy. She smiled and, with a shrug, mouthed, "I'm sorry."

Finally, Landru returned but stood at the back of the auditorium. Charlie could see the glowing tip of a cigarette, so he knew where the director stood. Mindy coughed and gestured wildly at Landru.

"I'm not technically in the theatre proper, so pretend you can't see me back here," he declaimed.

"But I can see you," muttered Mindy.

"Which is why you're not an actor," retorted Landru. "Because you can't pretend, and you can't enunciate!" Then he turned on Charlie. "Your turn! Let me hear you! Make me feel something back here!"

Charlie could bellow, but he doubted he could bellow and act.

The next morning, the sheet went up listing the members of the ensemble. Frank appeared first on the list. Reading his own name, Charlie pasted a placid expression on his face before facing the crowd of disappointed students pressing in around him.

A BARBED QUILL

"We're here to create art together," lectured Landru at the cast and crew at the first rehearsal. "I will inspire you with my words and you will inspire me with your choices. I feed you and you feed me like the snake of Ouroboros we will create a perfect circle."

Nothing prepared the actors for the rehearsal process. Landru handed out the script in random scenes. They veered from political commentary to the deeply personal.

Frank raised his hand and spoke when Landru ignored him. "Didn't the snake devour itself?"

The ripple of giggles brought a flash to Landru's cheeks. "See me when we're through," he directed.

As a background player, Charlie did not mind the haphazard script. The more scenes jumped, the more he could show his versatility: Secretary of HEW to bridge partner in a retirement community to a man in a bath house to a nurse in an emergency room.

Frank complained playing a lead held nowhere near the fun of the chorus. They could focus on types while he had to learn new lines every day without a throughline.

Finally, during notes after a grueling rehearsal, Frank burst out, "Look, this makes no sense. I don't understand if I'm playing an actor playing an actor. What am I supposed to feel? I don't understand why something this simple has to have all these layers. I'm not saying it's not any good."

Landru held up his hand to stop Frank from talking. His voice ran steady and deep. He should be the one on stage, thought Charlie. I could write for his type.

"Young Frank, life is complex. Three or four writers are running around to producers right now trying to sell their idea of the perfect AIDS play. But who did the producers come to when they wanted something with flesh? They came to me. I am complexity incarnate."

"You're Narcissus incarnate, too," said Frank.

Landru's eyes closed while his face passed through a series of reds until he settled back on the skin tone of someone who worked too much indoors. "Admittedly."

Mindy hurriedly dismissed everyone. The technical crew made for Landru, but he shooed them away.

"Mr. Flynn! To me!" bellowed Landru.

"Fuck," said Charlie, turning back.

Frank whacked him on the butt and said, "Better you than me."

Landru stood cross-armed mid-stage. "Mr. Flynn, I have been talking with your classmates and now it is your turn."

Charlie forced his eyes to open. He tilted back and eyed the older man. "I don't have class tomorrow afternoon."

"How about now? A little bird told me you wish to be a scribbler. Walk me back to the hideous apartment this school provides visiting dignitaries."

Discarding tomorrow's Philosophy and Stage Combat classes from his plans, Charlie shrugged and followed the thick shoulders and wide backside of the famous man.

Outside, Landru paused and lit a cigarette. "You're not much of an actor. You prop up the set well enough though."

"You're not much of a director," replied Charlie and cringed. "I'm sorry . . ."

"No, you're right. I do whatever all the slobs have done with my plays already. I cajole and chastise because they did." Landru turned and walked down the sidewalk. "Coming?" After Charlie rejoined him, Landru asked, "Are you a better writer?"

"I think so."

Landru stopped in the middle of a crosswalk with no cars in view. He emphasized his thoughts in the air. "Go, retrieve your latest masterpiece and we shall read it together."

"What? Now?" Charlie studied the older man's face. His early onset jowls impregnated his expression with a lack of seriousness.

"We shall drink wine, watch the sun rise and dissect your art. Now go. I will stand here until you return."

"Here? In the middle of the street?" Charlie shrugged as Landru turned to study the edifice of the local movie theatre.

For a week, Charlie missed over half his classes in favor of Landru.

Frank took him aside during a break in their rehearsal on Friday night. "Coming to the Downstairs when we finish here?"

"I don't think so," Charlie wanted to hear more about working with Mike Nichols. Landru had become his Scheherazade.

"Because you'll be busy finishing Landru?"

Anger blossomed in Charlie, "Jealous much, Frankie? We were

roommates. Then we had a fling. What if I do take a page from your book? You're the one who bragged about how he spent his summer."

Frank pushed him into a corner. "You're an idiot. Maybe I just want you to be careful. You know I was the teacher's pet first." He waited while Charlie studied the warning and discarded it. "I'll give you this much. His writing's a lot better now." He leaned in and gave Charlie a deep kiss. "But for your sake, remember some of us are your age." He turned and walked away.

Charlie thought how completely dramatic it would be to see Landru standing there as a witness even before he saw Landru 's silhouette.

In later years Charlie wondered if he remembered the reality the first time around or a version rewritten by the quill—a little self-immolation masquerading as self-justification.

When Charlie arrived outside Landru 's apartment building later in the night, a pile of paper drifted from above. He recognized the pages as his play. Looking up, he saw Landru leaning out of the window, benevolent and triumphant.

"You know something?" Charlie yelled up at the sad, sagging face bent down at him. "You set a scene a lot better out here than on stage!"

Landru 's large lips puckered scenically. "Good line. You should come up after you've gathered your scattered pages and we'll find a place to insert it."

Chanting "such a tiny dick, such a giant ass," Charlie collected the litter.

Landru's door lay open when Charlie finally arrived. He found his host lounging to solo jazz piano, beautiful and discordant. "Doesn't it sound like people?" commented Landru.

Charlie considered the paper pile in his hands and asked, "Why don't you ever show me what you're working on?"

"You never asked." Landru lowered his bare feet to the ground and said, "You won't find it in here. I do my best work in bed."

Charlie did not take the bait. Instead, he followed Landru into the bedroom.

Landru pointed at pages along one wall. "Each of those is a scene for this bastardization you and your fellow amateurs helped to create." Swinging out an arm for balance, he procured a page from the floor. "This one is the mess we worked on this evening. It featured your friend—Frank, is it? Let's do a bit of editing, shall we? Where did I put my pen?"

Charlie pointed to the nearby desk.

"No, I rather think I'll use my special pen." He went to his secretary desk and sat in his antique chair. "I had these shipped. Nothing is more important than a consistent work space." Opening the roll top, he pulled out a wooden box and extracted a quill pen. "No sense making a change unless you mean it." Landru bent over the manuscript and scratched at the paper like a signer of the Declaration of Independence and handed the page to Charlie.

In the original scene Frank portrayed a young actor confessing his homosexuality to his girlfriend. "You made him pledge his undying devotion," said Charlie. "I don't see how you're moving the plot along."

"Everything doesn't move the plot along!" erupted Landru. "Plot, plot, plot! They demand invention and art, but they only see art through archaic eyes!" He jumped at Charlie and waved the quill barbs under his nose. "The way to change minds is, first, you change the world!"

Charlie sneezed and walked out.

On Saturdays, they rehearsed in the afternoon. Charlie watched as Frank worked through the new scene with Janie MacAdoo.

—*"But I want to marry you!"*

—*"I've learned my life has been all a fantasy, boys being boys, but I'm ready to be a man with a family and a wife and children and a good job in the city."*

—*"I have faith in our love and your support."*

—*"We can hold off until they find a cure."*

Charlie felt his gorge rise as the actors tossed aside their scripts and played the scene for keeps. After Mindy dismissed the cast, Charlie found Frank catching onto Janie. Arm in arm, the pair walked outside.

Later, Charlie saw the new couple in a booth at the Downstairs. He waited until Janie left Frank alone and dropped onto the bench. "You two look cozy."

A BARBED QUILL

Frank peeled the label off the bottle in his hands. "I've been doing a lot of thinking."

"This is a new side of you. When did the urge come over you to think?" asked Charlie.

"We did the scene and it felt real." Frank glanced at Charlie. "The old fart can write."

By Tuesday night, Charlie charmed his way back into Landru's apartment. He waited until the second side of *Time Out* had finished before asking, "Did you do something to Frank and Janie?"

"I'm sorry, we speak of whom?" Landru slurped his third whiskey.

"My friends—they play the couple in your play?"

"I believe I did. I made them into something better."

"You made Frank into someone he isn't."

"Don't be ridiculous. He's a grasping, cloying little shit who'd do anything to get ahead." Landru went to his liquor cart. "It's the job of the playwright to make the actor into someone. They're our clay. You're not much of a writer if you can't imagine a world different from this one."

"But they're actually dating now."

"Shocking! Two actors playing a couple and they have the temerity to inhabit the roles! We must alert *Playbill*!" Landru wiggled his pinkie, "The magic is in the implement you use."

"Frank is gay."

"Shhh," spurted Landru as he plummeted back onto the sofa. "I established the fact a couple of weeks ago in there." Landru waved his glass at the bedroom, spilling whiskey on his smoking jacket. "As I recall, you once did also."

On Thursday evening, Mindy handed Charlie a new page with his first dialog. Off in a corner, he found his way to a sincere reading of the line. While playing a nurse, he turned to a doctor, "Did you hear, they're making a movie of the Broadway hit, *Fantasy of Life*?"

Back at Landru's apartment afterwards for an impromptu gathering of cast and crew, the phone rang, and the old man lumbered into the bedroom to answer. Upon returning, he announced, "I've been optioned for the big screen again! It's been a dry few years, but it's finally happened!"

Charlie drifted from the clutch of admirers surrounding the great man. He looked from the door to the bedroom and wondered where he wanted to end the night. If he left now, Landru would reach into his pile of admirers and extract a new toy.

Sidestepping his way into the bedroom, Charlie found the working script on the rolltop desk. The quill pen had been responsible for Frankie's transformation and Landru's success, but it had not been left out. The roll did not budge, so he searched the drawers. When he saw Landru's pants flung over a chair in the corner, he searched the pockets and found a likely key. The box beneath the roll held the quill. Caressing the barbs, the ink inside dripped.

He scratched out some asinine lines about an upcoming meeting of the Gay Men's Health Crisis and had the actor say he had heard a brilliant new playwright had recently been discovered and his powerful new play would be staged by Joe Papp next fall. "The playwright's name is Charlie Flynn."

Charlie's heart paused when his rewritten scene started. Then, the actor sniggered as he said Charlie's name. The few people around the theatre paying attention joined in giggles. Landru must be pulling a prank, perhaps a public kiss-off.

Charlie walked outside to relearn how to breathe. He argued with a dumpster until he collapsed against the side of the building. People walked past after the rehearsal finished. Frank stopped to look at him. Janie stood beside Frank. When she tugged on his arm, Frank followed.

Alan Landru exited into the alley last. He walked by alone but dignified in a way which exuded Manhattan at 3 am on a Sunday morning.

At the end of the alley, he bellowed, "To me, Mr. Flynn!" In the professorial abode, after more jazz, "I saw your clumsy change this morning."

Charlie dodged the conversation, "You should open a window in here or something. They sell incense in the college bookstore. Why didn't you erase it?"

"Because you needed to learn it's not only the pen. You have to give it your art and your brains. A playwright needs to give the actors the right words. Otherwise, nothing happens."

"It's a quill—how do you know it isn't the ink?"

"I don't. Besides, it's a modified quill, so it's a product of the last century. It holds its supply of ink."

"What can you do with this quill? How much damage can you do? Can you make people sick?"

"Why don't you ask if I can heal people?"

"Well? Is it so powerful?" Charlie felt those heavily lidded eyes watching him cogitate. "If you could really change the world, why haven't you?"

"I asked the same question of the previous owner."

"You're not a good enough writer either," accused Charlie.

"I said something in a similar vein to him except he was fucking brilliant."

Charlie's mind raced forwards and backwards. "You worked with . . . "

"I did."

"Someone beat him to death."

"I remember watching the ink bottle shatter on his floor."

Charlie rose from the sofa.

Landru cupped his glass to his chest. "Losing your stomach for the work? Don't leave now."

Charlie did not. Instead, he went into the bedroom and opened the desk. "I'm getting ready for bed." He retrieved the quill box and returned. Landru's snores stopped him in his tracks. The box warmed his belly like the touch of a lover asking him to stay in bed. He went back to the desk and sat. He had made a mistake with his first attempt. He could do better.

Conveniently for Charlie's plan, Landru lectured the cast before the next rehearsal, saying they had been losing the thread of the play all week.

The two actors playing patients in a medical waiting room put their hearts into their lines.

"Did you hear? The famous playwright, the one who wrote *Fantasy of Life*, he died. They're not giving the cause, but everyone knows he had AIDS."

Landru made it halfway up the aisle before collapsing.

Charlie rushed to his side. Numb with fear, excitement, and anxiety, he extracted the apartment key from Landru 's pocket while Mindy called for an ambulance.

By the time the chairman of the theatre department met with the cast and crew the next day to announce the cancellation of the show, Charlie, quill box in his lap, sat on a Greyhound bus headed for New York City. Flooded with ideas, Charlie wondered if an inanimate object could be a muse.

Charlie slept rough in Central Park for six weeks before the pen gifted him the monolog which placed money in his bank account. Charlie found a good enough actor willing to perform the piece for an Off-Off-Broadway audition.

When Frank appeared at his door, Charlie had gone to New Saint Marks Baths the night before and did not appreciate the noon wake up. He had not seen his old friend since the death of Alan Landru.

"They announced city health is closing down Saint Marks," announced Frank. "You walked right past me last night. I stood by the sauna."

"I didn't know to look," responded Charlie. Then he embraced Frank and tugged him into his studio apartment. "Do I have to ask what you're doing in New York? Becoming a theatrical powerbroker?"

"I know how Dustin Hoffman likes his coffee if you're asking. I thought you hid in your parents' house, licking your wounds, plotting a career managing a fast food restaurant."

"I'm plotting a lifetime of being turned down by off-off-Broadway houses who wouldn't know a decent plot if it slapped them in the face."

Frank shrugged. "You need one person to notice you. Our agency does a showcase with all the fresh faces the older agents like to litter their parties with. They're young and desperate. Give me a scene or three and I'll slip them in."

Charlie threw himself into Frank's arms. The kiss lasted long enough to establish Charlie had not brushed his teeth. He massaged Frank's crotch with his erection protruding from his pajama bottoms.

Then he stepped back and gave Frank a closer examination. "All tired out from last night?"

"I didn't do anything last night." Frank

Charlie shrugged, "Makes sense these days."

"I'm married now." Perkiness appeared on his face like a forced blossom. "Plus, I'm representing actors instead of suffering like one because the money is better. Greed is good, as they say. Besides, the agent stands off to the side while the artist announces they have AIDS, not at the mic doing the announcing."

"You're not like this because of Janie? Or anything else?"

Frank nodded. "I go to the baths because I've forgotten how to feel some things. I blame Landru for being such a good writer when he gave Janie and me that scene. You remember?"

Charlie backed away. "You ought to go."

Charlie crafted three comic scenes tracing his experiences since arriving in the city. holding the pen gave him such a rush, but the ink looked lower. The last scene he wrote projected his coming success.

As it turned out, the professionals enjoyed nothing better than the gentle skewering of their compatriots. Frank's boss signed Charlie. One month into rehearsal for his first off-Broadway play, Charlie's quill arranged his reassignment to the newly promoted Frank.

A week after winning the Tony award, Charlie sat with Frank in the Kimberly Hotel rooftop bar. "Here we are, two imposters," said Frank.

"Hmm?"

"You're some kid from the Midwest who's become the crown prince of Broadway." He sipped his pina colada. "I laid a lot of groundwork during my internship by doing a lot of laying. Then I come back a changed man and blow all that up because I'm not able to play ball anymore. Pretty fast, neither the boss men nor the boss ladies can recall my name. Honestly, when I ran into you, I had packed it in."

"I'm glad you didn't. This success has to make it a little easier."

"Janie's having a baby."

"Congratulations!"

"Okay."

They watched the sun set and sipped their drinks. Then Charlie told Frank about the quill pen.

"Prove it. Make me gay again."

"I think I like you asexual."

"You can always change me back if it isn't working out."

"I don't think you understand how it works."

"The quill?"

"I mean life. I don't think it's a great thing to change your orientation."

"Like when someone waves their magic wand and tells you to stop being gay?" They fumed together for a while. "What about making AIDS go away?"

"How about if I make Reagan gay? Or kill Hitler?"

"Interesting order of preference there." Frank stirred his drink.

"I tried. Do you remember during rehearsal when they tried that scene about AIDS never having existed. So bad we cut it."

"Nichols hated it."

"I think the quill isn't any good with changing major events because the actors can't perceive what they're saying as anything other than fantasy, at least for past events."

"Maybe you're a crap writer. Or you really don't want to change things."

"I'm the one the quill chose." Though he could not stop wondering if Frank had been right.

"You need to take responsibility for the quill, or I'll find someone who can do better than you!" screamed Frank.

By 1988, Charlie could predict Frank's behavior on the anniversary of his quill confession. They made a point of meeting on the rooftop of the Kimberly one week after the Tonys and hashing out the previous year. Frank hardly referred to Charlie's magic pen any other time.

With the quill in his possession, the award celebration could be a foregone conclusion, but Charlie stopped putting his finger on the scale after back-to-back wins. This year, he had arranged for one of Frank's other clients to carry off the medallion. The gesture had not prevented Frank's rant.

The real question haunting Charlie regarded the implications of a big change. The idea of curing AIDS with the quill always hovered slightly behind his ear. Next to it, a voice asked whether he would have come into possession of the quill without the epidemic. Landru might not have visited the college. He certainly would not have died as he did. Behind those voices, a choir sang out reasons not to solve any global problems. He would exacerbate rather than alleviate. The good he would accomplish would become a set of tumbling dominoes with the last one wrecking his life and career.

"I can't change election outcomes or stop wars. Don't look at me like I'm being selfish. I'm realistic. You can keep yelling about it, but my mind is set."

"I can see we're both children of the Eighties," said Frank. "Give the pen to someone who writes political thrillers! Or medical stuff."

"The pen belongs to me." Charlie rattled with anger.

"You're afraid of making a difference!"

"I've healed more people than Jesus did by my age," ventured Charlie. "A few dozen homeless from Times Square live in housing now."

"In Jersey City . . . " Frank shifted in his chair. "Fix me," he said softly.

Charlie had tried without telling Frank. His wife and child lived in Connecticut while Frank lived in a city apartment. Frank coped with Charlie's tinkering by cultivating a drug habit.

Charlie rose from his chair and walked around the table. He bent over and kissed Frank on the lips before leading him by the hand to the men's room, except Frank slipped free before they arrived.

Two years later, they met at Frank's uptown pad for their annual post-mortem.

"Bring back Haring or Ryan White," demanded Frank.

"We both know it's not a good idea, not after the experiment with my dad," said Charlie. "What if he came back and died again underground in a tiny box. He might have been a homophobic asshole, but not that for him." He walked out on the balcony. "You look like shit."

"It's my meds," said Frank as if he had pulled an all-nighter in college.

"You have to be shitting me."

"Janie comes into the city once a month and brings the kid with her. They stay here." Frank turned from the view and studied his reflection in the glass. "The first woman I ever fucked, and I couldn't believe in it. I didn't know I could do such a thing. I was gay at twelve."

"You had it lucky living here and not in the Midwest."

"Oh, yeah, fucking Long Island made it all very clear. Now I've screwed ingenues and secretaries and interns, and I feel nothing. You know, I fell in love like five or six time my first couple years in college—once with you."

"Really?"

"I haven't had sex in seven months."

Charlie wanted to go home and take out the quill. Lately, he had not needed much more than sitting at his desk with the pen resting on a blotter before him. As the ink grew drier, Charlie let it pulse with power in his grip.

"Don't do me any favors," said Frank as if he read Charlie's mind.

"I think the ink might be running out."

"Then buy more."

"I can't chance adulterating it."

The rest of 1990, Charlie watched Frank lose his job and his family.

Two days after Christmas, Frank walked into Charlie's condo and ripped the place apart. He wanted the quill, but Charlie had moved it to a safe deposit box. A limp, sad friend, the pen had needed protection.

A year later, Charlie created a one-act about single payer health care since he could think of no better way to use the quill to deal with the devastation of AIDS. Charlie brought the script to the bank and wrote key lines in the depository anteroom.

Then, he wrote another short piece about a powerful agent's downfall and his successful rehab stay.

During rehearsals off-off-Broadway for the latter, Frank appeared in the lobby and demanded to talk to Charlie.

When he saw and smelled Frank, Charlie led him out the door. They walked down the street in silence and turned at the next alley.

"I saw you made a show about me," said Frank. "You ought to

give the quill to somebody else." Frank's voice sounded raw. "You're not using it right. Maybe you never have."

"I practically etched the ending of this play onto the paper. The quill is running dry."

"You're a hack." He backed Charlie toward the dark end of the street. "You couldn't write well enough to save peoples' lives. You didn't care enough to learn how. You gave up once you got yours."

That winter, Janie called Charlie to let him know that Frank had died in a flophouse in New Jersey.

The ink had almost deteriorated to nothing. Frank had been the only person who knew about the quill. Mourning in his own fashion, Charlie attempted a last full-length play about the presidential contest, using the quill only for key words. He predicted a return to power for the Democrats on a wave of resentment for those currently in power.

Marketed as a return to form, the show opened on Broadway four weeks before election day.

After opening night, Charlie went with the show people to Sardi's to await the first reviews. He sat alone. He wore a velour tracksuit with a velour gym bag, containing the dry quill.

At the bank, he emptied the safe deposit box containing the quill and his stash of cash. Placing it all in the gym bag, he padded the quill's wooden container with the money.

Bowing reverently, the producer placed the critical praises on the table before him.

Above the fold on the front page, the big headline announced AIDS had become the number one killer of men between the ages of 25 and 44.

Charlie zipped the paper into the bag and walked four miles south to the underside of the Brooklyn Bridge where he had seen a homeless encampment.

In the middle of the night, none of the residents expected a well-dressed stranger. Ignoring catcalls and threats, Charlie joined a small group around a barrel fire. He opened the gym bag and removed the newspaper and added it to the flames. The faces of the others scanned the remaining contents of his bag.

Charlie pulled out the quill box and opened it. "I'm here for a cremation." He turned to the old woman beside him and presented the box to her. Then he held the quill over the flames and lit the barbs. He held onto the tip for a minute before letting the barrel accept the gift.

Picking up the bag, Charlie turned to walk away. Before he made ten yards, the residents attacked him for the money in the bag.

Charlie spent two days in the hospital and two more at home before he dressed in the outfit which he called Professional Playwright On Call. Sitting through the performance beside the stage manager in the booth, Charlie felt hopeless. The election would change nothing.

Stepping out of the Belasco stage door, he walked to the Macklowe Hotel.

THE THING THAT CRAWLS

AMANDA M. BLAKE

PERHAPS YOU STOP at *what is that thing?* and go no further, because there isn't anything left within the strangled scream in your mind or the shrillness spilling from your constricted throat as you cower against the headboard like a larval worm dragged from filthy, wet soil into clean light.

But as I clutch my spider-twitch fingers into your sheets, twist lungs and limbs over your legs, moan from a mouth too dark and wide, tongue lolling like a dead snake over my cheekbone and settling with a wet slap on my forehead, perhaps another thought crosses your mind—just enough room for a sylph of curiosity to slip through for the split second your terror can spare:

Who is that thing?

Have you considered that this creature invading the sanctuary of your bed once had a bed of its own and that it once had a name, that it is no mere projection of an apparition, no mimic, no illusion, that the thing that crawls before you once walked and talked and slept and ate toast and called its mother?

Or do you only consider the few paralyzed moments you have left, with the image of what I am now branded into your retinas, the last picture of the show—this thing?

No, you only scream for God, as though what giant carrion fly laid its eggs in the decaying guts of space has ears to hear or eyes to see the miniscule, pale, blue offspring among its billions. You scream for God, who never screamed for you.

Do not feel shame. I screamed once, too, and moaned, but not like this. I was not always like this. I should not be like this. If the god you scream for exists, what I am is how I know he is a man. A woman would have understood, would have twisted me for other uses; I could have made her scream instead.

In the intimacy of your bed and the island of your fear, I will pretend you asked.

Who?

They don't require it anymore, but I sat in the chair with the other male Navy recruits and watched with relief as my hair fell to the vinyl tile like cut grass. No one asked, and I didn't tell; none of us had to, but unspoken made things easier.

They hazed me almost as much as the other female recruits, but men didn't look at me the same way they did the women who, tough as nails though they were, wept over hair swept away and the awkwardness of regrowth.

Even though I was hardly the only dyke among us, I wasn't the kind of dyke that men liked to fantasize about—the wrong gait, the wrong posture, the wrong vocal burn. We are what we are, and some of us hide better, while some of us just cover our eyes and pretend no one can see us. The men were far more likely to haze me like they hazed their brothers, laugh when I took their money at poker, rib me when they beat my course times and rib the ones I beat again out of competitive spite.

Not everyone believed I was a brother-in-arms, but I left bruises where necessary, with my poverty of a childhood that had taught me to be strong. The write-ups, the aches, and the hangovers were worth it for the respect I earned from superiors who pissed down warnings from their greater height.

Those of us who made it through training came out the other side crudely stitched together with black twine. There was a specific kind of solidarity among Navy women, but I preferred the friendships of men, and they found a woman they didn't want to fuck refreshing. Our differences made moments awkward, but only moments, and when we came back from our first tour, the patchwork between us was sewn with a far finer and more thorough hand.

Back stateside, Navy women generally didn't mingle with Navy wives. The wives formed groups to support each other through the prolonged absence of husbands. Navy women created their own groups for their own purposes, but we shared more in common with our brothers than the sisters left at home. Michael, Rudy, Junior, and I were thick as thieves when we got back, drinking too much, passing money around the group through poker games, pretending we were fine when we weren't and pretending we weren't fine when we were.

Really, the only wives I knew were those of the men we served with, and the only wife who I cared to know better was Michael's. Lacey never asked me to shop with her, instead invited me to look at Michael's black Mustang baby girl in the garage. She didn't try to make me fit into the role of a Navy wife nor a work wife—some of us were, but I was a brother in almost all ways except in the latrine or running with a shirt on.

Lacey treated me the same way she treated Michael, Rudy, and Junior, passed me a beer and didn't request that I help her in the kitchen—for which her kitchen thanked her. But I would needle the guys to help clear up after, and brother or not, I couldn't make myself like football to save my life. Lacey would take me back to the den where the TV was smaller, and we would watch something else while I had a beer and she had a Diet Dr Pepper, or sometimes we didn't watch anything at all, just talked.

I didn't even care that she was lipstick and I was a pig. We didn't need to have anything in common. She showed me the boxes she'd been placed in without any expectation that I would join her, and she seemed just as interested in what I had to show her.

I kissed my favorite shipmate's wife for the first time during the Army/Navy game, when no one in our world was going to notice two women in another room—even one like me, even one like her. Or maybe she kissed me. That part is still a little fuzzy, whether she leaned in first or whether I drew her in or whether it all happened at the same time as though it had been meant to happen from the beginning, a new thread drawn painfully through skin to pull us together, with mingled blood on the needle's tip.

Soon after, I shipped out again with Michael. She sent letters and care packages to him, then a sonogram, which he displayed with pride in his bunk and showed to everyone who asked and almost everyone who didn't.

She sent me letters, too, printed rather than handwritten and as anonymous as the USPS allowed. The guys bothered the shit out of me, tried to steal the letters to glean more details than I was willing to share. I'd preferred when they hadn't asked or when I hadn't needed to field such questions as *It is a girl, right?* I'd depended on assumptions to keep some distance from matters of the heart and pussy so the others could convince themselves that I was as sexless as a Cabbage Patch doll under my pants. Romance made them see me differently, *imagine* me differently, and I didn't want my naked ass in any man's fantasy, even if they saw me with a strap-on on the other end.

In spite of them, I devoured the letters, innocuous and restrained though they were because she was another man's wife, and she would soon be a child's mother. On the one hand, we were friends. The letters read like those of a friend. On the other hand, we were everything short of lovers, and the odd phrase made my cheeks heat all the way to my ears and my clit twitch with unsettlingly matter-of-fact interest:

gloved hand

warmth at the edge of autumn

cozy

under the gray throw

My desire was positively domestic, but I was abroad with her husband, and she was stateside and going to have a baby. I wished her well with the other men in a video we made, reminded her to take advantage of every last casserole brought over, advised that she purchase a garage freezer just to make sure she had room, and bought her shower gift cards for restaurants, in case she got tired of casseroles.

I'd had all kinds of dreams in my youth, but I'd wanted to join the Navy more than anything else, and that was exactly where I was—married to the sea, like the officers who refused to retire. I didn't like to answer or tell, because I was a woman and didn't want to be seen as one, because I didn't want to be a consolation prize or a quota passed around from port to port. I'd followed the dream with a lighthouse and didn't have time for a wife. Still, I folded and unfolded the creases in her letters until they frayed.

Michael wasn't there when she went into labor, but she had her father video the whole affair from the less bloody side of the sheet. Tasteful editing, a warm glow over the blood, guts, and gore that made my fallopian tubes tie themselves in protective knots, the images instead as sweet as her child sleeping swaddled in the bassinet. Although he was damn cute.

Lacey gave Michael a son, and the Navy gave me the hook when

THE THING THAT CRAWLS

I tore my Achilles tendon during a morning run, of all things—sprawled in an ungodly mass of limb twisted all the wrong ways, cursing God, my body, and everyone and their mother to fuck themselves and each other if they dared try to help me up from the ship deck. Ultimately, Michael convinced me to use him as a crutch to the infirmary.

There, he told me he needed me to do something for him, that he wouldn't trust just anyone to the task, but if I couldn't serve at his side, he'd feel a lot better about my sanity and his wife's safety if I could keep an eye on Lacey until he came home.

I worked at the base during my rehab, then my old training officer offered me a job Trunchbulling the new recruits. I couldn't make my old times anymore, but I focused on strength training instead, winning medals in spite of a ginger limp.

But everything stateside smelled of the wrong kind of clean and a thousand chain restaurants. Machines and neon lights buzzed through the night, and I couldn't navigate by the stars anymore to save a life. I was surly, and Lacey was exhausted, but I still regularly came over, and we tiptoed around what we neither asked nor told, because she always carried with her a reminder of what we risked, tucked onto her hip with soft food crusted in the corners of his mouth.

Her next-door neighbor, however, loved children and was the unofficial babysitter of the block. She'd been trying so hard to get pregnant every time her husband was stateside and failing that sometimes mothers wondered if she would give the children back at the end of the night. As soon as Lacey didn't have to worry about breast milk, she handed her son to her next-door neighbor, poured herself wine, gave me her husband's beer, rested her head on my shoulder, and tucked herself closer and closer, first against the late winter cold and then against the chill of the air conditioner. I didn't know what she wanted, but her breast pressed against my arm, and of all the stateside smells, her shampoo justified the honorable discharge.

I did what I'd been tasked to do, looking in and looking after her. When I was with her and her son, I was Auntie, but when Lacey gave her son to the babysitter, I gave her permission to not be a mother for a little while, to not talk about her son, arrange playdates, monitor his cough, wipe his nose, or sweep up food he'd spilled on the floor. With me, she could be an adult for a few hours, and if that was my only purpose, I'd accept the fluke of her kiss. My dream had spit me out, but I didn't have to kiss her to like her, didn't have to fuck her to keep her in my life.

Then she crawled into my lap one night, blocking the psychosexual thriller we were watching, and murmured, "I didn't think I'd have to work this hard to give you a hint." I kissed her as the onscreen killer stabbed a knife into a college girl's abdomen. When she didn't let it stop there, because we didn't have to worry about who would burst in, I fucked her to pornographic moans on screen and off, her delicate legs in the air and strong thighs muffling the movie murder but not the bright red splatter in my periphery.

After that, we used the bed.

She was the romantic, with rose petals, Prosecco, and silk underwear, and I was the thing that crawled onto the foot of the bed and over her smooth, demure legs to part them roughly and feed, leaving marks on her thighs and bruises on her ass, teaching her spine to arch and crack, then teaching her to do the same to me.

Without clothes, it was harder to hide that I was a woman. No matter how butch I tried to be or how butch I was naturally, I was a woman in her eyes, soft in places when I was uncomfortable with being soft but resilient in places most men can never dream of, and I taught her how uncareful she could be with me.

For the first time, I didn't have to pretend to be something I wasn't, nor did I have to pretend to be something I was. I was unvarnished self, naked in a way I hadn't allowed myself to be in myriad locker rooms from when I was easier to puncture under a kitten heel. I wasn't her lesbian friend, her experiment, nor her substitute for a man, even when we broke out the strap-ons. I was simply Thea, a woman without any expectation of what a woman should be, and she was simply Lacey, a woman of every expectation of what a woman should be, but I didn't hold her to any of it.

I never thought of myself as the other woman. Lacey was simply mine. I knew what made her bite her fingers. I knew where she put the meat fork and the cheese grater. I knew how to put her son down in his crib. I knew the color of her manicure and her favorite wine. I painted her bedroom. I made myself vulnerable to her, a terrifying place to return despite all my strength, all my anger, all my growth, with other women and a few men under my belt and all of them held at a distance no matter how deeply I sank my fingers into them. Lacey welcomed me into her home and into her bed as exactly what I was.

If anyone whispered, they didn't do it to my face, nor did they telephone the message to Michael, as far as I knew. I was following orders from a friend, and everyone knew I didn't date. No one asked, and I didn't tell.

But with Michael off doing the things I couldn't do anymore, I stopped sharing his calendar.

He entered a house with rose petals on the floor like a trail of blood, moans in the bedroom like someone being killed. The scene: His wife on her knees as she grasped the headboard behind her, me crouched before her with my mouth fixed to her clit. She arched back and I arched down, my fingers buried inside myself and in her, moving to the same rhythm. I was a messy eater, no finesse, just enthusiasm mingled with very specific knowledge and memory.

I twisted to find the right angle. Michael's arm around my neck helped me for a fraction of a second before he snapped my spine—the crunch of a boot on puffed rice, but inside my head. The break was too low. I slumped on the bed, unable to move, unable to feel anything below the break, and above it, the worst crick I'd ever had in my life. But my mouth was functional, smeared, muffled when Michael pressed my face down onto the sheets, a little boy drowning a kitten in a bowl of milk.

Nothing muffled Lacey's screams until Michael swelled her lip with the back of his hand. She toppled from the bed, striking the wall, and dragging sheets down with her.

I couldn't turn my head, not without threatening the exposed cords. I couldn't lift my shoulders, couldn't shift my hips, might have shit the bed for all I could tell. I was a brain in the jar of a malfunctioned robot. And still I shouted the emptiest threats: *If you dare hurt her . . .*

Michael shook me by the back of the neck, lifted my dead weight up, pinched the large nipples at the tips of my breasts. It hurt to see, but it didn't hurt, not really, nor did the punch to the gut, although it knocked out what stifled breath I had. When he dropped me again, I fell like a marionette with cut strings, a mass of barely functioning meat. If it hadn't been for the sight of Lacey on the floor, crying and covering herself, I might have wished myself dead.

Michael left me there on the bed with a ball of sheets shoved into my mouth so that I was paralyzed and almost mute, just a pair of eyes and ears, a red plasma of fury, adrenaline, shame, and guilt swirling in the skull.

He grabbed Lacey by the hair. *Where is my* son?

Every time she tried to answer, he pulled whole hanks of hair out, kicked her diaphragm, her knees, punched her face, chest, gut, back. He spared none of his strength, struck her like an enemy combatant rather than an opponent in the boxing ring that we had sparred in more than once.

I wanted to surprise you. And this is what I find—a rancid, sloppy-tit slut tangle in my bed, in my home, in my wife. I swear to fuck I will kill you a dozen times, cut off your arms and limbs, leave you at a hospital, then take my son to Australia where you'll never get your disgusting hands on him again. I risked my life for you. I didn't dip my dick in anything that spread its legs for me, didn't even get to see the birth of our son, but all the sacrifices were worth it because of our promise. Then you toss my son away and whore yourself out to this Judas dyke like I'm six feet under? Maggots won't even find your remains, Lacey, if you don't tell me what the fuck is going on here.

Ropes of blood and mucus dripped from her nose and her mushed mouth. A cracked tooth nested within the cruor gelee in the carpet pile. Her beautiful, delicate body was unrecognizable, no longer beautiful, no longer delicate, barely human as she squinted through swollen eyelids, one eye underneath threatening to burst.

Sometimes it seemed as though my life was a serious of desert-set obstacle courses, a harsh, hostile terrain in which I had survived by being just as harsh and hostile. I'd survived primary and secondary education, I'd survived recruit training, and I'd survived four-month radio silence on a floating fraternity. I'd killed men. I'd killed women. I'd done my damn job, followed orders, busted heads, kicked ass, and took names.

But torture was watching the woman I loved beaten to a bloody pulp for something I had done. All my life I'd been able to throw punches with the best of them, and now I couldn't even move my middle finger to flip the bastard off. I couldn't hold her, couldn't shield her, couldn't stop him, couldn't end the nightmare playing in front of my face while I struggled to breathe.

THE THING THAT CRAWLS

She held up her hands in a vain attempt to protect herself, shedding bloody tears.

I didn't want to do it.

I jerked, the force of my twitch shuddering the mattress beneath me. My neck crackled, a live wire sparking in the bloody conductive matrix of my insides.

Michael bent down, almost nose to nose with her, teeth bared in a mask. *Could have fooled me, Lace.*

She threatened to hurt our son if I didn't. And then she threatened to tell you when I did. I never wanted this.

Both man and wife turned creaking necks to me. Inhuman faces melted, molded, contorted beyond unrecognizability into transformation, fraternal twin parasites of betrayal wriggling through gray matter and fixed upon me.

I read loathing, self-pity, and pleading in what was left of my lover, but she didn't reach for her husband to stop him as he thundered to his bed. Cheeks and ears florid and spittle flicking from his lip, he dragged my sandbag ass onto the ground and finished what he had started on his wife. I couldn't feel it any more than I could feel the piss that stained the carpet until he forced my cheek into the mess. Lacey huddled in the corner, biting the back of her hand and flinching at everything that he devised upon me.

I trusted you. I trusted you with her. I trusted you with my child. I trusted you to have my back. You twisted, perverted monster. You make me fucking sick.

Tear of fiber and crack of bone, impossible arch of back. He couldn't get a grip on my short hair, so he grabbed my foot instead to hold me up while he slammed steel toes into me over and over and over, gut, chest, pussy, back, until I exhaled bloody foam. Boot in face, another crunch from cartilage shards.

When he had finally exhausted himself from innumerable rounds with my broken, stubbornly living body, he bent over me and vomited onto my face. Bile dripped into my mouth and down my throat, stung my eyes. He coughed the sourness from his mouth, then gathered mucus in the back of his throat to spit into the slime.

Why won't you fucking die?

I opened my mouth to tell him *Because I want to kill you and your wife so hard they won't be able to identify your remains among the cockroaches and cow intestines,* but all that came out was a wordless moan.

He grabbed me by my slippery face, picked me up from the puddle of blood, piss, and sick, ground his heel into the base of my back, more crackling that I could hear but couldn't feel, and wrenched my head clean around.

And still, one-hundred-eighty degrees twisted, I could still see them through my wide-open eyes, a moan still howling from my wide-open mouth, and there was no more pain.

For me.

You see, I don't make idle threats. I may not be able to keep them at first, but when the means fall into my hands—by whatever means necessary—I clench them in my fists and keep my goddamn word.

They thought they burned me. They thought they scattered the ashes. They thought they cleaned every forensic trace of me. They thought they convinced my family, friends, coworkers, and their own neighbors that I had simply gone missing or moved or shipped out again. Lacey thought she could go back to normal once her face healed up and she could see a surgeon for the rest. Michael thought he had gotten away with coded justice, with a righteous hand that still made her flinch when he raised it.

But I never left. The thing that always sees and always moans and always crawls upside-down in painless contortion crawled across their floor while they slept, crawled onto the foot of their bed, panted over their still, huddled forms. My fingers twitched on their legs until Lacey woke to the warped shadow above her.

Her screams woke her husband as well as her child in the other room. I broke every bone in Michael's body that hands can break but saved his spine for last so he could feel every last one. Then I pulled open Lacey's chest and ripped out her gutless intestines, her fluttering lungs—finally, her shriveled heart. I held it, beating, before crushing it in my fist. My accusing face was her last living memory.

I'm not a ghost. There is no business for me to finish. I simply have new marching orders, and I will crawl the length of this wretched world on my hands and feet, hips to the sky and neck jerky and loose. I will continue to be the harsh and hostile terrain, the thirsty survivor, kicking ass and taking names.

You didn't ask, but I pretended you did. I spilled everything like viscera, and you didn't hear a word.

Hear this, cowering worm.

THE THING THAT CRAWLS

I will rip your tongue from your throat, split you chin to chest to clamp my fingers around your vocal cords. I will steal your words, your voice, everything you should have used, that I couldn't use, then snap the sticks of your ribs and impale them through your windpipe. I will take the grub of your prick and sew it to the remnant stump of your tongue. It's what you always led with anyway.

You didn't care what I was, but you should care what I am: I am the thing that crawls upon the beds of betrayal.

INKED IN DARKNESS

SARA TANTLINGER

LIZZIE STOOD OUTSIDE** of the main door to the archives, her fist hovering in the air to knock, but she couldn't bring herself to rap it against the alder wood. She swallowed saliva down into her desert of a throat, and summoned willpower from somewhere inside her nervous mind.

The campus archives were small, but contained a solid range of records, books, and artifacts. The university was located outside of Prospect, not quite the city and not quite suburbia. Somewhere in between it all, Lizzie found herself focusing on her graduate research for her master's in history. If nothing else, the wealthier people of Connecticut seemed to enjoy making donations to the private university. Perhaps it made them feel important, and the wealthier they were, the more important they wanted to feel.

One of those people had donated a rather special book, according to Clark, who had emailed Lizzie. Many graduate students had received good help from the archivist, so they claimed. For Lizzie, the few times she'd been down here, she'd mostly received uncomfortable stares. She'd always been with a group of peers, but today, she came alone. Her fellow students were gone or at work as the weekend approached, and Rose had decided to stay home because Lizzie didn't tell her she was going to see Clark. Otherwise, Rose would have accompanied her, but Lizzie would rather walk through fire than have Clark make Rose feel uncomfortable.

So, fire it was.

She knocked.

Clark opened the door so quickly, Lizzie could only assume he had been waiting on the other side the entire time, hand poised on the doorknob. He grinned at her, and it was a handsome grin by any standard, but to her, she felt like his mouth would spread into eternal teeth, then chomp away at her bit by bit. Light blue eyes regarded her, and she instantly missed the warm, earthy brown of Rose's irises. Everything about Clark sent cold spikes through her spine.

"I knew you'd be here soon." He ushered her into the archives, smile still plastered on his face.

She stepped inside, zipped her jacket up a little higher. "Bit brisk in here."

He chuckled, and the lifelessness behind that noise sent another chill to gnaw at Lizzie's bones.

"Yeah, the temperature and humidity are set to keep the records and artifacts we have preserved the best, so it can get a little cold in the winter."

He moved closer toward her, and she stepped back. Cleared her throat. "I'd love to see the book you told me about."

Clark stood in silence long enough for more discomfort to creep into the room, but then that Cheshire grin reappeared across his face. "Of course. One moment."

He disappeared into his office, and Lizzie moved about the room. The spaces in the back were lined with shelves supporting white boxes, all labeled. The stacks went pretty far back, and shadows waited on the other end. In front of the shelves, a few tables and display cases held featured objects that mostly pertained to the campus. Old university newspapers and photographs, even a 50-year-old stuffed toy mascot of an owl. Faded fur lined its body, and the orange eye bulged out like it'd been strangled.

Otherwise, it remained an ordinary room with a few desks for students to take notes, and a range of colorful pens in a plain white mug.

"Here." Clark emerged from his office and held a small object wrapped in a black cloth. He'd put on disposable gloves, and when Lizzie met his eyes, he finally unwrapped the book.

Her heart skipped a beat. "Wow," she whispered, unable to help herself. The cover was worn and looked, well, like it was hundreds of years old. It was intact, though, and the pages seemed worn, but legible. "How old is it?"

"The first entry is dated 1647, written by a woman who calls herself 'The Outcast.' She claims to have witnessed the execution of Alse Young."

"Really?" Breathless, Lizzie couldn't help but step closer to Clark. She knew as much about Alse Young as any research could tell her—the poor woman was sent to the gallows for supposed witchcraft, long before the Salem Witch Trials. She was the first documented case in the colonies when it came to witchcraft. Right here in Connecticut, a horrible hunt began that would turn the lives of so many women inside out.

And the book in Clark's hand, could it really be a firsthand account by someone who was there? Someone who witnessed the birth of the witch panic in Connecticut? Lizzie had spent so long trying to research details of women who escaped, women who found solace in each other, both in platonic and romantic ways, and the diary in Clark's hand could hold so many answers.

"Should I put disposable gloves on, too? Where are they?"

Clark closed the diary, and Lizzie felt her heart sink with the motion.

"What aspects of witch trials are you focusing on, exactly?"

He knew the answer. She'd explained before while accompanying peers to the archives.

"I . . . I'm writing about the relationships that took place between women during this time period."

Clark clicked his tongue. Lizzie wanted to rip the slimy thing out and throw it down into the shadows of the stacks. "I know what kind of *relationships* you're writing about, Lizzie. What use could that research really be of?"

"Please," she said, swallowing down her pride, and hating every second. "I appreciate your help. I would love to look through the book."

"Oh, I don't know," he said, but his eyes glimmered, and she knew he was toying with her. Playing with the prey he had all alone. The campus library was above them, and while students were still studying upstairs, it was unlikely anyone would come down here as the late afternoon stretched on into evening.

"I just want to do my research."

He stepped closer, forcing her to back up against the cold plaster of the wall.

"Are you still living with that woman? Don't you want to be saved?"

"What the hell is wrong with you? My life is none of your business."

"Let me help you. You belong with a man who can take care of you. A man who can help you get your hands on any research you want. I'd even let you write about your nonsense witches, as long as you keep your real life reflective of true virtues. Pure virtues."

"Stop."

Clark backed her against the wall, and then bent to whisper in her ear with breath that rank of old tea and stale lemons. "You're so beautiful, Lizzie. Let me show you the life you could have."

She hated the pinprick of tears behind her eyes, threatening to spill on her cheeks. Clark would love that. She wanted to kick him. To scream. Her limbs refused to obey.

A knock at the door, and Lizzie almost collapsed from relief.

Clark held a finger up to his lips, a warning to be quiet.

Fuck you, she thought, and something within her fear cracked, just enough.

"Come in!" She yelled, and the furious look on Clark's face told her she would never get a chance to look at the diary and learn about "The Outcast," whomever she was.

The door handle rattled. "It's locked! Everything okay in there?" A man's voice. A familiar voice.

Clark moved away; fury obvious in his every step as he went to unlock the door. When had he locked the door?

Dizzy, she leaned against the wall again.

"Can I help you?" he spat.

Danny stepped in, and Lizzie had never been so glad to see an ex before.

"Sorry to disturb you all," Danny said, standing tall in his campus security uniform. "We've had issues with kids from the downtown high school sneaking into the library. They've been breaking objects and leaving graffiti. I was concerned when I went to do my rounds and this door was locked. Usually, I lock it myself in the evenings."

Lizzie knew Danny was putting on an act, one she was grateful for, and Clark could probably tell, too. The campus security didn't carry guns here, but Danny was a huge dude who towered over Clark, and the archivist was probably smart enough not to risk a fight.

"Everything is fine."

Lizzie cleared her throat. "And I was just leaving." She unglued herself from the wall, hating how shaky she felt.

Clark had the nerve to laugh. "It's a shame, Lizzie, that you won't be able to do your research, after all." With the diary in hand, he traipsed over to a glass display case in front of the stacks. He punched a number into the keypad keeping the case shut, and then he locked up the donated book.

Anger made her lightheaded. He had no right to withhold information.

"I'll walk you out," Danny said, holding the door open for Lizzie.

"How noble." Clark didn't bother to hide the derision in his voice. Did he know Danny was her ex-boyfriend? What did it matter?

Still, she couldn't help herself from trembling as Danny followed behind her, closed the door to the archives, and walked with her back up the stairs to the library. Outside on the sidewalk, she let out a breath she'd been holding for the longest time, then breathed in the crisp air, trying to recenter herself.

"How did you know I was down there?"

"I saw you go into the library from the parking lot. I had to help a guy fix the streetlamp, and I had a bad feeling when I saw you were alone."

As far as exes went, Danny wasn't bad at all. He'd gotten a job with campus security right around when she started her graduate work here two years ago, right around when she'd started dating Rose, too. Before then, she'd dated Danny for three years when he had worked security at a small concert venue she frequented. They'd drifted apart, and something always felt a little off when they were together, but Lizzie never realized what exactly, not until she met Rose.

Danny had always been supportive, and it was good to have him around. She'd told him about the archivist giving her the creeps months ago, and apparently, he hadn't forgotten.

"Thank you," she breathed out.

He shook his head. "No need to thank me. I hope he didn't hurt you."

"I'm okay, mostly mad. He wanted to *save* me, whatever the hell that means. Sounded like he wanted to chain me in his room. I won't be seeing the book I wanted to study, after all."

"I'm really sorry." Danny frowned and tugged at his cap, his curly brown hair much shorter than it had been five years ago. He had always looked good in a uniform.

She shrugged, bid her farewell to Danny, and then got in her car. With the door locked, she called Rose. As soon as she heard her girlfriend's voice, the timebomb in her chest imploded.

"That freaking perverted creep," she sobbed, barely saying a greeting. The tears had started, and she needed to expel every piece of Clark from her memory.

"Oh no, what happened?"

She recounted the story to Rose, who would always listen. Would always believe her. Rose's soft voice soothed her.

"Are you able to drive? Come home to me, Lizzie."

An unsteady hand put the car in drive, and she sped past the campus as the December sun set into the silvery sky.

Back at the apartment, Lizzie picked out a movie while Rose made dinner. The scents of rosemary potatoes and salmon baking in the oven helped Lizzie temporarily forget the humiliation of the day. She hated how embarrassed she felt when her mind drifted back to Clark. Both Rose and Danny had encouraged her to report him, and Danny said he'd of course back her up and give a statement, but she waved away their advice.

Clark brought in big donors and even bigger checks for the small university. People would see her as an oversensitive woman exaggerating a story. A figure not to be believed. Meanwhile, Clark would gain sympathy and support, and he'd be callous enough to blame Lizzie and say she was the one who came onto him. The world loved a good liar, especially when he was good-looking enough for people to swoon over him. She could see the headlines now, calling her manipulative, or claiming she tried to seduce the poor lonely man in the archives for her own personal gain.

Lizzie had lived long enough in the world to see how this shit always went. From her research on women like Alse Young, to the modern day, she couldn't see how her story would be any different. Those furious thoughts lingered in the back of her mind throughout dinner and during the movie. At some point, she was aware of drifting off to sleep on the couch, Rose curled up next to her and their fingers entwined. A small moment of peace.

A shrill chime sang its way into her mind, but in the quiet of the living room after today's events, it felt more like a death knell.

Rose murmured next to her and shuffled away as Lizzie reached for her phone, the culprit of the sound. The screen read 11:32pm, and she groaned.

"We fell asleep," Lizzie said and yawned, then she opened the text from Danny that had woken her up. "Shit."

"Hmm, what?" Rose blinked sleepy brown eyes at her.

"Danny says he can get me in to see the book."

Rose untangled herself from the gray blanket she'd burrowed beneath. "Really?"

Lizzie nodded, and her heart beat a little too fast as she stood up on wobbly legs. Drowsiness vanished from Rose's eyes, too.

"When?"

"Now."

"*Now*?" Rose frowned. "It's almost midnight."

A small smile tugged at the corners of Lizzie's lips. She couldn't help it. "Exactly. He said everyone is gone. No Clark. Danny has the keys to any building since he volunteered to take over a night shift for a sick coworker. He usually leaves in the evenings."

Rose arched an eyebrow. "He's really been your knight in shining armor today, hasn't he?"

"Oh, stop it," Lizzie huffed. "You're going to tell me you don't want to see this book, too?" She moved to the hallway, and Rose followed behind.

"I'll go. You know I will. But I want it on record that I am not loving the general idea."

"Noted." Lizzie grabbed her black coat and boots. Early December in Connecticut had brought in bitter cold, but at least the place wasn't too buried under snow, yet.

She wrapped her arms around Rose, kissed her flushed cheek. "Thank you."

"Yeah, yeah," Rose said, but she smiled and it let Lizzie know she understood how important this was. "Let's go."

It was a clear night with an endless black sky and the white twinkle of winter stars. The drive back to campus would only take 20 minutes, and Lizzie let her mind wander. She'd put her heart into her research, so determined to give voices and life to queer and forgotten women in history, to those who were likely targeted and killed because some religious men were scared. When the threat of control no longer worked, they invented devil after devil to kill the women who they no longer held power over.

Clark would have fit in so seamlessly with the Puritans. Originally, Lizzie had hoped her master's in history would allow her to teach college courses or pursue something else in education, but now, she thought of how sweet it would be to push someone like Clark out of a job. She'd never deny knowledge to those who were eager to learn.

Her fingers ached as she pulled up to campus. The book was so close. According to an article in the local newspaper, the donor claimed to be an ancestor of someone who nearly died during the Hartford Witch Panic, but she wanted it to be used on campus as a tool, not locked away in a museum only to be glanced at. The woman had said in the article that her ancestor survived the hunts by disguising herself as a man and hiding out in the woods, and by having a proficient knowledge of which plants to eat and which to make into poisons. She'd rescued other women when she could and took a few as lovers. Lizzie could not rest until she knew more. If she had to steal the book away from Clark, she was willing to do it.

Rose's cold fingers entangled with Lizzie's right hand as she parked the car near the campus library.

"Is that him?"

Lizzie peered down the lot at a figure walking toward them.

"Yeah, that's Danny. Are you ready?"

Rose nodded.

Lizzie made quick introductions, and Danny's genuine smile at meeting Rose had an unexpected impact on her, like healing an old wound.

"You're positive Clark is gone?"

"Yeah, not even that jackass stays until midnight on a Friday."

Lizzie took Rose's hand and together, they followed Danny down the salted cement sidewalk from parking lot to library. The familiar brick building greeted them, surrounded by bald trees that reached from the earth like spindly, snow-dusted fingers.

"The security cameras to the archive are on the front entrance, but not the back door. Even so, Clark wouldn't have access to these tapes. Plus, I have the master set of keys to check on things, we're good to go."

Lizzie put her faith in Danny, but nerves still swooped around in her stomach, like an explosion of downy feathers.

Her hand still clutching Rose's, the dim library passed by in a blur. She'd never been here this late and hadn't even realized it locked up and kicked students out on Friday nights. Down the tiled stairs and to the back door, only pausing when Danny went to unlock it. Eerie darkness broken by Rose flipping the light switch on, and then the archives lit up.

"There it is," Lizzie whispered, not daring to raise her voice any louder. Just as it had been when she left today, the book sat tucked away behind a locked glass case.

"A keypad?" Rose let go of her hand and walked over to the lock.

The whole display felt mocking. A door slam behind her made Lizzie jump and spin around.

"Sorry," Danny said, "I wanted to check his office. Not much in there."

"You don't think he'd be here, waiting for us? Upstairs?" Rose shivered.

The very thought made Lizzie's flesh want to crawl off her skeleton.

"I can go have a look around," Danny offered. "Everything should be locked until morning, but I'd be glad to double-check."

Lizzie smiled. "Thank you."

"I'll be back in a few minutes. You can lock this door from the inside. I'll knock three times when I'm back."

Danny retreated up the stairs, back to the library where someone could easily hide in the shadows of shelves and the little corners of desks and beanbags where students liked to study. A shuffle by the door told Lizzie that Rose did indeed lock it from the inside.

"Any idea how to open the case?"

"One," Lizzie said. "Clark did mention the date of the book when I was here earlier. I suppose that could be a way to remember a passcode."

Rose shrugged. "Give it a try."

"It seems too obvious." Still, she tried. The lock was a digital one, keeping the doors of the glass case firmly pressed together. Lizzie pressed in 1-6-4-7, and her stomach swooped when the doors emitted a tiny *click*.

She looked back at Rose who had paled a little. "Maybe he just . . . kept it simple?"

"I don't like this."

It was too easy. The kind of trap someone sets when they're expecting prey to wander freely into a trap. She needed to move quickly.

Lizzie snapped on the disposable reading gloves, and then gingerly reached for the old book. It felt surprisingly solid in her hands. For something over 300 years old, she almost expected it to disintegrate like sand between her fingertips.

"It feels like a dream," she whispered, and then carefully, so carefully, opened the book. Her heart sunk with the turn of every page. "It's blank."

"What?" Rose stepped closer and peered down at the book.

"The pages are blank." Panic crawled up her throat with sticky feet, choking her with its glue. "It wasn't blank earlier. How? This is the same book. I know it is."

"You really think you deserve all of that information, Lizzie?" A voice twice as cold as it had been earlier today. Clark walked out of the shadows. He hadn't entered through any door. They were all still shut and locked. He'd morphed from the darkness, as if those shadows had birthed him from their gloom.

"No. No." Lizzie chanted, as if she could send Clark back to whatever twisted reality he had emerged from.

Rose went silent but stood firmly beside Lizzie.

Like a serpent, Clark glided forward. Something slow and purposeful possessed his gait. When he stood in the light of the room, Lizzie bit back a scream.

His pale skin had taken on strange tones of yellow and gray, not unlike the faded pages of an old, mildewed book. Handwritten letters in swooping cursive sprawled across his skin. Every place of exposed flesh bore the letters. Across his face, his neck, along his forearms where his sleeves were rolled up, down his hands, beneath inky fingertips . . . the words moved, shifted, impossible to read, as if they had all been turned upside down and out of order. He'd unbuttoned his white shirt, and there across his chest and belly grew symbols Lizzie had seen before. Symbols of witchcraft from the 17th century: charms and seals, drawings of different circles with instructions written in some combination of Latin and English. It all had to be from the diary of The Outcast. The diary that was now blank.

"What did you do?" Disbelief and anger swirled in Lizzie's skull.

Clark tilted his head to the left, and ink spilled from his ear in a sticky black stream. "I have taken the foul stories and charms in that diary, taken them away. I thought, at first, what kind of gift from God is this? But when my hands touched the pages, I was able to absorb the filthy lies from mad women. All of their hideous acts against God, their beliefs they could perform magic in the woods, that they could touch each other. And you, Lizzie, you will learn something by the end of this."

She tried to follow, and though Clark sounded insane, the moving ink beneath his skin was evidence something had happened here.

"No. Not God," she said.

Clark's eyes had turned form blue to the dewy black of spilled ink. Darkness rained from the corners, trailing sludge down his cheeks.

"You touched the diary with your bare hands? Then maybe she cursed you."

"Who?" He moved forward. Lizzie entangled her hand with Rose's, and together, they walked backwards, away from Clark, and toward the door that had been locked from the inside.

"The Outcast. You disrespected her stories. This is a curse, Clark. Not a Godly gift."

He laughed, and more midnight-colored sewage seeped from his body, blurring the words on his skin.

"Foolish Lizzie. No. This is how I will cleanse the lies of the world from history."

"How?" She prompted him, and then nudged Rose with her elbow, squeezed her wrist, hoped she understood through their language of touch that she wanted Rose to unlock the door while she talked to Clark. Rose squeezed her hand back. *Affirmative.*

"Does it matter?" Clark spat, and then a cold laugh followed by a black trickle of ink leaked from his mouth. He came closer, unhurried. Positive in his strength for whatever he was going to do. "The stories from those unholy women are gone, and soon, your story will be gone, too. I gave you so many chances, Lizzie."

The blank book in her hand trembled. Startled, she dropped it and backed away, nearly tripping Rose in the process. They were so close to the door.

A diary of stolen stories, of words meant to be read, but instead a man put it behind glass like a prisoner. Wouldn't The Outcast have had enough time spent feeling like a captive? All of the terrible horrors she must have witnessed in her time . . . .

A violence all its own belonged to that book, and it shook with such rage, even Clark stopped to stare with his oil-spill eyes.

Wraithlike figures erupted from the empty pages, specters who once resembled women, but one look at them told Lizzie more than she needed to know.

"Why do they look like that?" Rose said.

"It's how they died." Tears formed in Lizzie's eyes. She'd researched the witch hunts long enough to know. These apparitions, once women and young girls filled with life, now mirrors of their deaths.

Women hanged from Gallows Hill.

Women tortured until their minds and bodies broke.

Women burned.

Women drowned.

All here in the room, darting from wall to wall with their disfigured faces, broken necks, lips tinged purple and blue. They brought their past into the room, and the walls shifted from white plaster to a forest clearing where a noose swung from tall gallows.

Water trickled in from somewhere unseen, promising to bring a drowning.

Fire sparked within Clark's office, sending smoke to suffocate them all.

The glass display case rattled, and one more figure emerged. Her face and body seemed intact for a 17th century ghost, and her dress, too. White eyes glanced around, and the ghost focused on a drowned woman. The pain in that glance, it struck Lizzie through the heart like lightning. It was the kind of expression she'd have on her own face if anything ever happened to Rose.

"The Outcast," she murmured, and the creature cast its empty eyes toward her.

The writer of the diary. A survivor. All of these deaths she likely witnessed. Her friends and family, her lovers.

The woman's spirit shot through the case, and glass sprayed around the room, showering clothes, skin, and hair with sharp debris. Lizzie yelled along with Rose, bending to try and cover her face.

Three knocks on the door. *Danny.*

Lizzie kept her sleeve over her eyes, opened the door. Rose sobbed, groaning in pain.

"My eye."

A deep breath, and then Lizzie dared to look. A glass shard had wedged itself in the corner of Rose's left eye.

"Shit. We have to go. Danny, get Rose out of here."

Blood pooled on Rose's face, spilling over into her eye.

"Don't touch it. Run up the stairs, now."

Shadows shifted and Clark appeared behind Rose. He pressed a dagger of broken glass to her throat.

The ghosts tore through the room, and Lizzie understood their anger, but she desperately needed to focus on Rose. "You used your anger to create him!" She pointed at Clark, and then wondered what good shouting at ghosts would do. "I didn't need to see him like this to know the monster he already was. Help us, please."

They didn't seem to listen. Their stories had been stolen from them, along with their entire lives. All the futures they could have pursued.

Clark laughed.

"What the fuck is so funny?"

"They didn't create me, Lizzie. I told you. My gift is one from God. It has been for centuries. I will always be the shadow lurking behind you, trying to save you and people like you. But you'll ignore me, try to change history into what you want it to be. And I will change it back."

She shook her head, confused and lost in desperation.

The Outcast floated above Lizzie, cast its white eyes at her, and then the ghost whispered into Lizzie's head.

The first page of my diary details a woman I loved. The magistrate saw us kissing in the woods, by the river. The river they would then drown my lover in, calling her unholy. I escaped. I never meant to leave her behind.

The shadows got to her first.

"Help us," Lizzie pleaded up at the ghost.

Rose yelped as Clark pushed the glass harder into her neck.

"Let Rose go." She coughed, losing breath. The smoke grew thicker, cloying her senses. Water rose to her ankles. So many ways to die all in one room.

Clark grinned a row of blackening teeth at her. "Will you come with me in exchange? Let me save you?"

"I'd do anything for her."

Behind Clark, Danny lunged for the madman's arm, helping to get the glass away from Rose. Clark spun around, faster than he'd ever been before, and the shard slashed across Danny's throat. He didn't stop there—Lizzie darted to help, but Rose held her back as Clark stabbed the glass into the side of Danny's neck. Blood sprayed out like a heartbeat, staining the rising water with globs of scarlet.

"I'm sorry. We can't help him. Let's go!" Desperate coughs wracked from Rose's lungs; the smoke might kill them first.

"Why won't they stop?" Lizzie searched for the ghosts, but they'd disappeared.

The diary, this book that had survived since 1647, floated by atop a boat of glass. She wanted to laugh at how resilient the damned thing was, but then something clicked in her brain. Another keypad unlocked.

She turned to Rose, mouthed words at her so Clark wouldn't hear.

Distract him.

Rose nodded. As Lizzie waded through the knee-deep water, Rose picked up a cup of pens on a nearby shelf, spilled them everywhere, and launched the mug at Clark's head. Even with one eye filled with blood, Rose had a killer aim.

As the satisfying *crack* of ceramic colliding with skull hit the air, Lizzie grabbed the diary. The butchered ghosts remerged, rocketing about the room that seemed torn between flooding or burning.

Clark cursed, made his way toward Rose, but Lizzie was ready. She grabbed one of the pens floating in the water, and then dived toward the archivist. The Outcast swooped through Clark's head, further distracting him. With no hesitation, Lizzie jammed the opened pen into his neck. Rose caught on, joined her, and together they stabbed the pens as hard as they could into his body.

Ink floated from papery skin and onto the pages Lizzie held beneath him. All of the history he tried to steal, to rewrite, all of the catharsis he denied women like The Outcast, now trickled back into the pages where they belonged. Where they would be read and honored. Lizzie would make sure of that.

"We will learn your stories."

The ghosts seemed to accept her promise, and as the final ink leaked from Clark's dying body, the creatures disappeared back into the book. Fire and smoke stopped spreading, and water stopped rising, but it all lingered in the room even as forest morphed back into plaster walls.

A single noose swayed above them still. Lizzie shivered.

"Their bodies are gone," Rose said, her voice faint.

She was right. Danny and Clark both vanished.

"I'm sorry, Danny," Lizzie said to the silence of the ruined archives.

"Look." Rose pointed to the stacks, and there in the farthest corner, shadows moved in a twisted rhythm.

"I guess there will always be some kind of gloom. Always be people like Clark in the world."

She guided Rose away, wishing she knew how to stop those shadows. They had lived inside Clark, and with him gone, they'd move on. Find another. Whatever Clark had turned himself into, that power had not yet died. Its magic, or poison, whatever it was, lived on.

Lizzie took Rose by the hand. Bloodied and bruised, glass in her hair and in Rose's eye, she clung onto hope that the shadows could never eat away at everything. Darkness never stayed still, and its vanquishment could only ever be temporary, but hope lived on. Stories lived on. With the diary of The Outcast in hand, Lizzie made a promise to herself and to the spirits of women who came before, that she would continue to find hope even as the shadows crept onward.

LOOK AT WHAT YOU'VE LEFT OF ME

ERIC LAROCCA

*"**L**OOK AT WHAT you've left of me," he might have said, blood pooling in the velvet pocket of his cheek so that each word sounded watery and somehow rotted.*

"That's the point, faggot," they might have told him with an imitation of matter-of-factness that he probably despised. "The point was always to leave you this way."

"Do you hear that—?" I ask her, chewing on a small ice cube while it melts in my mouth. "There's—something—crawling in the wall."

But she shoos me away, pushing the phone between her shoulder and her ear as she loiters in the kitchen doorway.

"Dear, please," Claire says with that strained urgency I know all too well as she leans away from me to speak into the phone. "No, doctor. She's been complaining about hearing some sort of—gnawing sound. Must be the cabin fever. Unless you know if this—peroneal nerve dysfunction—inspires fits of deliria."

"You don't hear that—?" I ask her.

But she ignores me, turning away and pacing back and forth in front of the window lined with the plants we had intended to care for but instead neglected for the past month since the accident.

"Well, I was taking her to her physical therapy sessions, but I wasn't seeing any progress," Claire says to the doctor on the other end of the line. "They made it sound like this surgery was the only other option. What's it called again—? Reconstructive nerve transplantation. Well, those certainly are a lot of syllables for one mouth. I'm just curious to know the expected recovery rate with a type of procedure like this. I assume absolutely no type of exertion or physical strain?"

I call out her name, but she continues to ignore me.

"Dorothy mentioned that you pointed out there is the possibility that the operation will be unsuccessful," Claire says to the doctor. "Of course, we understand the procedure is rather delicate, but it's understandably difficult to think about investing so much money in a life-altering endeavor that might offer more damage than good."

I cross my arms, feeling more and more like a nuisance—a piece of waste corroding more and more each day the way a sheet of metal might that's been abandoned at the bottom of the ocean.

"For Christ's sake."

Claire suddenly looks nervous, as if worried the doctor has somehow heard my complaining.

"Dorothy is so eager, you see—?" she tells him. "She's furious that I'm even questioning this opportunity. I suppose I'm hesitant because it's nearly been a month since the accident, and she's only recently stopped griping about the squeak in her wheelchair. I only make her use it because I worry. Maybe needlessly."

Just as the oven begins to chirp, I wave my hands at her and motion to the timer we had set on the counter.

"Have a candy, dear," she tells me, passing across one of the expensive chocolate truffles her younger sister in New Hampshire had sent us last week.

Before I can say anything, she's barking into the phone once more:

"And then, of course, there's the issue of the price. Those certainly are a lot of numbers. Any kind of debt makes Dorothy itch terribly. So, we'd have to find a way to pay it in full."

I sense my skin heating and threatening to curl as if it could shrug and unspool itself from me at any moment.

"For Christ's sake, do I have to get it, myself—?"

"I'm sorry," Claire says, plugging her ear. "I have to run and pull her dinner out of the oven. But thank you for calling back. I'll be sure to give you a ring if I have any other questions. We'll be in touch."

LOOK AT WHAT YOU'VE LEFT OF ME

Claire sets the receiver in the cradle, hanging up.

"For Heaven's sake, Dorothy," she says. "I knew the oven was going off. You didn't have to yell. It's embarrassing."

I watch her as she kneels, prying open the oven and sliding the tray out.

"You're not calling him again," I tell her. "Do you understand—?"

Claire looks at me queerly. "Who—? Your doctor?"

"I want you to stay out of it," I say. "It does not concern you."

Claire can probably tell I'm itching for an argument. She brandishes the warm tray in front of me with a theatrical flourish, as if soliciting a truce from the pit of my stomach.

"It's your favorite tonight, dear," she tells me. "Roast lamb with mint sauce."

"Claire, do you understand me—?"

But she won't respond. She busies herself at the counter, prattling on and on as if I were invisible.

"I know we were saving it for a special occasion, but I was just dying to find an excuse to use this new electric knife I ordered. It certainly looked bigger on TV, though."

"Claire," I shout at her.

She falters for an instant, surprised at my brashness.

"I can't help it if I'm troubled by the whole idea of this operation, Dorothy," she tells me. "And I had questions. Even though this young Boston surgeon of yours is brazen enough to operate, he acknowledges that there's a risk of infection or permanent nerve damage. Don't get me wrong. I think he's very polite and well-spoken. But I never met a doctor who didn't carefully hide his horns or his tail. Now, hand me your plate, would you?"

Before I can do anything, she's already wielding the electric knife and slicing through the leg of lamb.

"I can't have you second guessing and making me wait any longer," I tell her.

Claire halts her work and turns to me to speak with a rehearsed gentleness, as if she had always expected my opposition.

"I know you're eager, dear," she tells me. "But we must be practical. This year hasn't exactly been successful money-wise. We can only spend so much."

I fold my arms, detesting the horrible reminder. "Get off your damn soap-box, Claire."

Before I realize it, she's at my side and tenderly stroking my hair. "Oh, please don't think I'm complaining. I'm just trying to stress the number of sacrifices we've had to make to—accommodate this—setback."

I sense my voice thinning to a whisper when I speak. "It's not my fault."

"Of course, it's not your fault, my darling," she tells me. "And thanks to a little extra sweat, we've managed keep the place. But if we did go through with this surgery and something horrible did happen, we wouldn't have a prayer of keeping the farm. That's just too great of a chance."

"It's not when you have to live by the hands and care of other people," I remind her, shaking my head.

Claire looks at me strangely again. "Certainly, you don't think I loathe taking care of you. You remember a couple years ago when we were going through our troubles, and I caught a bad fit of the blues?"

I find myself trembling at the dreadful reminder.

"When we—lost the—?"

"Yes," she says, cutting me off before I can utter the words. "After we had to—bury that small bundle in the white cloth out in the backyard. I could hardly eat or get out of bed. You remember. Over three years now and those blues are gone for good. I swear. Because now I look forward to getting up every morning and taking care of you. You give me purpose."

Presumably thinking she's pacified me for the moment, she returns to her labor and resumes slicing through the lamb with the electric knife as it hums gently and fills the kitchen with noise.

"The doctor said if we wait any longer, they won't be able to operate at all, Claire," I remind her. "I'll lose nerve function entirely. You can't expect me to ignore this kind of opportunity."

Claire won't look at me. She sets down the knife and stares blankly out the kitchen window into the back yard. I can't help but wonder if she's staring at the unmarked grave where we buried our horrible loss those few years ago. Part of me hopes she isn't. Part of me hopes she's staring off into the distant trees, searching for a sign that things will get better—a sign that will probably never come.

"Well, this kind of opportunity certainly doesn't come cheap," she says. "And I don't know how you expect to pay the whole thing in full with such a poor crop year. They'll still send us the bill whether you can walk or not."

Pulling her gaze away from the window, she makes a beeline toward me and motions for my plate.

"Now, stop your complaining. Give me your plate. Quarter inch slices, right?"

"Our savings will cover it," I say to her. "After all, that's what savings are for."

"But that would exhaust our investments entirely," Claire says. "We'd be left with less than nothing. And what if the operation isn't successful?"

I close my eyes, as if willing myself to walk, as if willing myself to be anywhere but here. "Try living at the mercy of someone else."

Claire reels from me, obviously hurt. "Why? Have I been so awful to you—? What didn't I do? Tell me. Was I too sparing with the chocolates? Did you not get enough—?"

"I don't want any more Goddamn chocolates, Claire," I shout at her after she pushes the bowl of chocolate truffles toward me again and again.

"You need to stay here—where I can look after you and make sure you're well," she says.

"If I stay here any longer, Claire, I'm going to lose my fucking mind."

"Language."

"I'm already going stir crazy sitting in this chair day in and day out," I tell her.

"Why, dear? Is the cushion not comfortable—?" she asks me, fussing with the pillow behind my back.

I push her away. "And that chewing. That—gnawing coming from within the walls . . . "

"An old house has sounds, dear," Claire says, rolling her eyes. "Things creak. Faucets leak."

"No," I tell her. "There must be hundreds of them. They must have—built a nest inside some of the old, rotten beams. They're famished and they must be collecting food because they don't know when it will come again."

"You think it's an animal—?"

"Rats—or maybe mice," I say. "Tell me you hear it, Claire. You must. They're crawling in the walls."

Claire shrugs. Her unresponsiveness vexes me like nothing

else. I glare at her, imagining all the different scenarios in which I could feed her to the starving creatures teeming inside the walls. I wonder if I'm a monster for thinking something truly so vile.

"Well, we'll just have to find some cats," she says. "Now, here. Have something sweet to calm you down. Your face is getting all red."

"I don't want something sweet, Claire."

"I find wrappers under the sheets almost every morning," she tells me. "You really shouldn't be eating these candy bars in the bed. You might as well have one now, dear."

"I don't want chocolates, Claire," I tell her. "I want out of this Goddamn wheelchair."

She pauses for a moment, visibly searching her mind for an excuse, an answer, anything.

"You're not ready," she says to me. "You'll hurt yourself and then we'll really be in sorry shape. I need to take care of you."

"I'm tired of being taken care of," I shout at her. "I'm going out of my mind."

"Dorothy . . ."

"I'm calling the doctor tomorrow," I tell her.

Claire looks at me with a glare of betrayal—as if I've somehow undone some of her grace, her charm, her resolve to remain affectionate and polite.

"I don't think you appreciate the kind of distress this decision will put upon us, Dorothy," she tells me.

"We'll close the savings account tomorrow," I say.

Claire thinks for a moment, her lips curling and her fists tightening a little. Finally, she speaks:

"I hate to remind you, but I offered my fair share to those savings. Half of that money—belongs to me."

"You'll see every penny back once we sell the farm," I tell her.

Claire looks at me, her mouth hanging open and begging for an explanation.

"Sell—? You never told me you were planning on selling."

I laugh, a little surprised by her foolishness. "You didn't really expect me to keep this place going with no children and no help—?"

Claire swallows. She returns to the kitchen counter, the electric knife whirring alive in her hand as she stands there and stares blankly out the kitchen window once more.

"You've made up your mind, I gather?" she asks me.

LOOK AT WHAT YOU'VE LEFT OF ME

For once, I don't answer. I know I've hurt her, wounded her far more than losing the child we had lost those few years ago.

"Let me just cut it the way you like it," she says, slicing another bit of lamb and ladling it onto a plate. "Extra sauce too?"

"I'm not hungry," I say to her. "I'll turn in early."

"All this lamb will go to waste," she says with a heavy sigh, as if it were a futile attempt to coax some pity from me. "At least let me help you."

With both hands, she begins to steer me out of the kitchen and across the living room. We pass the television set and as it plays, the screen rinses the nearby wall with a muted silver glow. I suddenly notice a familiar face staring at me from the television—a photograph of the young blonde-haired boy that had been murdered in a field on the outskirts of a small town in Wyoming. As soon as his photograph greets us, I notice how Claire slows until we come to a complete stop. We remain in silence for a moment, our attention fixed on the screen as we watch the news report from the town of Laramie.

"The poor dear," Claire says, her voice brittle-sounding and threatening to break apart at any moment. "His poor mother must be beside herself."

I straighten in the wheelchair, sensing how Claire comfortably rests her hand on my shoulder.

"I would never let something like that happen to my child," she tells me with a horrible look that seems to screech a warning at me, as if I had somehow questioned her motherly instincts.

I listen to the pain quivering in her throat—rattling incessantly like a small, black beetle that's crawled inside her and built a nest there.

"I'm sure his mother did everything she could to protect him," I tell her.

"No," Claire says, shaking her head and looking as if she wanted to hurl the thought from her mind. "I keep the things I love very close. I care for them. I would have never let something like that happen. If I had known he was going to be hurt, I would have hurt him myself . . . "

I find myself drawing closer and closer to the television set, my eyes fixed on the photograph of the butchered college student splayed in the center of the screen.

"Can you imagine their cruelty—?" I ask Claire, the corners of my eyes webbing with tears. "They just left him there. Tied to a fence post. Left him there to die. I heard they pretended to be gay to get him in their truck . . . I suppose you don't think your own kind will ever hurt you."

Without warning, Claire grips the handlebars and steers me away from the television set and toward our bedroom door.

"You know, if we have rats, we certainly can't expect an easy sell, Dorothy," she tells me in a patronizing tone the same way an adult might caution a child. "That's the first thing realtors ask about when they take on a commission. Vermin is a deal breaker."

Of course, I had expected her to question me. I had expected her belligerence, her frustration, even her sadness.

"An old farmhouse is an eyesore," I tell her. "They'll knock it down. Nothing wrong with the land. Just needs someone who's familiar with the end of a shovel. Some asshole with a family from New York City will take it off our hands. And then things will go back to the way they were before."

She stops for a moment, leaning toward me as if she had misheard something. "What do you mean—?"

"I won't need a caregiver anymore," I tell her. "I won't need to be taken care of."

Claire's eyes lower. Her voice begins to wilt.

"Sounds like you won't need me at all," she says, ushering me to the threshold of our bedroom and then leaving me there.

"Claire," I call out to her.

But she's already skirted back into the kitchen, taking most of the light with her and leaving me to find my way in the dark on my own.

It's three in the morning when I awake and hear the brittle noises of chewing, something gnawing.

"Claire . . . Claire—? It's back. It sounds like it's—outside the wall. Do you hear it—?"

Her voice answers me in the dark from across the room:

"Go back to sleep, my darling. There's nothing there."

I struggle to move my arms to reach for her, but I find them pinned at my sides.

"I—I can't move my arms," I tell her.

"I know you're in a lot of pain, dear," Claire says to me, drawing a little closer.

LOOK AT WHAT YOU'VE LEFT OF ME

I can scarcely make out the silhouette of her in the dark as she stirs in the corner of the room where the two walls meet.

"No. I—I can't move my arms, Claire."

"That's because I've bound them with wire, my love," she tells me.

"Why?" I ask her, screeching until I'm practically hoarse. "Where are you—?"

It's then she switches on the lamp on the bedside table, and I glance down at what she's done to me.

A swarm of rats weave in and out between my legs, screeching with glee. Some have already begun to feed, working the gristle from the bone as they chirp and make horrible squealing sounds. The white bedsheets are now dyed red, more blood leaking from the small holes they've pecked at in my calves.

"Get them off me," I beg her.

"It takes a while to get down to the bone, I imagine," Claire tells me, circling the bed and observing the rats while they feed. "I told you not to eat those chocolates in bed, dear. The poor little things were so famished. I did my best to look after them, but they had hardly anything to eat and had just been living off rations. Of course, they prefer sweets, but when they're starved enough, they'll scavenge for almost anything."

I cry out for help, but it's foolish to think anyone can hear me.

"Your legs pained you, my love. So, I did what I've always done. I took care of you," Claire says to me. "It just wounded me to watch you carry that cross day in and day out. Those limbs will never trouble you again. And when your hands grow heavy and tired, I'll take them too and I'll gladly be your hands. I'll be your eyes, ears and, mouth too, darling. You'll be my little worm. And you will want for nothing, I swear. I'll see to it that I'll always take care of you."

I scream, pleading with her to untie me and drag me from the bed, but she won't. Instead, Claire lingers in the corner of the room for a moment and then takes a seat in a small wicker chair facing the bed.

"Rest, my dear," she says to me with a voice impossibly delicate. "Let them finish eating."

When it's finished, Claire clears the vermin from the bed and lures them back into the walls. I tremble there, shuddering as if confused by the horrible ordeal and wishing it were somehow an awful nightmare.

She finally returns to me and begins to dress me with gauze.

I glance down and notice my legs are shortened and the remaining skin is pockmarked black with quarter-sized wounds.

Before I can speak, Claire passes a small ice cube into my mouth and lets me suck on it for a moment as she knows full well that's what calms me down.

"Look at what you've left of me," I say, the melting ice cube circling around my tongue and pinched in the velvet pocket of my cheek so that each word sounds watery and somehow rotted.

"My dear, that's the point," Claire says to me with a rehearsed matter-of-factness that I can't help but despise. "The point was always to leave you this way."

THE END?

Not if you want to dive into more of Crystal Lake Publishing's Tales from the Darkest Depths!

Check out our amazing website and online store
or download our latest catalog here.
https://geni.us/CLPCatalog

We always have great new projects and content on the website to dive into, as well as a newsletter, behind the scenes options, social media platforms, our own dark fiction shared-world series and our very own webstore. Our webstore even has categories specifically for KU books, non-fiction, anthologies, and of course more novels and novellas.

ABOUT THE EDITOR

Vince A. Liaguno is the Bram Stoker Award®–winning editor of *Unspeakable Horror: From the Shadows of the Closet* (Dark Scribe Press 2008), an anthology of queer horror fiction, which he co-edited with Chad Helder; *Butcher Knives & Body Counts* (Dark Scribe Press, 2011), a collection of essays on the formula, frights, and fun of the slasher film; the second volume in the Unspeakable Horror series, subtitled *Abominations of Desire* (Evil Jester Press, 2017); and the acclaimed *Other Terrors: An Inclusive Anthology* (William Morrow Paperbacks, 2002), co-edited with Rena Mason. His debut novel, 2006's *The Literary Six,* was a tribute to the slasher films of the eighties and won an Independent Publisher Award (IPPY).

He currently resides in the mitten-shaped state of Michigan, where he is a licensed nursing home administrator by day and a writer, anthologist, and pop culture enthusiast by night. He is a member (and former secretary) of the Horror Writers Association (HWA), International Thriller Writers (ITW), and the National Book Critics Circle (NBCC).

Author website: www.VinceLiaguno.com

CONTRIBUTORS

Matthew Blain-Hartung is a Berlin-based biochemist. The author of many scientific manuscripts, he has recently veered into the fictional realm. His short stories appear in press at *Kind of Like a Hurricane, Moonflake, Theme of Absence, Written Tales, Dark Rose,* and others.

Author website: https://mblainhartung.wixsite.com/my-site-1

Amanda M. Blake is a cat-loving daydreamer and mid-age goth who loves geekery of all sorts, from superheroes to horror movies, urban fantasy to unconventional romance. She's the author of horror titles such as *Nocturne* and *Deep Down* and the fairy tale mash-up series *Thorns.*

Author website: amandamblake.com
Twitter: twitter.com/AmandaMBlake1
Facebook: facebook.com/authoramandamblake
Instagram: instagram.com/amanda_mblake

Craig Brownlie's first published book was 1987's *Financial Commercial Loan Handbook* from Financial Publishing Company (uncredited). After publishing one short story in *Haunts Magazine* (Nightshade Publications, 1993), he went on a long hiatus from submitting fiction. Instead, he wrote for newspapers, websites, and stage, oh my! Getting his gumption back in 2022, he found editors receptive to his tales. He lives in western New York.

Author website: www.craigbrownlie.com
Facebook: www.facebook.com/craig.brownlie.3
Twitter: @brownlie_craig

James Cato is an environmental organizer and flips over logs in his spare time. Look for his work in *SmokeLong Quarterly, Pithead Chapel,* and *Daily Science Fiction,* among others. His short fiction often centers on rural Appalachia and certain works have been nominated for Best of the Net, Best Microfiction, and the Pushcart Prize.

Author website: www.jamescatoauthor.com
Twitter: @the_sour_potato

Dan Coxon is an award-winning editor and writer based in London. His non-fiction anthology *Writing The Uncanny* (co-edited with Richard V. Hirst) won the British Fantasy Award for Best Non-Fiction 2022, while his short story collection *Only The Broken Remain* (Black Shuck Books) was shortlisted for two British Fantasy Awards in 2021 (Best Collection, Best Newcomer). In 2018 his anthology of British folk-horror, *This Dreaming Isle* (Unsung Stories), was shortlisted for a British Fantasy Award and a Shirley Jackson Award. His short stories have appeared in various anthologies, including *Nox Pareidolia*, *Beyond the Veil*, *Mother: Tales of Love and Terror* and *Great British Horror 7: Major Arcana*. His latest anthology—*Isolation*—was published by Titan Books in September 2022.

Author website: www.dancoxon.com
Twitter: @DanCoxonAuthor

Michael Thomas Ford is the author of numerous books for both young readers and adults, most notably the novels *Every Star That Falls*, *Love & Other Curses*, *Suicide Notes*, and *Lily*. A five-time winner of the Lambda Literary Award, he has also been a finalist for the Shirley Jackson Award, the Bram Stoker Award, the Ignyte Award, and the Firecracker Alternative Book Award. He lives with his husband and dogs in rural Ohio, where he keeps bees, plants gardens, collects tattoos, and hangs out with Mothman.

Author website: www.michaelthomasford.com
Twitter: @AuthorMTFord
Instagram: michaelthomasford

Craig Laurance Gidney (he/him/his) is the author of *Sea, Swallow Me & Other Stories*; *Skin Deep Magic: Stories*; *Bereft* (a YA novella), and *A Spectral Hue* (a novel). He has been a Lambda Literary Finalist three times, was a Carl Brandon Parallax Award Finalist, and won the inaugural Joseph S Pulver Sr Award for Weird Fiction. *The Nectar of Nightmares* is his most recent collection. He lives in Washington, D.C.

Author website: www.craiglaurancegidney.com

Maxwell I. Gold is a multiple Pushcart and Rhysling award nominated author who writes prose poetry and short stories in weird and cosmic fiction. His work has appeared in numerous anthologies and magazines including *Space and Time Magazine, Startling Stories, Strange Horizons, Other Terrors: An Inclusive Anthology, Shadow Atlas: Dark Landscapes of the Americas,* and many more.

Maxwell is the author of the Elgin Award nominated poetry book *Oblivion in Flux: A Collection of Cyber Prose* from Crystal Lake Publishing.

He lives in Ohio with his partner and two dogs Marshall and Otto, and currently serves on the Board of Trustees for the Horror Writers Association as the organization's Treasurer.

Author Website: www.thewellsoftheweird.com

Instagram: @ cybergodwrites

Chad Helder is the author of *The Dead Mall Horror, The Vampire Bridegroom,* and *Pop-Up Book of Death.* With Vince Liaguno, Helder co-edited *Unspeakable Horror: From the Shadows of the Closet,* which won the Bram Stoker Award for Superior Achievement in an Anthology. Helder teaches writing in Fort Collins, Colorado, where he lives with a Bichon Frise named Biff.

Author website: Hauntedpoems.com

CG Inglis is a Stockholm-based writer and narrative designer.

Twitter: @viscereal

Vincent Kovar is often a marketer for game companies, periodically a playwright, as well as formerly a journalist and a pre-pandemic University professor. Vincent has previously appeared as an actor both on stage and in independent films such as the gay-zombie spoof, *Creatures from the Pink Lagoon.* His fiction has appeared in anthologies such as *Hardcore Hardboiled, Wilde Stories, Tales of the New Mexico Mythos, A Touch of the Sea,* and *A Study in Lavender,* also in periodicals such as *Icarus Magazine, Ellipsis Magazine,* and *The Oregon Literary Review.* He lives in Washington State.

LinkedIn: www.linkedin.com/in/vincentkovar

Eric LaRocca (*he/they*) is the Bram Stoker Award®-nominated author of several works of horror and dark fiction, including the viral sensation, *Things Have Gotten Worse Since We Last Spoke.*

A lover of luxury fashion and an admirer of European musical theatre, Eric can often be found roaming the streets of his home city, Boston, MA, for inspiration.

Author website: ericlarocca.com

Twitter: @hystericteeth

Instagram: @hystericteeth

Maryse Meijer is the author of *Heartbreaker, Rag, Northwood,* and *The Seventh Mansion.* She lives in Chicago.

Author website: www.marysemeijer.com

Oliver Nash's writing has been published in *The Offing, Spectrum Literary Journal, The Headlight Review,* the *Santa Ana River Review,* and *The Albion Review,* among others. In 2022, they were a finalist for the Headlight Review's chapbook contest and the Ohioana Library Association's Walter Rumsey Marvin Grant, a semi-finalist for the Tomaž Šalamun prize, and was longlisted for the Frontier Poetry Chapbook Contest. Their work crosses genres—from sci-fi and horror, to the new weird and the ergodic, to more traditional literary fiction—in order to tackle issues such as eco-anxiety, existentialism, and queerness. They are currently an MFA candidate at the University of Alabama, where their time is split between wandering the woods and trying to write the next great weird novel.

Author website: www.olivernashwrites.com

Hailey Piper is the Bram Stoker Award-winning author of *Queen of Teeth, The Worm and His Kings, No Gods for Drowning,* and other books of horror. She is an active member of the Horror Writers Association, with dozens of short stories appearing in *Pseudopod, Vastarien, Cast of Wonders, Cosmic Horror Monthly,* and other publications. She lives with her wife in Maryland, where their occult studies are secret.

Author website: https://www.haileypiper.com

Twitter: @HaileyPiperSays

Mathew L. Reyes is an attorney and copy editor based in Minneapolis. His short fiction has appeared in the NoSleep Podcast, *Bards & Sages Quarterly, Everyday Fiction,* and *Monsters Out of the Closet,* an LGBTQ+ horror-focused podcast.

When Mathew isn't working as an editing gremlin, he's jogging, writing, and killing his darlings at the advice of his wonderful critique group.

Twitter: @MathewLReyes

Zachary Rosenberg is a Jewish horror writer living in Florida. He crafts horrifying tales by night and by day he practices law, which is even more frightening. His forthcoming debut books will be published by Brigids Gate Press and Darklit Press. You may find his stories released or forthcoming at Air and Nothingness Press, Deathknell Press, Nosetouch Press and Seize the Press.

Twitter: @ZachRoseWriter

Yah Yah Scholfield was born in New York and raised in Atlanta. She's been published in *Fiyah Lit Magazine*, the *Death in The Mouth* horror anthology and a few other speculative fiction 'zines and anthologies. She self-published her debut novel, *On Sundays, She Picked Flowers*, in 2021.

Author website: www.fluoresensitive.com
Twitter: @yahyascholfield

Lucy A. Snyder is the Shirley Jackson Award-nominated and five-time Bram Stoker Award-winning author of 15 books and over 100 published short stories. Her most recent books are the collections *Halloween Season* and *Exposed Nerves* the apocalyptic horror novel *Sister, Maiden, Monster*. She lives near Columbus, Ohio with a jungle of houseplants, a clowder of cats, and an insomnia of housemates.

Author website: https://www.lucysnyder.com/
Facebook: https://www.facebook.com/lucy.snyder1
Instagram: https://twitter.com/LucyASnyder

NYC born and raised **J. Daniel Stone** writes urban horror with a queer focus. He sold his first story when he was 22-years-old and has since written three novels (*The Absence of Light, Blood Kiss,* and *Stations of Shadow*), as well as a short story collection (*Lovebites & Razorlines*) and a novella (*I Can Taste The Blood*). He writes under a pseudonym to keep the wolves at bay.

Author website:cwww.SolitarySpiral.com

Sara Tantlinger is the author of the Bram Stoker Award-winning *The Devil's Dreamland: Poetry Inspired by H.H. Holmes,* and the Stoker-nominated works *To Be Devoured* and *Cradleland of Parasites.* She has also edited *Not All Monsters* and *Chromophobia.* She is a co-organizer for the HWA Pittsburgh Chapter. She embraces all things macabre and can be found lurking in graveyards or on Twitter @SaraTantlinger, at saratantlinger.com and on Instagram @inkychaotics.

Author website: www.saratantlinger.com

A.P. Thayer is a queer, Mexican-American author based out of Los Angeles. He writes speculative fiction that blends horror, magic punk, grimdark fantasy, and science fiction. His work has appeared in *Space Fantasy Magazine, Dark Recesses Press, Uncharted Magazine, Los Suelos, Glitter + Ashes: Queer Tales of a World That Wouldn't Die, Made in LA: Art of Transformation, Murder Park After Dark*, and others.

He was a co-host on *The Genre Hustle*, a writing craft podcast focused on speculative fiction, and a staff member at *Constelación* magazine. He is also frequently a guest on other podcasts and is a full member of SFWA.

When he's not writing, he can be found cooking for his friends or running a game of Dungeons & Dragons.

Author website: www.apthayer.com
Twitter: @apthayer
Instagram: @apthayer

Kaitlin Tremblay (they/she) is a queer game developer and writer. Their writing (fiction and nonfiction) has appeared in a variety of print and digital magazines and anthologies, including *Rue Morgue* and *Playboy*. They were the co-editor of the Shirley Jackson Award-nominated anthology *Those Who Make Us: Canadian Creature, Myth, and Monster Stories* (Exile Editions, 2016) and the author of the critical examination of video game storytelling in *Ain't No Place for a Hero: Borderlands* (ECW Press, 2017).

Their full portfolio can be found on their website: www.thatmonstergames.com
Twitter: @kait_zilla

Paul Tremblay has won the Bram Stoker, British Fantasy, and Massachusetts Book awards and is the author of *The Pallbearers Club, Survivor Song, Growing Things*, and *A Head Full of Ghosts. His novel The Cabin at the End of the World* was adapted by M Night Shyamalan as the film *Knock at the Cabin*. His essays and short fiction have appeared in the *Los Angeles Times, Entertainment Weekly* online, and numerous year's-best anthologies. He has a master's degree in mathematics and lives outside Boston.

Author website: www.paultremblay.net
Twitter: @paulgtremblay
Instagram: @paulgtremblay

Carmilla Voiez is a British horror writer living in Scotland. Her influences include Graham Masterton, Thomas Ligotti, and Clive Barker. She is pansexual and passionate about intersectional feminism and human rights. Carmilla has a first-class bachelor's in creative writing and linguistics. Her previous work includes stories in horror anthologies published by Clash Books and Mocha Memoirs, a series of dark fantasy novels (currently out of print), a co-authored Southern Gothic Horror novel, and self-published graphic novels. Graham Masterton described the second book in her Starblood series as a "compelling story in a hypnotic, distinctive voice that brings her eerie world vividly to life." Carmilla also works as a freelance editor and English tutor and enjoys making language sing.

Author website: www.carmillavoiez.com

Holly Lyn Walrath is a writer, editor, and publisher. Her poetry and short fiction has appeared in *Strange Horizons, Fireside Fiction, Analog,* and Flash Fiction Online. She is the author of several books of poetry including *Glimmerglass Girl* (2018), *Numinose Lapidi* (2020), and *The Smallest of Bones* (2021). She holds a B.A. in English from The University of Texas and a Master's in Creative Writing from the University of Denver.

Author Website: www.hlwalrath.com
Twitter: @hollylynwalrath
Facebook: https://www.facebook.com/HollyLynWalrath
Instagram: https://www.instagram.com/holly__lyn/

Readers . . .

Thank you for reading *Unspeakable Horror Volume 3*. We hope you enjoyed this anthology

If you have a moment, please review *Unspeakable Horror Volume 3* at the store where you bought it.

Help other readers by telling them why you enjoyed this book. No need to write an in-depth discussion. Even a single sentence will be greatly appreciated. Reviews go a long way to helping a book sell, and is great for an author's career. It'll also help us to continue publishing quality books. You can also share a photo of yourself holding this book with the hashtag #IGotMyCLPBook!

Thank you again for taking the time to journey with Crystal Lake Publishing.

Visit our Linktree page for a list of our social media platforms.
https://linktr.ee/CrystalLakePublishing

Our Mission Statement:

Since its founding in August 2012, Crystal Lake Publishing has quickly become one of the world's leading publishers of Dark Fiction and Horror books in print, eBook, and audio formats.

While we strive to present only the highest quality fiction and entertainment, we also endeavour to support authors along their writing journey. We offer our time and experience in non-fiction projects, as well as author mentoring and services, at competitive prices.

With several Bram Stoker Award wins and many other wins and nominations (including the HWA's Specialty Press Award), Crystal Lake Publishing puts integrity, honor, and respect at the forefront of our publishing operations.

We strive for each book and outreach program we spearhead to not only entertain and touch or comment on issues that affect our readers, but also to strengthen and support the Dark Fiction field and its authors.

Not only do we find and publish authors we believe are destined for greatness, but we strive to work with men and woman who endeavour to be decent human beings who care more for others than themselves, while still being hard working, driven, and passionate artists and storytellers.

Crystal Lake Publishing is and will always be a beacon of what passion and dedication, combined with overwhelming teamwork and respect, can accomplish. We endeavour to know each and every one of our readers, while building personal relationships with our authors, reviewers, bloggers, podcasters, bookstores, and libraries.

We will be as trustworthy, forthright, and transparent as any business can be, while also keeping most of the headaches away from our authors, since it's our job to solve the problems so they can stay in a creative mind. Which of course also means paying our authors.

We do not just publish books, we present to you worlds within your world, doors within your mind, from talented authors who sacrifice so much for a moment of your time.

There are some amazing small presses out there, and through collaboration and open forums we will continue to support other presses in the goal of helping authors and showing the world what quality small presses are capable of accomplishing. No one wins when a small press goes down, so we will always be there to support hardworking, legitimate presses and their authors. We don't see Crystal Lake as the best press out there, but we will always strive to be the best, strive to be the most interactive and grateful, and even blessed press around. No matter what happens over time, we will also take our mission very seriously while appreciating where we are and enjoying the journey.

What do we offer our authors that they can't do for themselves through self-publishing?

We are big supporters of self-publishing (especially hybrid publishing), if done with care, patience, and planning. However, not every author has the time or inclination to do market research, advertise, and set up book launch strategies. Although a lot of authors are successful in doing it all, strong small presses will always be there for the authors who just want to do what they do best: write.

What we offer is experience, industry knowledge, contacts and trust built up over years. And due to our strong brand and trusting fanbase, every Crystal Lake Publishing book comes with weight of respect. In time our fans begin to trust our judgment and will try a new author purely based on our support of said author.

With each launch we strive to fine-tune our approach, learn from our mistakes, and increase our reach. We continue to assure our authors that we're here for them and that we'll carry the weight of the launch and dealing with third parties while they focus on their strengths—be it writing, interviews, blogs, signings, etc.

We also offer several mentoring packages to authors that include knowledge and skills they can use in both traditional and self-publishing endeavours.

We look forward to launching many new careers.

This is what we believe in. What we stand for. This will be our legacy.

Welcome to Crystal Lake Publishing— Tales from the Darkest Depths.

9 781957 133454